STARSHIP THUNDER

Joseph McRae Palmer

Prologue

Most people know me as Grand Admiral Drake. I am a man who daily walks the halls of power, shaking the hands of the influential, swapping stories behind closed doors with army generals and armada admirals and always followed by throngs of reporters. My official living quarters are lavish. Located in the government district close to the nexus of government power, they are paid for through a special dispensation in perpetuity invoked by the United Humans Executive as thanks for my decades of valuable service on behalf of our species.

The public assumes that I love my trappings of power. They celebrate my achievements just as much as they envy the ease with which I impose my will upon the UH Armada. But they do not know the price I and others have paid on their behalf to give them the freedoms most take for granted. Comrades lost in action; loved ones who've been ignored because of my duties; subordinates who've sacrificed themselves to carry out my orders.

On the other hand, my close friends and family—there are few—call me Kory, my given name. And they know that the happiest time of my life was when I was known as

Captain Drake, back in the day when I led my people into battle from the bridge of *Thunder*. As you well know, that old but glorious Dominion dreadnought is still around, though Grand Admirals like me lead from a desk, not from a bridge. *Thunder* is somebody else's command these days.

All the people who see me as a national hero forget that there was a time when *Thunder* was barely bigger than a fighter, and accounting for my crew required fewer fingers than I have on one hand. Back then, we had no fleet; nobody knew my name; we lived in a subterranean mountain base barely bigger than a garage, and we were seen as little better than cockroaches in the eyes of the Kergans.

But let me take you back further in my history, before even *Thunder*. My roots are buried in the orphanages of the old state of California and the streets of San Jose. In the beginning, I had never flown in a passenger airplane, let alone a starship. My daily fight was on behalf of my empty stomach, not humanity's freedom. I strove not for battle honors but a roof over my head. That is the condition I was in when Her Highness Zeta of the Nova Throne recruited me.

A diamond in the rough, Zeta would probably call me. I think unrefined iron ore would be a better description of me in my childhood. It took a great deal of fire, pressure, heating in the forge of life, and hammering on the anvil of battle to mold me into the man I am today.

I can point to a singular moment that set the trajectory of my life, the arrow in the dark with my name on it that woke me to the path that, over forty years later, led to this moment. That triggering incident was when the Kergan Military Authority captured my street sister, Destiny Austin. She was all I had, my only family and anchor in an uncertain life. I refused to give up on her. I *chose* to protect her. And that choice led to everything that followed.

2

Thus begins my story

1

The twelve-armed aliens held my sister captive.

Daylight leaked through the boarded-up windows of the abandoned office building, illuminating shafts of dust-filled columns that pierced the shadows in the ruined room. A moldy beige sofa pressed against one wall. Insulation lay exposed where vandals or contractors had pulled away drywall.

I knelt at the window, peeking through a gap in the board with one eye to spy on the detention cage where Destiny, my street sister, was being held with other detainees. I grasped the edges of the boards and yanked on them to try and expand the gap. I brushed my long brown hair over my right ear to keep it out of my eye, my faded leather jacket creaking as my arm moved.

Destiny stood in the back corner of the cage on the back of a small flatbed truck, her arms folded and her head up, appraising her captors arrogantly as if *they* were under *her* control. Her long black curly hair framed the chocolate skin of a face with sharp edges and slanted dark eyes. Four other detainees were trapped with her, some who I knew as other street people, though I no longer recall their names. The cage was made of low-tech chain-link fencing and steel bars—not the alien magic I expected of the Kergan military police.

The truck with the cage was parked in front of a seedy adult bookstore that had been closed for months. Next to it sat a smoking food cart doing a brisk business in hotdogs and sandwiches, ignoring the commotion down the street. The cart's owner was oblivious to his fellow humans imprisoned in the cage as he served a steaming hotdog heaped with relish to a customer.

I returned to studying the cage. Destiny stood ready, her vision locked on the alien MP—a member of the Kergan military police, of an alien species called *marac*—who loomed at guard near the cage door. The marac MP levitated several feet off the ground using advanced technology built into its armored suit. Its body was a nightmare of arms surrounding a spherical head with one pair of large eyes and another pair of smaller eyes resting just above those. Maracs looked like large twelve-armed octopuses with an extra pair of eyes.

The alien invertebrate gripped a ranged weapon of some kind with two of its arms. Down the street from the MP, a squad of four other Kergans—all maracs—were scuffling with homeless people, trying to round them up and bring them to the detention cage.

Soon, the cage would be packed, making it even more challenging to spring Destiny free. I had to try while only one guard was tending to the prisoners. She was my sister, even if only in name, not in fact. I met her on the streets of San Jose when I was thirteen. Over the last five years, Destiny and I had become inseparable and dependent on each other.

Why were the Kergans suddenly rounding up San Jose's

5

homeless people? I didn't know, but millions of other Americans had also been "detained" by the Kergans and promptly disappeared into their giant starships orbiting the Earth. I assumed that's where they intended to take Destiny, and I couldn't let that happen. If I did, it would probably be the last time I ever saw her.

The Kergans were advanced aliens from thousands of light years away, but the detention cage and its lock were familiar Earth tech. How foolish of them. I could break through that if only I could distract the MPs for a few seconds.

I hopped off the rotting table under the window and sprinted from the room. I entered a long, deserted hallway. At the end of it, I took the stairs down to the second floor, watching for soft spots on the floor where holes had rotted through some of the steps. Coming to an open second-floor window, I jumped out and hung by my hands from the windowsill.

Despite being only eighteen, I had grown into a big man, just like my father. I measured 6 foot 4, with broad shoulders, and weighed 225. It would be a lie to say I hadn't taken advantage of my size and strength to protect Destiny and me on the street. We were still alive because of the animal ferocity I could summon when it was needed.

At that moment, hanging from the windowsill, my long and sturdy body meant I had only a short drop to the dirty concrete below.

The courtyard was empty except for an overflowing dumpster and dead leaves that nobody had bothered to sweep up once winter had set in. It smelled of decay and rot mixed with a cold sea breeze from San Francisco Bay to the north.

I zipped my leather jacket against the chill but rolled the edge of my wool cap up to hear and see better.

Destiny was counting on me. She knew I would not leave her behind, even if it meant risking my own life. Despite her constant snarkiness, she was the only meaningful relationship in my life, and I knew she felt the same for me. This world may have been run by selfish adults who only cared about their own power, but at least Destiny and I had each other. When I summoned my few memories of my parents, I liked to think they would have been pleased with my protectiveness of her.

I ran through a narrow alley connecting the courtyard to the street parallel to the one where Destiny was being held. I moved to the opposite block from where the MP squad was battling the street people. They were as good a distraction as I was likely to get, and I needed to act before they returned to their lone colleague who guarded the cage.

Suddenly, the ground vibrated through my shoes. Then, the air seemed to throb. A shadow eclipsed the winter sunlight, and with a mind-numbing roar, a black circle flew directly over the city block about a thousand feet in the air. It had the appearance of an upside-down plate of stacked pancakes.

It was a Kergan ship, though I didn't recognize the type. Perhaps it was a warship, or just as likely, it could be an unarmed merchant ship. But its size and the noise it made were terrifying even after nine months of seeing them multiple times a day. I dropped my gaze and forced myself to ignore it. They wouldn't know I was down here stalking their MPs. I still had the element of surprise on my side.

I stopped at the corner leading into the street with the truck and cage. I poked my head around the brick edge of the building to sneak a look.

The Kergan squad was still fully occupied. Flashes of light signaled that the MPs were employing their stun weapons. Several humans lay motionless on the pavement around the squad. Fifty feet away from them, at least forty street people hid behind improvised barricades, throwing stones and garbage at the floating MPs. The one MP who had remained to guard the cage had its back turned to me as it focused on the chaotic battle. It held its weapon ready in two of its twelve arms.

I wrapped my hand around one of the last two Febreze bombs resting in the right thigh pocket of my cargo pants. Some months ago, a fellow human discovered that maracs were sensitive to hydroxypropyl beta-cyclodextrin, the primary ingredient of Febreze. Give them a big enough whiff of HPBCD, and it would knock the aliens out cold for several minutes.

The Kergans had quickly halted Earth's production of HPBCD, and now Febreze was becoming challenging to find. But if there was a time to use one of my precious bombs, now was it. I pulled the arming fuse, walked around the corner, and threw the bomb toward the solitary marac. "Destiny! Get down!" I yelled and broke into a sprint toward the cage.

Destiny's head snapped in my direction, making her braided hair fly. The dark brown skin of her round face opened into an expression of surprise.

The MP jerked up and turned around on its floats. "On the ground!" an electronic voice boomed from it, and it started to raise its weapon in my direction.

The bomb detonated with a *CRACK* just underneath the alien. Within seconds, the MP slumped in its levitation suit, and its weapon fell to the ground.

I didn't look to see if the other squad had noticed. There wasn't time. The lock on the cage was familiar to me, one I could bypass quickly. I fumbled my lock-picking tools out of my pocket and got to work on it. A shove here, a twist there, then a pull, and the lock sprang loose seconds later. I pulled the cage gate open. "Let's go!" I yelled at the five occupants.

Destiny strolled over with her hands in her pockets. "Took you long enough," she said with a bemused expression as she angled her body to jump around me from the truck bed. She froze there, looking down the street. "Uhm…" She suddenly shoved the person in front of her. "Move it!"

I turned my head to where she'd looked.

One of the members of the squad down the street had taken notice of the escaping detainees and was headed rapidly in our direction. "On the ground, or I will fire!" it yelled from its booming suit speakers.

Maracs were smaller in mass than humans, though they often made themselves look more intimidating by floating their armored bodies above us and spreading their arms out wide, just as the oncoming MP was doing.

The unconscious MP remained floating just to my right side, between the approaching MP and me. I shoved it down the street toward its colleagues, hoping it would slow them down.

I crouched down, grabbed the alien's fallen weapon, and turned. "Dest, follow me!" I yelled to my sister, who kneeled nearby. I ran back up the street toward the corner from where I'd emerged. The surprisingly heavy weapon slapped against my thighs as my legs pumped up and down.

I had little idea how to fire the weapon—which appeared to be some kind of gun or rifle. I was pretty skilled with my fists and blade but had only slight familiarity with firearms, mainly in the form of a cheap 9mm pistol I kept in our van. What I hoped to accomplish with the alien gun had not occurred to me.

The thudding of shoes against pavement sounded behind me. I glanced over my shoulder for a fraction of a second and confirmed that Destiny's petite, wiry body raced after me. A *crack* sounded in the distance, and then one of the other escaped detainees running ahead of me jerked and fell. That wasn't a stun round! They were firing real bullets!

"Go!" Destiny screamed.

We rounded the corner, and I slid to a halt.

"What are you doing?!" Destiny said as she jerked to a stop ten feet past me.

"We can't outrun them like this. We need to slow them down!" I patted the gun.

"Kory, do you even know how to use it?"

I looked down at the gun's unfamiliar controls. Where was the trigger? There were knobs in weird places that could be hand grips, though clearly not designed for a human. I noticed a large black stud that might be a trigger. I went to the corner, pointed the gun in the direction of the pursuing MP, and pushed the stud.

Instead of firing, I heard a *thunk* at my feet.

I jumped back in surprise. A solid black rectangle had fallen from the gun. "Ugh."

My sister rolled her eyes and said, "Brilliant, another Elon Musk."

Ignoring her, I picked up the box thingy and tried to stick it back in the most likely hole. After fumbling for a few seconds, it dropped in with a *click*.

"Kory!" Destiny screeched, tugging on my jacket.

"Hold on! Let me try again." I noticed a smaller stud on the other side of the gun in an awkward position for my hands, such that I had to adjust my grip and rest the rifle on top of my right shoulder like a rocket launcher. "This thing better not have a strong kick, or I'm going to drop it." There was no shoulder stock, per se, to absorb any recoil.

I stepped around the corner again. The approaching MP

fired a shot that snapped past my head with a *crack*. Why I didn't drop the gun and run, I don't know. My attention was entirely focused on the pursuing MP. I suppose I wanted blood.

I forced myself to ignore the missed shot. I might only get this one chance. The gun had no sighting mechanism I could see, so I made do and pointed it as best as I could at the MP, who was now only about thirty feet away. I couldn't miss it.

I pushed the smaller stud. The gun thudded straight back out of my arms, and then an explosion in front of me lifted me off my feet and threw me back onto the pavement. I landed next to the fallen gun.

A percussive roar echoed through the streets of downtown San Jose like a nearby lightning strike.

"Nice," Destiny choked out. White dust covered her from head to toe, and a cloud of it lifted into the street, cutting visibility to almost zero. "Now you've invited every Kergan in the city for pizza." She patted her chest and legs to get the dust off. "Are you done?"

I lifted my head off the pavement, coughed and spat dirt from my mouth, and looked toward my feet in the direction of the MP. Or what was left of it. All I could see were severed limbs and purple gore.

Destiny ran to me and tugged my arm. "Let's go, Schwarzenegger! I'd like to live!"

I reached over and picked up the gun, cradling it in my right arm like a football, and started in a loping, crooked run, following Destiny, with my ears ringing and my sense of balance knocked askew. "Musk, then, Schwarzenegger," I slurred. "I think you've got your similes mixed up."

She reached back and pulled me along, even though I towered over her and weighed twice as much. "Hyuck,

hyuck!" she mimed, not looking at me.

After a hundred feet of stumbling along, we finally exited the cloud of dust that had been raised by whatever detonation my stolen gun had produced.

A gentle thrumming reverberated through my chest, and a Kergan motor sang behind us.

Destiny looked back and froze. "You found a friend!"

2

An ellipsoid aircraft floated above us, following closely. It was one of the Kergans' many surveillance vehicles, or blackholes, as we called them. It was as big as an SUV, and its smooth black surface seemed to absorb light. If we didn't eliminate it, the MPs would soon be on us again.

"Mmm…" I hesitated, trying to decide what to do. We could try running, but blackholes were notoriously tricky to elude.

The blob of the vehicle just floated there, maybe a hundred feet above us. It had no visible sensor apertures or windows, no apparent means of propulsion, and no weapons.

"Stand back." I shoved Destiny to the side of the street. Then I again lifted the gun onto my shoulder and pointed it at the blob. It was a distant shot, and the vehicle wasn't all that big, but I thought I could hit it. Knowing only one way of firing this gun, I reached back and pushed that small stud again.

The gun jerked out of my hands with a *thud*. I visually

tracked a projectile shoot out of the gun muzzle, travel in a beautifully straight line, and connect with the blackhole. A *WOOMP* exploded above us, knocking me to my back. Pavement smacked into my head, making me see stars.

Something grabbed me and yanked me to the side. I looked. Destiny somehow was dragging my heavy ass through an open doorway as a black shape crashed into the street right where I'd been moments before. Smoke and dust enveloped us, blocking out daylight and muffling sounds.

We lay in a building vestibule of some kind. Coughing, Destiny shoved aside an interior door, then yanked on my arms to pull me through it and shut the door behind us.

"Dude, you need to go on a diet!" she panted.

The visibility began to improve immediately. We lay on the carpet of what looked like a building lobby, abandoned like so much of the city had become in recent months as the Kergans slowly enforced their repressive rule over the huddling masses of humanity. The businesses in this building had surrendered to the enemy just as had our militaries.

"Give me a second," I said. "I hit my head."

"If you don't get moving, *I'll* hit you in the head." She pointed back in the direction from where we came. "You called the entire city down on us, firing that gun like you think you know how to use it!"

I squinted at her. "I saved us!"

"Sure, you did. Tell me that later when we're both sitting in an octopus prison ship."

I smiled and gently punched her. "I love you too."

She deflected my fist and punched me back. "You make me sick!" But a smile snuck around her lips. "Pay attention. We need to get to the van."

"Where's that gun?"

"It's gone!" she said, pointing outside. "If you'd stayed lying on that street, you'd be gone also! Don't worry about it. How you handled it, you would have leveled half the city before you ran out of ammo."

A thank you from her would have been nice, but I knew it wasn't her style. She didn't need to say anything. We'd saved each other so many times from difficulties that it wasn't worth adding another to the list.

She shoved me. "Let's get out of here." She stumbled to her feet, pounding her hands on her clothes to remove the dust.

I got to my feet. My head throbbed, and I had a swelling bump on the back of my skull. Destiny finished cleaning herself and started on me, pounding on my back and legs and brushing my hair. Clouds of dust exploded around us.

"I'm finally a white girl," she said in a mumble as she wiped at her face.

"Okay, so you said, go to the van," I said. "So, let's go." I jogged down the hallway, looking for a rear entrance, with Destiny following close behind. We found a loading dock in the rear leading to the block's central courtyard.

"We need to leave San Jose," I said as we exited the building.

"Are you serious?" she said.

"Yes. They'll be looking for us."

"Where do we go?"

"I don't know. Right now, let's worry about escaping."

We trotted out of an alley and turned onto a minor street.

"We could stay here," she said. "We just need to go to ground for a few weeks."

"It won't work, sis. It's just a matter of time until they trap us." She was vigorously shaking her head. I grabbed her arm. "Listen! They almost got you today. I was lucky I got you out of that cage."

She rolled her eyes and took a step back. "It was fine. I knew you would get me out."

"Don't be stupid."

She folded her arms, and her face flushed. "Don't you dare—"

I reached up and cupped her head in my hands. "Dest! We can't stay here any longer. It's too dangerous. You know it!"

She reached up and grasped my hands but didn't shove me away. "But what about my mom and my sisters?"

"It's been how many months since you last saw them?" She looked down and squeezed her lips together. My throat constricted. "It's been at least four months."

She nodded, and a single tear ran down her cheek.

I touched our foreheads together. "It's just us two. If your family is out there somewhere, we'll find them, but I don't think it will be easy. We *must* take care of ourselves first. Right?"

She sniffled and wiped away the tears. "Yeah, I know. But, you know, it's my family and all..."

Her mother had lost custody of Destiny when she was eleven years old because of neglect and a string of abusive boyfriends. After that, Destiny had bounced around five different foster homes over the course of a year until she finally escaped and went to live on the street. I'd met her when she was twelve and still trying to figure things out. Despite all that her mother had done to her, I knew Destiny still loved her. On the other hand, we'd made a pact to always look out for each other first. Our own welfare always came before anybody else's.

"I understand how you feel," I said. "But we need to take

16

care of each other. I need to know you got my back. Do you?"

She pushed me away. "You don't even need to ask!" She threw her hands up. "Yes, of course I've got it." She took a deep breath and gazed at me for a couple seconds. "If you're gonna go all Marco Polo on me, then tell me where we're going."

I nodded. But I didn't know where we would find safety, only that it wasn't in San Jose.

Ever since the invasion of the Kergans nine months ago, I hadn't worried too much about the aliens. Even when the USA and the rest of NATO's military forces had surrendered unconditionally seven months ago, I hadn't worried. Why would I? I'd been living on the streets as a homeless teenager since I was thirteen, since the time I escaped from the orphanage. Society had done little to help me. In my opinion, the fall of the US government was irrelevant to my life. Indeed, the Kergans couldn't be any better or worse.

And for a while, after the collapse, things had been looking up. The local police had so many other things to worry about that they stopped pestering us homeless people. It became easier to loot food and find safe places to squat during lonely nights, what with all the missing citizens.

Then, about four months ago, the Kergans established martial law in San Jose and moved in with their military police. They showed none of the restraint or respect for the rule of law that human law enforcement had. Overnight, tens of thousands of people disappeared from the streets as they were deported into the skies.

Destiny and I had decided we wouldn't become victims, and with that determination, we'd procured some weapons, including the Febreze bombs and pistols. We'd had to hurt people to protect our lives, fighting with our fellow humans for access to limited resources. But until today, I'd never knowingly killed another intelligent being.

Now, that had changed. At least it wasn't a fellow human, but nevertheless, I'd killed a sentient being, blowing it to smithereens. Maybe I also killed some others when that blackhole crashed into the street, but I didn't know if it was a manned vehicle.

We took off jogging again, quickly covering several blocks, both of us huffing and puffing. We passed a video billboard on top of a three-story brick apartment building. It displayed the grainy image of a white octahedron with a message. *WANTED by the Kergan Military Authority: Z374 of the Collective Dominion for immigration crimes; $2,000,000 reward for their capture.*

With my elbow, I poked Destiny in the ribs and gestured at the billboard. "Is that a robot?"

She twisted her neck, looked, and guffawed. "What did they do? Overstay their visa?"

"Is that some kind of alien?" I asked.

She shrugged. "Do I look like David Attenborough? I don't know and don't care. Not our problem. Hurry up and keep running, you slug!" She picked up her pace, and I turned my head away from the odd message and focused on our path.

We continued our jog until we reached a sheltered side street where we'd parked our rusty 1988 Toyota Van. Its blue paint was almost completely faded, and the windows were clouded with age. But it was home. We had owned and purchased it with our own money. Earned mainly through panhandling, selling stolen or looted goods, and courier jobs for street gangs and other unsavory characters.

I pulled the keys out of my pocket, unlocked the driver's side door, and jumped into the seat. It was covered with faded and stained fabric. I cranked the starter, and the engine coughed with a *putt-putt-putt* accompanied by clouds of smoke from the tailpipe—the worn engine burned oil.

I saw that our gas tank was almost full, thanks to a hidden stash of gas cans we'd found in an abandoned garage two weeks ago. "We've got almost a full tank," I said as Destiny pulled her skinny frame into the passenger seat and belted herself in. "We should be able to get about 200 miles out of it."

I bowed my head to the steering wheel. "Where are we going?"

She sighed and bowed her head. "Highway 130?" she mumbled.

"East? To the Central Valley?" I lifted an eyebrow. "Are you sure?"

"Yeah. Where else? Let's get away from the coast and into the interior. Maybe we can find my aunt and cousin."

"Where do they live?"

"Wolf Jaw."

"Never heard of it."

"It's a small town in the mountains northeast of Fresno."

I nodded, but I didn't know this aunt and cousin of hers. "Are you sure?" I didn't have any other suggestions.

"It's as good as anywhere else. At least it's a long way from San Jose."

"True. Okay." Pulling out of our parking spot, I floored the accelerator, and we sped down the empty street heading eastward. "Wolf Jaw, here we come." In the rearview mirror, I saw two thick columns of smoke. I'd made those. And there was a swarm of human collaborator and Kergan aircraft circling them, undoubtedly looking for us.

We took the ramp onto eastbound I-280. Almost immediately, we came to a near stop. A miles-long traffic jam stretched before us. Our exit was only about a mile ahead. I should have paid attention and avoided the freeway.

Glancing over my shoulder, I saw a pair of Kergan aircraft closing in on us about a half-mile away.

3

The Kergan aircraft moved slowly toward us until I recognized them as more blackholes. Cars and trucks filled both lanes of the freeway. A semi-truck on the left had us boxed into the right lane, and several stalled vehicles ahead blocked the shoulder on the right. I could go in only one direction: forward, at a snail's pace.

The blackholes seemed to be searching. They moved slowly and irregularly, sometimes stopping to hover, then moving forward again, but always coming in our general direction. I sensed their eyes searching, making my back itch and my pulse throb.

"Get ready to jump out and run," I said.

"And leave all our stuff?" Destiny said with wide eyes.

"Would you rather be the guest of the Kergans?"

She cursed under her breath, unbuckled her seatbelt, moved to the back, and began pushing our belongings around and packing a pair of backpacks.

The blackholes approached and flew over the freeway several hundred yards behind us. Their thrumming engines made the chassis of the old Toyota vibrate, but they continued in motion and passed us, leaving the area.

Tension flowed out of my muscles, and I released a sigh. "I think we're okay."

Destiny left the packs in the back, returned to the passenger seat, and buckled in again. "We've got enough food to feed a mouse."

"That much?"

"A *tiny* mouse."

"We'll find more on the road."

She glared at me. "I'm not eating roadkill. I'm not that desperate."

I slapped the steering wheel. "I didn't mean literally on the road!"

She pointed at the semi-truck that still had us boxed in. "Speaking of roadkill, that's what we're about to become if you let that jerk squeeze us anymore."

"Yes, I know! I'm trying to get around him."

Destiny was quiet for a minute, staring off into the distance. "We should have gone by my mom's house again before we left."

I didn't respond. Destiny already knew there would be nobody there. In the preceding three months, we visited her mother's apartment weekly. Located in a government-subsidized housing block, it was empty every time. Her family had left no evidence behind of where they'd gone or when. I didn't understand why it was suddenly so important for her to know where they were. She hadn't lived with them for over five years. From the little I knew of her mom, she was a complete and total loser. However, I'd never say something like that to her. It would hurt her too much to hear the truth.

After the invasion, one of the first things the Kergans

did was to destroy human telecommunications infrastructure. The Internet: gone. Cell phone service: gone. Broadcast television: gone. Broadcast radio: gone, except for a couple Kergan-approved stations. Much of the telephone network had been left intact, but access was tightly controlled. Our new overlords had systematically destroyed satellites, fiber trunks, switches, data centers, cell towers, microwave relays, and they continued the campaign, seeking to control humanity by limiting the exchange of information. Contacting friends and family was no longer a simple matter. Indeed, if cell service still worked, Destiny could have gotten a text through to her mother or one of her siblings. I knew she felt disloyal by leaving without any word to or from them. But what other options did we have?

I had no family other than Destiny, but that didn't mean I was precisely happy about leaving. Though San Jose wasn't much of a home, we felt secure there after living on its streets for years. It was familiar. We knew the people, the geography, available services, and resources. The rules. Boundaries. Expectations. Though we lived day-to-day, life was usually predictable.

Now, we had left it all behind, becoming two teenagers on the road in a rust bucket with a tank of gas, almost no money or food, and wanted by the authorities. We had to find somewhere isolated with shelter, food, and water to go to ground and disappear.

An hour later, with the traffic crawling forward, we finally reached our exit. Thankfully, traffic from that point onward was very light, and we soon left the outskirts of San Jose behind us.

Destiny dug around in the clutter under the dashboard and found an old cassette tape. It was a mixtape that came with the van when we bought it. The music wasn't the kind

I typically liked, but it had some excellent tunes. She put it in the dash tape player—the van was too old to have even a CD player, let alone an MP3 player—and pushed the play button.

Not too long after that, we listened to Journey playing *Don't Stop Believin'*. I liked the song. Especially the verse that said, *Streetlights, people livin' just to find emotion, hidin' somewhere in the night*. The words seemed to describe my own life and search for satisfaction.

I clung to the steering wheel as we drove eastward up Highway 130, which twisted through the foothills east of the city. I intently watched the rearview mirror for somebody following us. Several times, I thought I caught a glimpse of a distant blackhole trailing us, but it was never close enough to be sure. All I saw were fleeting signs.

After about 10 miles of driving through the hills, we pulled into a small Chevron gas station. We didn't have enough cash to buy more gas, but Destiny reminded me she hadn't used the bathroom since she was detained. And the gas didn't matter in the end because the place was abandoned.

The empty station and its small, attached convenience store had been thoroughly looted. Most of the windows were broken, the store shelves were bare, and any useful furniture had either been smashed or taken. So, I sat in the van while Destiny found somewhere private to take care of her business. At times like this, I was glad I wasn't a girl. It made me nervous having her out of sight, even for a minute, knowing how vulnerable she'd be squatting behind some bush with her pants bunched up around her ankles.

Despite my anxiety, after a minute, my thoughts wondered. I remembered the last time I had been on the road like this. Five years ago, when I was thirteen, I escaped the orphanage. To this day, I don't know precisely where the orphanage was, only that it was somewhere in California's southern Central Valley, probably south of Fresno.

The night of my escape, I'd been locked into solitary confinement after Mrs. Brown found one of my secret stashes containing a horde of food, cash, and a knife. In truth, it wasn't much of a horde. But it was *mine*, carefully collected over months. The self-important, power-hungry adult had confiscated it and thrown me into the orphanage's basement punishment cell.

The cell was familiar to me. The latch of the locked door was mounted to a brick wall. The last time I'd been there, I'd noticed the bricks were loose. Even though it was pitch black, I went to work on the wall instead of sleeping. Over several hours, I picked and pried at it until my fingers were a bloody mess. But finally, a brick came loose. And then another. And another, until the latch fell out of the wall and the door swung open.

It was the middle of the night, and the orphanage night watchman was asleep in the ground-floor drawing room with an open book on his lap. I snuck up to my dormitory and emptied my other stash. It was much smaller than the one they'd found, but at least it had enough food for a few meals and dollars. I also collected my warmest clothes and stuffed them into a backpack.

I snuck out of the kitchen service door and ran to the nearby highway. It was a cold winter night with wisps of fog obscuring the road. I began walking northward and hung my thumb out at every passing car, hoping for a ride but fearing that, eventually, one of them would be somebody who'd been informed of my escape. After an hour, a trucker stopped for me. She looked at my young face with concern but only said, "Where're you headed?"

"San Jose," I said, having already planned it out.

She said, "You're in luck. That's where I'm headed. Hop

in!"

A few hours later, she dropped me off at a service station on Story Road south of downtown San Jose.

A few weeks later, I met Destiny, who was twelve and had recently escaped from her fifth foster home. We made an odd pair: a plain-looking white orphan boy and a skinny black girl from a broken family. But in trying to survive on the streets, we found common cause and formed an unlikely relationship. She was the first person I let myself become close to since my parents had been killed on that fateful night.

These recollections were interrupted by signs of movement behind the station building. Worried that somebody might be stalking Destiny, I reached behind my chair and picked up my pistol. I didn't know how to use it but had noticed that showing it was usually enough to get somebody to back off.

I climbed out of the van, locked it, and crept to the wall of the building, white paint peeling and shaded by wisps of black mold. A crow standing on the roof made a *caw-caw* sound. Scraps of empty plastic wrappers drifted by on a stiff westerly breeze.

Glancing around the corner of the wall, I saw a rusty dumpster and somebody in rags digging through it. Their back was turned to me, so I couldn't tell if it was a small man or a big woman. The important thing is that they weren't stalking Destiny. Instead, their attention was focused on the dumpster. I recognized this as an opportunity instead of a threat. This lonely person might have something useful we could take.

There is no denying that the street had turned me into a criminal. Yes, I planned to rob this person. Looking back on the experience now, I'm not proud of it, but when you're a street kid, you survived by any means possible. Looting and stealing were just two of the many ways to earn the cash needed for food and shelter.

I stepped around the corner, held the gun up, pointed it at the figure, and said, "Show me your hands!"

The figure started to turn around.

"Freeze!"

They stopped, holding their body in a hunched-up crouch on the ground.

"I've got a gun on you. Don't make any fast moves. Now, drop whatever you're holding and put your hands up nice and high." They hesitated. "Do it!"

Something metallic landed on the cracked pavement next to the dumpster with a *thud*. The person slowly lifted their empty hands above them.

I ignored the fallen object. "Turn around, real slow."

They shuffled on their feet until a face appeared. An old man dressed in stained mechanic's coveralls with a ripped puffy coat over that and a stocking cap on his head. His face was gaunt, empty, and spotted with sores. A meth head, it looked like, with his teeth almost completely gone.

Footsteps sounded behind me, and I caught Destiny's familiar scent. "What's going on?" she said from the right of my shoulder.

Without looking at her, I said, "Just exploiting an opportunity. Search him."

"Yuck! You search him!"

"We don't have time for this, and I've got the gun."

"Then hand it over. I'm not touching him."

I sighed. Destiny was better with the gun than me, anyway. At least she'd fired the thing before. I passed it to her.

She took it and pointed it at the man, who glanced over his shoulder at us. Destiny cursed and said, "Just cuz I'm a girl don't mean I won't shoot yo' ass. Face away, and don't move a muscle!"

I stepped up to the man, and his odor made my stomach turn. Urine, old sweat, and rotted teeth.

"I don't have nothin'!" he said with a thin voice. "Why do you think I've been diggin' through the garbage."

"We'll see for ourselves," I said. I began emptying his pockets. I found a worn pair of gloves in one pocket, a pack of cigarettes with only four left, a lighter, sixteen dollars and change, and two small plastic baggies full of white powder, which I recognized. Crank.

I pocketed the cigarettes, lighter, and money—the rest I stuffed back in his pocket, including the drugs. Destiny and I had been clean for two years now. There was no reason to start again, though I felt the old cravings as the powder texture teased me through the thin plastic. I ignored it and dropped them into the man's breast pocket.

I was about to turn around when I remembered the object he'd dropped. Double checking that Destiny still had the gun pointed at our Toby—the euphemism we called our targets—I stepped behind him and crouched down.

A dirty white container lay on the pavement. It measured about a foot long on each side. It was the shape of two pyramids whose bases had been glued together. An octahedron is what I remembered the shape was called.

I touched it, and its surface felt warm. In fact, it was pretty hot and felt like ceramic or glass. I picked it up, and it was heavy, maybe forty or fifty pounds. It looked familiar. I turned to the man and said, "What is this?"

"Got me," the Toby said. "I thought it might be valuable. If we go to the Kergans, maybe they'll give us money for it."

"There's no 'we'," Destiny said.

The man shrugged. "Are you done? Can I drop my hands?" He didn't seem at all bothered that we'd just robbed him. He was probably high on something.

Destiny gestured at me with her head. "What is that thing?"

"I don't know, but it's heavy and hot," I said. "Let's not talk about it here. Come on, let's take it to the van." I returned to the parking lot, hefting the heavy object in both arms.

"It's not radioactive or something like that, is it?" she asked.

"How would I know? How would you?"

"I don't know, but I thought I saw something like that in a movie once." She shrugged. "Well, if you start glowing in the dark tonight, remember that I tried to stop you."

Destiny backed away from the Toby until the building was between us and him. We heard the man go back to digging in the dumpster.

Back at the van, I unlocked it and opened the rear hatch. I set the object onto the rusty floor of the tail, which caused the old suspension to compress slightly.

"What are you going to do with it?" Destiny asked.

I closed the back hatch and then motioned for her to get in. I wasn't going to talk about it out here in the open.

Once seated, she said, "You going to answer me?"

"Don't you recognize that thing?" I said in almost a whisper.

She looked at me for a few seconds, then her eyes suddenly opened wider, and her mouth dropped open as she recognized it as the thing we'd seen on the Wanted billboard back in San Jose. "But we can't go to anybody about it. They'll arrest us for what we did back there with those MPs."

"We'll figure something out."

"You really think it's that alien robot thing they're looking for?"

I shrugged and shook my head. "Probably not, but it's worth a try." I whispered, "Think of what we could do with that reward."

"I can think of a lot, but we're just sitting here out in the open. Let's get moving before we're seen."

I started the engine and pulled out of the pot-holed parking lot in a cloud of blue smoke, heading east again on Highway 130.

The tape player started a new song. Bon Jovi's *Livin' on a Prayer*. I tapped the steering wheel in rhythm with the music as I drove us around a sharp bend in the highway. On the left, tall hills covered with dead grass loomed over us, and a basin filled with winter-naked trees lay to our right. We hadn't seen another car on the road for at least 30 minutes.

Abruptly, I caught a flicker of movement in the rearview mirror. I stiffened and let up on the gas pedal, but whatever I'd seen was already gone when I looked again.

Then, something behind me shouted in a woman's smooth, contralto voice. "Well met, humans! I am Z374!"

4

"Son of a monkey!" I screamed, nearly losing control of the van.

"Ah!" Destiny yelled and grabbed her seat's armrests.

The van's tires squealed on the pavement as I slammed my foot on the brakes and pulled us onto the shoulder. I shifted the transmission into park and turned around in my seat.

The white octahedron floated in the air just behind us. It hadn't moved a millimeter when I slammed on the brakes. The object rotated on its vertical axis ninety degrees, showing me a different face, and then the voice spoke again. "The fates have brought us together, and Zeta is indebted by the timely rescue by such brave humans as yourselves."

"Who are you?" I said.

"*What* are you?" Destiny said.

"This sentient's designation is Z374, from the Collective Dominion, though, in practice, worthy persons such as yourselves may call Z374 by the name Zeta. Alas, a description of Zeta's species is beyond the limits of your

31

language, but you may call Zeta an igna, as well as a Templar of the Heliacal Order, decreed a military adviser to Earth until Zeta's venture quest is fulfilled. The aid you have rendered to this humble servant has freed Zeta from the depredations of a mysterious foe who, through fickle luck, stumbled upon her encampment."

"Mysterious foe...?" Destiny snickered. "You mean that druggie back there?"

"Zeta is unacquainted with the creature known as druggie," Zeta said. "What were the intentions of that fell beast?"

Destiny giggled. "He probably wanted your cash."

"Alas, Zeta carries no coin or script. Nay, neither shelter nor arms, only her keen intellect does she possess—which is not insubstantial—and the promise of manufactured goods and apparatuses."

I looked at Destiny, and she looked back at me. What was this creature? Zeta radiated heat inside the car, and a smell of ozone and chemicals wafted from her. I also noticed a soft glow of light emitting through the edges of her octahedral body.

"Are you a robot?" I asked.

The strange being laughed. "Nay, Zeta is a biological creature, though undoubtedly of a nature foreign to your experience, Zeta dares to admit, for her noble body is composed of a phase of matter that human science has not associated with life. Furthermore, the sentient artificial intelligences you refer to—these so-called "robots"—are prohibited under the Galactic Machine Intelligence Treaty."

I noted that we were exposed on the shoulder of this open road. "Let's not talk here. We're in the open, and there are spies around. I'm going to find somewhere to hide."

"If you can find a junkyard, it would perfectly match

our camouflage scheme," Destiny said.

"I'm not sure about that," I said. "The rust on the right side needs a little more work."

"I defer to your judgment, oh wise humans," Zeta said.

"The name is Kory," I said.

"Well met, Kory of the Humans."

"It's just Kory."

"And you, lass?" Zeta said, gesturing as if looking at Destiny.

I pulled the Van back onto the highway and drove eastward, looking for a place to pull off under some trees.

"My name is Destiny," Destiny said.

"Kory and Destiny. Heroic names! The fates have united our prospects. The world will yet see the day when our valorous feats of arms are told by all!"

Destiny and I looked at each other again. Destiny's face twisted into a mocking smile, and I knew I had a similar expression. What was this creature talking about?

"Okay, Sir Lancelot," Destiny said, "you're getting ahead of yourself."

"This being is called—" the alien said.

"Zeta. Yeah, I got it. What do you mean by…valorous feats of arms?"

I saw a copse of trees off to the side of the road at the end of a muddy path off the shoulder. I braked and pulled us down it, hoping we didn't get stuck in the mud. But once under the trees, we were completely hidden from view unless one stood directly at the roadside. I set the parking brake and turned off the engine. I turned around and faced the alien creature. "What the blazes are you talking about, Zeta?"

"Brave Kory, Zeta witnessed your selfless acts of valor in the settlement known as San Jose. Numerous foes wearing the Kergan livery were thwarted by your cunning and courage. Zeta hopes to call you friend and join our causes against our common enemy."

As Zeta spoke in her strange manner, I felt something warm vibrating inside my chest like a steel thread tied around my heart, pulled tight, and somebody was strumming it with their finger, making it thrum. It was an odd sensation, unlike anything I'd ever felt before. My jaw relaxed, and I felt...content. I was left momentarily speechless.

"What trash are you going on about?" Destiny said. "All we did was steal you from that druggie back there."

Zeta laughed. "Zeta cannot be abducted, being the mighty Heliacal Templar she is. As the daughter and heir to the Nova Throne of the Collective Dominion, Zeta would rather return to the Ancients than be held captive!"

Finding my voice, I said, "That's what the Kergan are trying to do. Don't you know they've posted a two-million-dollar reward for your capture?"

"I know. Just think what we could do with that money!" Destiny said sarcastically. "We could finally afford a bag of Doritos!" With wide eyes, she held a hand to her mouth. The dollar had become almost worthless, making two million not worth much.

"Indeed, they fear Zeta," the alien said, "as they should. Undaunted Zeta's quest demands that she unite in partnership with a worthy human companion, that thereby together they may confront the threat posed by the Kergan Empire without exposing the Collective Dominion to Kergan claims that Zeta's people have committed acts of war."

I laughed. Loudly. "You're barking up the wrong tree."

"Zeta does not bark up any tree, seeing as none are nearby."

"There're several just outside," Destiny said, gesturing out the window.

"Zeta is confused," the alien said. "How are trees and barking relevant to the topic?"

I groaned and glared at Destiny, who smiled innocently at me. "Zeta, it's just an idiom. It means that you're looking in the wrong place. What I mean is this: if you're looking for human freedom fighters, then you shouldn't be talking to us."

"We're not free," my sister said. "We expect to be paid."

I jabbed her with my elbow. "Shut up, you're confusing her!" I turned to Zeta. "We're not fighters."

"Nay, friend Kory, your courageous acts on behalf of friend Destiny have proved you worthy of Zeta's regard. This very hour, humanity awaits the unveiling of those heroes who shall put such fear into the breasts of the treacherous Kergans that they are obliged to give up their unjustified occupation of this world and grant your people their right of self-determination. For the purpose of revealing these heroes has noble Zeta exposed herself and her urgent quest."

Destiny held up both hands. "Time out! Time out, you two!" She sighed. "Look, Lancelot, we don't even know you, and yet you suppose we're friends. You don't know anything about us. You're a *stranger*. No offense, but I don't give kisses on the first date."

"Cautious Zeta is not seeking amorous relations. She expresses confusion."

I knew Destiny was having difficulty containing her wit with such a naive target like Zeta, but it annoyed me. I glared at her again, and she shrugged and held her hands up defensively. "Zeta, it was a metaphor. Destiny does not expect actual kisses."

"Aah...mmm..." Zeta rotated on her vertical axis and bobbed forward as if nodding her nonexistent head. "The wise lass reveals her piercing intuition. Noble Zeta must offer gifts of information that will ease suspicions. Very well, Zeta shall disclose her background. As she previously stated, she has begun a Heliacal Templar's venture quest."

"Venture quest?" I said.

"Indeed, it is a right of passage required of all noble-born youth from the Collective Dominion ere they reach their majority. Zeta shall complete her venture quest and prove herself worthy of the Nova Throne of the Collective Dominion."

"You're a...princess?" Destiny said.

"Aye, Zeta is the provisional crown princess to the Nova Throne. She must prove herself through brave and honorable deeds. For this purpose, young Zeta has chosen to cast her lot into humanity's war of liberation."

"So, that's why the Kergans are after you," I said.

Zeta bobbed up and down once. "Indeed."

Destiny pointed at Zeta. "Is that your body? Or are you just shy?"

"Zeta doesn't... Oh, the lass expresses more humor. Zeta understands. Zeta is an igna. Her humble body consists of stellar plasma held by the containment capsule that friend Destiny has joked about. Zeta cannot survive outside this capsule. Now friends Kory and Destiny know of Zeta's fatal weakness, yet she trusts you will protect this knowledge."

After a lengthy pause without further explanation, I said, "And what else can you do?"

"Brave Kory is quite justified in inquiring about Zeta's talents, which are not insignificant. Zeta's capsule serves other purposes beyond containment. It also is equipped with a nanoforge capable of manufacturing consumables, arms, and most important for your purposes, warships."

"Warships? You mean, like spaceships with weapons on them?"

"Indeed. This very hour, wise lad, you have obliged Zeta to reveal her intentions. Kory ought to join Zeta as her heliacal consort. Once such a union is realized, Zeta is authorized to construct a single armed starship from which you and your chosen comrades in arms may ride into battle and face your Kergan foes on equal footing."

"Ewww... Consort?" Destiny said. "Like marriage?"

Zeta emitted a very human-like sigh. "Nay, ignorant lass. Kory would be Zeta's *heliacal* consort, a special partnership between an igna and a worthy alien ally. Zeta's consort becomes the pilot and captain of the armed starship, and together, they go forth to destroy their common enemies using all their cunning and courage."

"Why?" I said. "Why do you need me?"

"Zeta's people, the Collective Dominion, are not at war with the Kergan Empire. Zeta is forbidden to take up arms against any member of the Kergan armed forces. Nevertheless, the Order of Heliacal Templars trains and sends forth military advisers, such as noble Zeta, who are oath-bound to aid other alien civilizations who suffer at the hands of predatory species. Though Zeta may not take up arms against the Kergan, she is empowered to train and equip a small force of humans who wish to resist their enemies."

"Like I've already said, you've clearly made a mistake," I said. "You can't just pick the first human who comes around. Not all of us are fighters. Not all of us want to throw off the Kergans."

"Friend Kory, your humility is acknowledged and yet is unjustified. In this regard, perceptive Zeta is not mistaken in her judgment and offers you a heliacal consortship in exchange for your willingness to bravely face your enemies."

What Zeta was offering sounded pretty awesome. My own starship? Not only would it be the most remarkable thing to do—like living in a sci-fi movie—but it would undoubtedly be a safer place for Destiny and me. But I felt strangely guilty about misleading Zeta. Yeah, me, the guy who just a few minutes ago had robbed a poor druggie of all his money. Leading Zeta on didn't feel right.

"What if I don't want to be a freedom fighter?" I said. "What if I don't want to fly around and fight in some kind of...guerrilla starship? And what would happen to Destiny? I'm not going to abandon her."

"Friend Kory must choose comrades in arms to crew the starship. Friend Destiny may join him, if such be your mutual wish. You fear you lack the desire to fight for your people. Zeta believes you will find that purpose in time, though in this hour it be merely a seed buried in your heart. But Zeta has sensed its potential."

I felt that twang again around my heart like somebody was again thrumming on the string. "So, just like that, if I say yes, I'll be your *consort*?"

"Indeed."

"Then I'll be captain, and you'll have to do whatever I say?"

"Within Kory's domain of responsibility, indeed, Zeta must obey his commands."

"What are the limits?"

"Kory shall not destroy Zeta or aid your foes in capturing her. Alas, if such were to occur, Zeta is permitted to use violent force to protect her noble self."

"What else?"

"Kory and his comrades in arms shall not take up arms against the Collective Dominion or its allies. Neither shall they undertake banditry against civilians."

"Oh! You mean we can't be space pirates?" Destiny said.

"Anything more?" I said, ignoring Destiny's question.

"Zeta must reveal certain limitations imposed at the start of the consortship. Kory and his comrades in arms shall prove themselves worthy through feats of arms against humanity's foes before the Collective Dominion will grant access to certain technology upgrades and larger ship hulls."

"So, what you're saying is, if Destiny and I are lazy, we won't earn a good ship."

"Indeed, and Zeta should note that the maximum size of Kory's crew is limited by the ship hull. The first hull Consort Kory shall be granted is the Raider strike fighter, which may be crewed by three humans and is capable only of entering low orbit around Earth. However, the Raider is a superior atmospheric fighter, at least compared to current human technology."

"But no flying to other planets."

"Nay."

"What about the moon?"

"Nay, though according to the latest Dominion intelligence, Kory's enemies do not currently possess any lunar facilities."

"Not much of a starship, is it?" I said, looking at Destiny.

She shrugged at me innocently. "I know, it's kind of a letdown, actually. All we get to do is eat, sleep, and blow up Kergans. In our very own spaceship. Zeta drives a hard bargain."

I held up a hand as if I could deflect her cutting sarcasm. "Alright, alright, I get your point."

Zeta said, "Through feats of arms, Kory shall unlock upgrades according to how quickly you and your comrades in arms gain the trust of the Collective Dominion. Through your worthy efforts, you shall eventually obtain a powerful starship capable of traversing the galaxy and fighting humanity's most deadly foes."

"You keep saying that phrase. 'Feats of arms,'" Destiny said. "What does that mean, specifically? You sound really old when you say it that way, Lancelot."

"Young lass, Zeta means that by employing the weapons systems she shall provide Kory for use against humanity's enemies, in well-chosen battles, pursuing worthy objectives, you will undertake feats of arms."

She nodded. "So, if we blow up Kergan stuff, we get credit. Got it."

"What do you think?" I said to Destiny.

Her gaze pierced me. "It sounds like it's your choice, not mine. You're the one Zeta is dating."

I sighed. "Don't be silly, you know what I mean. And you know I would never choose to do something like this without thinking of you first."

"Fine," she huffed. "It sounds like it'll mean a roof over our heads and regular meals. I'm okay with that. I mean, what do we have to lose?" She flicked a hand. "And don't worry, I'll get over my jealousy, eventually."

I ignored the jibe, threw up a hand, and snorted. "It could cost us our lives."

She shrugged. "Not necessarily. Zeta never said we would be forced to fight. I think we should try it out."

"If you can get over your jealousy," I said with a grin.

She made a mock scowl. "How *dare* you make me the third wheel! I'm *so* hurt!" She touched an eye like she was wiping away a tear. "Maybe I'll just *walk* home, you insensitive jerks!"

I smiled at her playing and looked back at the igna. "Hey, Zeta, suppose I become your consort, and then a little while later, I decide it's not working out for me, and I want out. What happens?"

"Once heliacal consorts have formed a union, it may be dissolved if either party—Kory or Zeta—decides that it should end. The relationship must be mutually beneficial. For Zeta's part, she seeks success so that she may return home with her venture quest honorably fulfilled."

"How long will that take?"

"In human temporal units, Zeta allows for at least one year, three months, and twelve days."

I took a moment to consider. I looked out the windows of our old van, observing the trees that enshrouded us and the hints of overcast sky peeking through the leaves. A stiff breeze shook the van with occasional gusts. The inside would already be cold if Zeta weren't emitting so much heat.

The unknown awaited us in the Central Valley. With so many local governments collapsing, the towns and cities had reverted to chaos. Some authorities had established martial law while waiting for the Kergans to arrive and take charge. Destiny and I would not find safety for long, if at all. The local authorities and citizens would not welcome two street kids into their towns. And even if they did, it would only last until the Kergans arrived.

We needed to find our own way. I had no wish to fight the Kergans. Sure, I wished they were dead and gone. I admit that now. They were actually worse than the US government, that had been proved. But I didn't want to be the guy at the end of the gun that did the killing. And yet, Zeta's offer might be an avenue that provided us shelter, safety, and food for the next few months. If not for myself, I owed it to Destiny to try it.

Free food. Free shelter. Safety. What more could we ask for? I couldn't refuse.

"Yes," I said. "I agree to be your consort."

5

"Zeta shall formalize the consortship after completing travels for the day," Zeta said.

"Okay, this evening then," I said.

I started the engine, backed us out of the grove, and continued eastward on 130. We drove for a further 45 miles until we were a bit west of Patterson but still in the foothills and away from populated areas. We found a place to pull off the road and camp for the night.

The reason for not entering Patterson was that I didn't know the situation there and didn't want to arrive in the middle of the night. Many local towns, feeling abandoned by the national government—and because of the surrender they truly had been abandoned—and lacking oversight from the Kergans, had taken the law into their own hands; martial law had been imposed; habeas corpus suspended; local police and militia granted the power of summary judgment. Unfortunately, not all towns used these powers wisely, and we'd heard rumors about communities cleansing themselves of undesirables for weeks. There were hundreds of towns and small cities in the Central Valley, and we'd pass through dozens of them over the next day or two. I wanted us to be prepared for cold receptions.

I parked the van in a depression in the ground behind some brush that hid us from the view of the highway. Dusk had already arrived, and the quickly diminishing twilight left the arid terrain around us looking gray and lonely, like a landscape from an old black-and-white Western movie. The sky was gray and smelled of rain and perhaps even snow.

Our Toyota Van was our home, literally. It's where we slept and ate and where we stored our belongings. This made camping on the road very convenient, even though we were low on water and food. There had been no time to restock before we fled San Jose.

"Zeta, what do you eat?" I asked as I unbuckled my seatbelt. Destiny had already left her seat and was rummaging through our belongings in the back.

"Zeta wonders what food the lad thinks she would eat?" Zeta said. "Do not trouble yourself, for all Zeta's small needs are satisfied by this excellent capsule."

"Well, that's convenient because we don't have much food." I moved a stack of Destiny's books under the bench seat. "Just some bags of trail mix and a little beef jerky."

"The water cooler's half empty," Destiny said as she picked up the cooler and shook it.

"You want to see if you can refill it? There're still a few water filters left."

Destiny snorted. "Just a second while I walk over to that giant lake over there."

I could tell by her sarcastic tone that I'd suggested the impossible. "No nearby water?"

She patted me on the shoulder. "You catch on fast."

I looked at the dry hills that surrounded us. We were

probably miles away from the nearest water hole. "Good observation," I said. I didn't know what we would do about food and water. We had barely enough for the next day, though water wouldn't be a problem once we got to the valley floor and its dense network of irrigation canals. At least the Kergans seemed to have left the water infrastructure mostly intact.

"Perhaps Zeta can give you aid," Zeta said.

"With what?" I asked.

"Friends Kory and Destiny hunger and thirst, if Zeta is not mistaken. She wishes to satisfy your needs."

I inclined my head to her. "How's that?"

"Clever Zeta possesses a nanoforge. With it, she can harvest local resources and synthesize many different forms of matter and chemical compounds. Within her data archives, she possesses the formulation for a nutrient solution that can indefinitely sustain human life. Her nanoforge can also extract water from the local environment, even in this desiccated setting."

"Say again?" Destiny said, pausing in her unpacking.

"Resourceful Zeta can mine this habitat for the food and water you humans require. This ability is intended for constructing the starship and weapons, but also for acquiring and synthesizing consumables, such as fuel, food, and ammunition."

I listened to Zeta with a growing sense of astonishment. Destiny and I were driven by two principal needs: shelter and food. I'd signed up for this consortship because it would ensure regular meals, but I hadn't realized it could be this easy. If the strange alien could manufacture food for us, that would remove a colossal uncertainty from our lives. "How does it work? What do you need?" I said.

"Zeta need only position her capsule on the ground

adjacent to this vehicle."

I stepped over to the side door, slid it open, and stepped out onto the dirt, sparsely covered by patches of brown grass and weeds. "Show me."

Zeta flew out of the van, her capsule emitting a soft whining sound and dim glow of white light, hovered about a foot above the ground, and moved back and forth for a minute as if she were looking for something. Then she abruptly stopped and glided down until the bottom pyramid of her body pressed with its tip penetrating the ground. "Zeta needs two vessels for collecting the harvest. One for water, another for the nutrient solution."

I dug around in the back of the van until I found two empty plastic containers we normally used for food storage. They were reasonably clean. I returned to Zeta. "Where do you want them?"

"Zeta shall be satisfied with the vessels resting next to her capsule," Zeta said.

I set them next to her capsule, then stood back and watched. Destiny came over to stand next to me. After a minute passed with no sign of activity, she said, "Is something supposed to be happening?"

"The lass grows impatient. Zeta's nanoforge employs nanobots. These are presently surveying the environment and locating concentrations of suitable material. Harvesting and synthesis will commence momentarily."

"So, you can make just about anything," Destiny said. "Why not just synthesize me a cheeseburger?"

"Zeta does not possess the formulation for the complex ingredients needed for making meat, bread, and other components of a cheeseburger."

Destiny cocked her hips and folded her arms. "Oh, so *now* we get to the fine print. Not so resourceful after all, are you?"

The alien responded in a steady voice, seemingly unmolested by Destiny's criticism. "Zeta is capable of synthesizing over four million different compounds and—"

I held up my hands. "It's okay! Zeta, she's just goading you. Ignore her." I eyed my sister reproachfully.

It was quiet after that. I started thinking about what I'd agreed to with this consortship. We'd been promised protection and shelter in exchange for our willingness to resist the Kergans. Was I taking us into a scheme that would leave us dead?

"So, Zeta," I said, "tell me more about what it means to be your consort. You don't know anything about me or Destiny, but you want to be partners or something. Right?"

"Zeta has collected numerous facts about you, friend Kory. You rescued Zeta from danger. According to Dominion intelligence sources, Zeta knows you fought the Kergan military police and eliminated several members of their armed forces using improvised weapons." The whining sound coming from her increased in pitch. "You evaded capture using rudimentary human technology. Zeta has concluded that you are resourceful, brave, bold, and capable of selfless, heroic acts when called for."

"I rescued Destiny." I shrugged. "That's all I did. Then we saved our own hides by getting out of Dodge."

"In doing so, you have demonstrated the qualities the Heliacal Templars look for in potential insurgent fighters. You are honorable and humble."

I nearly choked. Honorable? I contemplated my life as a petty criminal. No, I couldn't say I was honorable. I would cheat and steal without a second thought if it meant eating and having a safe place to sleep.

Was I humble? I was poor and needy, so in that way, I

was humble. However, I didn't think that was the kind of humility Zeta was talking about.

"Honorable and humble? Sure. I can be those things," I said, glad that Zeta couldn't sense the irony in my statement. Destiny poked me with her elbow.

"Then Zeta and Kory's relationship is settled on a firm foundation that shall yield worthy deeds. Zeta humbly predicts success from this consortship."

Inside, I felt something bending painfully at the facade I was trying to fake. I was not an honorable human being. I had done no heroic deeds. Sure, I had put myself in danger to save Destiny, and it wasn't the first time I'd done so, but she was my sister. I would never have abandoned her to the Kergans and whatever they'd intended to do to her after abducting her along with the other homeless people. But Zeta seemed to think I was some kind of human hero. She would be in for a rude surprise when she realized the truth, but it was her choice to believe these things. It wasn't my fault if she had poor judgment.

I noticed tendrils of some kind of liquid had appeared on the ground surrounding Zeta. They looked like a network of gelatinous veins that covered a circle of the ground about four feet in diameter.

"Gross. What is that stuff?" Destiny said.

"Friend Destiny is pointing to the nanoforge nanobots," Zeta said. "Those have begun to reproduce and are transporting materials from the soil. Zeta's nanoforge also collects oxygen, nitrogen, and small quantities of carbon and hydrogen from this planetary atmosphere."

"Each of those threads is a nanobot?" I asked while pointing at one of the veins.

"Nay, the individual nanobots are too small to see with a human eye. Each of those threads is composed of billions of nanobots. Collectively they have the consistency of a scum, much like the bacterial mats some of your terrestrial microbes form."

Just then, I saw something drip from the edge of Zeta's capsule into one of the containers. It was a clear drop of water. Then came another drop, and another followed even more quickly.

"I am beginning production," Zeta said.

Over the next thirty minutes, the drip increased in rate until it was a trickling flow of water. At the same time, another dripping flow began into the other container. This one was of a gray viscous fluid. It must have been the nutrient solution Zeta had mentioned.

By this time, darkness had settled in, and our only illumination was from the van's dome light and Zeta's soft glow. Zeta's nanobot network had thickened and spread further until it enveloped the ground under the van, trees, and everywhere except where we stood. A strange smell hung in the evening air. Earthy, like somebody had plowed wet soil and fertilized it.

"It stinks," I said. "But I'm strangely hungry."

"You eat enough for both of us," Destiny said. "Lordy, you eat so much that they had to build a Walmart Supercenter just to keep you fed."

I maintained a straight face and said, "Yeah, they have to open a checkout lane just for me so I don't block all the other customers."

Destiny smiled and shook her head. "But you never have enough cash to pay at the end. It takes six employees an entire shift to restock everything you tried to buy."

I held up a finger at her. "No, you are sorely mistaken, madam. It's eleven employees. And they have to work overtime."

Destiny started giggling. It made me smile.

"Zeta has noticed humans exhibit some unusual behaviors," the alien said. "She is trying to understand the purpose of this exchange. Zeta concludes that friend Kory consumes large quantities of food. Is this correct?"

Destiny and I laughed.

"So, when's it gonna be ready?" I asked Zeta.

"The nutrient solution is ready now if you can swap vessels for an empty one," Zeta said.

I did as instructed, placing a pair of empty pans in place of the plastic boxes. Zeta had produced about a gallon of water and a few quarts of the nutrient stuff. I sniffed the latter, holding the gray liquid close to my nose, but smelled nothing. "Time to test it."

I tipped the box back and let a few drops of the liquid drip from a corner into my mouth. Smacking my lips and allowing it to settle on my palette, I detected a slight sweetness and a fatty taste. It tasted a little like butter with a floral aftertaste. "Not bad," I said. Then, I consumed several gulps. The consistency was about the same as a lukewarm smoothie. "Here, try some." I handed the box to Destiny.

She tested the liquid, then tilted the box back a moment later and started gulping it down.

I tapped her on the shoulder. "Hey. Not so much, you pig. Save some for me."

She stopped for a breath and sighed with a smile. "Zeta, that's pretty good." She gave me the box. "It's sort of like thick milk. Hmm... I'm calling it...zetamilk."

I chuckled. "Zetamilk?"

"Yeah, you know, because we milked it from Zeta. Zetamilk."

"Zeta is overjoyed at the satisfaction her friends have

found with the...zetamilk," Zeta said. "It provides all the nutrients, minerals, and vitamins needed by the human body. In theory, you could survive off it indefinitely. Unfortunately, it is the only kind of complete food Zeta knows how to synthesize."

I chugged down the remaining zetamilk. I looked at the pan I had replaced it with, and it already had half a quart of the substance. "How much of that can you make?" I asked.

"Lad, Zeta can produce it endlessly as long as she has access to raw materials."

"Like what? Be more specific."

"The principal four ingredients are carbon, hydrogen, oxygen, and nitrogen. Zeta also requires access to small quantities of chlorine, sodium, potassium, phosphorus, calcium, sulfur, and magnesium and trace amounts of a dozen or so other minerals. All are widely available in this planet's crust. Not surprising, given that your species evolved here."

That's how plants make food. I had never considered it until then. All the ingredients for food were just sitting around. Air, water, and a source of energy were enough to produce the main components of any kind of food. Add to that pinches of other elements, and you have your electrolytes, vitamins, and minerals. If it was that easy, why did so many humans have such trouble keeping themselves fed? The Earth was like a big chunk of unprocessed food. Take the atmosphere, ocean, and sunlight, and there should be enough to feed literally trillions of human beings. And yet, somehow, people were starving. We humans can be such idiots sometimes, not even capable of feeding our species even though the building blocks are lying around us waiting to be processed. No wonder we lost to the Kergans.

"Thank you, Zeta," I said. "This means a lot. We'll ask you to do this again. Finish filling up that pan. Then I think you can stop. We'll store some to eat for breakfast."

"The task was simple," Zeta said.

"Is this the same way that you construct the starship? You sit in the ground, harvest materials, and build it?"

"It is one way to do it, though slow for something the size of a starship. The nanoforge contained in Zeta's capsule is necessarily small. Nay, before Zeta begins construction of the ship, you ought to help her locate a suitable place to excavate and build a base."

"A base? Like a...building?" I said.

"Indeed, precisely that. Using her internal nanoforge, bold Zeta shall fabricate multiple large nanoforges. Then she shall use those to construct the base and the ship and any other consumables our noble mission demands."

Zeta was like a completely self-contained universal factory. She could build almost anything. She could harvest the environment for the required materials. With something like that, Destiny and I could become rich. Wealthy beyond imagination!

"Can you teach us to operate the nanoforge?" I asked, hoping we could get our very own nanoforge.

"Nay, unfortunately," she said. "Zeta's race, the igna, have a particular talent for nanotechnology that other races and civilizations have never mastered. The skill and knowledge are an innate attribute she cannot teach. Attempting it would be like you trying to teach her how to breathe."

Which meant that Zeta would always control the nanoforges. We would need her compliance to exploit this opportunity to its fullest.

"Don't worry, you're not missing anything special," Destiny said. "Breathing is kind of overrated."

"And, yet, Dest blows enough hot air for all of us," I said

with a straight face.

She punched me in the thigh. "But, Zeta, you could build anything," She'd seemingly had come to a similar conclusion as me.

"Not anything. But if it is within the technological bounds of the Collective Dominion, then yes, Zeta could fabricate it, given sufficient time and resources."

"So why not build us a massive flying battle station powerful enough to destroy the Kergans here on Earth?" I said. "Why do we need to start out with a small starship?"

"Firstly, by Zeta's reckoning, the sort of weapon Kory refers to—this battle station—would demand one or two years to construct. Time constraints do not allow for this. Secondly, building such a powerful weapon would give humans access to technologies you are not ready for. Thirdly, if you can threaten the Kergan Empire, you can threaten the Collective Dominion."

"So, you're saying that you don't trust us," I said.

The network of nanobots had disappeared, seeming to have been absorbed into the ground. Or perhaps Zeta had consumed them. She rose from the ground to float level with my head. Her body slowly revolved on its vertical axis. Destiny picked up the pans of water and zetamilk and carried them to the van.

"Friend Kory, trust ought to be earned through worthy acts," Zeta said. "But Zeta trusts you sufficiently to initiate a partnership. Now it is time to formalize our relationship and make you Zeta's consort in truth."

6

Destiny strolled over to stand by my side. I looked at her and said, "What do you think?"

She shrugged. "It's weird. You've never seemed interested in a girlfriend before," she said with a smug grin.

I punched her softly in the shoulder. She flung herself back as if I had walloped her and rubbed her shoulder with mock offense on her face. "Jerk. You shouldn't hit girls."

I ignored her comment. "Okay, Zeta, what do I have to do?"

"It is simple," Zeta said. "You must agree to the terms as previously described. Then Zeta will implant you with a small device that will establish a sydereal link to her. The link also registers you with the Collective Dominion's Ministry of War as an insurgent partner and begins to maintain a record of your deeds."

I didn't know what a sydereal link was but didn't want to ask. "What about Destiny? She's as much a part of this as me."

"Zeta can only have one consort. But you shall be

authorized to delegate some of your responsibilities to other humans."

I nodded. "To anybody I want?"

"Yes, whomever you choose. However, you are limited in the number of subordinates you may recruit. Initially, you shall be limited to just two others. With time, as you undertake and succeed through heroic deeds and feats of arms, you will be granted a larger number of subordinates from whom you can staff your base and crew your ship. You will also be granted access to more advanced technologies, better weapons, larger ships, and base upgrades."

So, I would have to prove myself to Zeta and her people to gain access to the best capabilities and comforts. Obviously, they wanted me to fight the Kergans. The promise of upgrades was undoubtedly an incentive to keep me aligned with their interests. But what if my interests didn't? I only wanted to find a safe place for Destiny and me to live where we had reliable access to food, shelter, and perhaps some simple comforts. I wanted to watch Destiny grow old, for her ribs to disappear under layers of healthy fat and muscle. Living on the streets had exhausted me. For the last two years, I had been working toward our independence, trying to get us off the street. With the Kergan invasion, I had assumed that goal was lost, but a consortship with Zeta might allow me to achieve it.

"I understand," I said. "I accept. What do I do?"

"Remove the clothing from your upper body."

I shrugged out of my leather jacket and pulled my sweatshirt over my head until I stood bare-chested in the chilly wind. I hugged my arms to my chest, trying to contain my body heat. "Is this going to hurt?"

"Kory, Zeta does not know. She has never done this

before," Zeta said.

I squeezed my knees together and jumped back a step. "What?!"

Destiny laughed.

"As Zeta has said, she just began her venture quest. She has never had a previous consort; therefore, she has never performed this implant procedure. But do not concern yourself. It is perfectly safe." She tried to fly around behind me.

I pivoted to hide my back from her. "Are you going to cut me open? Is this like surgery?"

Zeta held her position in front of me. "Nay. The implant shall assemble itself in place beneath your skin. Competent Zeta shall release a stream of nanobots onto your skin. Those shall burrow and complete the construction."

My skin felt clammy, and a lump hung in my throat. "Burrow?"

"It should not be painful. The nanobots are small enough to pass between the cells composing your body tissues." She tried to fly around me again—this time, I allowed her. "Please hold still. You may relax, but do not move."

I was *not* going to relax, but I sucked in a breath and faced forward, looking at the darkening sky.

I felt a tickle on the skin at the base of my skull in the back, like an insect was crawling on me. Then, the pressure on my skin began to grow in intensity. It wasn't painful, but my imagination went wild. Billions of nanobots were penetrating my skin, crawling under it, invading and implanting me with alien technology. My imagination went rampant, conjuring images of Kory Drake as one of the Borg.

The pressure suddenly released.

"Done," Zeta said.

It hadn't taken more than thirty seconds to complete the operation. "That's it?"

"As Zeta already stated, the procedure was minor. How does friend Kory feel?"

I didn't respond immediately. I stood still and sensed my body. I reached behind my neck and pressed against it. I felt nothing under my skin. But inside me, I felt a tug, somewhat like earlier in the day when I felt like a string was pulling my heart. This time, it was persistent and had a direction to it.

I pivoted on my feet. The tug's direction didn't move with me. I walked several paces away until I stood at the front of the van. The direction of the tug shifted. It was always pointed at Zeta. "I can sense you, Zeta. Even with my eyes closed, I know where you are."

"Indeed," Zeta said. "That is what Zeta meant by us being linked. Zeta, too, can sense your location. She is glad that your body has accepted the implant."

"What happens when our consortship ends? Does the implant stay in me?"

"No. Zeta would send a command, and the implant would dissolve to be absorbed by your body and expelled through your urine."

Destiny chuckled. "Watch out, now you've been marked with the Sign of the Beast."

"So, are you saying that makes Zeta the devil?" I said.

"I'm just joking. I'm just glad it's not me."

"Now we must discuss next steps," Zeta said. "Zeta asks Consort Kory to establish a base from which to operate."

"I don't even know where to begin," I said. "I'm not a pilot or a soldier. I still don't understand what you see in us, Zeta."

"Zeta is most interested in worthy Kory's natural attributes. The skills you lack can be taught. Once the base is established, Zeta shall train you and your crew."

"My crew." That term would take some getting used to. "And what is this base?"

"It shall be hidden from the Kergans. Preferably subterranean. Zeta shall excavate it and construct its rooms and equipment, which ought to be completed first before Zeta can construct the ship. We ought to find a location remote enough to have open lands unlikely to be searched by others but close enough to human communities so we can obtain information and provide protection from the Kergans."

"So, we're going to build an underground base. In a remote area, but with nearby humans."

"Aye."

I didn't like the idea of living underground, but I understood why Zeta needed that. The Kergans or human collaborators would easily detect anything above ground. It would be safer. It would become our home. It would be like a bunker, protecting us from the collapse of civilization. With Zeta, we would always have food, water, and shelter.

I looked at Destiny. "Any ideas about where to go?"

"Remember I told you about Wolf Jaw?" she said.

"Yeah. Where's it at again?"

"My aunt Judith and cousin Earline live there. It's up in the mountains northeast of Fresno near Huntington Lake."

I stepped toward the van. "Do we still have that road atlas?"

"Yeah, it's in the front." She ducked into the van and groped under the passenger seat. A moment later, she pulled out a ragged bound set of maps.

I took it from her and opened it to the map of Southern

California. I found Fresno and drew my finger on a line to the northeast until I found Huntington Lake. Wolf Jaw was a small town a mile or two west of the lake. The Sierra National Forest surrounded the town. It was a pretty isolated area, with only one road in and out of town. A half dozen other forest service roads were in the area, but they only took one deeper into the National Forest.

"I think this would be perfect," I said.

"What is?"

"What about setting our base up on national forest lands? That's pretty remote. Nobody lives there."

Destiny nodded and scratched her forehead. "Sure, and the federal government isn't around to kick us off, even if they found us."

"Yeah, we could set up a small camp like homeless squatters. Then Zeta could build her base underneath us. And Wolf Jaw is near the Sierra National Forest." I looked at Zeta. "Would that work?"

"Zeta concurs. Destiny's suggestion seems wise."

I closed the atlas and tucked it under my arm. "Then, Wolf Jaw it is. Destiny, does your aunt still live there?"

"The last I heard, she did. That was about six or seven months ago when I last exchanged texts with my cousin, Earline. They've lived there for like twenty years."

"How come you never went to live with them?"

"They wouldn't take me in. Aunt Judith and my mom never got along, and my aunt didn't think it was fair for her to have to take care of me. But even though she wouldn't let me live with her, I still like her. She's independent and responsible. She's nice, though stubborn."

"Well, maybe we can use her as a contact for getting into town," I said. "A lot of small towns like Wolf Jaw aren't letting strangers into them. We may not be welcome."

"We'll cook that rabbit after we catch it," Destiny said.

I considered the trip. To get to Wolf Jaw, we would have to drive through Patterson and pass south of Modesto over the breadth of the Central Valley. We likely didn't have enough fuel, so we would have to find more.

"Zeta, can you make gasoline?" I asked.

"Indeed," Zeta said. "It is a mixture of basic hydrocarbon compounds. Zeta requires only water and a carbon source, such as plant matter."

Wow, it really struck me at that moment how valuable a resource Zeta was going to be. Being partnered with her removed so many uncertainties. And as with anything valuable, she also needed to be protected. Nobody else could know about her. Not the Kergans, obviously, but also not any other humans who would try to steal her and exploit her if they learned of her capabilities. Could she even protect herself? Would she? She hadn't tried to with that druggie back there. Which meant she also wouldn't protect Destiny or me.

I now had *two* people I was responsible for.

My new link with Zeta tugged at me, reminding me she was floating just a few feet away. Through the link, I sensed her contentment with the situation. She was profoundly satisfied. Would I always sense through the link what she was feeling?

7

The next morning, we awoke before dawn. Zeta was awake and, in fact, didn't appear to have slept.

The sky was gray and overcast, with a chill breeze from the west, and a light but unrelenting drizzle of rain fell on us. The temperature had dropped below the dewpoint, leaving a thick sheen of water and fog on the van's windows. My breath steamed in the cold and clammy air.

We drank the rest of the zetamilk for breakfast. It wasn't as satisfying as bacon and eggs, but it filled our stomachs and kept the hunger away.

We got back on the road and continued eastward to Patterson. With the rising sun in my eyes, we drove under the I-5 overpass west of Patterson, and I noticed a line of stopped vehicles ahead. I let my foot up off the gas.

"Checkpoint ahead," I said.

"Hide the beer cans," Destiny said, joking because we didn't actually have any alcohol in the van. "You're a liability, Mister Drake. One look at you, and they'll stop us."

"Well, *Miss* Austin, you're welcome to drive instead. I

dare say you exude trustworthiness."

She shrugged. "Do you think they'll let us through?" Destiny said.

"I don't know. Zeta, hide yourself. Make yourself inconspicuous."

"Very well," Zeta said, floating onto the floor behind my seat.

The line of vehicles advanced slowly. A large semi-trailer moved before us, blocking my view of what awaited us. Finally, the truck accelerated forward with a growl and puff of exhaust, and I could see the checkpoint.

Four men armed with automatic rifles stood at the side of the road just before the bridge over the first canal. A half dozen vehicles were parked in the highway lanes so that one could only pass by slowing down and weaving between them. After the truck passed, one of the blocking vehicles was driven forward to block my lane.

One of the men signaled to me to move forward next to him. Just like the other guards, he was dressed in combat fatigues, armed with a semi-automatic rifle hanging from a shoulder strap and a pistol in a hip holster.

I drove forward as ordered and lowered my window. The man's expression was severe, and his hand gripped the trigger guard of his rifle, though he kept it pointed at the ground.

"Where are you headed?" he said. His clean-shaven face studied the inside of the vehicle. Two other men on Destiny's side walked around us, looking through the windows and checking underneath the chassis.

"Just passing through," I said. "Our destination is near Fresno."

"Are you a resident?"

"Of Patterson?"

The guy looked annoyed. "Where else?"

"We're from San Jose," I said.

He shook his head. "Sorry, I can't allow you to pass."

My face heated up. "Why?"

"Sir, I need you to turn your vehicle around and return the way you came."

I thought about where we were going to go. "Look, we only need to get through Patterson so we can head southeast."

"Do you have an entry permit?"

"No."

The guard shook his head.

"How do I get one of those? An entry permit?"

"They're issued by the town council for residents and official visitors." He studied our car, clothes, and belongings visible through the windows. He didn't look impressed. "I doubt you'll get one." He took a step back and waved his hand at us. "I need you to turn around, sir. You're blocking traffic."

I didn't move. "Where are we supposed to go?"

"Anywhere but here. Now move it." This time, he gestured threateningly with his rifle.

I put the van in gear, pulled a U-turn, and headed west, back under the I-5 overpass, where I pulled over to the shoulder. "You got the map, Destiny? Where to next?"

"Do I look like Magellan?"

"No, not Italian enough."

Destiny gave me a flat look. "Magellan was Portuguese. Where'd *you* go to school?" she said as she opened the atlas and studied it.

I felt my face flush, and I swallowed an angry retort. I'd dropped out of school when I escaped the orphanage and ever since I'd been sensitive about my lack of education.

Over the last couple of years, I'd taken steps to make up for it, working toward my GED through a community outreach program and making good progress until the Kergans invaded, forcing me to stop and focus on more important things, such as food, shelter, and avoiding being knifed by some desperate refugee.

"If we go south down I-5 about three miles, there is supposed to be another crossing over the canal," Destiny said. "There's a town called Crows Landing. We could try that."

"Okay."

I was annoyed at the roadblock. This was America, or at least it used to be. Who were these people who thought they could stop me from entering their city? They must have had the entire city of Patterson encircled and protected. They were probably operating under local martial law.

We took the on-ramp for southbound I-5 and began driving south. I checked my fuel gauge. We had about a half tank, which was not enough for the entire day. We'd need to get Zeta to produce some more.

The I-5 freeway was almost deserted. Dozens of abandoned cars rested on the shoulders of the road, left there months ago during the Great Panic when everybody was trying to flee from the invading Kergans after the federal government collapsed. That was until they realized there was nowhere to escape to. And with fuel so hard to come by these days, many hadn't bothered to return for their abandoned cars.

We passed by orchards that looked overgrown and unkept, with long grass growing between the trunks and stretches of fence falling down. I swerved around a massive puddle in the middle of my freeway lane where drainage had obviously failed.

Soon, I spotted the exit ramp for Crows Landing and took it. We turned left to head eastward under the overpass. After a short stretch of country highway, we crossed the west canal bridge. Thankfully, there were no roadblocks.

And no roadblocks at the east canal either.

The small, two-lane highway was empty of all traffic. After a mile, we entered Crows Landing without incident, a small farming town surrounded by fields. I saw one home with a man sitting on the front porch cradling a shotgun. We drove straight through and left the town behind as we continued eastward.

We found ourselves driving through farmland, endless fields in all directions, most left fallow either because it was winter, or the farmers were gone. A thin morning fog hung over the ground, and I had the windshield wipers running to deal with light rainfall. It was a dreary winter morning in the Central Valley. I was glad to be inside our van with its heater.

A bend in the road took us toward the northeast for a few miles. As we drove by yet another field full of unidentified crops, I noticed a person walking along the highway backward with their hand hung out and their thumb up. The hood of their coat was up, and their other hand rested in a pocket. They must have been miserable walking in this weather. As we came closer, I saw it was a man with a thin black beard, wearing a stocking cap and a backpack.

Usually, I wouldn't stop to pick up a stranger. I wouldn't even consider it, especially having Zeta in the van with us. But when I saw that hitchhiker walking on that lonely highway in the fog and rain, I remembered that night five years ago when a kind lady trucker had stopped for me. Who knows what would have happened to me if she hadn't? I could have been picked up by the police and forced to go back to the orphanage.

I didn't have long to think about it. We were approaching quickly. I came to a decision, took my foot off the gas, and pressed down firmly on the brake. "Zeta, get under cover. We're going to have some company for a little while."

"Aye, lad."

Zeta had such an antiquated manner of speaking. Did she learn her English from old Victorian texts? I hadn't bothered correcting her since it didn't bother me and was endearing, but her habits were odd.

My seatbelt pressed firmly against my chest as I rapidly brought the van to a stop on the shoulder.

"Uh...are you crazy?" Destiny said.

I looked in the rearview mirror. The man was running toward us in a jog, his backpack bobbing up and down behind him. "Just for a few hours," I said. "Maybe he's not even headed in our direction. But I figure if we can save him a hundred miles of walking, then we'll have done a good turn."

She snickered. "Since when did you become Mister Goody Two-Shoes?"

I rolled down my window and poked my head out as the man stopped beside my door. "Where you headed?"

"Just trying to get away from the coast," he said. "Are you headed east?" He was so bundled up it was difficult to make out his features, but he was medium height—shorter than me by about eight inches. Medium build and appeared to be Hispanic.

"Yeah, we're headed to the Fresno area."

"That works for me."

"Okay, hop in. Door's on the right side."

A few seconds later, the sliding door opened, and the

man stepped in with his backpack at his feet. He sat on the bench behind ours and slid the door shut again. "Woo! It's chilly out there but nice and warm here. Thanks a bunch! I really appreciate it." He extended his hand. "Clemen Busto."

I accepted it. "Kory Drake." I gestured to my sister. "This is my sister, Destiny Austin."

Busto looked back and forth between us. "Sister, yeah?"

I know we didn't look at all related to each other, but it wasn't his business. "It's a long story," I said. I pulled us back onto the highway and accelerated.

After that, it was quiet for a while. Our passenger didn't seem to have anything to say, and Destiny and I had nothing to talk about we would want to speak in front of this man who we didn't know. Had I made the right decision to pick him up like that? What if he was armed? If he had a gun and wanted our van and possessions, he could just take them; there was little we could probably have done about it.

I studied Busto through the rearview mirror. He had unzipped his wet jacket and removed his cap. He wore his hair about shoulder length and had a scruffy thin beard, though his build was lean and wiry. His age was hard to determine, but he could have been thirty, though his eyes betrayed a greater age. They looked haunted.

Soon, we crossed the San Joaquin River and then came to a highway junction, where we turned right and started driving eastward again.

"What the hell?!" Busto abruptly cried out.

I glanced behind me. Zeta was floating next to Busto's shoulder. "Zeta! Ugh."

"Zeta is greeting this stranger," Zeta said.

Destiny had turned around in her seat and was shaking her head. She shook with concealed laughter.

"I thought I told you to hide yourself." I threw one of my hands up in the air and sighed. Now, what were we going to do? Zeta was like a friendly dog. She didn't seem capable of hiding her curiosity about other humans. Thank the stars she'd kept quiet when we were at that roadblock.

"What is *this*?" Busto said, pointing at Zeta, who was practically touching his shoulder. He didn't appear scared, only slightly surprised.

"That is Zeta," I said. "She's an igna."

"A what?"

"An igna. She's an alien."

"This being is named Z374," Zeta said, "also called Zeta, of the Collective Dominion. These humans are Zeta's comrades."

"You have strange companions, Kory," Busto said. "Very interesting. Zeta, are you friends with the Kergans?"

"Zeta does not enjoy friendly relations with any member of the Kergan Empire."

Busto nodded. "Good. That's the right answer. I myself am trying to get as far away from them as possible."

"The Kergan authorities have issued a reward for Zeta's capture because she illegally entered Earth territory," Zeta said.

It's just what we needed, for Zeta to tell people she was valuable to the Kergans. If she had a mouth, I would describe it as a big one.

"Let's not share too much information, Zeta," I said. "Only what he needs to know." I glanced at Busto. "No offense, but it's safer this way."

"I understand," Busto said. "You can't be too safe these days, what with so many humans having turned into collaborators who are now happily licking Kergan boots. Or tentacles, anyways. But what are you doing with an alien traveling with you? I don't mean to pry, but you don't look like the sort of people who're on good terms with aliens. You know what I mean?" He studied the dilapidated state of the van and our belongings.

I didn't respond. Instead, Zeta did.

"Mr. Busto," Zeta said, "Curious Zeta wonders about your history. From whence do you come, and what deeds have you wrought?"

I didn't know how to shut up Zeta without causing a scene. And on balance, she was collecting some valuable intelligence on our new acquaintance.

"Sure, I don't mind," Busto said, looking pointedly at me. "I'm from Oakland. Grew up there. I had a rough childhood but enlisted in the Marine Corps after finishing high school. I served for twelve years and reached the rank of gunnery sergeant. People who know me call me *Gunny*. I've been out for three years now and been trying to make my way in life. At least, I was, until the Kergans invaded. I'm on reserve status but never get called up. The U. S. Government collapsed so quickly that they couldn't activate all the reserves. It was just crazy to watch it all fall apart so fast.

"Since then, I've just been trying to survive. My brother was killed in the fighting. My mother and father disappeared two weeks ago during one of the Kergan police sweeps through Oakland. It's just me now. I don't know where any of my family are. I'm just looking for somewhere in the middle of nowhere that the Kergans will ignore, and I can hopefully live in peace."

As Busto told his brief story, I found myself nodding. His background was so much different from mine, yet I could empathize with what he had passed through, seeing as how Destiny was almost taken from me.

Busto looked at us expectantly, as if waiting for us to share our stories. But neither Destiny nor I responded though I croaked out, "Sorry, that sucks big time." Then, I turned my focus back on the road.

Zeta and Busto continued chatting for a few more minutes. Gunny Busto asked some probing questions, and I worried that Zeta's big mouth would get us into trouble. But after a while, I became satisfied that she wouldn't reveal our plans or that we planned to become guerrillas.

8

We made good time on the highway for the first hour after picking up Gunny Busto. We drove east until we arrived in Delhi, and from there, we turned southeast on the highway toward Fresno. Delhi was quiet, and we passed through it without any drama.

There were thick patches of fog in places, and the highway was beginning to show the effects of a lack of maintenance by the State of California, so I kept our speed below the posted limit. The old van couldn't comfortably go at freeway speeds anyway. Above 50 MPH, it began to shake like it would fall apart.

In Merced, we encountered heavier traffic and many roadblocks. Just as we had encountered in Patterson, the city authorities had closed the city to non-residents. Armed militia manned checkpoints and patrolled every single little back road around the small city, forcing us to take a long detour around the north side of the city limits. Most of it was through muddy tracks that threatened to trap the van and leave it fossilized, to be encountered by some

71

archaeologist in a thousand years with our mummified bodies still strapped into the seats.

Obliged to make a considerable detour, we circled to the east of Merced all the way to a tiny town called Planada. It had suffered far worse than others. Most of the town looked like it had been looted and burned. As we drove through the center, we passed decomposing bodies lying in the streets and the skeletons of burned-out buildings. There wasn't a living human in sight.

"Most of these towns have been unwelcoming," Destiny said, "but these people in Planada are alright in my book. They just lay around all day."

I groaned and shook my head at her dark joke.

"That's harsh, girl," Busto said. "You could have been one of those people."

"Naw, I lack a *grave* personality."

Busto shook his head and snorted.

I didn't say anything 'cause it would have just encouraged her. Instead, I thought about what had happened here.

Who could have done this? It didn't look like the work of the Kergans. They didn't leave dead people in the streets like that and didn't indiscriminately destroy property either. I'd never heard of them undertaking a terror campaign. The Kergans didn't pillage and burn just for the sake of causing suffering. No, Planada had been attacked by somebody else.

By this time, the sun had already crossed the sky and was in the west. Getting through Merced had really slowed us down, and the fuel tank was less than a quarter full. We wouldn't make it to Fresno before dark, and definitely not all the way to Wolf Jaw, especially if we didn't get more gas.

"We're going to have to find a place to camp for the night," I announced. "Gunny, you're welcome to spend the night with us and share our food."

"Thanks, I'll take you up on that," Busto said. "I wish I'd some way to contribute to your expenses. I've got some protein bars I could share."

With Zeta helping us, we didn't need his. I shook my head. "Don't worry about it, we got you covered."

Destiny laughed. "You'll get to try the zetamilk."

"Zeta-what?" Busto said.

She turned around and smiled in a secretive way at the former Marine. "I'll give you a hint where it comes from. The creature has no legs, no mouth, and sounds like a Charles Dickens character."

Busto sniffed. "You are a strange child."

"Hey, soldier, watch who you patronize," she said, turning her back on him.

"I'm a *marine*, not a soldier." Busto abruptly leaned forward from his bench seat and tapped me on the shoulder. "I know this area. I've got a suggestion for a camping spot. Somewhere safe and off the road."

"Sure," I said. "Destiny, why don't you have him show you on the atlas." Though they were twenty years old, I was glad we had the old paper maps. The Kergans had destroyed Earth's satellite-based navigation systems. GPS, Galileo, and GLONASS were all gone. Even if they had still been there, smartphones would not have worked anyway, given that the cell networks and Internet were also gone, and we'd never owned a stand-alone GPS receiver.

The location Busto had chosen was a large lot to the northeast of Madera on the banks of the Fresno River.

The drive from Planada to Madera went quickly. We drove through two more villages that had been looted and burned, but the highway was passable.

During that stretch of road, I again caught flashes of a

very distant blackhole seeming to follow us. It was no bigger than a black dot and was never out in the open long enough for me to know for sure what it was, but it worried me that we'd been followed.

I tried to suppress my anxiety and focused on the road. To our surprise, Madera's roads were open. Unlike the other small cities, there were no roadblocks. We soon learned why.

We slowly drove through the north side of Madera, heading east to a bridge over the Fresno River. Light rain fell from the overcast sky, making a *pitter-patter* sound on the van's roof. The road traffic was sparse, and what we saw moved slowly, well under the speed limit.

"Is that a checkpoint?" Busto said.

I jerked my head up. "Where?"

"Up there ahead, beyond that red pickup truck."

I saw it. Expecting more human guards, I was surprised instead to see the floating bodies of Kergan marac MPs carrying weapons, stationed next to an armored ground vehicle of some kind. The latter blocked one of the lanes of eastbound traffic. They were forcing cars to stop in the other.

I pulled over to the right shoulder and parked behind an empty SUV.

"We can't go through there," Destiny said. "They know my name."

"What're you talking about?" Busto said.

I needed to tell him what had happened to us in San Jose. He should know that being with us was a risk. And then there was Zeta. We couldn't let her be found.

"We're wanted," I said.

"Who?"

"All of us, including Zeta." I turned around in my seat to

look at Busto. "Sorry, I didn't say anything. I didn't expect to encounter the Kergans out here in the Central Valley. Maybe it would be best if you got out here. That way, they won't think you're an accomplice if we're caught."

Busto held up a hand to stop me. "What did you guys do?"

"Well, Zeta is wanted for illegal entry into Earth. There's a fairly large reward on her head. At least it was large at one point, though not now with this hyperinflation.

"Destiny and I are coming from San Jose. Back there, they tried to round us up. Destiny was caught and put in a detention cell. I broke her out. We killed at least one Kergan MP while escaping and destroyed one of their spy ships."

Busto grunted. "How the hell did you do that?"

"There's no time to tell you. The important thing is that they know Destiny by name because they detained her. And they know me by association, though I doubt they know my name. If we go through that checkpoint and they see Destiny's ID, we'll be arrested, and the car searched. Then they'll find Zeta."

The former marine settled back into his seat and looked into the distance at the checkpoint. He didn't say anything right away.

"Zeta," I said, "You better hide somewhere. Get out of sight and stay there."

Zeta's octahedral body floated behind Busto's seat and disappeared under my dirty laundry pile.

"Maybe I can help you," Busto said.

I didn't want to get the man mixed up with our problems. "No, you don't have to do that."

"I want to."

"No, this is our problem. Sorry we couldn't get you all the way to Fresno, but this is the end of the road."

Busto chopped his hand into his palm. "Look, dude, I was a Marine Raider. I received extensive training in SERE."

I looked at Destiny. She shook her head and shrugged. "What does that mean? Raider? SERE?"

He rubbed his chin. "Marine Raiders are the Corp's special operations regiment. At least they were. They're probably disbanded now. But I was basically a commando. SERE is an acronym that stands for survival, evasion, resistance, and escape. What it means is that I'm trained to operate behind enemy lines. I want to help you. Please."

The pleading in his voice compelled me to consider it. If Busto indeed had all that experience, then he knew what he was about to get himself into. Probably far better than either Destiny or me.

"What did you have in mind?" I said.

Busto pointed at the checkpoint ahead, which was a couple hundred yards away, thanks to his sharp eyes seeing it long before the MPs could see us. "While we've been chatting, I've been watching the checkpoint. The guards are bored. They're only making the most cursory check of people's IDs and vehicles. They won't search your van unless you give them a reason to. Therefore, I propose hiding Destiny and Zeta in the back under your belongings. Then you and I sit in the front. Let me drive and do the talking. We'll say we're roommates relocating from the Bay Area to Fresno."

"Why not let me drive?"

"Because you're so young looking. I know, the Kergans probably won't catch onto that. Most of them don't know how to tell humans apart, but just in case they do, it would be better if I looked like the one in charge. I know how to talk to soldiers. I know how to put them at ease."

It seemed really risky. All they would have to do is

search in the back, and within seconds, they'd find Destiny and Zeta. "It seems really audacious to me," I said. "To just drive right through the checkpoint with them hidden under some junk."

"That's why they won't be expecting it. I'm not saying it's risk-free, but it's our best chance. And regardless, if they happen to catch us, then I can take down those guards before they can do anything about it. Maracs are slow. I'm surprised they beat us in battle, honestly."

I realized that Busto might be a little bit nuts. The bravado he was putting off was not what I would expect of an unarmed human facing several armed and armored Kergan soldiers. *But, wait, maybe Gunny isn't unarmed,* it suddenly occurred to me. I looked his body up and down but saw no signs of obvious weapons hiding under his bulky winter clothes.

We needed to get out of California's populated areas where the Kergans and human collaborators liked to lurk. I was forced to admit that we needed Busto's help. Maybe he was just an arrogant braggart who was about to get us captured and maybe killed. But I wouldn't know for sure until we tried it. It was a risk, but Destiny and I were used to taking risks.

"Okay, Gunny, we'll do it your way," I said. "Is that okay, Destiny?"

"Can't we just go around?" she said. "Find another way around the city?"

"We need to get across the Fresno River," Busto said. "Any bridge west and south of here will be either watched by the Kergans or too far away. The only other bridge is ten miles away to the northwest."

She folded her arms. "So, you're gonna put Zeta and me at risk just to save some time."

He shook his head. "No, it's not like that. What I'm proposing is a measured risk. We're in danger no matter what we do. At least here, I know what we must deal with: a couple bored Kergan MPs. I *know* we can handle them, and I'd rather manage a known situation like this than take the chance of going somewhere else and running into an unpleasant surprise."

She shook a finger at him. "Well, easy for you to say, it's not *your* ass that's gonna be in the clinker if they catch me."

Busto's frown made his whiskers droop. "If you think that, then you don't understand the Kergans. If you're caught, we're *all* going to prison. I'm taking the same risk as you."

Destiny huffed. "Fine. I just want to get out of here, eat something, and sleep." She unbuckled her seatbelt, stepped out of the car, went to the rear, opened the back hatch, and started shifting around our belongings. Busto and I got out and helped her.

We rearranged boxes around to make a small nest in the middle of which were piled our bags of clothing and other loose items. Destiny lay on the rusty floor with Zeta cradled by her belly. Then we laid the bags on top of them until they couldn't be seen.

I handed the keys to Busto, and he went to the driver's side. I took the passenger seat.

Busto started the engine and shifted the van into gear. "Everybody ready?" he said.

The rest of us called out our affirmations. I took my California driver's license out of my wallet.

Busto pulled into the traffic and started driving toward the checkpoint. There were three cars ahead of us. Busto brought us to a stop behind them. He looked calm and unconcerned, but his eyes never stopped watching the

Kergan guards as they checked papers and observed the vehicles.

Three maracs were floating in their armored suits. There were probably more of them sitting in their armored truck. The latter had a heavy weapon of some kind mounted on the roof. That gun, or whatever it was, constantly tracked back and forth, pointing at the surroundings. What if it had a special sensor that could detect lifeforms? What if they could look through the skin of our van and see Destiny and Zeta hiding in the back? I didn't have a clue what Kergan sensors were capable of. But we couldn't pull out of line now. It would look too suspicious.

The line slowly advanced, one vehicle at a time. The guards acted bored and disinterested in the humans, but I didn't know how to read marac expressions. Twelve-armed octopus-looking monsters whose technology far exceeded that of humanity.

The last car in front of us drove off, and Busto glided us to a stop next to one of the guards and rolled down his window.

"IDs and vehicle registration," the marac soldier said from a speaker with a synthetic voice.

"Oops," I said with a whisper. "My registration is expired." I opened the glove compartment and grabbed the registration, which expired four months ago. I handed it and my license to Busto. At least the vehicle was registered in my name, which should avoid too much suspicion.

Busto added his ID and gave the documents to the guard.

The Kergan studied our licenses, glancing up to look at our faces. It said something loudly, but not in English or any other language I recognized. It sounded like a jumble of trumpeting and whooshes interspersed with staccato chirps. A response came from another marac guard who floated back and forth on the van's passenger side, obviously studying the interior.

"Your registration is expired," the guard said. "But I don't care. Just take care of it soon. California state laws are still in force."

Nominally. Yeah, right.

"Yes, sir," Busto said.

The guard continued to hold onto our documents. "What is your destination, and where are you coming from?"

Busto nodded, looking at the guard in the visor of its helmet. "My friend and I are roommates. We're relocating from the Bay Area to Fresno. We've got new jobs at a food processing plant. A cannery."

"Excellent. With your food production having fallen so low, we need to keep you humans fed and healthy."

Of course, it didn't admit anything about who was at fault for human food shortfalls.

The guard returned the documents to Busto, who returned my registration and license. "Madera's city limits are now under Kergan martial law. You will obey all orders given by Kergan MPs. Curfew is at 7 pm."

"Curfew?" Busto said.

"Yes. Human looters and bandits are a problem. If you are caught on the streets after 7 pm without a pass, you will be detained and possibly executed. Curfew ends at 7 am."

"Yes, sir. Then we better get going." It was already 5:30 pm, and the winter sun was low on the horizon.

The guard waved an armored tentacle at us. Busto put the van in gear, and we advanced, easing around the front end of the hulking armored truck.

When we had put a couple hundred yards between us

and the checkpoint, Busto said, "Okay, you can come out now."

There was a *thump,* and shuffling sounds as Destiny and Zeta dug themselves out of their nest.

We crossed the Fresno River a few minutes later and turned northeast to follow the southern bank.

"The camping spot I had in mind is about a half mile ahead," Busto said.

We passed a sizeable bridge-looking structure that crossed above the road. Its gray concrete looked new.

"That's a viaduct to carry the incomplete California High-Speed Rail," Busto said.

Destiny was now sitting on the bench seat where Busto had been sitting earlier. "Hooray for government projects!" she said. "Look at our tax dollars at work!"

I chuckled. "When did you ever pay taxes?"

"Hey, buster, they're mine by association."

California no longer had the budget to complete the ambitious project. They couldn't even keep the existing highway system running correctly, let alone continue with their dreams of high-speed rail. Everything in the state was beginning to fall apart—governments, infrastructure, and especially the people. The Kergans were ruling a defeated and increasingly destitute people.

Was the rest of the United States in a similar situation? So little information flowed now. News organizations had been banned. Only rumors and gossip remained, passed via word-of-mouth, the one remaining means of knowing what was happening in the world. I didn't know if the US existed as a government entity anymore, though the Kergans seemed to support the state governments if California was any evidence. But how long would that last?

Soon after passing the viaduct, Busto slowed and pulled

off to the left of the road into a large gravel lot. It was partially filled with abandoned construction equipment and supplies, some of which looked to have been looted. A gate covered the lot's entrance, but the chain on it was broken, and the gate was pushed open.

The Fresno River lay to the north, and at this time of the year, when it was cool and wet, a decent amount of water flowed down it.

As we pulled to a stop under some trees at the edge of the lot, tension released from my chest. "Thanks, Gunny," I said. "You did good back there."

Maybe the man had utterly bluffed his way through the checkpoint. Perhaps he wasn't all the things that he said he was. I didn't know because we never had to put his skills to the test. But we had made it, and it was because of his advice. It would be a mistake not to give him credit for it.

"Anytime, my friend," Busto said. He held out a fist, and I bumped it with mine. Then, he did the same for Destiny.

"Are your hands clean?" she said.

It was a pretty crummy thing to say, and Busto's face turned red. "Probably not." He dropped his hand.

"Zeta has concluded that friend Gunny is resourceful," Zeta said. "My compliments."

Gunny smiled and said, "Thanks."

9

That evening, Zeta again settled onto the ground next to the van and extended her nanobots into the lot's soil and the river's bank. She produced enough water and zetamilk for the next day. Then, she started to make gasoline. Only a trickle, but she produced it all night while we slept, and by morning, she had collected 10 gallons. Throughout the night, those on watch swapped and emptied the full containers into the van until we had a nearly full tank.

Zeta also produced a small quantity of motor oil, which we needed because the van burned through nearly a quart of oil per tank of gas.

After dinner, before going to bed, I leaned back in a camp chair in front of a small fire of broken pallets we'd lit to keep the winter chill away. Destiny sat in another chair, and Busto rested on a tarp lying on the ground, his back propped up against a tree trunk.

Busto had been studying Destiny and me for a minute. I knew he was about to ask some questions. "No offense," Busto said, "but you two seem awfully young to be alone.

What happened to your families?"

"We're old enough," I said.

"I saw your driver's license. You're eighteen. And if Destiny is older than that, I'll eat my right ear." He leaned forward and shoved a burning brand deeper into the fire. "But it's none of my business, and I've spent time with young kids in the Corps who, nonetheless, are old enough to carry a rifle and kill with it. I'm just curious what happened to you, is all."

Destiny went first and told the marine an abbreviated version of her story. She talked about having a happy family when she was very young. Then came her mother's entrapment by drug addiction. Her father disappeared and never returned. Family life got slowly worse until child protective services took her—and only her, because they didn't consider her younger siblings to be at risk from her mother's steady stream of slimy boyfriends—and put her into foster homes.

Her story naturally led to mine since we'd met on the streets and been together for five years. I kept the detail sparse—not that I remembered much of my childhood, as it was. I'd been part of a family, an only child, happy as far as I could recall, but my parents were both killed in an auto accident. Their car went off a bridge with me strapped into a booster seat in the back. The car's front end was submerged, with me hanging in my seat just above the water. My parents drowned, and I survived. I had no extended family in a position to take me in, so I ended up in a state-run orphanage. Then, I escaped when I was thirteen and had lived on the streets ever since.

Destiny and I were a family. As dysfunctional as one could be, without a home or steady employment, but we depended on each other. I didn't expect somebody like Gunny Busto to understand us. So, I was surprised when he tossed wood in the fire and said, "I wish I were as strong as you two are. I can't imagine living through what you have. You're both survivors. That's what you are."

That wasn't the typical reaction we got from strangers when they learned of what we were. Usually, we were ignored, and when we did get somebody's attention, it was generally because they wanted to exploit us in some way. But I'd learned years ago to use my physical size and strength to convince predators that we weren't worth the trouble. It was a relief to have the companionship of an older man who wasn't looking to steal something from us.

Be that as it was, we'd talked long enough about ourselves, more than I wanted, and Gunny hadn't reciprocated with much in the way of his own history. So, I picked a different target.

"Zeta," I said to the alien, who rested on the ground nearby, "I suppose you must have a family, right? Seeing as how you're a princess and all. Is your father a king?"

Busto stiffened and pointed a thumb at Zeta. "She's a princess?"

I nodded.

"Aye, lad," the alien responded. "But it is Zeta's mother who is the reigning sovereign of the Collective Dominion. She is Z373, Matriarch of the Realm and the Nova Throne. Ignas do not grow up knowing their fathers. Zeta is ignorant of his identity."

"So, your family is just your mother and your siblings?"

"Aye, though Zeta has but one younger sister, Z375."

"And she's still at home?"

"She is abroad studying at what you would call a university. A place of higher education. One day, she will become a lawyer unless something were to happen to Zeta or if Zeta were to prove unworthy of inheriting from her mother."

"You must be very wealthy," Destiny said.

"Nay," Zeta said, "that is not the igna way. The monarch serves the people. Zeta's mother possesses no property. She relinquished all when she took the throne. If Zeta becomes queen one day, she shall live a life of asceticism wholly dedicated to serving her people."

"But your mother must be a very powerful person," Busto said.

"Indeed, she is. Zeta's very life is in her hands, as are all the soldiers of the realm. The ignas of the Collective Dominion subscribe to a practice called Inverse Wealth Governance. Those who hold political power must surrender their wealth in proportion to the number of people they govern. The monarch, being the highest power of the realm, holds the least amount of wealth. Zeta's mother, her Highness Z373, depends on the charity of the people she rules over for her daily upkeep."

"That's an interesting way to govern," Busto said.

"I wish our world were like that," Destiny said. "Imagine if our politicians had to give up all their wealth before they were allowed to rule. How different our world would be! If people don't like your job, they just stop feeding you."

"I don't know," I said, "it still seems like a corrupt politician could still exploit such a system. In fact, wouldn't it make them vulnerable to being influenced by the wealthy? Wouldn't we just end up with a bunch of puppet rulers? Those who hold all the riches *always* find a way to grasp for power. Sorry, Zeta, but I don't see how a government you described could be stable over the long term."

"Lad, it is ingrained into the culture of Zeta's people,"

Zeta said. "It is part of the igna religion."

"You have a religion?"

"In a manner of speaking, though not like you humans. Unlike you, we igna are in contact with those who live in the afterlife."

"What?!"

Zeta shifted around on the ground as if excited. "Zeta's people call them the Ancients, those who have finished a life within a material body and have moved onto the next existence, what we call sydereal space, or the syderealium."

"You know them?"

"Nay, Zeta is too young to speak with the Ancients. And not all who speak with them return to the world of the living. For this reason, the Dominion rarely allows young igna to converse with the Ancients."

"But you must have priests then, right?"

"Nay, at least not in the sense you are thinking. Every female can commune with the Ancients once they come of age."

"When will that happen for you?"

"Once Zeta completes this venture quest and Zeta's mother approves the outcome, she shall be granted the privilege of communion. It is a prerequisite to assuming the Nova Throne, for the queen answers to the Supreme Council of the Ancients."

"Ha," Destiny laughed. "So even she isn't all-powerful. Even she answers to somebody."

"Indeed, friend Destiny speaks the truth. The Supreme Council may overrule the monarch, and it happens frequently."

I tried to imagine humanity being watched over by the ghosts of our past and granting them the power to veto our dumbest decisions. I could see how a system like that could work. But in all honesty, what Zeta had described sounded like mystic nonsense. I imagined Zeta sitting—or floating—at a table in some kind of seance so she could speak with the dead. But I didn't say anything. It was her culture and their beliefs, and it was none of my business how they chose to govern themselves.

I realized that Zeta had mentioned her venture quest, and Busto had not asked about it. I didn't want him to know about our actual goals. Though I wanted to keep listening to Zeta's stories about her world, I worried it would reveal too much, so I suggested it was time for bed. The conversation quickly ended after that.

Despite my wariness of Busto, the help he had given us with the Kergans and his openness to our unconventional lives increased my trust in him. I began to see him as a potential ally, as a person who would be worth keeping around. We'd been quite lucky to encounter somebody like him with his former military experience.

The next morning, a little after 8 am, we left our camp and drove east with the rising sun in my face. We didn't want to go any further south because none of us knew what was happening in Fresno. Being a large city, it had probably been taken over by the Kergans by now.

We crossed the San Joaquin River —again—several miles north of Fresno city limits at a small town called Friant. From there, we continued east on small country roads in increasingly hilly terrain as we entered the foothills of the Sierra Nevada Mountain range. We were headed toward a junction with Highway 168, which would take us northeast to Wolf Jaw, hopefully arriving by that evening.

I drove us down a narrow paved country road at about 35 MPH that twisted through and over the hills. The area was solitary. We hadn't seen a building, home, or other road for several miles. Busto sat in the passenger's seat, and

Destiny lay on the rear bench napping.

We came around the base of a hill on a blind turn, and I saw several vehicles blocking the road. I braked hard to avoid colliding with them. Destiny crashed to the floor.

"Ugh!" she cried out.

"Idiots!" I yelled. "Who would park on a blind corner like that?"

Busto held up his hand to me. "Careful. This wasn't stupidity."

That's when I noticed men getting out of two pickup trucks carrying what looked like assault rifles.

"It's a roadblock," Busto said. "And I don't think they're friendly. Keep your hands visible, where they can see them."

10

Two of the strangers—a man and a woman—had their rifles pointed at us, tracking us through the windshield. A second man lowered his rifle to hang from his shoulder on its sling and drew an automatic pistol, which he pointed at me. He approached the driver's side of the van in a very aggressive shooter's stance.

I kept my hands raised, as did Busto and Destiny.

The second man stood outside my door and yelled, "Turn off your vehicle!"

Conscious of the menacing pistol pointed at my chest, I did as ordered and reached down to the ignition and turned off the engine. I put my hand back up, holding the keys in it.

"Zeta," I said softly, "Hide yourself. They will find you but act like an inert object."

"Already done, Consort," she said.

Busto gave me a strange look.

"Everyone, exit the vehicle now!" the man ordered. "Keep your hands up and visible!"

"We're in deep trouble," Busto said. "I think these are

bandits."

"Damn," I said. My only thought in that moment was for Destiny. What would they do to her?"

"Now!" the man yelled again.

I slowly reached down for the door latch and opened it. Busto and Destiny did the same. I stepped out and turned to face the man. I had no weapon on me. My pistol was behind my seat, and I hadn't had a chance to grab it. Not that I would have stood a chance against these people. They looked dangerous and carried their weapons with confidence.

"Walk to the front of the vehicle," the woman said. "Keep your hands up. We will shoot to kill if you give us a reason."

I stepped over in front of the van's grill and was soon joined by Busto and Destiny, with Busto in the middle.

"We're friendly," I said. "I assure you we're just passing through."

The first man stepped toward me and swung his rifle buttstock into my belly. With a bellow, I dropped to my knees, clutching my guts, gasping, feeling like I was going to asphyxiate.

"Nobody asked you!" the first man said. He followed this with a kick to the thigh and a laugh. "But, please, talk some more if you want to meet my other foot."

The woman pounded on the bed of another pickup whose diesel engine was idling. A few seconds later, the engine shut off, and two more men got out. They also carried assault rifles. Now, there were five heavily armed strangers facing us. We were entirely under their control.

"Search their van," the woman said to those two. "Confiscate everything."

When I heard this, I came to my senses, lurched back to

my feet, and was about to object. But the first man stood there with a grin and a look in his eyes that told me he was just waiting for an excuse to hit me again. Swaying on my feet like a drunk, I kept my mouth shut.

The two new men walked toward us. When they were a few yards away, one of them looked at us and stopped. He was staring at Busto. "Gunny? Gunny Busto?"

Busto chuckled. "Well, I'll be damned. If it isn't Whistlefoot."

Whistlefoot ran forward and grabbed Busto in a bear hug. They were both soon slapping each other on the back and laughing.

"Dude! How long have you been out for?" Whistlefoot said.

"Three years," Busto said.

"Three years? That long? Why didn't you reach out to me?"

"Oh, you know how it is. There's a lot of things I've been trying to forget."

The other man looked at him with sympathy in his eyes and nodded. "Yeah, I get it." Then he turned to his colleagues, gesturing to Busto, and said, "Hey, you guys, this is the most badass Marine I ever met. Instant death on the battlefield. We were pals in Syria."

"Do you vouch for him, Rojas?" the woman said, who seemed to be in charge.

Whistlefoot/Rojas turned to Busto. "What're you doing with these other two? Where're you going? What brought you all the way out here? You really shouldn't have come this way."

I was so hoping that Busto was about to get us out of the situation. That he would be our ticket past these people. I sucked in a breath with my bruised diaphragm, praying for freedom.

"Oh, these two? Well, I'm hitchhiking across the state. I don't know them. They picked me up and were taking me as far as Fresno. But I don't know anything about them. They're strangers." My mouth dropped open. "But you should know, they're wanted by the Kergan authorities. There's probably a reward for their capture." My mouth fell open even further.

So much for making a new friend. This situation showed that you couldn't trust anybody those days. I tried to let the sense of betrayal eat at me, but honestly, I'd suffered so many setbacks during my life that the only thing I could feel was defiant acceptance. My expectations had been met.

Whistlefoot told the woman, "Yeah, Gunny is good. Let him go. You have the others and their van. But let Gunny grab his belongings first."

Busto patted his friend on the back and said, "Thanks, dude. I'm good to grab my pack, then?"

"Yeah. Are you armed?"

"What do you think?"

"Yeah, of course you are. What am I thinking? I don't want to know. Just keep it holstered, a'right?"

"Yes, of course. I'll grab my stuff." The woman nodded and gestured with her head for him to move along.

Busto left our line-up, leaving just Destiny and me standing alone with our hands up. He went to the van's side door and picked up his backpack and jacket.

Strangely, Busto never said anything to these bandits about Zeta. Why had he told them Destiny and I were wanted but said nothing about Zeta? It didn't make sense.

Whistlefoot and the other man were soon emptying our van of all our belongings. They found Zeta. One of them came forward and showed the others.

"What is that?" the woman asked, looking at me and Destiny.

"I don't know," I lied. "We found it in a dumpster a couple days ago. Thought it might be valuable."

"Just put it with the rest of the loot, Davids."

Once our van was emptied, the woman lowered her rifle and approached us. "You two are lucky. You get to live. Normally, I wouldn't waste my time on garbage like you. I've got too many mouths to feed as it is. But the Kergans want you. That means I can exchange you for a reward."

She turned to Whistlefoot and said, "Rojas, you and Davids, restrain them. Gags and blindfolds, too. Then lock them into the backseat of your truck."

"Yes, ma'am," he replied.

Busto stood to one side with his pack hanging from his left shoulder, watching, not saying anything, as the other two men bound our arms and legs with zip ties, stuffed a stinking rag into my mouth, and tied a blindfold over my eyes.

I heard a scuffle next to me. "Keep you stink'n hands to yourself, asshole!" Destiny screamed.

I could see nothing. A man laughed and said, "Ooh, she's squirmy. God, I love how she moves like that. This is gonna be fun."

Another man laughed, and I heard what sounded like a clap.

I tried to yell. "If you touch her, I'll kill you!" But all that came out was, "Mumm, mmm, mmmm, mm mmm!"

Somebody pushed me, and my bound legs made me fall to the ground, smacking my head painfully against the hard pavement. My head rang, and lights flashed in my eyes.

"Did you say something? No? I thought not," somebody said.

A boot kicked me right in the balls. I cried out and doubled over my groin as agonizing cramps roared through my belly like a thousand needles.

There was more scuffling on the ground and what sounded like the muffled screams of Destiny. My sister never screamed like that, even when she was super pissed. She always kept her anger contained inside and released it in slow, deliberate, well-planned moments. What were those bastards doing to her?

"Davids, stop screwing around with the prisoners!" the woman screamed. "Do what you're told."

"Sorry, ma'am," he said. "Right away, ma'am." Then, in a quieter voice, I heard him say, presumably to Destiny, "Don't worry, we'll have some playtime a little later."

Blast it. I wanted to murder the guy. I wanted to wrap my hands around his neck and squeeze him until his eyeballs popped out of his head. I wanted to claw his chest open with my fingernails and yank his heart out and stomp on it.

Two pairs of hands picked me up and carried me. I was shoved up and onto the bench seat of a vehicle. Then, something was tied to my wrist ties in such a way that my hands were held above my head against the ceiling or back wall of the truck we were in. It was very uncomfortable.

The only sense I had was my hearing and touch. Despite the cool air outside, it was hot in the truck. The doors were shut, and soon, it was completely quiet, like the inside of a coffin, except for soft cries coming from Destiny. She wiggled and moved, making the truck shift on its suspension. I assumed she was tied up just like me.

We were bound so tightly that there was no chance in hell we could escape. My hands were already numb from the zip ties cutting off my circulation and being stuck hanging over my head. The only way to take tension off my wrists was to sit ramrod straight in the seat, but that was difficult because of my bound legs. My feet also soon became numb.

It was quiet in the truck. The closed doors insulated us from all but the loudest sounds. Occasionally, I'd hear the roar of an engine. At some point, I'm pretty sure somebody departed. Then another vehicle arrived, though I couldn't tell if it was the same people or not.

Several hours later, my door opened, and somebody shoved me. "Do you want some water?"

I nodded and tried to say, "Yes, please," but it came out muffled. My mouth was dry like the desert from the rag soaking up my spit.

"I'm going to lower your gag. Don't speak, or I'll gag you again and give you no water. Do you understand?"

I nodded.

The gag was lowered roughly, tearing at my lip. I cried out. Then, the rim of a canteen or cup was pressed into my mouth, and water gushed out of it. It came so fast I choked on it and started to cough.

The cup was pulled back, and the man laughed. Water had spilled all down the front of my shirt until it was dripping on the seat and wetting my legs. "You look like you pissed yourself!" He continued laughing.

I wanted to curse him, but I was still coughing.

Before I could recover and get more water, he said. "I'm tired of waiting." The gag was raised back into my mouth and retightened until my cheeks were grinding against my teeth.

The same thing that happened to me also happened to Destiny. She was soon coughing, too. Then I heard what sounded like her spitting the water out.

"You bitch!" the man screamed.

"Creep!" Destiny yelled back.

The sound of a smack, and Destiny cried out.

"No more for you," the man said. A moment later, the door shut, and we were alone again.

Who were these monsters? Torturing innocent civilians like this. Robbing us and betraying their own species. They couldn't be collaborators. As bad as such people were, at least they still obeyed the laws. No, these people were of another sort. These were opportunists, taking advantage of the collapse of so many law enforcement agencies. These were the sort of people who looted, burned, and murdered, like we'd seen in Planada and other towns. Maybe even the same people who'd committed those crimes.

We hung in our bindings for hours in that hot truck. The minutes ticked by ever so slowly. I no longer had any feeling in my hands or legs.

Our captors only came once more to give us water. Fortunately, it was a different person this time who treated us a little more gently. At least they didn't force the water down our throats, and from Destiny's behavior, nobody tried groping her. Either that or she was so exhausted and out of her mind that she no longer cared.

At one point during the ordeal, I heard Gunny Busto's faint laughter somewhere nearby. He and his good ol' friend must have been swapping stories. It made me furious how he was letting us be treated, especially Destiny. It went to prove what kind of a human being he was, that he would allow us, people who had helped him, to be exploited, robbed, and probably murdered without raising a finger to help—the man had disavowed us! And I found it even harder to believe he had the stomach to stick around and watch us be destroyed. Was he some kind of psychopath?

Many hours later, it had begun to cool off in the truck. There also seemed to be less light leaking around the edges of my blindfold. Night was settling in. They must have been nearing the time when they'd have to do something about us.

Destiny had shifted her body, so she sat sideways on the bench and rested her legs on my lap. The warmth of her body reminded me that we were still together. I was suffering, but so was she. If she could survive, then I damn well could also. But I didn't know how much longer I could take this. And yet, what could I possibly do about it? I couldn't even kill myself if I wanted to.

Why had that traitor, Busto, given us up like that? Why had he turned his back on us? Why hadn't he used his friendship with one of the bandits to try and get us free? I couldn't stop thinking about these questions. But honestly, if our roles had been reversed, would I have acted differently? If it had been Destiny and me who were recognized by our *own* friends, who then set us free, I wouldn't have hesitated to turn over Busto in exchange for our freedom. I shouldn't blame him for what he did. He was like us, homeless and just trying to survive from one day to the next.

That was depressing when I realized I was just as selfish as Busto. It was pure chance that things had turned out the way they had, with him free and us captive. Indeed, one could argue that Busto was the lucky one. Shouldn't I be happy for him?

And what about Zeta? Why didn't she do something for us, her new partners? I could feel my tie to her. If my hands had been free, I could have pointed my finger precisely in the direction where she was currently located—about fifty feet to the left. But unfortunately, our link didn't allow the passing of any kind of information. I imagined she must be hiding somewhere, staying inconspicuous like I ordered her to. I sensed her feelings of stillness and watchfulness, though weirdly no anxiety. I wished I could cry out to her now and beg her to do something. Surely, there was help she could provide, given her incredible capabilities and all the knowledge she possessed from the Dominion. Didn't it mean anything that I was her consort?

Many hours had gone by. Night arrived. I hung by my bindings in a half stupor. With my blood boiling this entire time, my mind, by that point, was well-stewed and tender.

Suddenly, the door on Destiny's side opened. I heard rope rubbing and felt the weight shifting on the bench. Moans. A muffled squeal.

"Lord, oh, how I love it when you wiggle like that!" a man said softly.

11

It was that asshole creep again. Davids. If I ever set my eyes on that man and had the means to do it, he would die by my hands. "Little Darl'n," he crooned like he was wooing a lover. "Just calm down. I'm going to pick you up nice and gentle. Yes...just like that."

The truck shifted on its suspension as Destiny's weight was lifted from the bench. I wanted to turn and kick out with my legs but couldn't see, and I feared I would hit Destiny instead of Asshole. Instead, I tried to shout. So forcefully my throat felt like it would burst. But the gag soaked up my cries of rage like a dry sponge.

The truck door shut with a slam. I found myself completely alone.

My will to fight collapsed. They had Destiny and were going to do something wicked-awful to her. I wouldn't let my imagination go down that path. Just looking at the entrance of that dark alley made me lose it. I broke down in sobs. But the blindfold absorbed all my tears and the gag, my cries. It was pointless. There was no cathartic release to be found. There was nothing I could do, though I cried out for what felt like an hour.

Some guerrilla leader I made! I was so pathetic. Not even capable of protecting what was mine. I didn't deserve my sister. What could Zeta have possibly seen in me? Imagine me trying to fight on humanity's behalf. This was the result. Taken down by common highway robbers on an isolated country road, without putting up any resistance.

I sensed Zeta moving away from me quite rapidly. I sensed she was feeling anticipation and excitement. Had they taken her? Was she in a vehicle?

The door next to me opened. Somebody pushed me to the side. They were breathing hard. A hand reached up and grabbed my wrists. There was a yank, and then my bindings came loose. Another tug, then my legs were free. What was this? I flung my arms out, pushing the person away, and tried to jump out of the truck, but my legs were useless, and instead, I fell to the ground. I shoved the blindfold up onto my forehead but saw only shadows.

"Shh! Dammit, keep it down," somebody hissed.

"Mm, mmmm, mmm," I said through my gag.

"If you would just hold still for a second, I'll take it off. Chill, dude! It's me, Gunny!"

Gunny?! What was he doing?

"I'm going to take your gag off, but don't cry out. In fact, don't say anything. You ready?"

I nodded.

The gag was pulled from my mouth. I spat out. Feeling was beginning to return to my hands and feet. A million needles poked at my extremities as blood began to flow again. I moaned and squeezed my eyes shut, pushing the pain into the background.

"Destiny!" I yelled.

"Dammit, I said to be quiet!" Busto hissed. "Destiny's okay. Well, at least she's going to be okay. Two of these creeps were about to have their way with her. I took them both out. She's safe. For now."

Do you remember all those evil thoughts I'd had about Busto? They disappeared instantly, and I only thought about how grateful I was to him. I grabbed him and hugged him tight, squeezing him until he could probably not breathe. "Thank you," I whispered.

"We're not free yet, bro," Busto said, pushing his hands between us. "I took care of those two, but they'll be discovered soon. Two others are on watch up the road about fifty yards from here. I will take you to Destiny, then I need you to hang tight while I hunt down the others." He pulled out of my grip and grabbed my arm to help me gain my feet. "Can you walk?"

"I think so." I placed my wobbly legs under me and pushed myself up until I stood unsteadily, leaning against the side of the truck.

"What did you do to those two who had Destiny?" I said.

"They're dead," Busto said.

He said this without emotion, and I didn't know him well enough to read his body language, but I sensed his unease. But all of this was overwhelmed by my feelings of relief at having been rescued. The man hadn't betrayed us! My instincts about him had been accurate.

We moved in a crouch in the dark around the front of the truck and behind some bushes on the side of the road. We passed the outlines of two people lying prone and motionless on the muddy ground. Something dark pooled between them. I was pretty sure it wasn't water. The smell of feces and urine assaulted my nose.

Another thirty feet beyond that, under a small oak, we found Destiny squatting and hugging her knees to her chest. When she saw me, she jumped up and folded me in a hug, sobbing into my shoulder. "Thank, God!" she said.

"Shush, now, you idiots," Busto said. "Keep quiet."

Suddenly, a dark shape moved in the shadows behind Busto. He jerked up and around, a wicked-looking knife suddenly appearing in his hand, its edge flashing in the starlight.

"All enemies are incapacitated," Zeta said.

"Blast you!" Busto cried out. "Don't sneak up on me like that. I just about shoved my knife into your...whatever that is. Body. Capsule...thing." He waved his hand out.

"A very unlikely outcome."

"Whatever. What did you mean? Incapacitated? There were still two of them out there on watch."

"The two humans up the road are unconscious. Zeta witnessed bold Gunny slay the other two men and liberate Destiny and Kory. Cunning Zeta judged the moment opportune for her to seize the initiative and render what aid she could. Though in this form she is no warrior, Zeta knows of many ways to undermine a foe even though she lacks weapons."

"So, they're dead?" Busto said. "Be specific. It's important."

"Incapacitated. Zeta rendered them unconscious using a potent anesthetic injected via a remote delivery device she manufactured in secret. The foes shall be unresponsive for a lengthy spell. They are in peril of dying from exposure. Zeta favors bringing them to shelter."

"They're not getting that," I said. "These sorts of people don't deserve to live. They're predators. Parasites living on the rest of humanity. Even worse than the Kergans, in my opinion. If I'm going to be fighting the Kergans, there's no way I'm letting garbage like these bandits get away with their crimes. Let them freeze. The rest of us will be the better for it."

"What are you talking about? Fighting the Kergans?" Busto said.

I realized that in my degraded mental state, I had said too much—more than I had intended. But if we got out of this alive, Busto deserved to know what we were planning. Maybe he would even offer to join our effort. We could use somebody like him, and I owed him. Both Destiny and I owed him our lives. The least we could do would be to tell him the whole truth.

"I'll explain everything," I said. "But let's get out of here first, before backup arrives. Any idea when they'll be relieved?"

"I don't know," Busto said. "I tried to learn their operations schedule, but they were closed mouth. They trusted me, thanks to Whistlefoot, but only a little. I'll tell you what I know."

"You fellas, feel free to relax," Destiny said. "I'm out of here. But first, I'm gonna find our stuff. They managed to steal everything except my virginity." She brought both hands to her face, took a deep breath, and was about to say something else, but then stopped and froze. After a few seconds, she dropped her hands and slapped her thighs. "It's darker than Dracula's guts out here. Anybody got a flashlight?"

"I do," Busto said. A few seconds later, a red light appeared, lighting the way. "This light will protect our night vision. Come on, I know where they put your stuff. And your van is still there."

As we returned to the road, I said, "Maybe we should

steal one of their trucks. They look a lot better than our van."

"I wouldn't," Busto said. "They may have some way to track them, and I don't have time to give them a clean sweep. Your van is fine. In fact, in some ways, it's perfect for the sort of life you've been living. And in a piece of junk like that, you won't attract attention."

"Okay," I said, feeling let down. It would be great to have such a massive upgrade as one of these powerful diesel pickups. With four-wheel drive. And who knows how many accessories. And think of all the cargo space and how we could put it to use.

We found all our stolen possessions in the back of one of the trucks. And more loot that wasn't ours. Clearly, these monsters had been robbing travelers on this road for some time.

We stuffed everything into the back of the van, taking no time to organize it or identify the articles that weren't ours. We'd sort through it later.

Destiny found the keys and handed them to me. I hopped into the van's driver's seat and cranked the engine. It roared to stinky life with a cloud of smoke.

My sister and Zeta got in the back.

"Where's Gunny?" I asked.

"He said he'd be right back," Destiny responded.

I waited impatiently, anxiously watching the rearview mirror for the shine of approaching headlights. A few minutes later, Busto appeared out of the shadows carrying a large duffel bag and opened the passenger door.

"Dude, did you need to take a crap, or something?" I said.

Busto laughed. "No. I slashed the tires on the trucks. If they pursue us, it won't be in those."

I felt terrible for doubting him and not thinking of it

myself. "Good job." I gestured to the road with my chin. "Shall we?"

"Open the back. I grabbed some of their guns and ammo."

I hopped out and helped him. He had four assault rifles, bags full of ammo and loaded magazines, and other materials. When the stuff was stowed, we got back in.

"We ready?"

"Hell, yeah," Busto said.

"And good riddance," Destiny said.

I pressed the pedal to the metal, and we putt-putted away from that hellacious roadblock. But I knew the experience wouldn't soon be left behind, especially for Destiny. I wished I could resuscitate those two wannabe rapists and murder them all over again.

I reached back to Destiny, who sat on the rear bench, blindly searching for her hand with mine. She seized it and hugged it to her breast. Drops of warm water fell onto my forearm, and a shudder rocked her body. But as we drove down that lonely path into the night, I never heard a whimper from her.

12

We had about 40 miles to go until we reached Wolf Jaw. It was about 11 pm. Not far by car, but this trip across the Central Valley had already taken us three times longer than anticipated.

Soon after escaping the roadblock, we arrived at another small town called Prather. The highway was blocked by two armed men who told us it would be opened again at sunrise. We backtracked a half mile to an open area we'd seen at the side of the road and parked there.

"Let's get some sleep," I said.

"I'm starving," Destiny said with a hoarse voice. "And we're all out of zetamilk."

"Zeta will make more," the alien said and floated over to the side door, where she began dancing slightly in the air like a little kid needing the bathroom.

Busto opened his door and stepped out. "I'll take first watch." He opened the side door for Zeta.

"Go ahead and sleep. I'll take the watch. I'm too wound up to sleep," I said. I went to the rear to get one of our folding camp chairs.

"I'm the same," Busto said. "You got another one of those chairs?"

"Yeah." I handed him the other one, shut the rear hatch, and followed him to where Zeta was settling into the sandy surface next to a patch of grass.

There was no moon, but the sky was clear of clouds, unusual for this time of the year. A million stars covered the sky. I gasped. Living for so many years in the Bay Area with all its light pollution, I had become accustomed to skies saturated with the backwash of city lights. I'd never seen a truly dark sky before like that night.

I unfolded my camp chair, settled into it, and zipped my jacket all the way up to my neck. We were 1,500 feet above sea level and in the foothills of the Sierra Nevada. The chill of the night rushed through my clothes and made me shiver.

Busto dropped some wood on the ground and started kindling a fire. He was pretty good at it, and I learned some things about starting fires while watching him. After he was done and had a small blaze going, he sat next to me with something gleaming in his lap, but it was too dark to make it out.

"What is that?" I asked him.

"An M4 carbine. I recovered four of them from those pricks. Don't know where they got them. This is a military-grade firearm. They must have gained access to a National Guard armory. Or maybe they were all deserted military."

"You think?"

"Yeah, I think it's likely. All of them had been in the service. The few who talked to me confirmed it. The others gave it away by the way they moved and carried themselves and their weapons."

"Damn. And preying on their fellow citizens. What

happened to your friend?"

Busto looked at me abruptly. "Who?"

"The one who recognized you."

"Whistlefoot? He's dead."

I felt bad. He'd killed his friend. If we hadn't been stupid enough to make ourselves into victims, then his friend would have never been tempted, and he'd still be alive. "Sorry about what happened."

"Don't be. He wasn't *my* friend. He got what he deserved. This isn't the first time I've witnessed one of his atrocities. At least this time, I could do something about it."

"Really?"

"Yeah. We were in Syria together. Whistlefoot has always skirted the rules, and in that war zone, he was out of control. I witnessed him execute prisoners and rob them. Not a very good marine either. I'm surprised he ever made it to become a Raider, but there's always a few worthless slimeballs who fake their way through the gauntlet."

"How'd he get that nickname?"

Busto chuckled. "He accidentally shot himself in the foot on the shooting range."

We both laughed.

"Well, I still feel bad about it," I said.

Gunny leaned forward. "Sometimes there are bad people who force you to kill them. They can't be reasoned with. Psychopaths, sociopaths, megalomaniacs. They get a hold of a little power—or sometimes a lot—and start manipulating and hurting people for no reason other than because they enjoy it." He held up a finger. "About 1 in 20 people are pure evil. Take 100 people out of the general population; five will be misfits who only care about themselves and have no reservations about committing crimes. They only fear the law and getting caught, and sometimes not even that. Many are good at conforming to social standards, masking their intentions from others, but when society collapses, the worms crawl out of the woodwork.

"That's what we've seen happen these past months. The Kergans don't care about humanity's comfort, so they won't do anything about bandits and gangs. And the local governments are falling to pieces. Right now, if you're a sociopath, Earth is a heavenly place to be."

I thought about this. Was I a sociopath? I'd been homeless for years. I was a nonconforming citizen who wouldn't hesitate to commit petty crimes if it meant food in my stomach and shelter from the rain. I cared about Destiny, but she was my sister, so it was different. Then I thought about seeing Busto on the highway, all alone, hitchhiking, and my reaction to it. I remember feeling the desire to help him, not to exploit him.

The conclusion I drew from this was that I couldn't truly be a bad person. There must be something inside me that made me a worthwhile human. Though we had guns now, I felt no desire to use them to go out and find victims to rob. Maybe there was hope for me. Perhaps I could become a good person if I wanted to, and there wouldn't be anything wrong with that. I'm pretty sure my parents would have agreed with this assessment, and though they were gone, I still wished to live up to their expectations. I didn't want to die someday and find out they'd existed in an afterlife like Zeta's Ancients, watching me this entire time. I wanted them to be proud of me, not ashamed. I was their legacy, the only thing they left behind in this life. If I could live a meaningful life filled with worthy deeds—as Zeta would call them—then maybe it would be a little like bringing Mom and Dad back to life again, to live vicariously through each breath I took and each beat of my heart. I wanted them to be proud of that life I would live.

Something changed in me at that precise moment. Though it has been forty years since then, I can still point my finger at that conversation with Gunnery Sergeant Clemen Busto as the moment when I decided I wanted to live to be more than just a homeless petty thief. I don't know why, but I believed both my parents had been good people. I have no evidence to support that conclusion because I lost everything of them when they died except for my few precious memories of them. I don't even remember their first names. But they had loved me, of that I was sure, and it was *good* love. In that moment, I suddenly felt a driving need to prove myself worthy of their memory, and since then that need has not left me.

The memory of my mother and father's love for me is what drives me and defines who I am. As you will discover in subsequent tales of my life, I very nearly lost that memory forever to a thief, to Ban'ach the marac Soul Ravager. Perhaps that is why I value it so much. But that is another tale for another time.

Going back to my conversation with Busto, then I asked him something that had been bugging me ever since we were captured. "Why did you give us up like that?"

He sighed and rubbed his cheek. "It was the only way to save you."

I snorted.

"Look, I had seconds to put a plan together. When I recognized Whistlefoot, I realized I had a way to stay free. And as long as I was, and you two were kept alive, there was a chance to escape."

I shook my head. "You sounded like you were having a good time with them."

"It was all an act. I was terrified, actually," he said.

"Though I'm deadly, I couldn't have taken them all down simultaneously. I saw my chance when two of them got distracted by Destiny. They were supposed to be keeping an eye on me, but I made sure to put them at ease by acting like one of them. Boss lady had gone back to their base with another soldier. Two others were down the road, watching it. I just had these two. They thought I was sleeping, even though I was watching. They took Destiny into the bushes, and at that point, I didn't hesitate. Neither of them had a chance to scream."

"Thanks for rescuing us. Still, it was close. My muscles are gonna hurt for a week."

"Usually, war is like that."

"Is that what this is?" I reached down and pulled a burning stick out of the fire, watching orange flames dance along its length like faeries.

His eyes gazed into mine, gleaming slightly in the reflected starlight. "Well, why don't *you* tell me? You're the one who said you would fight the Kergans."

That's right. I had promised to tell him what this was all about. Zeta hadn't said a word this entire time we'd been sitting here chatting. I'd forgotten she was just a few feet away. "Zeta, is it okay for me to tell Busto?"

"That is your decision, lad," she said. "Zeta's mind is that Clemen Busto has practiced superior judgment and revealed fine ethical behavior. A worthy candidate, is he."

"Dude, don't talk about me like I'm not here," Busto said. "Just tell me what's goin' on."

So, I told Busto how we'd met Zeta. The invitation. The consortship. The planned secret base and starship. "We're supposed to become some kind of guerrilla force backed by the Collective Dominion, with Zeta as our military adviser."

Busto nodded. "That's actually really cool, man."

"Well, not much has happened yet. And we're not off to a very good start. Our entire guerrilla unit almost got taken out by a half-dozen highway robbers. It's...embarrassing."

"But you didn't get destroyed, and most of those bad guys are dead now."

"Because of you," I said.

"And Zeta," the igna said.

"Yeah, sorry, Zeta. You, too." I picked up my chair to pivot it so I almost faced Busto. "Look, Gunny, we could really use somebody like you. You're a soldier who actually knows something about...weird ways of fighting."

"It's called unconventional warfare," he said. "And your group is what we marines call an irregular military unit."

"Okay. I'm glad to hear we fit somewhere into the known universe, at least."

Busto reached out and patted me on the shoulder. "Sure, I'll join you guys."

I threw my arms wide. "Just like that? You don't want to hear more about what you're getting yourself into?"

"I've heard enough," he said. "I know there's a lot of uncertainty, but there always is in these kinds of situations. It would be inappropriate for me to demand assurances from you."

I had hoped that Busto would accept but hadn't thought it would be this easy. It was *too* easy like he'd been planning on staying with us all along, no matter what. What was his agenda? I'd just asked him to join the war against the Kergans, and he'd barely paused before agreeing.

Busto nodded and said, "You're probably wondering why I didn't hesitate. I'll tell you why. The Kergans invaded, and I sat with my phone in hand for days, waiting for the call from the Marine Corps to reactivate me. Then it became weeks. Nobody called. I was ready to go and fight for my country. I've been floating around without purpose for the last three years since I got out. Finally, there was a situation precisely of the type for which I had been trained, and my country needed me. But they never called. Then, the mighty USA surrendered, along with nearly every other military power worldwide. And I was left feeling useless like I had betrayed my country. The Kergans destroyed my country, and I never fired even a single bullet at them."

He was silent, but I could tell he was thinking, so I didn't reply. Then, leaning forward, he said, "Secretly, I'd been hoping to find insurgents somewhere in the country's interior who were still fighting. Americans, Mexicans, Canadians, I don't care who, as long as they were humans. That's why I was headed east." He spread his arms to encompass Zeta, me, and Destiny, who was sleeping in the van. "You three aren't exactly what I had in mind, but I'm not sure I'll find anybody else. And the sort of capabilities you described sounds impressive. I know you have none of that yet, but just the little I've seen from Zeta over the last two days has floored me."

"Thank you," Zeta said.

"You're welcome," he said. "If you can truly construct an armed warship made with advanced alien tech, then maybe we have a chance at hurting the bad guys. Even if we only kill a few dozen Kergans before I die, it'll be worth it."

As I've said already, the honest truth is that I didn't really want to fight, despite my sudden change of heart. I continued to insist to myself that I was in this consortship for guaranteed access to shelter, food, and safety. And having somebody like Busto with us would only add to our safety. He'd already rescued us once and, on another occasion, helped us slip by Kergan MPs. Yeah, I wanted him around, and I knew my reasons were selfish, but I didn't care. I just wanted to live in peace and quiet. If the Kergans got in the way of that, then maybe I'd have to shoot at them. But I hoped it could be sniping done from a position of safety. Call me a coward if you want, but I thought of myself as a survivor, just as Busto had correctly assessed the previous night.

I held my hand out to Busto. He took it, and we shook. "You're more than welcome to join us, for whatever it's worth," I said. "Destiny and I owe you our lives."

He released my hand and waved away what I said. "Get used to it. We're going to be comrades in arms. There will be lots more of saving each other. I'll keep watching your backs if you watch mine."

"It's a deal."

13

We went to bed a little after 1 am when Zeta told us she could keep watch without us. Busto didn't seem so happy with that, probably because Zeta didn't have a gun, but I could tell he was dragging almost as much as me.

We awoke well after sunrise. My muscles ached, especially in my shoulders and back. When I stood, it felt like something was tweaked in my spine, and my vertebrae didn't want to settle right. I rolled my shoulders and stretched my back to get the bones in my spine to align properly.

During the night, Zeta had made more zetamilk, water, and gasoline, filling each container we left her. She also fabricated three surprises: Two five-gallon gas cans and a three-gallon insulated jug for storing zetamilk. The containers were made from some kind of woven material she called nanofiber, which was light and flexible but very strong. We needed these, and I didn't know Zeta could make something like this. I suppose it made sense. If she could build a starship, then these containers were pretty easy.

After eating breakfast, we departed. This time, we found the checkpoint at Prather open.

At that moment, we were about 20 to 25 miles away from Wolf Jaw. The land became less and less inhabited as we penetrated deeper into the mountains and the forest thickened. We began to see snow in the shaded areas under trees. Then, before long, most of the land was covered with a carpet of snow, though the highway had fortunately been kept plowed.

About 8 miles before our destination, we left Highway 168 and began ascending a narrow two-lane road. It was the only way in and out of Wolf Jaw. According to the map, we were at about 5,500 feet elevation. The road was slick and icy. It wound around a mountain and then descended into a broad valley. Occasionally, we passed turnoffs onto dirt roads that led deeper into the forest, most of which were unplowed and covered by over a foot of snow.

I wish we had taken one of the trucks, I thought, looking at the deep white blanket that the van would never be able to traverse if we needed it to. We didn't even have a shovel to dig us out if the worst happened and we were trapped in the snow.

But it was nearly all uninhabited.

"This will be perfect," I muttered to myself.

"Did they borrow all their snow from Antarctica?" Destiny said. "Lord almighty, I've never seen so much white in my life. How's a black girl supposed to feel? I swear, the weather god's a racist."

I snickered. "What? Didn't you ever visit your aunt when you were younger?"

"A few times, but always in the summer. I've never been up here in the winter."

We began descending a steep hill, and I shifted into a

lower gear. The old Toyota Van's engine revved in protest. We seemed to be driving down a tunnel of trees, the rising sun still hidden behind the mountains.

"Roadblock," Busto said.

I looked where he pointed and, in the distance, saw armed people standing in the road with a jersey barrier in the middle. The only way around it was to drive on the shoulders, which were guarded.

"We're here," Destiny said. "I guess I'm not surprised they've blocked the road."

I slowed the van as we drew nearer, coming to a stop when somebody dressed in a uniform and armed with a shotgun made a signal. I rolled down my window.

"Good morning," I said, trying to put a smile on my face.

A man wearing a heavy police jacket and a cowboy hat looked at me sternly. A short, dark red beard framed a lean face of about thirty. He kept his shotgun pointed at the ground. A second person, a woman, paced on the passenger side of the van, studying Busto and Destiny through the windows.

"What're you folks doin' out here so early for?" he said.

"We slept in our van about twenty miles to the west last night," I said. "We're headed to my sister's aunt's house. She lives here in Wolf Jaw."

The man smacked his lips and eyed me up and down. "Doesn't that make her your aunt also?"

I wanted to smack my head. Now, I looked like an idiot. Not a good way to set first impressions. "Yeah, I suppose so." I didn't want to explain that Destiny wasn't my real sister, but it was obvious by comparing our skin colors. "She's my...foster sister. So, her aunt's not really my aunt."

"Are you residents? I don't recognize any of you."

"No, sir, just family."

He folded his arms and mashed his lips together. "Only residents are allowed past the gate." He waved his hands at their improvised guard point.

"Well, we were actually hoping to pass through town to get to the national forest lands on the other side."

"Why?"

I didn't have an explanation prepared, and the question stalled me.

Busto leaned forward to look at the guard. "We're just campers, sir."

"In the middle of the winter?" He shook his head. "I can't let you through."

Destiny unbuckled her seatbelt and knelt between the front seats to see the man. She said, "But what about my aunt? Her name is Judith Fulton, and my cousin is Earline Fulton. Can you at least tell me if they're still here? Are they okay?"

"Let me see your ID, miss," he said, holding out a hand.

She took her license out of her wallet and gave it to him. He studied it, comparing the photo with her face. "Destiny Austin. You don't share the same last name."

"Fulton is her married name. Her full name is Judith Austin Fulton. My Uncle Phil died about eight or ten years ago. Aunt Judith and my mom are sisters."

The guard nodded and handed her license back. "Yes, she still lives here, as does your cousin. I remember your uncle, Phil. He was a good man." He sighed and rubbed his chin. "Look, I can't let strangers into town. We've been raided several times by bandits, and the county and state no longer provide law enforcement resources. But this is what I'm going to let you do." He pointed at me and Busto. "You two gentlemen are going to remain behind the gate with your vehicle. I'll allow Miss Austin to walk into town and meet with her aunt. Then you can walk back. It's not very far. I'm assuming you know where she lives."

I was worried Destiny would let her wit get the better of her and make some sarcastic comment that got us all into trouble. But she responded like a well-socialized heiress. "Yes, sir, I can find it." She nodded. "I can do that."

"Are you sure?" I said. "I don't want to separate."

"It'll be okay, Kory," she said. "I won't be long. It's like a ten-minute walk. I'll be gone one or two hours, at most." She dropped her voice to almost a whisper. "I'll talk to my aunt and see if she can help us get through town." She opened the side door and stepped out.

The female guard met her there and said, "Miss, I'm going to have to pat you down."

Destiny rolled her eyes but said. "Fine."

"Are you carrying any weapons?"

"Yeah, I've got a pocketknife and a loaded automatic in a shoulder holster."

"The knife is fine, but you must leave the pistol in your vehicle."

Destiny huffed. "Buckets of monkeys. You guys know it isn't safe now these days, right? Especially for a black woman out walking alone in all this...whiteness."

The female guard smiled sympathetically. "You'll be fine. That's why we're blocking access to the town. It's for everybody's safety."

Destiny took off her jacket, then slipped out of her shoulder holster and folded it under the bench seat. She put her coat back on and turned to the woman.

The female guard briefly patted her down. She nodded and said, "Okay, you can go."

Destiny waved to us and said, "See you later, guys. I won't be long."

"Be careful, Dest," I said, feeling anxious. It had been months since we had last been separated.

She slid the door shut, turned on her heels, and started walking down the middle of the paved two-lane highway. In the distance, through the trees, I could see the outline of buildings and roads. A few houses.

I turned to the male guard. "How many folks do you have living here now?"

The man smiled. "I'm not at liberty to give you that information. Sorry, I'm sure you can understand why."

Everybody was so careful these days. If you got into trouble, you couldn't just call up 911 and wait for the police or firemen to appear five minutes later.

"Okay, we're going to park over in that turnoff there," I said, pointing to an open area next to the shoulder about a hundred yards behind us.

"That's fine. We'll send your sister to you when she returns."

I nodded, put the van in reverse, executed a three-point turn, and drove to the open area.

"What do you think, Zeta?" I said.

The Igna floated up from her hiding place. "This land looks promising. Indeed, the mountains shall mask our business from the eyes of our foes."

Rocky soil covered with trees rested on inclines to both sides of the road. The south side climbed up a hill, and the north fell into a gully. Below it, I could hear the roar of rapids.

"From the maps, it looks like there are a few flat areas nearby in the national forest north of town. We just need to get there. I hope the roads have been plowed."

I kept the engine running for the additional warmth. We had plenty of fuel and no foreseeable shortages in the future now that Zeta was supplying us. It felt good not having to worry about things as basic as food and fuel.

"I'm going to take a look around," Busto said.

"Like where?" I said.

"Around. I'll take a walk in these woods and see what kind of perimeter they've got. I doubt they're guarding anything else except the road."

"Can I come?"

"No, stay here and guard the van. I'm going to be moving quietly and quickly. You don't know how."

His comment stung me. It made me conscious of my vulnerability. "I need to learn."

"Yeah, and I'll teach you, but not yet. Just stay here. That way, I don't have to worry about you. Okay?"

I nodded. "Yeah, I understand."

Busto slipped out of the van on the passenger side, which was hidden from the view of the guards. I studied them. They looked bored and cold.

When I glanced back to Busto, he was already gone.

"Well, it's just us two now, Zeta," I said, feeling uncomfortable and awkward. My sister and my new friend were doing the hard work, and I was just sitting here idle. Some commander I was starting out to be.

I tapped my fingers on the steering wheel. Maybe now would be a good time to get more details from Zeta. "So, how long will it take to build this base and the starship?"

"That depends on access to materials," Zeta said. "Under ideal conditions, Zeta foresees nigh on two weeks to build the base and another week for the ship. Then she shall need to train you lads."

"You're going to train us?"

"Indeed, as a military adviser, that is worthy Zeta's primary purpose."

"What about missions? How will that work? Do we just go out and look for Kergans to kill? Or is it more organized than that?"

"Your crew forms a cell of human insurgent warriors. You shall receive mission recommendations directly from the Dominion War Ministry. From these recommendations, you may select whichever deeds you feel prepared to undertake."

"Are there other cells?"

"Aye."

"How many?"

"Humble Zeta does not know. Maintaining human resistance efforts in cells improves security, and informing Zeta of others would defeat that. By keeping each cell ignorant of the others, if one were captured, the others would not be compromised because they do not know about the others."

"So, we'll always operate alone."

"Nay, there shall be occasional multi-cell endeavors. Those shall be coordinated at the War Ministry level. You will undoubtedly encounter friendly cells in the field of battle, but conversing with them shall be restricted to within the time where cooperation is necessary."

"Right, I got it. So, we don't give each other away."

I liked the setup. Being on our own was the way I wanted to do this. I didn't want some commander over me, laying down the rules and telling me what I could or couldn't do with my ship and crew. I liked the idea of being the boss of my own crew.

"And what about the ship? How big is it? What kinds of weapons?"

Zeta spun and moved closer. "As Zeta has said, the first ship hull Consort Kory and his crew will have is the Raider hull. In its basic form, the Raider masses 50 tons fully loaded, is powered by a 10 TJ chromatic battery, and requires a crew of four, including three humans and one igna."

"You'll be one of the crew?"

"Indeed, Zeta will serve as the ship's engineering officer."

"What about weapons?"

"In its basic form, the Raider is equipped with one 1 MJ annular plasma cannon, four 1,000 pound missile tubes, twenty 200 pound missile tubes, and atomic bolsters."

"What are atomic bolsters?"

"They are powered by the chromatic battery and reinforce the atomic bonds that hold the hull in a solid state. The bolsters enable the hull to resist damage and stress which would otherwise cause a breach or vaporize it."

"So, the bolsters are like a shield."

"Nay, the bolsters reinforce the existing bonds between neighboring molecules of the crystallized solid of which the hull is formed."

"Okay, I think I understand. They make the hull stronger."

"Indeed."

"Why two different sizes of missile tubes?"

"The 1,000-pound tubes carry anti-ship or ground attack missiles. The 200-pound tubes carry intercept missiles for use against enemy missiles or small vehicles."

"You said this is the basic configuration. We'll be able to upgrade the hull?"

"Aye. You shall earn tribute points upon completing worthy deeds that advance the war effort. These tribute points may, for example, be used to add additional missile tubes, upgrade the cannon, and add improved defensive systems."

The spaceship fascinated me, but I knew it was pointless to dream about it if we didn't first have a safe base for it to operate from.

Zeta and I continued chatting for the next hour about how we would operate as a guerrilla cell. To me, the toughest part seemed to be right now at the beginning. We were starting with almost nothing. Zeta needed an isolated, open area with plenty of resources where she could begin to excavate the base and construct its infrastructure. Besides crew quarters, the base would contain a power plant, hangar, armory, shop, nanoforge, and command room. All of it would be located below the ground with two small openings to the surface, plus the hangar doors.

A figure suddenly moved to the side of the van. My head shot up, and my teeth clenched together.

Busto stood beside the passenger door, holding something in his right hand. The door opened, squealing on its rusty hinges.

I held my hand to my chest. "Dude, you gave me a heart attack!"

Busto grinned. He held up his hand. Something dead and furry hung from it. "I got a rabbit."

"I thought you were scouting?"

"I was, but I wasn't going to ignore a target of opportunity like this." Busto looked at Zeta. "Zetamilk is plenty fine, but I like some meat in my diet. Don't you want some rabbit stew?"

"Okay, but you kill it, you clean it. I don't even know what to do with a dead animal."

"Don't worry, my friend, I've got it taken care of. I'll get a fire going."

Fifteen minutes later, Busto had a small fire burning

next to the van and a pot with chunks of meat in it simmering. He had mixed several cups of the zetamilk into it. "I think it'll make it creamy," he said.

I lifted an eyebrow, but he seemed to know what he was doing.

Before long, the smell of the cooking stew began to waft over us. My stomach growled at me. Busto tasted it and said, "It's done." He grabbed four bowls and started filling them.

"Why so many?" I asked.

"For the guards," Busto said. "Look at them."

I did. They appeared cold. And envious glances indicated they could smell our meal.

"Why? They don't deserve any," I said, still annoyed because they wouldn't let us pass through town.

"Kory, listen. I live by the maxim that what goes around comes around. You do nice things for people, and karma guarantees that somebody will do you a good turn in the future. Besides, wouldn't it be great to have them in our debt? They'll feel guilty about turning down our request when we again ask them for permission to pass through."

"Okay. But I want my bowls and spoons back."

Busto and I each carried a full bowl over to the freezing guards. They accepted with smiles. "Coney stew!" one of them cried.

"It's not much, but you're welcome to it," Busto said.

The male guard who had questioned me in the van shook his head. "Hot damn! It's hard to get meat these days. Thank you, sir." He raised a heaping spoon into his mouth and sucked air while he chewed. Steam poured out. "I thought I heard a gunshot. Was that you?" he said, looking at Busto.

"Yes, sir," Busto said. "I hope I didn't startle you."

"Nah. Plenty of people around here have been hunting for small game lately. It's been a month since we've had any fresh meat at One Stop."

"One Stop?" I said.

"Best One Stop," the man said through a mouth full of stew. "It's our local grocery store and gas station. Not much gas in it these days, though. And what's there is reserved for official use only."

Busto and I looked at each other. Maybe there was an opportunity here. If the town had needs, and we could provide them, perhaps that could help us establish a relationship with them. Maybe we could trade.

"No fresh milk either," the man said. "From the taste of this stew, you've got milk." He held out his hand and shook mine and Busto's. "By the way, the name is Archibald Andrews. Wolf Jaw Police Department."

"Nice to meet you, sir," Busto said. "Clemen Busto."

"You a veteran?" Andrews said.

"Yes, sir. Marine Corp gunnery sergeant. I've been out about three years."

"I could tell by the way you carry yourself. I was Air Force, myself." Andrews looked at me and said, "And you, young man?"

I looked at my feet and thought about what to say. "Kory Drake" is all I could think of.

We chatted with the guards for a few more minutes, then returned to our fire and waiting lunch.

"Mission successful," Busto said with a grin and slapped me on the back. "See how they opened up to us?"

"Sure," I said.

"It's hard to be grouchy and suspicious when somebody offers you a warm meal."

Maybe he was right about that. Few people had done

the same for me in my life. I'd scrambled for every crumb of my meals since I was a small child, even at the orphanage. Especially at the orphanage—I'd put on weight when I got onto the streets if you can believe it. Maybe that's why I was so suspicious of strangers.

We stood next to our fire, eating our stew. A few minutes later, I saw Destiny come walking around the bend in the road she'd gone down earlier. An unfamiliar young black woman walked with her. Their breaths clouded in the cold air. Their jackets were unzipped to release body heat as they hurried.

"Dest is back, and she brought company," I said.

14

Destiny walked up to the checkpoint in the company of another pretty black girl. They talked with the guards. A heated discussion soon ensued between the pretty girl and Andrews.

I started to walk toward them, but Busto stuck out his hand and grabbed my arm. "Hold on, Dude. Give them a chance."

I wanted to go and help if I could, but maybe Busto was right. Now Andrews held his hands out as if to say, "Sure, fine, do what you like."

The two girls turned toward us and walked over. The pretty girl wore a thick winter jacket that stood open in the front. Her dark brown skin glowed in the chilly air, and her curly black hair fell freely down to her shoulders like an obsidian waterfall.

Destiny walked up. Breathing hard, she said, "Hey, guys. This is my cousin, Earline. We call her Earl."

Busto and I both said, "Hi."

"What was that all about back there?" I said.

"Good news," Destiny said. "They're going to let us pass through town. Earl vouched for us."

I looked at Earline. She looked about twenty and had a pixie face on top of a petite body. I could see the resemblance to her cousin. "How did you manage that?" I said.

"My mom's the secretary for the mayor, Mrs. Best," Earline said. "The mayor sent a message to Andrews asking them to let you through. The only thing is that you can't stop, and you'll be under police escort."

"That's fine. That's all we were asking for. Thanks for the help." I turned to Destiny. "Did you get enough time to visit with your family?"

"No. Never," she said with a smile. "It's been over five years since I last saw them. But it was good. I hope we find a way to visit again soon."

"Well, let's get going, then." I went to the van and checked if Zeta was hidden—she was. Then, I started the engine. "Earl, you want to ride with us into town?"

"No, I'm good. I'll walk from here," Earline said. She and Destiny hugged and chatted for a minute. Then Destiny got in, and we drove up to the checkpoint.

"You have the permission of Mayor Best to pass through the town under police escort," Andrews said through my side window. He pointed to the female guard. "Miss Hampson here is going to drive that truck"—he pointed to a black pickup truck parked nearby—"down the road. You are to follow her. Do not deviate from her path or stop for any reason unless it's absolutely necessary. She'll wave you past once you reach the checkpoint at the other end of town. Any questions?"

"No, sir. Thank you, this is great. We really appreciate it," I said.

Andrews waved at me. "It's fine. Don't make us regret

it." He looked over at Hampson, who was walking toward the truck. "Okay, you can pass. Just wait for her to back out and drive in front of you."

I eased forward, then stopped so I could wait for Hampson. Soon, we were moving down the highway at about 30 mph. I stayed right on the tail of her truck.

Before we saw the first house, we began seeing what looked like campgrounds. Areas of the forest near the road had been cleared, and tents covered them. I saw hundreds of people dressed in ragged clothing. Children too. Skinny, dirty, with haunted eyes.

As we drove through town, I counted the homes we saw. "There can't be more than a thousand people in this town normally. But look at all the refugees," I said. "Where'd they all come from?"

Busto shook his head.

"My aunt said they've been accepting people from nearby towns that have been attacked by bandits," Destiny said. "A lot of them have lost everything. There are about four thousand people inside the town limits now. Many are ranchers and farmers who've been pushed off their property in Fresno County."

"Their population has quadrupled?" I shook my head. "How can they possibly sustain that?"

"And how are they feeding them?" Busto said.

"By the skinny faces I've seen, I don't think they're eating much," Destiny said.

We drove through the tiny downtown area, which consisted of a half dozen businesses and offices. What looked like the local elementary school had a line of people snaking out the door and all the way down the street for a quarter mile. There were women whose only winter clothing was a thick blanket wrapped tightly around their upper bodies.

Children stood forlornly next to their parents without displaying any of the energy they should. And why weren't they in school?

We passed Best One Stop. It looked like a large convenience store with four gas pumps out front. Its parking lot was mostly empty of cars but packed by a crowd, with people coming and going with sacks, some empty and some full.

The people we saw looked defeated. There was no prideful gleam in their eyes. They were a powerless society that had been beaten on the battlefield by the Kergans and had submitted to the inevitable. It made my blood hot enough to boil.

At the end of Main Street, Hampson turned right onto a residential street with a dozen houses. We drove to the end of it and arrived at another checkpoint guarded by armed men and women. Hampson stuck her hand out her window and waved us past her.

I waved at her as we drove by, and we passed the guards, who eyed us with a great deal of distaste and puzzlement.

The road into the national forest stretched before us, barely wide enough to permit traffic in both directions. Unlike the highway leading into town, this road hadn't been recently plowed. The snow was packed down from other vehicles, and it was icy. I could sense the van's wheels slipping and sliding on the uncertain surface, and I had to drop our speed down to just 5 mph. The road twisted and turned up into the mountains, rising above Wolf Jaw.

"We made it," I said. "But I honestly don't know where we're headed from here."

Zeta floated forward, coming to rest between the two front seats. "Continue driving," she said. "Zeta shall observe."

The land was rugged. The road's shoulder was almost nonexistent. Cracked rock covered the ground with pine and cedar trees poking out of gaps. The mountain incline came right down to the road's edge on the right and continued down on the left.

After a half mile of negotiating this slippery path, the terrain opened up a bit, and we found some flat areas, although all were heavily forested. We saw a few campsites with vehicles parked on the side of the road, but nowhere near the density of refugees we'd seen back in town. I wondered how people were surviving out here in the middle of the winter.

We drove around and scouted for a couple hours. Some of it was done on foot when we found promising areas that were only accessible by unplowed dirt roads buried in feet of snow. My cotton pants quickly became wet and cold. I was not dressed for this kind of weather, and neither was Destiny.

Later, well into the late afternoon, we found ourselves studying a sizeable shallow bowl in the terrain close to the main road but hidden behind a rock outcrop. The outcrop consisted of bedrock projecting out of the ground into a 30-foot plateau behind which hid the sheltered bowl. A little valley. A glen with a brook running down the middle of it. It was bordered by the mountain on the west and the outcrop and road on the east, with forest on the northern and southern ends.

"This is the place," Zeta said.

"Finally," Destiny said. "You're pickier than a toddler at mealtime."

Zeta ignored her comment. "This site is protected yet has easy access to the road. Zeta senses plentiful resources and a ground suited to subterranean construction."

"You can tell all of that from just floating here?" I said.

"Nay, Zeta has remote nanobots surveying up to a thousand feet out. Though still collecting information, she needs no more. The decision is made. This is the place."

"Nice," Busto said. "But one problem: there are people already here."

My eyes shot into the distance, scanning our surroundings. "Where?"

Busto tapped my shoulder and pointed to a gap in the trees about a hundred yards from the outcrop. That's when I saw something blue that didn't belong there. Then I noticed garbage strewn on the ground. "Campers?" I said.

"Maybe. But somebody is living here and has been for weeks, at least," Busto said.

I grumbled. "Son of a monkey. We just can't get a break." I scratched my head under my stocking cap. "Let's go take a closer look. Maybe it's abandoned."

"Okay, but move slowly and make lots of noise. We don't want to startle anybody, or we're liable to get shot. Zeta and Destiny, why don't you stay here and guard our rear. Kory and I will check it out."

Busto reached inside his jacket and pulled out a pistol, confirming my suspicions I'd held ever since we met him that he had a concealed firearm. He pulled back the slide, held it in both hands, pointed at the ground before him, and then began creeping through the forest.

I followed in his footsteps, wishing I held a weapon of some kind. "Hello!" I cried out in the direction we'd seen the flash of blue. "Hello?! Anybody there?"

We continued forward, calling out greetings. As we penetrated deeper into the glen, we passed piles of refuse. It stank. Several beaten dirt paths crisscrossed under the trees, well worn by the passage of feet.

Out of the trees appeared three improvised shelters. I wouldn't call them tents. Instead, they were blue tarps hung from the trees, sheltering rickety structures built from fallen logs and lumber scraps.

A branch snapped. Busto jerked his gun up, pointed it at a clump of bushes, and froze. "We mean you no harm. Come out with your hands in the open."

"You first!" yelled a voice. "You're on *my* land. Lower your weapon before I put a hole in your head."

"Okay, stay calm. I'm putting my gun down." He lowered his pistol until it pointed at the ground before him. "Alright, I'm not pointing it at you. Can't be too safe these days. We intend no harm."

A man stepped out from behind a tree. He was bundled up in so many layers of clothing it was challenging to make him out. From under his hood, I saw a ruddy face covered with long blond hair and a graying beard that came down to his chest. He held a hunting rifle pointed at us. From behind him, two women looked at us suspiciously.

"What're you doin' here?" he said.

"Sir, please lower your weapon," Busto said.

"I'm not the one who's trespassing."

I laughed.

"What ya think is so funny, kid?" the man said with narrowed eyes.

"These are public lands. You can't live here," I said.

The man's face became even redder than it already was. "I claimed them. And who're you to tell me otherwise? This piece"—he shook the rifle—"in my hands is all the paperwork I need."

Busto looked at me and shook his head as if telling me to shut up. He looked back at the man. "We're just scouting the area. We wanted to know when you folks were thinking about leaving. Can we help you with anything?"

"Who said anything about us leaving?" the man said. "I'm not telling you anything."

One of the women poked the man in the shoulder and whispered something at him.

"Dammit, Lynda," he said, "I'm busy. You and Phoebe go back into the tent." He turned back to us. "I'm only going to say this once: Go back the way you came from, or I'll shoot you both. This is my land. You don't belong here."

"Okay, we're leaving," Busto said. He backed up and waved his hand at me. We moved backward under the trees until we'd put twenty yards between the man and us. Then we turned around and hiked out of the glen quickly.

"What happened?" Destiny said when we rejoined her and Zeta.

"Squatters," Busto said. "They've taken up residence and don't seem to have any plans to move."

"Zeta, how about we find another location," I said.

"Nay, Zeta insists on this one. These humans have no right to be here," Zeta said.

If there was one thing I'd learned from living on the streets, it was that possession was the first rule of ownership. Never challenge anybody about what they had, unless you were prepared to die for it. Even if they had obtained it illegally. "Well, neither do we. This is a national forest. And I don't want to get shot. They were here first."

"There is a seam of rich tungsten ore resting sixty feet below us," Zeta said. "And the water table is comfortably high. Those are two crucial materials Zeta ought to have for the base and the ship. Relentless Zeta insists on this location."

It was the first time Zeta had ever pushed me so hard

with a request. Up until then, she had been agreeable and flexible. If she said we needed it, we'd have to figure out a way.

But I felt terrible about it. I'd been a squatter on many occasions. Nothing was worse than somebody with a greater claim of ownership appearing and tossing Destiny and me from our home. That's why we'd eventually pulled together the funds to buy the van. It was so we could have a home that we truly owned and couldn't be kicked out of.

I didn't want to kick these people off their claim, even if they had no legal right to it. They were clearly just trying to survive, just like us. They had found a place that worked for them.

But we had a social right to it. We were going to fight on behalf of humanity. Zeta had special requirements pertaining to the base and access to resources. This glen met those requirements, and we needed it.

In the distance, I saw the man standing in the woods and watching us. Hostility poured from him like waves of heat.

"Come on," I said. "Let's go talk in the van."

We stomped through the deep snow back to the van and climbed in. I cranked the engine but didn't immediately drive away. Destiny sat in the passenger's seat, and Busto on the back bench.

"If Zeta says we need this spot, then I think we should take it," I said.

"Kory," Busto said, "put yourself in these people's shoes. You'd be taking their home from them. And if they don't want to move, what will you do?"

"Shoot them," Destiny said, still facing forward.

Even I was shocked by her response. I knew she couldn't be serious but instead was just pushing Busto's buttons. She definitely got what she wanted.

He gasped. "I can't believe what I'm hearing! I just rescued you from people who tried to steal everything from you. And now you want to do the same to others?"

"We're stronger. Gunny, the world has changed, if you haven't noticed. If we want to survive, there's no place anymore for feel-good behavior. The strong are taking from the weak. And that's what we should do here."

Busto shook his head. "I can't believe you. If the real world worked like you just described, no child would ever reach adulthood alive. The human species would go extinct. You hold to fallacious ideals."

Destiny turned around and grimaced at the marine. "So, what do you suggest, Gandhi? That we just move along until we find whatever ground happens to be free and settle there, without regard to what Zeta has to say about it? If we follow your suggestion, we'll end up unsafe, frustrated, and probably dead. Still, you can feel good about yourself because you didn't hurt anybody. Get real!"

"That's not what I'm saying. I'm just—"

"Don't tell me you never hurt anybody when you were a marine. Or did the Raiders go around the world secretly undertaking humanitarian projects?"

"You don't know anything about—"

"Who cares. I've lived on the streets for years. That's a place where you won't survive if you're weak. You don't make it unless you're willing to prey on the vulnerable."

"That's harsh, girl." Busto rubbed his hands through his hair.

What Destiny was arguing for was based on the truth. When the world falls into chaos, resources are limited, and people are suspicious of each other. To survive, one has to be willing to hurt the weak. And yet, at the same time, I hated that life. In it, too many people with lots of potential were destroyed before they could make their mark on the world only because another greedy person wanted their food, shelter, clothes, or money. They weren't strong enough to hold onto it.

I nodded and turned to Busto. "Gunny, I recognize how you feel, yet Destiny has a point." I looked at Destiny and held her eyes. "But, first and foremost, we are not bandits. I'm not going to start using violent force against humans to get what I want. Therefore, we need to think this through." I looked at each of my crew members, hoping for suggestions. "We need to oblige these people to leave this land while causing minimal harm to them. And preferably none."

"I'm sure Gunny knows all about that, being the big bad Marine he is," Destiny said.

Busto blushed. He folded his arms and sighed. "I admit that we in the military could sometimes be heavy-handed."

Destiny snorted. I held a hand up at her. I needed them to stop arguing, and at least Gunny was trying to make peace.

There had to be a way to make the squatters leave voluntarily, under their own power. To make them pack up their stuff and abandon the glen. I'd seen their truck parked on the road. They clearly weren't trapped here. They had a way out.

"What if they left because they *wanted* to?" I said.

"What?" Destiny said.

"Yeah, think about it. What if we made them want to leave."

"Like bribe them? Purchase it?"

"Something like that, though I suspect their asking price will be too high. No, I'm thinking of doing something that would make them want to leave."

I thought about the Febreze bombs we'd used against the Kergans. It was a nonlethal weapon that incapacitated the aliens without killing them or hurting humans. It was a chemical weapon. Zeta seemed to be pretty good at manufacturing chemicals.

"Zeta," I said, "Can you make any known chemical?"

She bobbed up and down once. "Kory must be more specific. Zeta has access to formulations of millions of compounds whose synthesis is limited only by access to resources that yield the needed atomic components."

"Okay, I think I have an idea. Something that'll make them want to leave. We're going to stink them out."

15

"What do you mean by 'stink them out?'" Destiny asked.

"Let's get something to eat first, and I'll tell you what I'm thinking."

I drove us a half mile down the road to a clearing on the side of the road and parked. We broke out the zetamilk for dinner. After several days of eating Zeta's synthetic food, it started getting tiresome, though none of us complained. Having a secure food source made it taste better than a supersized bacon cheeseburger with all the fixings and a side of onion rings.

"I think I know what he's thinking," Busto said. "He wants to employ a nonlethal weapon."

"That's right," I said. "In fact, I'd call it a nonviolent weapon. I want Zeta to produce some kind of chemical that stinks so bad that deploying it in that glen will drive those squatters out of there."

"Don't call something like that a nonviolent weapon," Busto said. "It will still cause them distress and make them run like hell."

"Whatever. Zeta, can you make something like that?"

"Indeed, she can," Zeta said. "Zeta's database suggests an effective chemical targeted against humans called thioacetone. It requires carbon, hydrogen, and sulfur. Zeta can easily synthesize it from the local environment."

"Thiacetote?"

"Thioacetone. It causes nausea, panic, and, in sufficiently high doses, unconsciousness. It is related to an odorous chemical contained in the spray of the species you call skunks, though considerably stronger."

"Stinks worse than a skunk. Yup, that'll do it."

"It'll contaminate the site," Destiny said. "I'm not goin' to sleep in the middle of that. Beds, food, and skunks don't mix. And I know because I've had to deal with Kory's stinky socks before."

My mouth dropped open. "It was just that one time, but you won't let it go, will you?"

She held a hand to her chest. "I've been traumatized for life." She smiled.

"Zeta can neutralize the chemical with ease after you are satisfied with the result," Zeta said.

"I still don't understand why we need that particular land," Busto said as he pulled his stocking cap off and rubbed his dark hair. "Why can't we put the base somewhere else?"

It was the same argument as before. "We need it more," I said. "This is about protecting humanity. We shouldn't compromise our capabilities just because those people got there first. They could camp in plenty of other areas on this mountain."

"I don't feel bad about it," Destiny said. "I didn't appreciate having a gun pointed at me and told to get off land that wasn't marked as private. Those squatters are going to accidentally kill somebody someday."

Busto leaned back in his chair and sighed, staring out the front window. "It still feels wrong."

"Sorry, Gunny, but we're doing it," I said. "We'll make sure it doesn't get out of hand."

He pressed his lips together and stared into the forest. "Okay. Then let's make a good plan." He turned his head to the alien. "Zeta, after you make this stuff, how are we going to deploy it."

"Thioacetone is highly unstable and volatile. Zeta counsels synthesizing it in situ," Zeta said.

"Say again," I said. Sometimes, Zeta used big words that my brain couldn't translate.

Busto answered. "She's saying the stink spray is too difficult to control and that she should manufacture it and release it directly into the environment. Correct?"

"Aye, astute Gunny," Zeta replied, "that is a fine description of Zeta's proposal. Consort, Zeta wants you to lead her to the edge of that little valley. She shall plant herself in the soil and send her nanobots into the ground surrounding the illegal tenants. The bots will begin manufacturing the chemical and releasing it into the environment. Using this method, our foes cannot find the source and extinguish it. It also gives Zeta a fine degree of control over the production such that she can modulate thioacetone levels so they don't become so high they incapacitate them."

I imagined Zeta sitting out in that forest all alone, exposed. "The problem is that it'll be dangerous for you," I said. "We'll have to keep our distance. You'll be all alone."

"Zeta can care for herself."

"Like you did back at that dumpster where we found you?"

"A different situation, lad. Zeta was attempting to put herself in a situation where you would find her. Revealing her true nature to that vagrant would have possibly led the Kergans to our trail."

"And you're not worried about that in this situation?"

"Nay, not if they fail to find Zeta," Zeta said. "She shall burrow into the ground, for she excels at that."

"How will we stay in contact," Busto said.

"Zeta hasn't had an opportunity to fabricate portable comms terminals. We shall make a plan and follow it as best we can. And Consort Kory will be able to sense her location through our link."

"True," I said. "Okay. Let's schedule the operation for sunset. I want there to be enough light so the squatters can see well enough to collect their belongings."

Another pang of guilt poked me. These people were homeless, just like Destiny and me. They were our unofficial allies on the streets. What we were planning to do was against the rules of the street. They'd done nothing to us. It was us who had intruded on them and were planning to run them off. I wished there was something we could do to compensate them for their loss. I honestly didn't want the coming confrontation.

I remembered a shelter Destiny and I had found about three years ago. It was an empty shed on the roof of a three-story apartment building. We discovered a broken fire escape that gave us easy access from an alley in the back. The shed was dry and warm because of the heat rising from the building, and it even had an electrical outlet.

We took up residence and moved our few belongings there. We brought some old mattresses, a table, and some chairs. A couple lamps and a space heater. A nearby exterior faucet provided water from the building. Best of all, nobody else seemed to know about it. We were safe.

We lived in that shed for about six months. Then, one day, a curious building tenant discovered us and reported it to the landlord, who called the police. We fled before we could be arrested. Being juveniles, they would have put us into a group home. But we left behind most of our belongings.

One minute, we were safe and secure in our shed, and then suddenly, we were back on the street again. Ever since then, I had dreamed of having our own place that was truly ours, that we could defend. To have a home is what I most wanted, and it was why I was following Zeta. She had offered us a place to live and become independent.

And now we were going to kick these squatters off land they'd been living on for many weeks, if not months. Were we indeed the Good Guys?

16

About an hour before sunset, we returned to the granite outcrop that bordered the glen. Busto opened the van's sliding door, and Zeta floated out.

"Consort," she said, "Zeta recommends waiting for her back at that clearing. She will find you."

"When?" I said.

"Zeta will wait for the illegals to depart. If she encounters a problem and can move in secret, Zeta shall come to you at midnight."

"Fine. We'll wait for you. Good luck."

Zeta didn't respond but instead flew around the base of the outcrop and disappeared into the forest.

"Let's go before they see us," Busto said.

"Don't be shy, Gunny," Destiny said.

His eyes shot daggers at her. "I don't want to get shot."

Destiny tucked her curly black hair behind her ear. "And I thought you were such great friends with them. I'm sure they wouldn't want to hurt you. After all, they're just innocent people trying to live in harmony with the land and other creatures."

Gunny mumbled something. "I never claimed they were."

"That's not what—" she started to say.

"Right, knock it off, you guys," I said. I didn't need these two at each other's throats.

We drove back to the clearing. The sun was low on the horizon, and the sky was mostly clear. Long shadows were cast onto the road, with the sun occasionally peeking out from behind the trees as we traveled down the narrow forest service road. At the clearing, we did our best to hide the van under some trees, though if anybody looked closely, they'd see tracks we'd left in the snow leading right to us.

We relaxed in the van seats and kept the engine running for warmth. Nobody spoke for a while. I played with the radio, searching the AM and FM bands for stations. There was nothing on the FM, and I only found one AM station.

A synthetic-sounding human spoke over the radio. "*The Kergan Military Authority has authorized the distribution of humanitarian supplies to California and Nevada counties affected by recent cold-weather power outages. Citizens in need of assistance are to contact their local government representatives to see if they qualify.*

"*Citizens are warned about a recent spike in highway robberies in Central Valley counties. Authorities are investigating the incidents and taking steps to apprehend the suspects. In the meantime, citizens are urged to travel in large groups and avoid rural areas during darkness.*

"*Today, the California State Assembly authorized an emergency $237 billion increase in the budget for the California Department of Transportation. The increase offsets unplanned shortfalls in the Caltrans budget due to inflation in the value of the dollar. Governor Hut—*"

I switched off the radio. It was all useless news that had

been carefully censored by the Kergans. The reports never released national or world news and little information about neighboring states. The only way we had to learn about those things was through rumors shared by word of mouth.

There was no normal anymore. The Kergan invasion had disrupted human lives so much that things would never return to normal, even if the Kergans were to up and disappear tomorrow. They had destroyed so much of our infrastructure and institutions that humanity's progress as a modern society had been set back at least a century.

What I would give for some decent music. I shifted around in my seat, trying to find a more comfortable position, and shut my eyes.

I must have fallen asleep because, the next instant, I noticed it was dark outside, and Busto was talking.

"Somebody's coming," he said.

The air stunk horribly. I covered my nose.

I sat up and looked through the window. A vehicle's headlights moved slowly, coming down the road toward Wolf Jaw. From its height above the ground, it looked like a pickup truck.

I sensed Zeta through my link; she was still in the same position as she'd been before I fell asleep. She felt focused.

"Hey, I think it's the squatters," I said, pointing at the lights.

"Well, your head is no box of rocks, that's for certain," Destiny said.

The clock on the dashboard said it was 8:36 pm.

The truck drew closer and passed behind us without slowing. It was so dark I could barely see its outline, but it did indeed look like our squatters.

After they passed, I opened my door. I immediately

regretted it. An overpowering stench nearly knocked me onto my knees. It smelled like somebody had mixed skunk spray with spoiled eggs and feces, let it ferment for a week, then cooked the concoction over an open flame.

"Ugh!" I retched and got back in, closing the door.

"Good lord!" Busto said.

"No!" Destiny squealed, holding her jacket up over her mouth.

We almost had to flee ourselves because the smell was too overpowering, even at our distance and with the van sealed. But over the next hour, the stink gradually dissipated to tolerable levels. Soon after that, I sensed Zeta was moving toward us. "Our friend is on her way back," I said.

A few minutes later, Zeta appeared and tapped on the side door window. Busto let her in. This time, only fresh mountain air came in with her.

"Zeta has succeeded," she said immediately. "The illegal tenants have vacated their campsite and taken most of their belongings with them."

I wanted to celebrate, but we were so exhausted by the stench that the only responses I heard from Destiny and Busto were mumbles and groans.

"How are we going to keep them from coming back?" Busto said.

"Yeah, this seemed too easy," I said. "I can't believe they'd give it up without fighting it."

Destiny snorted. "Dude, Kory, we were like half a mile away from Ground Zero, and even we were almost overwhelmed. I think you give these people too much credit."

"Maybe you're right."

"My clothes are gonna stink like skunk for the next six

months."

"Sometime," Busto said, "I'll tell you about the time somebody let a female hamster in heat loose in our barracks in Syria. The smell was so bad, we had to sleep in our trucks."

I drove the van back to the glen and parked it behind the outcrop. It was too dark to move into the narrow valley, so we made camp there, the three of us lying crammed together in the back of the van with our sleeping bags.

At first light, Busto and I were both up. Leaving Destiny to sleep, we explored the glen with Zeta. She showed us a hollow in the soil where she had burrowed not too far away from the van. I could smell nothing of the stink that had been there last night.

The squatters hadn't taken everything. They'd left behind all their refuse and a great deal of discarded junk. Broken chairs, electronics, ratty clothing. An open latrine pit.

"Gross," I said. "I don't want to dig our base in the same ground that soaked up their piss and crap."

"Do not fear," Zeta said. "Zeta shall recycle all this discarded material. It shall be valuable."

"Okay, but just do me a favor and put the base far away from their latrine. It smells so bad I'm surprised they didn't stink themselves out without our help."

I walked to the other side of the glen, further away from the brook, about halfway between it and the outcrop. "How about here?"

"A fine plan, Consort," Zeta said, coming to rest on the ground. "Zeta shall begin excavating here."

17

I felt elation. We were finally going to do it. We were going to build our home. I ran back to the van to wake up Destiny.

"Ah!" Destiny sniffed as she squirmed in her sleeping bag. "I still smell like a skunk!"

I shifted on my legs. "Come on, Dest. We'll rig up some kind of shower today. I promise."

"Do we have any more Febreze?"

"I have one bomb left if that's what you're asking for."

"Give it to me."

I did. She disarmed it and removed the compressed gas can holding the chemical. Then she opened the valve and sprayed herself and her clothes with a liberal amount. It seemed to help, so I sprayed myself and the van's inside surfaces.

By the time Destiny and I returned, Zeta had already begun digging. Tendrils of a nanobot network stretched out on the surface of the rocky soil in all directions. I tried to take care of where I stepped so I wouldn't tread on the threads. Zeta hadn't said anything about not walking on them, but it couldn't be good.

While Zeta worked, us three humans constructed a temporary camp. I had suggested we just continue camping in the van, but Busto said it wouldn't be safe if the squatters returned. It would be too difficult to conceal ourselves.

Fortunately, Destiny and I had a three-person tent we'd saved for situations when we couldn't sleep in the van or when we didn't have enough space in it to rest. We set that up. It was worn out and wouldn't last long in these harsh conditions, but it was better than sleeping out in the open.

By the time we had our camp set up and a small campfire burning, Zeta had already dug up a pit about 3 ft square and 6 ft deep in the rocky soil. And her work seemed to be accelerating. The tendrils of nanobots had expanded and grown into a slimy mat that oozed over the ground like scum on a pond. Heat wafted from it, melting the surrounding snow and ice, turning the nearby ground into a muddy soup that threatened to suck in anybody who unwisely stepped there.

I saw no visible chunks of soil being moved, and yet it was clear that the dirt being dug out of the hole was being deposited to the side. The slime mat covered the ground between the pit and a growing mound of spoil where the excavated material was being left. Trillions and trillions of nanobots were moving the dirt one microscopic particle at a time from the pit to the spoil mound. Though a little disgusting, I still found it fascinating to watch, like observing an ant colony at work, only amplified by several orders of magnitude.

Destiny walked over and stood by me. "This is an illustration of your intestines at work."

"That's gross, Dest," I said.

She giggled. "That's what it reminds me of. Pretty

nauseating."

"But maybe you're right. Our intestines extract nutrients and energy from food. Maybe that's what Zeta's nanobots are doing."

"It looks like it's alive." Destiny rested a hand on my arm. "Watch out. Today, a small pit; tomorrow, the Gray Goo!"

"The gray what?"

"The Gray Goo."

"What's that?"

"Years ago, some scientist predicted that out-of-control nanotech could accidentally digest the Earth, leaving behind a blob of goo made of nothing but self-producing nanobots. He called it the Gray Goo."

My eyes opened wide. "That's terrifying!"

She nodded. "But I also read that it would never happen in practice because the nanobots need too much energy and resources. They'd run out of fuel, so to speak, before they got far."

"Well, I sure hope Zeta has these things under control."

She patted me on the shoulder. "I'm sure you're completely in control of the situation."

"You are making me feel so much confidence."

"That's what I'm here for!" She laughed and started to walk away.

"Friend Destiny's explanation is technically incorrect," Zeta said as she flew out of the pit. "The nanobots are machines fabricated by Zeta's nanoforge and are not alive. Furthermore, they require a working fluid within which to move efficiently, much like your bodies require blood and water to transport nutrients. Zeta believes this is why it looks alive to you humans, but in truth, the nanobots may replicate themselves only under Zeta's direct command.

This so-called Gray Goo catastrophe is impossible."

Destiny wagged a hand at the alien. "Zeta, you're no fun. I was just giving Kory a hard time."

"Ah, yes, Zeta understands. Friend Destiny was playing with Consort Kory. Very well, Zeta will return to her task." She rotated and flew back into the pit.

The air smelled of wet soil and rotting matter. Zeta was tearing up the center of the glen. As the pit expanded, she felled trees and consumed the surface vegetation, leaving behind naked soil adjacent to the pit. All of these materials were then decomposed into microscopic particles and stored in spoil mounds that would later be used as resource caches. The nanobot slime also acted as a barrier to Earth microbes, such as bacteria, who would try to invade the mounds and consume the raw and easily digestible stock.

Later in the day, Zeta had disappeared from sight. I could sense her location underground in the pit she was digging. Waves of a muddy substance flowed out of the hole, guided and propelled by the slimy veins of nanobots. The flow burbled and boiled, steam rising from it in the cold air before stopping on the spoil mounds and hardening to a consistency like concrete. The air smelled of rock dust and decomposing plant matter, just like a garden that was being worked.

The excavated pit had deepened and widened into a subterranean cavity. But insufficient light penetrated for me to see its layout, and hot gas bloomed out of the hole, rushing straight up into the sky, condensing into a fog, and further obscuring views of the interior. These water vapors produced localized clouds that drifted down the glen and over the Wolf Jaw valley.

The people down in the town must have seen the clouds and suspected that something was happening up there. I hadn't considered this. We were going to draw attention if this went on for much longer.

"Zeta, where are these clouds coming from?" I asked.

"Hydrated silica," her voice came from deep in the hole. "Processing it for the silica is releasing high levels of water that exceed our requirements. Venting it to the atmosphere is the most practical means of disposing of it."

"What's the silica for?"

"The load-bearing structure of the base will be constructed of crystallized silica. What you call quartz. It is exceedingly plentiful in your planet's crust."

I had no opinion on the decision because I knew nothing about construction materials. A rock was a rock. If quartz is what Zeta wanted to make the base out of, that was fine by me.

I shrugged and walked to the edge of the glen, feeling bored. Destiny sat on a log, staring into the distance. I saw Busto on the other side of the small valley, hiking along the forest's edge.

Abruptly, a man walked out from under a tree about fifty feet behind Busto. He held a rifle cradled in his arm.

18

I recognized the man as one of the squatters we'd run off last night. He stood there studying the excavation with wide eyes, his greasy, long blond hair falling past his shoulders. His beard came down to his chest.

"Hey!" I yelled, trying to get Busto's attention. When he turned to my voice, I pointed at the man.

Busto turned around, but just then the man saw us and took off running back into the forest.

"Find cover!" Busto called out. Then he turned and ran diagonally toward where the man had disappeared.

Destiny and I dropped to the ground behind the log. Moments later, a *boom* sounded as somebody fired a gun.

"No!" Destiny screamed. She tried to stand but I put my hand on her shoulder and held her to the ground.

"Do you have your pistol?" I said.

"Yes!" she barked, her eyes narrow and sharp.

"Well, what are you waiting for?" I replied, wishing I had one on me, but I'd left mine in the van. Regardless, I didn't feel safe when carrying it because I didn't know how to use it.

Destiny opened her jacket, drew her pistol, and cocked it. Then we lay there silently for the next few minutes.

"You can come out!" Busto yelled.

I raised my head above the log. Busto stood inside the glen with the man in front of him, his hands bound, and his face flushed and frowning.

Destiny and I hopped over the log and ran to Busto.

"Watch him," Busto said when we arrived. He passed me a hunting rifle. "Keep a hold of that. It's his. There are more people back there. I'm going after them."

"They're just women and children!" the man screamed. "They're unarmed!" He stomped his foot to emphasize.

"Who fired the gun?" I said.

"I did," Busto said. "It was a warning shot over his head." He hefted his M4. "I'll be back. Keep him under guard." He pivoted and marched in the direction of the road.

Destiny raised her pistol at the man. "Have a seat." When the man didn't respond, she roared, "I'm not asking! Sit down!"

"You've no right to do this!" he screeched but then shuffled around a few times until he found a stone that wasn't covered with snow and sat on it. "This is *our* land."

"You vacated it," I said. "We moved in."

"Only because of that stink. Afterward, I returned, and now I see you're ripping up this clearing!" He sat hunched over with his hands ziptied behind him, but he still glared at me. "You know what I think? You people were somehow behind that smell. You did it on purpose!

"You had no right. We've been livin' here for a long time and never bothered nobody. You can't just march in and take a man's property!"

"What's your name?" I said.

He didn't reply at first, and I thought now he might clam up, but then he sighed and said, "Baxter Brooks."

Everything Baxter said was correct. We were behind the smell; we did it on purpose; we ran him and his people off the land and took it for ourselves. Technically, it wasn't his property, but in this new Kergan-governed era, possession was 95% of ownership. Still, we needed this glen more than they did.

The three of us remained quiet for the next five minutes. While Destiny kept her eyes on Brooks, I paced around thinking about what to do with these people. Clearly, they didn't plan to abandon their land like I had expected they would. This operation wasn't going to be as easy as I'd hoped.

This is why I wanted Destiny and me to live on our own, independently, with nobody else nearby. People make things complicated. You set two men down next to each other, and within a minute, they're arguing. Then in an hour, fighting. Then, in a day, maybe trying to kill each other. For there to be peace, people required space. We'd found a place for our home, and yet there was no peace because we took it by force.

At that moment, Busto marched out of the forest behind a line of three people: two women and a boy. One of the women was middle-aged, and the other appeared to be about twenty. Both were plain-looking and thin. The boy was perhaps thirteen or fourteen years old, about five and a half feet tall, with black hair that had been hacked into a ragged haircut. All were dressed in thick winter clothing, including gloves and stocking hats. None were armed, at least not visibly, and Busto had left them unbound.

The younger woman and boy stared at their feet and avoided looking at us. But the older woman, upon seeing Baxter, broke into a run and fell at his feet. "Thank God! I heard the gunshot…didn't know…are you okay?" She grabbed his arm.

"Back away from him, ma'am," Busto said.

She clung to Baxter's arm, her face flushed, glaring at Busto.

Gunny shifted his weight, his hand tightened on the trigger guard, and he started to raise the muzzle of his M4.

The woman flinched, let go of the man, and stepped back next to the other woman and the boy.

"He's not hurt," Gunny said. He looked at me. "This is all of them. Their truck's parked up on the road."

I stepped over to Baxter. "Mr. Brooks, is this your wife and children?"

He nodded.

We were congregated about a hundred feet away from Zeta's excavation. A gurgling sound came from it, followed by a cough, then a puff of steam rose out of the hole.

"I'm Lynda Brooks," the woman said, twisting her hands together, her eyes bouncing between us. "I swear he didn't intend to harm you. My Baxter would never hurt a fly except to put food on our table. *Please* don't hurt him." Her eyes grew shiny. "We just came back to see if that stink was gone, and you surprised us. That's all. Please let my husband go. We'll leave and won't come back, I promise."

"Lynda, shut up!" Baxter hissed.

She turned on him. "No! You're the one that got us into this mess."

"I'm tired of runnin'. First, the Kergans, then the bandits, and those assholes in town. Now, these thugs!" He gestured at us with his chin, his eyes finally landing on mine and boring into them. "You hear me?! I'm not gonna let you run us off without a fight!"

Lynda stood there watching us, washing her hands. She

wrapped an arm around her son and daughter and held them close.

I shifted the unfamiliar rifle in my arms, turned my back on all of them, and stepped several yards away. What were we going to do with these people? An entire family. Their thin faces betrayed their hunger. It was impossible to tell under all that clothing, but I'm sure their ribs were showing. How they were surviving out here in the national forest in the middle of the winter was a mystery to me, but clearly, they had been getting along somehow. If we chased them away, they might starve, freeze, or get picked off by bandits. Or even worse, Baxter might sneak up on us with that rifle of his and murder us from a distance. The fact that he hadn't done that already meant he knew how to restrain himself.

I turned back to them and faced Baxter. "What do you do for a living?"

"I'm a diesel mechanic," he said. "Or I was until everything fell apart. I'm also an outdoorsman. We thought we'd find safety out here in these woods."

"And you, Lynda?"

"I managed a diner in Tollhouse," Lynda said. Tollhouse was a small town to the south of Wolf Jaw.

Destiny approached me and whispered, "What are you thinking?"

I looked at Busto. "Gunny, keep an eye on them. We'll be back in a sec." I grabbed Destiny's arm and tugged her away so we could have a private conversation. I already knew that Busto would like the idea I was considering, but my sister wouldn't.

I sighed and looked into Destiny's eyes. "Maybe they can stay."

She tilted her head to the side. "You're kidding. Right?"

"Look at them, Dest! It's a family. It sounds like they've been chased around until they finally landed here. They thought they were safe, and then we pushed them out."

She stabbed a finger at the ground. "It's their problem, not ours!"

I needed to take a different approach with my argument if I was going to get Destiny on my side. "Look. We're building this base, right?" She nodded. I rubbed my chin. "We can't defend it by ourselves. My thinking is that this Brooks family can join with us. Not as part of the ship crew but as custodians for the base. In exchange for their help, we provide them shelter, food, and safety."

"That is *way* too generous! You're nuts!"

"Maybe I'm not. Remember that with Zeta's help, we're no longer short of those things. We can afford to be generous with others. Why not use that to our advantage?"

She was quiet for a second. I could see the wheels turning behind her eyes. She nodded. "Maybe you're right. Okay, I see your point. You're thinking there is safety in numbers."

"Exactly!" I said, grinning. "But we need to make sure they're loyal to us. What do you think is the best way to do that?"

Destiny grimaced and nodded. "We control the food and supplies and most of the weapons. So, they would depend on us."

"That's right. Now, I'm not planning to be some kind of tyrant. I honestly want to help these people. But if we do that, we do it in a way that also benefits us. Are you on board with that?"

"Sure, okay, it makes sense. But I don't know if Busto will like it."

I waved a hand. "Don't worry, he will. He never wanted

to run the family out of here in the first place. The stink bomb was a horrible idea, and I should have thought this through better."

"I *also* agree with that," she said with a small laugh. "This smell! It's goin' to be months before it goes away."

"Well, I'll chalk the experience up as a lesson learned. Okay," I nudged her on the shoulder, "let's go back and tell them."

We came back to the group. I spoke to Busto. "Gunny, untie Mr. Brooks."

Busto did as I asked with only a questioning look. Afterward, Baxter stood and rubbed his wrists, watching us. I still held his rifle.

"You're right, Mr. Brooks, we did take this land from you," I said. "But we need it."

His jaw muscles flexed. "Look at the mess you've made! It's not even been one day, and you've ripped the hell out of the ground."

I remembered all the trash they'd left behind. "It's not like you were taking any better care of it."

"What are you going to do to us? And I need my rifle back. It's our only means of eating during the winter."

I looked at the gun I held. I didn't know enough about firearms to tell what kind it was, except it was bolt action and had a scope. "How many rounds do you have?"

"What's it to you?"

I shifted my weight from one leg to the other. "You're gonna run out eventually. Then how are you going to get more?"

Baxter folded his arms. "We'll cross that bridge when we reach it. And it's none of your business."

I sighed and looked away. "And what if I made it my business?"

He gaped. "What's that supposed to mean?"

"Mr. Brooks, I think I'd like you to stay here. Let us share this land with you. We can offer you safety, food, and maybe even shelter and power. But I need to know you can keep a secret."

A change came to Baxter's face. The stubborn gleam in his eyes transformed into submissiveness. His mouth relaxed and his jaw dropped open. "I don't understand."

"Can you keep our activities secret?"

"Like what?"

"Let me just say that we're no friends of the Kergan Empire. I don't want them to find out about us."

Baxter shrugged. "You and me both. Why do you think we came out here into the woods?"

"That means you can't be saying anything about our activities to other humans either. We don't know who we can trust or who might be collaborating with the Kergans."

"So, why trust me?"

"Mr. Brooks, I get the feeling you and we have similar goals. I won't say anything to others about you if you don't say anything about us."

Baxter nodded. "Yeah, I could do that. And call me Baxter."

I handed his rifle back to him, and he took it with a nod. "So how are we going to share this here land?" he said.

"As you can see, we're in the middle of constructing a facility. It's almost entirely underground. As far as I'm concerned, you can have everything above ground except for our doorways. It's going to be a mess for the next couple of weeks, but we'll get it cleaned up so good you won't be able to tell we built something underground."

"That's some pretty amazing machines you've got running. How many people are down in that hole?"

"Baxter, the less you know, the better."

"Okay, I get it. You said something about shelter and food?"

"Of course. It'll be a few days, maybe a week until we can do something about shelter. But we have food and water to share. Also fuel."

Baxter's face split into a grin, and he held out his hand. "You got a deal." I took his hand. "What's your names?"

We went around the circle and exchanged names. Busto relaxed and slung his M4. Now that the tension was released, there didn't seem to be any hard feelings between him and Baxter, which I was glad to see.

The Brooks' daughter was named Phoebe. She was nineteen, just a year older than me. She'd looked plain when I first saw her, but now that she was up closer, I could see that she was actually quite lovely. Maybe a little too skinny for my tastes, but she was tall, with long, straight brown hair, peanut-colored eyes, a little delicate freckled nose, and a graceful manner of walking and carrying herself.

The boy, Ricki, was fourteen. He had wavy hair the same color as his sister's. He was skinny and short but had started growing into a man. He had a cautious but intelligent gleam in his eyes and watched us constantly. Especially me, for some reason. I caught him staring at me every time I looked toward him, though he would quickly avert his gaze.

The Brooks unloaded their truck and reestablished their campsite on the southern edge of the glen under the trees. Baxter seemed very skilled. With just an ax, rope, and tarps, he soon had their little shacks constructed again and a warm fire burning. We shared our zetamilk, telling them there was plenty of it and to eat their fill.

With food in their stomachs, they seemed content. How

would they respond when they met Zeta?

In less than one day, I had doubled the size of our group. Of course, the Brooks weren't part of our crew, but I had taken responsibility for them, even if nobody else realized it. Why had I done it? Because I couldn't turn that family out into the cold. Because I felt guilty about kicking them off their land. Because I could see myself in them and knew how I would have felt in their place. Every time I looked at Lynda and Baxter, I instead saw Mom and Dad.

I had started trying to find a way for Destiny and me to live independently, but I was failing miserably at it. In working to secure our living, I had bound other people to us. First, Zeta, then Busto, and now the Brooks family. Who would be next?

I thought about the people in Wolf Jaw. Did we truly need them also?

The ground vibrated. At first, I thought it was something Zeta was doing. Then, I noticed a shadow passing over us.

A massive ship flew overhead, blocking out the overcast sky. The thrum of its engines resonated inside my body, making my teeth feel like they'd shake right out of my skull. Everybody in the glen halted what they were doing and looked up.

The Kergans!

19

The ship filled the sky, making it appear closer than it actually was. As we stood there watching, it continued its course without slowing. I held my breath as if that would keep the Kergans from detecting us. Its blocky shape soon receded into the distance, shrinking in size like an ocean-going vessel on the horizon.

"Must be headed to Las Vegas," Baxter said.

Maybe that was the case. The ship must have just finished entering the atmosphere from orbit. Come to load up with our planet's wealth and carry it away. Maybe they were also after people.

Trying to forget about the ship, I picked up my chair, carried it over near the excavation, and sat. Watching the nanobots move the material was mesmerizing, and I didn't have anything else to do at the moment.

A few minutes later, Destiny came over with a second chair and plopped beside me. She threw her arm over my shoulders. "Bro, how does it feel to be like Mother Teresa?"

I lifted an eyebrow. "How's that?"

"If you're not careful, the next time you look, you'll have, like, a thousand people you're caring for. Your grocery bill alone must be like a million bucks a week."

"Yeah, you know how it is." I grinned. "Some people just aren't happy without their cheeseburger ration."

She shoved me. "Cheeseburgers are underrated. I consider them a vital part of a well-balanced diet."

I shook my head. "Heavens, what I would do for a Big Mac right now."

"Or Pizza Hut."

"Taco Bell. I would kill for some soft tacos with all the fixin's."

She giggled. "You would probably eat like ten of them."

"I would!" I bellowed with a wide grin.

She leaned back in her chair and stretched. "When're we going to try and go back to town?"

I removed my cap and ran my hand through my long hair. "Why should we? It seems like we're just fine here."

"My aunt and cousin are down there!" She tugged on my ear painfully.

"Ow!" I shoved her hand away. "Seems to me that they're doin' just fine."

"Didn't you notice the state of that place when we drove through? My aunt answered her door with a shotgun in hand. No, she's not doing okay. Nobody in that place is. They're overrun with desperate refugees."

A rumble and a sound like a falling rock sounded from the dark pit. "What did your aunt ever do for you all those years you lived on the street? She should have taken you in, but she didn't. You don't owe her anything."

She dropped her arm from my shoulders and leaned away. "She claims she didn't know. She hasn't heard from my mom in years. She didn't know I was homeless."

"You mean the state never contacted her?"

She shrugged. "I guess not. She was shocked when I showed up at her house. I told her what happened to me. She seemed genuinely sorry. And even *if* she'd intentionally left me to rot, there's still my cousin."

I rubbed my face. I didn't need even more people to worry about. "I don't see that we can do much for them."

"Don't we need to go to town anyway? Don't we need stuff?"

"Like what?"

"Do you want to eat nothing but zetamilk? And I could use some better winter clothing."

Trying to think through Destiny's argument and curious about what would happen if I did it, I tossed a nearby pebble into the pit. I didn't hear it hit the bottom. "I'm not sure the town people will let us back in."

She stopped my hand as I prepared to toss another pebble in, grabbing my wrist. "They will if we bring something to trade. You think they'll turn us away if we come with food and gas?"

"What? You're thinking about offering the zetamilk as a trade item?"

"Sure, why not? Or gasoline. You heard that policeman say they no longer had fresh milk and meat. I bet the zetamilk makes a good substitute. And what about fuel? Zeta makes gasoline pretty quickly. I bet she can also make diesel and heating oil. There's got to be demand for that."

I thought about what she proposed. It was an interesting idea. Use Zeta's manufacturing capabilities to produce items we could trade to Wolf Jaw for other goods. But it would mean having to establish a relationship with the town people, and there might be Kergan agents among them.

The sensation of the passing Kergan ship still hadn't left me. We were supposed to go forth and fight the enemy aliens, like that huge ship. I didn't see how it was possible to do so without dying a quick and permanent death. Furthermore, anybody who lived near our base might be endangered, including all of Wolf Jaw. What would the townies think if they discovered a band of guerrillas were operating near them? Definitely nothing good. They might even betray us to the Kergans.

But Destiny was right. We couldn't just cut ourselves off from human society. At the bare minimum, we needed a place to make trades for supplies so we didn't have to live off just zetamilk and whatever game we could kill in the forest. And Wolf Jaw was also a potential source of information.

Destiny also had her aunt and cousin to worry about. Betraying them would be the same as me betraying Destiny. Just as I would never dream of doing that, I would not do it to her family, because her family was mine. Period.

"Yo, Zeta!" I yelled.

A moment later, the igna flew out of the pit and stopped in front of me. Splatters of mud covered her, and she emitted waves of heat. "Aye, Consort?"

"How much spare fabrication capacity do you have?"

20

It turned out that Zeta did not have much to spare.

"Consort, until Zeta completes the base's nanoforge, we possess only the one in her capsule," Zeta said. "That is presently occupied."

"But you still can produce enough food and fuel for us, right?" I said.

"Aye, though doing so diverts diligent Zeta's attention from the base construction. However, it is a necessary duty."

After some discussion, we agreed to hold off on producing any excess consumables for trading for a few days until Zeta made more progress on the base.

We had a surplus of gasoline in our supplies, and with little to do, the next day Destiny and I decided to take 5 gallons to Wolf Jaw and see what we could get in exchange for it. Busto and the Brooks stayed at the glen to watch over things.

We drove the two miles down the mountain to Wolf Jaw's north gate. The temperatures had warmed, and the main forest service road was clear of snow. Blue skies covered the heavens, and the warm, yellow sun cast shadows from the forest on our path as I drove the van.

I wondered at the progress Zeta had made on the base construction overnight. While we had slept the night away, my consort continued excavating. I don't think she ever stopped to rest or eat or sleep. Her stamina was phenomenal. That morning, she told me she had completed the first chamber and corridor and was working on the next chamber. By the end of today, she would have completed an entrance stairwell and would let us in to look around.

Wolf Jaw's north gate was guarded by two men dressed in body armor and armed with AR-15-style rifles. Upon their order, we came to a stop.

"Residency license?" the first guard asked me through my lowered window.

"We don't have one." I didn't see any reason to tell him about our business unless it became necessary. "We live a few miles away up the mountain. We'd like to drive around town a bit. Maybe go by your market."

The guard shook his head. "I'm sorry, sir, I can't let you into town without a license or a permit."

Here we go again. "And how do I get one of those?"

"Residency licenses are for town residents who live within the town boundaries."

"You mean, all those refugees living here in tents have licenses?"

"Yes, they were already here when the residency ordinance was passed and were grandfathered in."

I scratched an itch on my leg. "And this permit? How do I get one?"

"Those are issued to people coming to town on official business."

I glanced at Destiny. We were bringing a valuable trade good to town. This was a business trip, not for pleasure. "We'd like to trade 5 gallons of gasoline for supplies. Is that official enough?"

The guard's face lit up with interest. "Yes, sir, it is. Can you show me what you have? If it checks out, then I can issue you a temporary permit right here."

I jumped out, went to the back of the van, and showed him the filled gas can. The other guard strolled around the van, looking on with curiosity.

"Sure, this will work," the first guard said, looking up from the open can. "Not many residents still have running cars. There's not enough fuel. You're fortunate." He looked at me searchingly as if hoping I'd reveal where I got the gas from.

I didn't say anything in reply; I just smiled at him. The less he knew, the better.

The guard shrugged and screwed the cap back on the can. "I'll fill out that permit for you. I need both of your IDs."

We returned to the front of the van, and I handed over Destiny's and my driver's licenses. The guard pulled out a paper tablet and began filling out a form. "Keep this on you while in town," he said while writing. "It's good for today. If you want a long-term permit, then talk to Dora Best, the town mayor."

"Where can I find her?" I asked.

"During the day, she's usually helping out at the town store, Best One Stop."

"Okay." I remembered the large convenience store we'd seen when driving through town. "Is that where we go to trade our gas?"

"It's probably easiest to go there. The Bests will exchange inventory for your fuel. Talk to Neal Best. He owns and manages the store."

"Related to the mayor?"

The guard nodded. "Uh-huh. Her husband."

So, a husband and wife ran the town and its largest store. Most of the political and economic power was in the hands of one couple. Typical. This should be interesting. Maybe Wolf Jaw was on its way to becoming a dictatorship.

The guard snapped his thumb on his pen to close it, tore the permit off his notepad, and passed it to me. "Okay, Mister Drake and Miss Austin. Enjoy your stay." He stepped back and signaled the other guards to open the gate.

The gate consisted of heavy sheets of plywood mounted onto a wheeled platform. The guards pushed it to the side. Not much of a barrier if somebody wanted to force their way into town. One could drive a vehicle right through it and only scratch the paint.

I accelerated away from the guards. "We made it," I said, smiling. "You want to stop and see your aunt and cousin?"

"Of course," Destiny said. "But let's go check out this store first."

As we drove down the center of town, I noticed again the long line of people leading into the local school. Was it being used as some kind of shelter? Were they distributing food?

The street was deserted of motor vehicles, but we saw dozens of residents riding mountain bikes. Many of them had cargo bins strapped over the rear wheels. Others carried multiple passengers, either sitting on the rear rack, on the crossbar, or standing on axle pegs. We got lots of envious looks as we passed in our rusty van.

The homes we passed were in good repair. They were mostly small, detached houses with carports or one-car garages, though we also passed an apartment complex and a row of duplexes.

We saw a hardware store, a small bookstore, a thrift store, and a medical clinic. Most had a long line of customers leading out the front door and onto the sidewalk. Business seemed to be booming. That is, if you were a business owner, but few people in this town would be.

We arrived at One Stop and pulled into an empty parking space between a yellow Jeep Wrangler and an old green Subaru. A large sign on the window we parked in front of said, "*DEER VENISON in STOCK!*" Four gas pumps sat idle in the front of the store under a steel canopy. A small crowd milled around in front of the store. They seemed to be waiting for something. The sidewalk and parking lot had been cleared of snow.

"Are you armed?" I asked.

Destiny patted the left side of her torso. "Yup."

I needed to talk to Busto about getting some training with my pistol. I didn't know how to use it, which put the rest of my crew at risk. Though this crowd didn't seem threatening, my inability to competently use a firearm was going to get us in trouble one of these days. The crowd watched us passively as I picked the gas can up and carried it into the store, followed by Destiny.

The lights inside the store were on, and the temperature was warm. They had power. I wondered why those people were standing idle out there in the cold. Then I saw why: a large sign at the entrance that said: *NO LOITERING!!!*

The store was larger than a typical convenience store, more like a small department store. One side sold food; the other had housewares, clothing, and sporting goods.

Many of the shelves on both the food and housewares sides stood empty. Far fewer customers walked around than stood outside. I walked toward the checkout counter and passed a stand selling $200 candy bars and $300 bags of chips. That's what hyperinflation had done to us. It had destroyed the value of the dollar and the rest of the world's currencies, all thanks to the Kergans and the reckless policies they employed to loot humanity's wealth.

A woman in her thirties, thin and tired-looking, stood behind the cash register. "Can I help you?" she said. A tag on her chest said her name was Cherice.

"Hi. I was told I could find Dora Best around here," I said. In a large, locked display case behind Cherice, I noticed firearms and ammunition were for sale.

She folded her arms. "Maybe. What's this regarding?"

"We're seeking a long-term permit to visit town." I patted the gas can I'd grounded on the floor. "And we have some gasoline to trade for supplies."

"Can I see your permit?"

I passed her the paper the guard had given us. She studied it, then said, "Just a minute." Carrying it, she turned and walked away.

For the moment, we were alone. Destiny and I browsed through the selection of food. Despite the empty shelves, there was still an abundance here. Fresh fruit and vegetables. Stacks of canned food, bags of beans and rice and flour. Boxes of prepackaged meals. A bank of refrigerators and freezers held a few items, though they were mostly empty. A few cases of Pepsi and Mountain Dew. No milk, cheese, or meat. No ice cream, though there was plain ice.

I was mistaken. There *was* meat, but it was venison like the sign had said in front, labeled as *Mule Deer Steaks*. Next to those were a few small packages of rabbit meat wrapped in butcher paper. This indicated some people around her must have been hunting for small game and trading their catches here at One Stop.

Footsteps sounded behind me, and I turned around. Cherice returned following an older woman. The latter exuded confidence, and her plump proportions betrayed easy access to food. Blue eyes studied me and Destiny through a pair of glasses. Her gray hair was cut into a bob.

She frowned at my mud-caked hiking boots, which had tracked dirt into the store, but didn't comment. "I'm Dora Best, town mayor. I hear you want a long-term permit. That right?"

"Yes," I said.

She studied the permit Cherice had given her. "Dammit, I can barely read Lewis' handwriting," she mumbled. She looked at Destiny. "You must be Destiny Austin." She turned to me. "And you're Kory Drake. Did I get that right?"

I nodded. "Yes, ma'am."

"What brings you to town? They don't just let anybody in."

"We have things we want to trade for supplies," I said. "And Destiny has family in town."

Dora's eyebrows raised, and she studied Destiny more closely. "Oh, how nice. Who, may I ask?"

"Judith and Earline Fulton," Destiny said. "They're my aunt and cousin."

"Yes, of course. Judith is the town secretary. Everybody knows her. She's wonderful. And yesterday, she told me about you." Dora said this with a sad look and held up the paper. "Why the permit? Why aren't you staying with her?"

Destiny said, "We've set up a camp to the north of town in the national forest. I didn't want to put a burden on my aunt."

"Oh my." Dora held her hand to her chest. "Do be careful. Dangerous people are living up there. You should have petitioned to live here in town. I'm sure we could have fit in a family member of Judith."

"It's okay. We've got our own plans. You said there were dangerous people?"

"Yes. Why don't you come back to my office, and we'll chat there instead of standing around out here in the front." She waved at us with a welcoming smile.

As soon as she'd heard that Destiny was related to Judith, her demeanor had changed entirely, becoming warm and open. Maybe the town didn't like strangers, and that's why they had been so unwelcoming toward us. Don't misunderstand me. I wasn't eager to make more friends, but I did not want to be on these people's bad side, especially if we needed to trade with them.

We followed Dora's footsteps toward the back of the store.

21

The door to the office had a sign that said *Neal Best, Manager*. The office was small, with a desk and leather executive's chair behind it and two cushioned chairs in front. She pointed us to those and sat behind the desk, leaving the office door open.

"Welcome to Wolf Jaw," Dora said, smiling and seeming sincere. It was such an odd response, considering how the police had treated us like we were guilty of some crime until proven otherwise. But not Dora. Maybe it was because we were putting ourselves forward as a source of trade goods.

"Thanks," I said. I patted the heavy gas can, which I was still lugging around and had put down on the floor next to the chair. "We also have some gasoline we'd like to trade you for supplies."

"Fantastic! As soon as we're done here, I'll have you talk to my husband, Neal. He's somewhere in the back storeroom right now but should be back shortly. You want a long-term permit to visit town, correct?"

"Yes. For Destiny and me and another friend," I said.

"Where's your friend?"

"We left him back at our camp. He's keeping watch."

"That's a good idea. There are dozens of groups living in the national forest, but no law enforcement. I've heard of some ugly things happening. You kids need to be careful!"

"Ugly things, like what?" Destiny said.

Dora waved a hand. "Oh, it's horrible. Burglaries, robberies, and at least one instance of murder. And these are the things we've only heard of. The town police don't have jurisdiction all the way out there. Back before the Kergans came, there should have been forest rangers keeping things in order, but they've all left. And the county doesn't care. You're on your own, I'm sorry to say."

"We'll be careful," I said. I was confident we'd be able to take care of ourselves. If we couldn't, then we didn't deserve to be guerrillas. However, it did remind me we had weapons that needed ammunition. "I'd be interested in trading some of this gas for ammo."

"Yes, talk to Neal. Now, about this permit. You want it for you two plus your friend?"

I thought about the Brooks. But I didn't want people in town knowing they were living with us, and the Brooks likely had no reason to come here. Maybe we could get them on the permit later, but I wanted to keep it simple for now. "Yes, just us three."

"I need an official justification for your visits. What should we put down?"

"I don't suppose saying we have family in town is enough?" Destiny said.

Dora shook her head. "No, sorry. There has to be a purpose that benefits the town."

I held up my hand. "Like I said, we have gasoline to trade. And there will be more. Also, food and perhaps some other consumables. If we could, we'd like to visit a couple times a week to trade."

"I see." She pushed back in her chair and folded her arms. "Fuel is almost impossible to get these days. Where are you getting these supplies?"

Questions. Of course, they were going to want to know. I hesitated with my answer. Destiny saved me. "I'm sorry, that's proprietary information," she said straight-faced.

Dora snorted. "Well!" she cried out. "That's a new one." She tapped on the keyboard of a laptop computer sitting on the desk and began clicking at something. "But I understand. You can't be too careful these days. Everybody has secrets. Don't worry, I don't need to know. It was just curiosity. As you can imagine, keeping the store well stocked isn't easy, so I hope you understand why I'd want to know. But if you have fuel to trade, we'll take it, and no questions asked. I just hope you obtained it legally."

She looked down at her laptop screen. "Let me fill out these permits for you and print them." She started typing.

I tapped Destiny with my elbow and looked at her from the corner of my eye. She smirked and shrugged. *Proprietary information.* That was a good one.

Judith tapped a button on her mouse, and a printer in the back corner began to make *whirr* sounds. She looked at my sister. "Judith told me about you, Destiny. That you've been homeless for some years and living on the streets. It came as a shock to her." She held a hand to her forehead. "You're so young! I'm so sorry!" Her eyes drilled into mine. "And you, Kory? Is your situation the same?"

How should I answer? *No, ma'am, mine's even worse because I have no family. At least Destiny has people she could have fallen back on if she'd become truly desperate.* But I didn't want this lady to know about my personal life. "Yes, ma'am, something like that. Destiny is my sister."

Dora's eyebrow popped up. "Sister?" She pivoted on her chair and picked up several pieces of paper from the printer. "I don't understand."

"Ever since we've met, we've been looking out for each other," I said.

She set the papers on the desk and signed them one by one. "How did you end up on the street?"

Sheesh, this lady is nosy! People weren't supposed to ask homeless people these kinds of questions. But we needed her on our side if we were going to be on good terms with the town. I evaded by asking a question. "How do most people end up on the streets?"

She shook her head. "But you two are not *most people*. You're kids. I don't understand."

My face burned, and I looked at my feet. It's not like I had any choice in the matter, at least not one that let me live free. The government orphanages and group homes were little better than prisons, and in some ways, they were worse. At least out on the street me and Destiny were in control of our lives. Yes, bad things sometimes happened, but at least we could do something about them.

A lady like this could never understand that. She'd probably come from a stable home, never been hungry in her life. Gone to college, all of it paid for by her parents. Married into money. Had so much leisure time she became bored and decided to get into small-town politics and became mayor.

She watched us, waiting for a reply, but we didn't give her one. I just couldn't bring myself to open my mouth and attempt to explain. I had raised myself, and I was proud of it. I had protected Destiny and made sure she had the necessities of life; however poor those might have been, she had them. My relationship with her was something I wouldn't trade for anything, not even for a luxury estate on an island in paradise.

Dora's lips pressed together, and her eyes became shiny. She sucked in a deep breath, sighed, and nodded. "So many things in this world are broken now. I suppose kids like you, who need help, can't avoid falling through the cracks."

"We're going to be fine, ma'am," I said. Destiny nodded. "But thanks, all the same."

The mayor huffed. "Call me Dora, please." She handed the permits to Destiny. "Keep these on you whenever you're in town. They're good for one year. If you lose them, just let me know, and I'll print them out again."

I stood, and Destiny followed me.

"Why don't you two come over to my home for dinner tomorrow," Dora said. "And bring your friend...uhm... Clemen."

"We call him Gunny," I said. "Thanks, but that won't be necessary. We've got plenty of food."

"But you have no friends and are new to the area. Maybe you don't have any parents to watch out for you, but I feel like I should get to know you." She chuckled. "You never know when you'll need something. I can't help you if I don't know you. And I want to. Please, come to dinner with Neal and me. We'd love to have your company. You seem like interesting people."

I opened my mouth to rebuff the offer, but Destiny jumped in and said, "Sure, Dora, we'd be pleased to join you. Thanks so much! What time?"

I snapped my mouth shut and glared at Destiny.

Dora clapped her hands. "Excellent! Oh, let's say 6:30 pm tomorrow... But that'll be after dark, won't it? And you'd have to drive into that forest at night."

"That'll be fine," Destiny said. "We've got our van. We'll see you at 6:30."

Dora smiled and held out her hand. "I'm so glad," she said. We shook her hand and walked back into the store. She noticed the gas can I was still lugging around. "That's right. Let me go find Neal. Be right back." She turned and walked through a nearby set of double doors, her short gray hair twirling on her head.

"Dest, I don't want to go to dinner with them," I said softly.

She propped a hand on her hip and scowled. "Too bad. She's being hospitable. These small-town people are like that. Get used to it. We couldn't turn her down." She tilted her head and torso forward until her long curly black hair hung almost to the floor. "And, besides, think of all the intel we can learn from her." Then she snapped her body up, caught her hair in her hands, and tied it back with a band.

"Intel? That sounds like something Gunny would say." I eyed her suspiciously.

"Well, maybe he and I had a little chat. And maybe he gave me some tips. And maybe I listened. Hmmmm?" she said in that snooty way she did when she was annoyed with me.

Destiny and Gunny had had a private conversation? Just the two of them? It surprised me. I'd gotten the sense that they didn't like each other. When they weren't ignoring one another, they were constantly arguing. But maybe they'd discovered they had some common interests.

Dora walked out the door, followed by a portly elderly man. He was short, perhaps just five-three or -four, and his tanned, leathery skin was covered in deep laugh lines.

"Hi, there, I'm Neal Best," the man said. His eyes darted between Destiny and me. "I hear you've got some gasoline you want to trade?"

"Yes, sir," I said. I patted the can. "Five gallons of 85 octane. I have more than that but not enough cans to carry it in."

"That's fine," Neal said with a smile. He looked at his wife to the side. "I've been instructed not to ask where it came from, but we'd happily accept it in return for in-store credit. Would that work for you?"

"I believe so. I'm particularly interested in fresh fruits and vegetables and ammunition."

Neal crossed his arms and pursed his lips. "We might be able to do that. What ammo do you need?"

"9mm parabellum."

"How many rounds?"

"Let us pick out the fruits and veggies we want, then exchange the balance of our credit for as many rounds as we can pay for."

"Fine. Ammo is precious these days, but so is gas. I'll make it work, but I'm warning you that it will only be like a hundred rounds. Maybe even less."

"How much is our gas worth?"

Neal guffawed. "Are you kidding? It's priceless. I can't even put a price on it. When it comes to fuel in this town, it's barter only. Nobody has enough of the worthless cash to buy even a pint of gasoline. If you'd come to me wanting to buy gas, I'd say no. The town has embargoed it, reserved only for official business. But I will definitely buy it from you and even give you some of my limited stores of ammo in exchange."

This was excellent news. My pistol was a cheap Taurus 9mm. It was not nearly as nice as Destiny's Colt 38 super, for which she had plenty of ammo. I didn't, and I wanted Gunny to teach me how to use it properly. For that, I needed ammo, of which I currently only had half a magazine. "Okay, that works for us. We'll go pick out our produce."

Neal took our gas can to empty it into the store's tanks. Destiny and I went to the produce section. There were no plastic bags, so we filled up my backpack. We grabbed 20 pounds of potatoes, carrots, apples, cabbage, and pears. There were no bananas. Destiny picked out several pounds of beets, which she loved, but I hated. I also picked up a 25-pound bag of oats, a 25-pound bag of rice, and a 10-pound bag of sugar.

All of this food was in plentiful supply. We barely made a dent in the shelves. Thank goodness for living next to California's breadbasket Central Valley. But how were they shipping this food in if fuel was so precious? Maybe that's the sort of thing they were reserving the fuel for.

We placed our purchases on the checkout counter, and Neal began to scan them.

"You all in need of diesel or gas more?" I asked.

"Diesel," Neal said. "There've been weeks when we've missed food shipments because we had no diesel left. And it can also be used as a heating fuel, in a pinch."

"Okay. I can't promise anything, but next time we come to trade, I'll try and bring some diesel instead of gas."

"Very good. Very good indeed," he said. "I'm curious to know where you're getting it from."

"Have you had problems with bandits coming into town?"

"A few months ago, yes. Right after the federal government collapsed, there was real chaos around here. But we got it under control. That's why we've got the town blockaded like we do. I know it doesn't seem very neighborly, but ever since we did it, we've had much fewer problems with gangs and other undesirables."

His face suddenly turned redder than Destiny's beets when he realized he'd said something insensitive. He turned his back on us, unlocked the case behind him, picked out a box, and then, after thinking for a moment, added a second.

"That's 100 rounds of 9mm parabellum. I was gonna offer you fifty, but I'm tossing in an extra fifty just because your business is so welcome."

I smiled genuinely and said, "Well, thanks, Neal. We're glad to be here, too." Destiny and I started packing our bags with our purchases. We each took one of the 25-pound bags of grain under our arms.

"You folks, stay safe now, you hear?" Neal said.

"Thank you, sir."

"We'll see you tomorrow for dinner."

We waved goodbye and walked out of the convenience store. I held a bag of oats under one arm, the empty gas can in the other hand, and my backpack filled with purchases strapped to my back.

The crowd outside had not dispersed. If anything, it had grown. The people looked destitute. But what were they waiting for? Why did they congregate here, of all places? I hadn't remembered to ask Dora or Neal.

The hungry eyes studied us intently like a starving pack of wolves.

A woman approached me in ragged clothes, her greasy blond locks hanging past a gaunt, hollow face. "Please, son, won't you give me some food? For my kids. They're hungry."

Having panhandled on countless occasions as a child, it surprised me to be petitioned by a beggar. It wasn't that I didn't want to share. But I didn't know how to respond. Me, give up our hard-earned supplies? Wasn't I supposed to be the one begging?

Before I could say anything, the store door opened, and

Neal came out. "Hey! Knock that off, Mrs. Monroe." He waved his hand at her. "You know the rules. Leave my customers alone, or I'll kick you off my property."

The defeated woman bowed her head and dragged herself away.

There was a tale here, and I wanted to know about it. How could the store have so much food, yet people just outside complained of hunger?

Maybe having dinner with the Bests wouldn't be so bad after all. We might learn some things.

22

Next, we went by Destiny's aunt's house, but nobody was home. Disappointed, my sister wrote a note saying we had visited and missed them. She hung it from the front door.

We returned to the forest, driving slowly through Wolf Jaw and leaving by the north gate. Contrails crisscrossed the blue sky from the frequent Kergan atmospheric traffic. What were they after? Why had they invaded our planet? The only thing I'd heard regarding Kergan intentions were rumors, none of which I trusted one bit.

We drove up the narrow mountain road, and as we came around a sharp bend, I noticed the glimpse of something matte black drifting behind the tops of the trees to the side of the forest. Though I caught the edge of it, it looked like a blackhole, one of the Kergan spy bots.

I slammed the brakes and brought us to a stop. "Did you see that?"

Destiny's right hand was inside her jacket, gripping her pistol. "No. What?"

With the engine still running, I opened the van door,

jumped out, and ran to the road's edge. But whatever I'd seen was gone.

I moved to the other side of the road and up the shoulder incline to find a higher perch from which to see over the trees. The forest stretched down into a valley. I saw thousands of trees. A few clearings with snow visible. But nothing else.

Maybe it was nothing. But that was the fourth or fifth time I'd seen that flash of black in the distance since we'd left San Jose. I couldn't shake the feeling that somebody was watching us and had been doing it for days.

I got back in the van and shook my head. "It's nothing. Guess I'm just jumpy."

"You're just hungry," Destiny said, patting me on the shoulder and yawning. "I remember something about how our senses become more sensitive when our stomachs are empty. That's why you're jumping at shadows."

"It wasn't a shadow!"

"You're just trying to catch a ghost with a butterfly net. Hauling air with a bucket. Jumping upstairs—"

"Okay, okay! I get it. But I know I saw something."

Back at the base, I expected a celebration when we returned, but our reception was the opposite. The Brooks looked scared, and Busto acted anxious.

"What happened?" I said.

Busto rubbed his face. "We had visitors. And they caused a scene."

Destiny and I moved closer to the former marine to talk softer.

"Who was it?" I said.

"All I got was his last name. A Mister Patton. He and three other men tried to come into the glen. I caught them at the gap by the outcrop and made them stop. All of them were armed."

"So, what happened next?"

"They put on a show of friendliness, but at the end, the leader, this Mister Patton, made *completely* unsubtle hints that we'd have to provide him some kind of payment or something unfortunate would happen to our campsite."

"You're kidding, right?" Destiny said. "Racketeers here, in the national forest?"

"Yup, it appears that way. They're trying to run a protection racket. Baxter told me he's had several run-ins with those people before, but the Brooks owned so little that it was easy to turn them away." He scratched his ear and shrugged. "But somehow, they got wind of the fact that new people were here in this glen, and they're trying again."

I rested a hand on his shoulder. "Well, I'm glad we didn't take you into town, Gunny. Who knows what would have happened if you hadn't been here."

"Sure, but they'll be back, or they'll try something. The guys looked like complete slimeballs." His face turned red. "You should have seen how they were leering at Phoebe, Lynda, and even Ricki."

I nodded. "Okay, we'll just have to ensure everybody is alert and armed. I'll talk to Zeta about ways we can improve our security."

The unwelcome visitors were disturbing, but we had other reasons to be happy. While we were gone, Baxter had shot a partridge. It was small, but Lynda took our new supplies and soon had a partridge stew simmering on the fire. Destiny used zetamilk, sugar, and rice to cook a batch of rice pudding.

"No beer?" Busto said.

"Do I look like the kind of person the townies are gonna sell alcohol to?" I said.

"I bet Zeta could mix up a fine batch of ethanol."

"I bet Zeta could mix up many excellent narcotics if we asked. Let's not go there. We have other supply needs." I'd have to remember to talk to Zeta about limiting what people were allowed to have fabricated. However, thinking about it made me feel suddenly like a dictator. But I was responsible for these people now, and I wasn't goin' to allow drunkenness and intoxication in our little community. I'd seen too much of that on the streets, watching it destroy people's lives.

I told Busto about the reaction we'd received in town and handed him his permit. I didn't think Busto was much for socializing, but maybe he'd find it helpful to go to town occasionally. He didn't seem annoyed when I told him about our dinner engagement for the next evening.

"Hey, Gunny, I acquired ammunition for my pistol. Can you teach me how to use it?"

"You bet!" my friend said. "Come over here with me."

I spent the next few hours with Busto, learning how to use a pistol to defend myself. It wasn't long before Destiny joined us, even though she was far more skilled than I.

Thus began our first session of what became a regular tactical combat training regimen with Gunny as our instructor. The man was extremely knowledgeable. I didn't have anybody to judge him against, but he exuded confidence and seemed always to have an answer to the questions Destiny and I posed to him. I could tell we weren't the first people he had trained.

I didn't know if the tactical training would ever be valuable. After all, we were creating a starship crew, not a ground combat unit. But we had a base to defend. If somebody attacked our home, nobody else would push back except for us. I wanted to be prepared.

The tireless Zeta worked for hours on end without ever stopping. But she popped up for a few minutes in the evening while we sat around the fire eating more stew and pudding. I decided now was the time to talk about beefing up our security.

"Zeta," I said, "Can you manufacture small arms for us? For protecting ourselves?"

"Aye, lad," she said. "Base defenses are within Zeta's duties."

"Good to hear. So, given that you're from an advanced alien race, I have to imagine you can make us something better than our Earth rifles and pistols."

"Indeed, though, like the starship, available small arms technology shall depend on how well you are judged in the conduct of your missions."

"Can you be more specific? What can you make for us today that's better than this?" I showed her my crappy 9mm pistol.

She twirled on her vertical axis. "In this hour, Zeta's primary constraint is not technological but the availability of a nanoforge. Hers is fully occupied with the construction of the base. Our manufacturing capacity will expand significantly once Zeta completes the base's nanoforge. But a firearm, even a small one, is complex and would demand much more investment of time than synthesizing chemicals and excavating soil."

I thought about the glimpses of blackholes I'd been seeing and of Dora's warnings about hostiles in these mountains. Then, there was the imminent threat posed by Mister Patton and his thugs. "What kind of time frame are we talking about? Where are we at right now?"

"It is a fine time to discuss this. For this purpose, Zeta halted work and came to you."

I smiled. "And here I thought you came for our company."

"Forgive Zeta, friend Kory, for her lack of manners. Human customs are known only a little by the igna. If it be your wish, Zeta shall spend more time conversing with you and your people."

"No, it's okay, Zeta. Only if you want to. I don't want us to get in your way if you have more urgent things to take care of."

"As Zeta was saying, she came up for a purpose. The stairwell is complete, and the first two chambers are ready for your inspection."

I set down my empty plate. "Great!" We would finally get to see our new home.

"While Kory inspects it, Zeta shall tell you what tasks remain."

I signaled to Busto and Destiny to follow Zeta and me. We walked to the center of the glen where the hole in the ground lay.

It was no longer just a pit. I could see steps leading down into the darkness.

"It yet lacks power," Zeta said as she flew at my shoulder. "Thus, the absence of internal lighting. You should bring a flashlight."

"I'll get the lantern," Destiny said. She ran to the tent and, a minute later, returned with our battery-operated camping lantern. She gave it to me, and I turned it on.

"So, I just walk down these steps like a normal person?" I asked.

"Aye, yet no safety railing has been added. Take care not to fall," Zeta said.

I studied the naked hole in the ground with the stairs easily visible and unprotected. They were light gray, shiny like they were wet, and smelled of hot rock. "These steps seem kind of exposed."

"Zeta shall construct a small building around the stairwell to serve as an entrance. But as yet, no."

"Okay, it's on the todo list. I get it." Holding the lantern at eye level, I stepped onto the first step. It felt like stone or concrete. Solid. Cold.

I took another step, then another, slowly descending into the darkness.

When my head descended below ground level, I saw I was entering a vestibule of some kind. Two openings in the walls led out of it.

"Those holes in the wall shall, in time, have doors installed in them," Zeta said.

I nodded. The walls looked slick and smooth, like glass. As I stepped down the stairs, I rubbed my hand on the adjacent wall. It felt the same as it looked. Slippery, cool, and flawlessly smooth. All the walls were made of the same material, even the internal ones. "What's it made of?"

"As Zeta has said, it is made of crystallized silica or quartz. The entire base shall be constructed of it."

Busto and Destiny came behind me. "It's warm in here," Destiny said.

"That is due to residual heat released by the nanobots in their work," Zeta said. "Consort, the next door leads to the armory."

I walked through the doorless opening at the bottom of the stairs and stood in a long rectangular room. There was no furniture yet, but holes in the floor and walls indicated mounting points for benches, tables, and cabinetry. The walls were made of the same gray quartz. Our footsteps echoed in the empty chamber.

At the far end of the room, we entered a hallway. One

end was a mass of what looked like molten rock covered with slime. It must have been Zeta's current working position. The other end had another doorway. I passed through it.

"This shall be the base control center," Zeta said.

"Where is that unfinished hallway leading to?" Destiny asked.

"It is the base's central corridor. It shall branch off into living quarters, the hangar, workshop, power plant, nanoforge, life support, and several other small facilities."

"What's next?" I said.

"Zeta's present priority is constructing the power plant, followed by the nanoforge. Upon their completion, Zeta can greatly accelerate the construction of the base and your ship. In this hour, our pace is limited by the lack of sufficient power and a larger nanoforge."

"What kind of power plant are we getting?"

"A class 1 proton-proton fusion plant. It is small but sufficient to power this base and charge the ship within a few hours."

"Charge the ship?" I looked at Destiny and laughed. "Is it battery-powered?"

"Indeed," Zeta said. "Recall that Zeta said it possessed a 10 TJ chromatic battery."

"What?" Somehow, an image of a toy spaceship popped into my brain with me as a little kid, making it fly in my hand. "We don't get a fusion plant on the ship?"

"That would be absurd," the alien said. "Only the largest starships, designed for independent operation far beyond existing infrastructure, have installed fusion plants. And even so, ships with them use helium-3 plants, not proton-proton. The latter's low power density demands too much volume and weight. Nay, just as with most ships in existence, yours shall use a chromatic battery as its power source."

"Chromatic battery?"

"Indeed. It is a compact energy storage device that exploits small variations in the strong nuclear binding force within radon gas atoms trapped in a temporal stasis field. When these are subjected to—"

"Whoa there, Nelly!" I held my hands up. "Time out. I didn't follow any of that. Some other time. These chromatic batteries are better than a Duracell. I get it. That's good enough for me."

I stood with my hands propped on my hips. "When will the fusion plant be completed?"

"In approximately six days time."

"Until then, we're stuck camping in the tent."

"Aye, Zeta is sorry, Consort."

"It's quite all right. Aren't knights supposed to be good at roughing it?"

"Zeta admires your stoicism, lad!"

"Until you get the new nanoforge up, we're stuck with our existing firearms. Understood."

"It's alright, Kory," Busto said. "We've got enough firepower to scare about anybody away who comes to bother us."

I sure hoped he was correct. "Maybe we should include Phoebe in the firearms training so she can help secure the base."

23

The next day, Destiny and I mainly spent it training with Busto. Phoebe Brooks, who Destiny had befriended, also joined us. She borrowed her mother's Mossberg pistol, which used the same ammo as my Taurus, so that I could share some of mine.

Busto made us review his instructions from the previous day. We practiced safely loading and unloading our weapons, maintenance procedures, and clearing malfunctions. Then Busto set up a firing range, and we each proceeded to fire two ammunition magazines, first from a standing position and then from lying prone.

My Taurus gave me plenty of practice in clearing malfunctions because it often failed to eject expended rounds or would try to feed two rounds simultaneously. It wasn't a good firearm and had already been well used when I procured it on the street a year ago.

Busto sat with me and taught me how to disassemble the pistol and inspect its parts. We found much crud built up on some of the components, causing cartridges to stick. I cleaned them with a rag and solvent and reassembled my gun. After that, it fired much more reliably.

For targets, we used scraps of paper. Busto drew target circles on them with a marker and hung them on trees a safe distance from the camp with the mountain behind them to catch any wayward rounds.

He placed us only 7 yards away from our targets, which I thought was awfully close.

"Most self-defense scenarios where you'll need your pistol will happen at that distance or less," Busto said.

"I don't intend to let a bad guy ever get that close to me," I said.

"That's what a rifle is for," he said. "I'll start training you guys in using one of those in a few days, but you'll find a pistol is most needed when it comes to covering your immediate surroundings. My purpose is to teach the three of you enough so you can quickly draw your sidearm and fire accurately at an opponent in less than three seconds."

And he was true to his word. By the afternoon, we'd moved on from safety and accuracy drills to one that practiced drawing and firing from a holster.

Destiny had a shoulder holster, and Phoebe a hip holster, but I had none. Busto showed me how to use the inside of the belt line of my pants, just forward of the hip bone, as an improvised—if uncomfortable—holster.

While we were doing our tactical training, Baxter and Ricki went hunting, and Lynda took care of the campsite and cooking. It wasn't my idea to delegate tasks like this. It's just what the people decided to do on their own initiative.

Baxter had expressed his gratitude for the food we'd shared, but I could tell he preferred to be self-sufficient. I didn't begrudge him his habits. If he caught any more game, it would just be added to our growing menu.

But when Ricki wasn't busy helping his father, he followed us around as we trained. It seemed like half the time I stopped and looked around for a moment, there Ricki would be studying us. He especially hung near me.

I didn't know what to make of him. It wasn't annoying. He didn't get in the way or ask questions. But I got the sense he wanted to be included. Think about it. At fourteen, he was only three years younger than Destiny and five years younger than his sister. If he had been a couple years older, I'm sure that Busto would have included him in our training, and Ricki probably had realized that.

Zeta continued with the excavation, which seemed to have accelerated. The piles of spoil lying on the ground outside the hole doubled in size. By the afternoon, it looked like a miniature of the rock outcrop north of the glen. I asked Zeta about the growth in one of the rare moments when she appeared above ground, and she said she was opening up the power plant chamber.

We finished up our training at about 5 pm. Lynda heated buckets of water from the brook over the fire, and we took turns bathing behind an area we'd screened off for that purpose. It was the first proper bath I'd had in several weeks.

While doing this, I wondered whether I should tell Busto about the sightings I'd had over the last week of those black objects in the sky. The problem was that they had proved so elusive that I was not confident in my own judgment. What was I going to say to him? *Gunny, I think somebody's spying on us, but I can't describe them.* He would think I was seeing things. And maybe I was.

Dressed in our cleanest clothes, we left for town to make our dinner appointment. But first, we took 10 gallons of diesel that Zeta had produced overnight and stopped by One Stop to trade it for more ammunition. Neither Neal nor

Dora was there, but another employee was on shift and helped us. Walking out of the store with 250 rounds each of 9mm and 0.38 super, we headed to the Bests' home.

24

The Bests lived in a two-story Craftsman-style home painted blue with white trim. The yard was small—like all the homes I'd seen in Wolf Jaw. A flower garden in front bordered the entrance, though most of it was covered by recent snowfall.

Busto, Destiny, and I exited the van and walked to the front door. A wreath hung on it with sidelights and a mud mat with the message "*hi friend*" woven into it.

I pressed the doorbell, and chimes sounded. A few seconds later, Neal opened the door and greeted us.

I introduced Busto to Neal. "We call him Gunny," I said as the two shook hands.

"Oh? Were you in the Marine Corps?" Neal said.

"Yes, sir," Busto said. "I served for twelve years, and I've been out for three."

"Semper Fi, my friend."

Busto's face broke out in a wide smile. "You served?"

Neal nodded. "I put in twenty years and retired in 2002 as a Master Sergeant."

The two veterans soon took up a conversation about their time in the service as Neal invited us into the foyer and led us through a spacious family room. Beyond that was their dining room. Through a door, we saw Dora cooking in the kitchen.

"Hi, guys!" she yelled and put down a spoon. Wearing a green apron over tan slacks and a blue shirt, she came over to greet us. "Dinner's not quite ready." She looked at Neal and said, "Come and help me finish, honey."

"Okay," he said. He gestured to a pair of sofas in the family room. "You folks make yourselves welcome."

Destiny and Busto sat on one of the sofas, but I remained standing to study the many framed photographs on a sideboard. There was a wedding photo of Dora and Neal from what looked like the mid-2000's. They appeared younger—perhaps by only twenty years, in their early forties. Other photographs were from family vacations. None included children, so that answered one of my questions. They seemed to have married when they were older, and Neal was already out of the service.

There were photos of other people I didn't recognize and must have been parents or other relatives. I saw one of a much younger and thinner Neal dressed in desert camouflage standing in the tan sand of the Middle East and holding a long M16.

Neal walked into the room. "Gunny, can I get you a beer? And sodas for Kory and Destiny?"

Busto glanced at me with laughter in his eyes. "Hell, yes."

"I'll take a coke if you have any," I said.

"Me too," Destiny said.

"You betcha," Neal said and left. A minute later, he returned with three cans. "Here you go."

The soda felt fantastic going down. It had been several weeks since I'd drank anything besides water and zetamilk. The sweet, tangy, fizzy, and very cold drink was a glorious treat.

Not long after that, Dora called us to the dinner table. We found it covered with a meal fit for a feast. Roasted yams, brussels wrapped in bacon, pork roast with mustard, and onion soup. I wondered where they'd gotten the bacon and roast from, seeing as how One Stop had no pork in stock. I felt a little wrong about us eating like this when so many people in the town were starving. But this was the Bests' home and their food, so I didn't ask any uncomfortable questions.

Sitting at that table, I felt like the odd man out. The honest truth was that I didn't know the proper etiquette for the occasion. I'd never been invited into somebody's home for a dinner invitation. At least not one which was for the purpose of socializing. On the many previous occasions I had eaten with a family, it was their way of helping a young homeless boy.

For the first fifteen minutes, Neal and Busto dominated the conversation with stories about their respective times in the Marine Corps. I heard a lot of jargon I didn't understand, though I learned that Neal had served in Desert Storm and had been some kind of specialist in logistics.

"And what kind of news have you heard out there in the Bay Area?" Dora asked us after becoming subtly annoyed with the two former Marines talking shop.

"Well, there're rumors that the Chinese nuked some of their own cities," Busto said.

Dora's eyes went wide. "You're kidding, right?"

He shook his head. "The story is that some rogue parts of the Chinese military refused to surrender to the Kergans, managed to hide some of their nuclear weapon stockpiles, and then a month ago nuked Beijing, Shanghai, and some other cities." Busto shrugged. "I guess the Chinese have a scorched earth policy to deal with the enemy. But these are just rumors. Nobody knows if they're true."

"But still, it means that some people are still standing up to the Kergans," Destiny said.

"They're not the only ones," Neal said. "We've heard rumors that El Paso is under mandatory evacuation because of insurgent activity."

"Why?" I asked.

Neal finished chewing a bite and said, "The Kergans can't find the insurgents, so they're forcing all the civilians out of the city. They're probably thinking that once all the civilians are gone, anybody left must be guerrillas, and they can just level the city."

Busto pointed at him with his fork. "I heard something like that happened also up in Boise."

"Oh, yeah?"

Busto nodded. "The Kergans moved everybody out of the city and then demolished it."

"God, help us." Neal shook his head.

"There's a price to be paid for resisting invaders." Busto took a sip from his glass. "We've seen that over and over again throughout human history. Look at what the Romans did in the Jugurthine War."

"Never heard of it."

"It was a war between Rome and Numidia around 100 BC. Rome invaded following a coup that overthrew the allied Numidian king. Afterward, they had huge problems with insurgents. But they eventually won the war because they undertook systematic looting, pillaging, and burning of the Numidian countryside. I think the Kergans follow a similar philosophy."

Dora shook her head. "That's terrifying. I can't believe they'd ever do something like that to us."

"They're just rumors, dear," Neal said. "We don't know if they're true."

"There's probably a grain of truth," Busto said. "I can't believe that everyone in the old USA just went and accepted the surrender and moved on with their lives. There *must* be plenty of angry people who still want to fight. Why do you think the Kergans have so restricted our communications with the rest of the world? They're terrified, that's why. They worry that the willing fighters among us will get into contact with each other and coordinate. There must be active insurgents in the country, otherwise the Kergans would have relaxed the restrictions."

"This is depressing," Dora said, "and I don't want to talk about it at the dinner table." She suddenly looked at me. "And what about you, Kory? Where did you grow up?"

I knew this question would arise, and I had prepared an answer that I hoped would deflect further inquiries. "I don't have much of a background, Dora. I was raised in an orphanage, and there isn't much to say about it." I looked away and dug into my yams.

My dismissive response didn't deter her. "What happened to your parents?"

"We were in a car accident when I was three years old. They both died, and I survived."

Her face crumpled. "And you had nobody else?"

I shook my head, not wanting to answer these questions. I didn't like talking about my past. My memories of my parents were extremely vague. Just impressions of them. One of my father tossing me in the air while I laughed with joy. Another of snuggling with my mother in bed while she read me a book. I couldn't remember their faces at all, only how it felt to be with them. To me, my parents were more of a feeling than a true memory. One of being loved. "No siblings. Both my parents were only childs, so no aunts or uncles. My grandparents were either deceased or too elderly to take me in, so the state got custody of me, and I was placed in an orphanage."

"I am *so* sorry," Dora said with genuine sympathy behind her words. "I just can't fathom something like that happening to a child. I'm amazed you were never adopted. There are so many women in this world left childless through situations out of their control. It's such a shame that somebody like you has to grow up without parents."

I tilted my head. "Yes, ma'am." I couldn't think of any better response and just wanted the topic to go away.

Destiny sat stiffly across from me. Even with her, I'd never talked about my parents and very little about my time in the orphanage.

But the busybody wasn't about to let the topic rest. "What orphanages were you in?"

"I don't know precisely. I ran away from the last when I was thirteen." Then, I added what I hoped was a hint that I didn't want to discuss it. "I don't like to think about it much."

Destiny came to my rescue. "Then he met me," she said.

Of course, that only opened up the conversation even more, but at least now, two of us could respond to the questions.

We had to respond to a flood of them. How did we eat? Panhandling, running errands for other street people, petty crimes, digging recyclables from garbage, and soup kitchens.

Where did we sleep? In vacant buildings, under

overpasses or bridges, sometimes on the couches of acquaintances, occasionally on park benches, but never in a homeless shelter because we were underage and would have been turned over to the state.

Did criminals ever victimize us? All the time. Maybe once a week. We shared no details because neither of us wanted to think about those experiences.

Did law enforcement ever catch us? A few times, but we always managed to escape. They would turn us over to a group home to await a hearing with a judge, but the homes always had poor security.

This Q & A session went on for almost an hour. By then, we'd all finished our meal and moved on to apple pie. It was all delicious, at least under other circumstances it would have been, but the food sat heavily in my stomach. Why was this woman so inquisitive? What did she actually want from us?

I decided to change the subject. "When we last saw you at the store," I said, "you mentioned there were dangerous people up in the mountains. Could you elaborate? As you can imagine, living out in the woods, we're concerned about securing our home." I decided not to say anything specific yet about our encounter with Mister Patton.

"Most of them aren't dangerous," Neal said. "I expect they're like you. They want to be left alone, want to get away from Kergan-controlled areas and don't bother anybody. But there's a clan of survivalist militia types named the Pattons who have a compound about five miles into the mountains. We've already had problems with them in town."

Busto smiled and chuckled. "Yeah, we know about the Pattons. We had a recent encounter with a Mister Patton."

"What happened?" Dora asked.

Busto told the story of Mister Patton arriving with several other men and making subtle threats.

"I'm sorry to say that your story doesn't surprise me," Dora said as she sipped a glass of wine. "Which of the Pattons was it?"

"He didn't give me his full name. I just know him as Mister Patton."

"What did he look like?"

Busto leaned back and rubbed his chin. "Let me see... Wavy black hair that's going gray. Skinny. About forty or forty-five years old. His clothes were dirty and ragged."

"Might have been Odell Patton. He's one of the grandchildren."

"Grandchildren? He was middle-aged."

Neal waved a hand and grinned. "They're like five generations living up at that compound."

"How many are there?" I asked.

"I'm not entirely sure. The father died some years ago, but the mother is still alive. Golly, she must be in her eighties by now. Then there's the two sons, George and Paul, and their children, who have their own families—Odell is George's son, and over the years, he's always been the ringleader of their slimiest schemes." Neal sniffled and rubbed his nose with his napkin. "But there must be about twenty adults living in the compound and maybe a dozen or fifteen children of various ages. They're all cousins and aunts and uncles, but every single one of them is mean as sin and only cares about the survival of the family. The kids are home-schooled, supposedly, but I doubt any of them could read a newspaper."

"But they know how to shoot a rifle," Dora said.

Neal chuckled. "Even the children are taught to fight."

"Yes, they're well-armed," Dora said. "That's what

makes the town so nervous. There are enough of them that they could overwhelm the Wolf Jaw police department if they ever became ornery enough."

Neal scratched his ear. "They're drug traffickers too. They've been fined on several occasions for keeping illegal marijuana crops. George Patton is rumored to have ties to one of the Mexican drug cartels."

The Pattons sounded like an organized crime family. And these were our neighbors! I was no longer surprised we'd had a run-in with them. I'd have to ask the Brooks more about them.

"What kinds of problems have they caused you here in town?" Busto asked.

"Not much, so far. But they've threatened all sorts of things. They blame the hyperinflation on the town officials and have said someday they'll just come to One Stop and take what they want. We tried to get a restraining order, but the state courts are completely broken now. And the Pattons live on county land outside the city jurisdiction."

"What about the county? The sheriff's department?"

Dora leaned forward, her silver bob bouncing above her shoulders. "Fresno county has stopped giving its aid to anyone outside Fresno city limits."

With that theme overshadowing the otherwise friendly conversation, our dinner party broke up soon after. Dora sent us away with leftover pie and hugs for each of us. I got the feeling she must be like that with everybody.

I tried not to think about the danger our guerrilla activities would put these people and the rest of the town in. This was a war, and civilians always got caught in the middle of fighting. I could do little about it except avoid fighting where the townies lived. We'd have to take our fighting somewhere else and hope the Kergans never came to Wolf Jaw looking for us.

25

It wasn't quite bedtime when we got back to the camp, so we sat by the Brooks' campfire and chatted. After a few minutes, Ricki approached me and said, "Hey, Kory, you want to play checkers?"

I felt too tired for anything but talking. "I'm not any good. You should probably ask somebody else."

"It's okay. Maybe I can teach you some tricks." His voice was so soft I could barely hear him over the crackle of the fire.

The hopeful gleam in his eyes was too much for me to resist, and I felt bad for how we'd been ignoring him the past few days. "Okay, maybe one game."

Ricki set up a small table near the fire and placed a checkerboard on it and the pieces. He let me be white, which was good because I liked to react to the other player's moves.

He moved one of his pieces diagonally, and I responded with one of mine. He moved another, and I another. Then he captured one of mine, I captured one of his, and then he captured two.

Ricki won the first game with five of his pieces still on the board. I didn't feel bad about it because I hadn't played checkers in years, not since the orphanage. And Ricki was pretty good.

After finishing, he told me what I'd done wrong that had made me lose to him. It was helpful, and I used it in our next game. I still lost, but Ricki only had two pieces left this time.

Ricki had a contagious laugh and a dry sense of humor. "Don't be so jumpy," he said to me with a straight face at one point after I made a dumb move.

It took me a second to catch the checker pun. When I did, we had a good laugh, even though it was pretty juvenile as jokes went.

"You want to go shooting with us sometime?" I asked him after our third game.

His eyes lit up. "Could I?"

"Sure, why not? If your parents are okay with it."

"Yeah," Baxter said, "that's fine, as long as Gunny's supervising."

Ricki nodded with satisfaction.

"We're short on guns and ammunition right now," I said, "but we'll have more in a week or two. Then I'll invite you along."

"I'm actually a pretty good shot," Ricki said.

"He sure is," Baxter said. "He's probably killed more rabbits than I have. Ricki's got a real sharp eye and a steady hand."

I nodded and pursed my lips. "Well, there you go. I should have asked you before."

Ricki's face beamed.

About then, the graveyard watch was about to start. Lasting from midnight to 4:00 am, Destiny was scheduled to take it. But I felt restless after all the talk today about Kergans, insurgents, and the Pattons. I told her I'd swap with her, and she accepted with a smile.

All the talk had left me with a sense of pending doom. Something terrible would happen, and I didn't want to be asleep when it did. So, I sat out in the freezing dark for four hours, waiting, letting the anxiety eat away at me.

Snow began to fall sometime in the middle of my watch and quickly accumulated. Zeta continued working on the excavation. A dim red glow leaked out of the hole, and the gurgling stream of spoil slowly accumulated as the nanobots dug up more and more material.

A few times, I got up and walked around the perimeter of the glen, keeping to the edge of the woods. I could barely see anything because of the overcast sky, but what little light there was reflected off the winter scene that surrounded us.

At the end of my watch, it was Phoebe's turn. Feeling sleepy and foolish because of my worries, I crept over to the Brooks' shack, slipped through the entrance, and shook her awake. In the dark, the pretty girl suddenly grabbed my hand and hugged it to her chest. Feeling awkward and not knowing what she wanted, I patted her on the shoulder with my free hand and pulled away from her. She released me with a sigh and began to stir from bed. Seeing that she was rising, I left the tent.

Tall pine trees loomed over me from the white snow-draped shadows. Each of my steps pressed into the fresh snow with a soft squeaking sound. The silence was so profound I could hear the impact of individual snowflakes striking the ground as they fell from the heavens like an angelic armada.

I trudged through the snow as I crossed the glen, passing the hole out of which drifted clouds of steam and the smell of wet soil. Our tent was staked on the other side of the glen, on the leeward side of the outcrop.

Out of the corner of my right eye, a shadow abruptly moved in the forest.

I halted and dropped to my knees, watching in the direction where I saw movement. Had it been my imagination? The shadows were so thick and the night so dark I could barely pick out the largest trees along the eastern edge of the glen. If not for the weak light reflected off the snow, I would have been blind.

I crouched on the ground for several minutes, watching. Nothing moved except for Phoebe coming out of her shack and going to the latrine.

Then I felt pressure waves rippling the air, gently kneading my insides. So softly that if I hadn't been awake and standing still, I likely wouldn't have noticed them. It was the unmistakable signature of a Kergan ship drive!

I leaped to my feet and started to run for the tent, but I stopped after sensing movement again at the forest's edge. I froze, holding my breath, willing my eyes to suck in the faint light and reveal what was hidden.

The Kergan drive was still there, somewhere. Without knowing the size of the ship, I couldn't tell how far away it was. It could be a small ship somewhere nearby or a large ship in the far distance.

Footsteps sounded behind me, crunching in the snow. I pivoted and saw a shadow approaching me. I reached under my jacket and drew my pistol, thumbing off the safety.

"Kory?" came a whisper. It was Phoebe.

I sighed, thumbed the safety on my pistol, and holstered it under my belt. "You startled me."

Phoebe came closer, stopping with her chest almost touching mine. I could smell her sweet breath, and the heat of her face warmed me. "What are you doing?" she said.

I took a step back. "I thought I saw something move. Do you feel that throbbing sensation in the air?"

She stood quietly for a moment. "Yes."

"A Kergan ship."

"Where?"

"I don't know."

The pulsing became weaker, tapering off until it disappeared.

My need for sleep had evaporated, and my anxieties renewed. In this fresh snow, there would be tracks left by the spy. "I'll be right back. Stay here and cover me," I whispered to Phoebe.

"From what?"

"I don't know. That's the problem."

She nodded. I removed my headlamp from my coat pocket and stretched it over my cap but didn't turn it on yet. I drew my pistol, cocked it, and held it aimed forward as I marched through the snow toward the direction where I thought I'd seen the movement. It was about thirty yards to the edge of the forest.

I flipped on my headlamp's red light as I approached the first tree. Details of the trees jumped out at me. Thick trunks spaced irregularly with patches of fresh snow lying between them and covering the thin undergrowth. I paced up and down the edge of the trees, looking for tracks.

Nothing.

I went deeper into the trees. My headlamp played weird tricks with the shadows, which seemed to leap around as I moved. The snow on the ground was undisturbed everywhere I looked. I started to relax.

But what if it was a Kergan? They don't walk. They float. They don't leave tracks, at least not normal ones.

Blast it! I raised my eyes to look up higher at the low bushes and the snow clinging to the sides of the trees. I backtracked through where I had already explored.

Then I saw it.

Places where something had rubbed against some bushes and knocked the fresh snow onto the ground. There were no animal tracks, so it couldn't have been an animal. I only saw my own footprints.

I moved closer. The snow on the side of a nearby tree showed signs of having been brushed up against, pressing it into the bark.

But it could have been me who did that. Did I touch that bush? That tree? When I was searching for tracks, did I bump up against them? I couldn't remember. I mentally kicked myself for being so careless.

I moved even deeper into the woods, behind the bush and tree, showing the marks. I was looking for a trail left by something floating through the trees, but the forest opened up slightly, and the ground became rougher, covered with boulders and narrow cracks. In the dark, I was at risk of falling and breaking an ankle.

I came out of the woods, turned my lamp off, holstered my pistol, and skipped through the snow back to Phoebe.

"Anything?" she said when I got back to her.

"I don't know. Maybe," I said.

"What?!" she hissed.

"I'm tired. I might be seeing things." I rubbed my face with my gloved hands. "I've been up all night."

She seized my arm. "You're not goin' to leave me alone out here, are you?"

"I don't think it was anything. And you're the one who wanted to be on the watch schedule. Remember?"

"Yeah, but I didn't think I'd have to be out here in the

dark alone with something hiding in the woods!"

I took a long breath and looked straight up until I felt snowflakes falling on my face. Was I becoming paranoid? Were these sightings of hidden things spying on me simply delusions?

Suddenly, it felt like I couldn't keep my eyes open any longer. "I'm sorry, Phoebe, but I need to sleep. If it makes you feel better, I'll wake Gunny when I return to the tent."

She pressed her chest to my arm in a distracting way. "No, don't do that, please! I can do this." In the shadows, her head seemed to lean toward mine.

Her body was inviting. Before I tried something I'd regret, I pulled away from her for the second time that night and said goodnight. I returned to the tent, opened the flap, kicked off my boots, and crawled into my sleeping bag at the side. It had been in the middle, between Destiny and Busto, but somebody had swapped it with Destiny's. I noticed she was snuggled up close to Busto. That was *really* weird.

The next morning, I quietly told Busto about what I'd seen in the woods in the early morning. He returned with me to the spot where I'd searched.

We found nothing. Snow had continued falling for hours since I'd been there, and any evidence there was had been covered. The investigation of my sighting was inconclusive.

26

The following week passed uneventfully, and I and my people settled into a routine. Zeta continued with the base construction, requiring no help from any of us humans. The heaps of spoil grew ever more prominent.

Zeta opened a second, larger hole, which she said would be the hangar opening, about thirty feet away from the stairwell. It was broader and deeper than the stairwell, making it a danger, especially to those on watch in the dark. Baxter and Gunny constructed a makeshift fence around it using fallen logs and rope.

Destiny, Phoebe, and I trained with Busto every morning and also sometimes into the afternoon. Occasionally, Baxter would join in with us, though he seemed to do it more out of the need for company than for the learning. He taught us some things about tracking and stalking prey.

We switched from training with the pistols to the M4 assault rifle. Busto had stolen four of them from the bandits the night we escaped, along with about 300 rounds worth of loaded magazines. We quickly used all that up and had to make a special trip into town to trade diesel for more of the . 223 ammunition that the M4s used.

In the afternoons, if we weren't training, then we worked on cleaning up the glen and creating a clear fire zone between us and the edge of the woods so nobody could sneak up and ambush us. That was hard work, given that our only tools for the job were a pair of axes. We tried to purchase a chainsaw in town, but nobody was selling. So many people were heating their homes with wood that chainsaws had become treasured possessions.

One thing the town of Wolf Jaw did have in abundance was electrical power. On the southern edge of town sat the turbine halls that generated power for the Huntington Lake hydroelectric plant. It could output 800 Megawatts, enough to power all of Fresno County. This critical piece of infrastructure, which the Kergans had left intact, was the only reason Fresno hadn't completely cut ties with Wolf Jaw. It ensured that the town continued to receive adequate shipments of food and other supplies despite its remoteness and small population.

Unfortunately, no power lines carried electricity into our neck of the woods. But by the end of the week, the point became moot. Zeta completed the base's fusion plant, and overnight, we suddenly were swimming in electric potential. With that came lighting and heat. There was no working plumbing yet, and the crew quarters remained incomplete, but that didn't stop Busto, Destiny, and I from moving into the base and out of the crowded tent, taking up residence in the empty control room for the time being.

The Brooks remained in their shack at ground level. Their campsite was our cover for the base, though, at the moment, not a very good one considering the ripped-up state of the glen. But Zeta assured me that soon she would be constructing camouflaged covers for the stairwell and hangar.

A couple days after finishing the power plant, Zeta completed the base's nanoforge. I had imagined the nanoforge would be some kind of sophisticated machine composed of millions of parts. The actual device's appearance underwhelmed me. It consisted of nothing but an empty cube-shaped chamber about the size of a small bedroom.

After the nanoforge was completed, base construction accelerated tremendously. It had taken Zeta nearly ten days to excavate four chambers and construct the fusion plant and nanoforge. After that, she completed the rest of the base in just four days. New rooms, fully equipped with furnishings, seemed to appear every hour.

The massive mound of spoil collected from the excavated rock and soil also disappeared. Zeta converted it into ground-level structures that protected and camouflaged the stairwell and hangar. She also constructed a dwelling for the Brooks that was made to look like a part of the landscape but was, in fact, a complete three-bedroom house with plumbing, electricity, and heating.

Lynda cried when she saw it. "I thought I'd never have a home again," she said. Her sentiments echoed mine.

The nanoforge could construct almost anything we would ever want and do it often within a few minutes. But it struggled with complex foods, though it could individually synthesize many simple food ingredients. This reduced our dependence on trade with Wolf Jaw. But by then, we had developed a friendship with the Bests. Destiny also had her aunt and cousin in town, so we continued to visit a couple times a week, bringing diesel with us each time to trade for fresh produce and meat. These were examples of foods the nanoforge couldn't synthesize. But we could produce such large quantities of diesel and other fuels that it was practically like printing money when it came to trading with the townies.

With the base completed, Zeta began fabricating the ship. Threads of nanobots streamed out of the nanoforge into the hangar and started forming the outline of a structure on the hangar floor. The cockpit would be produced first so that Zeta could begin training us while the rest of the ship was being constructed.

The day after ship construction started, I was training with Destiny and Busto in the woods when we heard Baxter yelling. He sounded frightened. I remembered that he and Ricki had gone out hunting. Thinking that somebody was hurt, Busto halted our training, and the three of us picked up our weapons, slung them on our shoulders, and raced through the woods down to the glen.

"Kory! Gunny!" Baxter yelled from the center of the glen, his face flushed, his hands cupped around his mouth to amplify his voice.

We ran up to him. "Baxter, what is it?" Busto said through panting breaths.

"They took him!" the man screamed. His eyes were wild, and saliva ran down his chin. "Help me!"

I stepped to him and rested my hand on his shoulder. "Calm down, you're safe. Explain to us what you're talking about."

Lynda came running toward us from their home. "What is it? Where's Ricki?!"

Baxter saw his wife and abruptly burst into sobs. "I tried to protect him, but they're going to hurt him if I don't come back with fuel!"

Lynda held a hand to his face. "What are you talking about?"

"Honey, they took our boy hostage!"

27

We convinced Baxter to sit on the ground. Slowly, his story came out. He and Ricki had been out hunting up the mountain to the north. They were following the trail of a deer when five or six armed men suddenly materialized out of the woods and surrounded them.

"They said they knew about all the fuel we were providing Wolf Jaw and wanted some. To make sure we did, they took my Ricki! They said if we don't pay, they'd punish him!" Baxter jumped up and grabbed me by the jacket. "Oh, God, Kory, you got to help me!"

Lynda stood close to her husband, arms folded stiffly, her face pale as death.

"Who was it?" I asked. "People from town? Did they take him?"

"No, it was the Pattons," Baxter said. "Those scumbags who came a while back and threatened us."

I remembered Busto's and the Bests' stories about them. "And they want what?"

"We have to bring them diesel and gasoline."

Ricki was a quiet kid. When I first met the Brooks, I'd thought he would be an annoyance, always getting underfoot and wanting to hang out with us young adults. But he'd been nothing but a joy to be around. His soft laugh and dry humor made it easy to like him. I looked forward to including him in our training soon.

A skinny, fourteen-year-old kidnapped by the Pattons. How must he be feeling right now? He must have been wondering if anybody would free him. He must have been terrified that nobody would care enough to fight the Pattons for him.

I instantly felt an ache in my chest as I thought about what it was like to be imprisoned. It had happened to me before in the orphanage. I had no desire to get mixed up with the Pattons, but it seemed that fate had taken that decision out of my hands. The Pattons had made their expected move, and now we had to respond appropriately, or they would continue trying to exploit us.

"Baxter," Destiny said, tipping her head up, "this is why you shouldn't have been taking Ricki out hunting."

Baxter's face flushed. "It's part of his education, and my family has to eat."

"We have plenty of food. It was an unnecessary risk, and I told you that before. You knew the Pattons had threatened us."

The angry father took a threatening step toward my sister. "Look here, little girl, I won't have you telling me how to raise my own children. Especially from somebody who's been living on the streets for who knows how many years."

Destiny's draw dropped open. If Baxter thought he could intimidate Destiny, he didn't know my sister. "I'm not going to let some hillbilly like you talk to me like that!"

Before the situation got even more out of control, I

stepped between them and raised my hands. "Baxter! We'll get him back. I promise." I gestured to Phoebe, and she came closer, her eyes full of fear. "I need to talk to Gunny and Destiny. Why don't you take your mom and dad back home and try to help them rest."

She nodded. "Okay. You really are going to try and get him back?" she said with a pleading look.

"Yes, of course we are. Ricki is one of us. We'll do what we have to."

Phoebe grabbed me in a quick hug. "Thank god!" Just as quickly, she let me go and went to her parents. "Mom and Dad, come with me. We need to let them talk. They will figure this out, but we need to let them think." She tugged on her mom's arm. "Come home. I'll make some coffee."

Baxter glared again at Destiny, then turned around and followed Phoebe.

When Destiny, Busto, and I were alone, I asked Destiny, "Why did you have to say those things to him?"

She rolled her eyes. "Because they needed saying!"

"All you did was put his back up against a wall."

"He screwed up, got his son into trouble, and now we have to get him out of it. I've a right to be angry with him."

"It could have happened to any of us," Busto said. "Destiny, you've got a big mouth and need to learn when to keep it shut."

Destiny puffed herself up. "Oh, you think so? Why don't you step a little closer so you can find out how big it is? Watch out, or this mouth'll take a bite right out of your Mexican ass!"

I pushed them apart. "Guys! Stop!" I turned to Destiny and held up a finger. "Just shut up for a minute."

She glowered at me.

"You can do that, right?" I said. Busto's criticism hadn't

been too far off the mark. Destiny needed reminding of that.

I sighed. "We need to focus on Ricki right now. Arguing with each other isn't going to help with that. So, my question to you is this: What do you think are the chances the Pattons will let Ricki go if we bring them the fuel they demanded?"

Destiny grunted. "Depends on how desperate they are. And how twisted. My thinking is they won't release him. They'll just keep asking for more and more—Ricki's within their power now. I know you want to help, but I don't see what we can do about it. We should talk to the Wolf Jaw police department."

"Nah, they won't do diddly-squat," Busto said. "The Pattons are outside their jurisdiction. I suppose there's the county, but like the Bests said, the sheriff no longer comes to these parts. I think we're on our own." He unholstered his pistol and began inspecting it. "That means it's up to us." He looked between Destiny and me. "I would think you two were used to solving your own problems without the law's help."

"So, we're just going to put ourselves in danger?" Destiny looked at me. "Kory, we're supposed to be keeping safe and surviving. I'm not even against fighting the Kergans like you promised Zeta. But this crosses the line. We're not responsible for the Brooks. You should have never invited them to stay."

"You agreed to it too. Remember?" I said.

"Yeah, I guess it was one of my stupid days. It happens every year or two."

Busto held up a hand. "We're a community now, those of us inside this glen. For better or worse, we accepted the Brooks family into that. We have a commitment to them."

Destiny folded her arms. "What, you think they would

lift a hand to help rescue you if the Pattons had caught you?"

"Maybe they would, maybe they wouldn't, but it's not their decision." Busto thumped a finger into his chest. "It's ours, and I believe in Karma: What comes around, goes around. If you help Ricki now, I know the Brooks will become loyal friends for the rest of your life. That's something worth fighting for. Those are the kinds of ties that hold communities together. It's what makes armies into cohesive fighting forces. Soldiers aren't there to fight for the greater good. When the bullets start flying, ideals are the first casualties. In those moments, you only care about the guy fighting next to you in the same foxhole. I'm telling you that the Brooks are in our foxhole, Destiny, whether you like it or not, and they're wounded. I can't speak for either of you, but I'm *not* going to abandon them."

I rested a hand on Destiny's shoulder. "Sorry, Dest, but I agree with Gunny."

She threw my hand off and turned away. "This is what I get for hanging with a bunch of idealists."

"That's not what Gunny is saying. He's actually being pretty practical if you'll listen to him. He's saying that the Brooks are our allies, and we need to treat them like such if we ever want to count on them in the future. And regardless of that, I like Ricki, and I won't abandon him to the Pattons."

She turned back around. "I get it. Can we stop talking about this now and actually make plans?"

"So, you're with us?" I said.

"Well, I'm still here, aren't I?"

Busto stood there watching Destiny with a clenched jaw. I turned to him and said, "You can trust her, Gunny. Like you said, Destiny is not shy about sharing her opinions. Please don't hold it against her."

The marine nodded, cleared his throat, and spat on the

ground. "Okay, do what she said. Let's talk about the plan."

"Gunny, you've probably done stuff like this before. What do we need?"

Busto looked down and kicked a rock. "We need information about this compound and the Pattons. Even if they don't release Ricki, I think we should take them some fuel. It'll give us an excuse to get the layout of their land and meet these assholes."

"So, we just drive up there with a couple cans and see what happens?" I said.

"Yes."

I looked at my sister. "Dest?"

"Sure, I don't have a better idea. It'll buy us some time. And, who knows, maybe we'll discover that Baxter overreacted, and Ricki's been at a slumber party this entire time."

I thought about Zeta's nanobots and wondered how much she could sense through them. She'd discovered a lot when we'd been surveying these woods. I walked over to the excavation and yelled. "Zeta! You there?"

No matter how deep she was inside the base, the igna always seemed to hear me somehow when I called her. About 30 seconds later, she flew out of the hangar opening. "Zeta is here, Consort."

"How much did you hear?" I said.

"Everything. Ricki Brooks has been taken captive by local hostiles who are demanding fuel in exchange for his safety. Zeta recognizes it as a straightforward hostage situation."

"You're pretty good at sensing things from a distance."

"When Zeta's nanobots are deployed, aye, she can sense the environment through them."

I told Zeta about our plan to accept the Pattons'

demands and take the fuel so we could scout their compound. "I want to take you. While we distract the Pattons, you deploy your nanobots to see if you can locate where they're holding Ricki. Could you do that?"

"Given sufficient time, aye, it is possible."

"How much time?"

"Zeta cannot foretell. It depends on how close you can get worthy Zeta to the enemy dwellings and whether Ricki is present. Zeta estimates at least five minutes."

"Okay, we'll buy you the time you need. Destiny, I want you to do what you can to hide Zeta next to the van while Gunny and I go in to talk to these Pattons and distract them."

"So, us four are going?" Destiny said.

I nodded.

"Armed?"

"Hell, yes, we'll be armed."

"But we don't have to show it," Busto said. "We don't want to escalate the situation by threatening them. What they don't know will help us. Let them think we're weak."

"Gunny, are you suggesting something specific?"

28

About an hour later, the four of us departed in the van. None of us had seen the Pattons' compound before, but Baxter knew of it and drew us a map. It was about three miles deeper into the mountains from our base.

I drove with Busto in the front passenger's seat. Destiny and Zeta sat in the rear, with Zeta staying out of view. We planned to park the van as close as possible to the Patton's primary dwelling, with the side door facing away from the house and the igna embedded in the soil next to it. Then Destiny would stand behind the van armed with an M4 and shield the view of Zeta on the ground next to her. Busto and I would do the talking and try to keep the Pattons eyes away from Destiny and Zeta.

As we neared the compound, the mountain road became rougher. We drove up deep valleys over the winding path, the van's poor suspension protesting at each of the many potholes its wheels found. We had to stop once and clear a path past a recently fallen tree, probably brought down by a buildup of snow on its branches. The sky was overcast, and the wind blustered away with icy fingers reaching past the minute gaps in the old Toyota's doors and windows. I was grateful for the heater blasting away in our faces.

I found myself watching the rearview mirror, looking for glimpses of blackholes tailing us. But I never saw anything suspicious, and it had been a week since the last incident. Maybe my paranoia was tapering off, and I'd finally get some peace.

The Patton compound was at the end of a quarter-mile dirt path through the woods leading from the highway. We crept down it, at one point crossing a rickety bridge over a creek. Fearing it wouldn't take the weight of the van, I finally decided the Pattons must use it regularly, and therefore, so could I. We passed it safely and continued on our way until we spotted two single-wide trailers and a double-wide in a clearing. The three trailers were parked in a ring enclosing a loose triangle. A barn and a couple sheds stood outside the ring and near the forest's edge.

As soon as we spotted the first trailer, I slowed the van until we were moving at barely a walking pace. Busto had a notebook and began quickly drawing a crude map and taking notes on the compound's layout.

A pair of angry German Shepherds bounded from behind the double-wide and started barking savagely. They ran toward us, pacing the van and showing plenty of teeth.

The three homes were old and in poor repair. The double-wide trailer had once been painted white and trimmed with green but was now patched with rust and faded colors. One of its windows was broken and repaired with a plywood plug. Thin threads of smoke trailed from the chimneys of all three trailers.

"How can thirty people live here?" I said.

The double-wide had a porch constructed in front of it

that looked like it was about to collapse. I aimed to park in front of that. As we approached, a middle-aged woman stepped out the front door holding a shotgun and trailed by two dirty kids. She yelled something I couldn't hear over the sound of the engine.

"Call the Rats of NIMH," Destiny said. "We found their lost colony."

I laughed. "Careful, you might offend the rats."

Destiny shook herself. "This family might just be a medical experiment gone wrong."

"Don't judge them too harshly. We haven't met them yet."

"Busto has."

"Give Destiny some credit," Busto said. "I think she deserves a prize."

A moment later, a burly man in overalls and a stained undershirt came out, taking the shotgun from the woman. He said something to her, and then she grabbed the kids and went back inside.

The man had long, graying brown hair lying on his head in greasy ropes. His face and neck were dirty except for a clean patch around his eyes and nose. His clothes were even filthier. But his shotgun looked shiny and well-maintained. And he had it aimed at us.

Understanding the implied message, I stopped about twelve feet from the porch. I rolled down my window and said, "We're here about Ricki."

"The Brooks boy?" he said. He still hadn't lowered his weapon nor called off his dogs, who stood outside my door, barking savagely and threatening to leap at me. "Who are you?"

"I'm not saying anything else until you lower your gun," I said.

Two more men walked out onto the porch. I couldn't tell if they were armed. Several children appeared at a window, including the two I'd seen earlier.

The man with the shotgun spit, nearly hitting the van's front tire. Then he lowered his gun until it pointed at the ground, relaxed, and nodded condescendingly.

"I'm Kory Drake," I said. "Baxter Brooks is a friend and told us about you abducting his son. Who are you?"

"Odell Patton. And we didn't kidnap nobody. We found Baxter and his boy trespassing on our land and demanded compensation. He couldn't pay, so we took charge of his boy to be our guest until he does. It's as simple as that. And I don't see how it's any of your damned business, boy."

If our plan was going to work, I needed to get Busto and me away from the van so Zeta could get going with her spying.

"If you want payment, then I'm the man you want to talk to."

Odell chuckled. "You're barely old enough to have hair on your balls. Why isn't Baxter here?"

I felt my face become heated. "If you don't want to be paid, then talk to Baxter. If you want to be paid, then talk to me. And I don't want to talk here."

Odell's gut projected over his belt like the prow of a ship. "I don't see that there's much to talk about. Show me what you got."

I shook my head. "First, we talk."

The middle-aged man rolled his eyes and grimaced. "Fine." He pushed himself off the wall he'd been leaning against and walked down the porch steps. "Follow me." He turned at the bottom of the steps and started walking to the end of the trailer.

I glanced at Destiny, who nodded and said, "Go with

Hillbilly Jim. We got this."

Busto and I got out of the van and followed Odell. We ensured our holstered pistols were visible but kept our hands away from them. I cast my vision around, looking for anybody else with weapons, but I didn't see any.

We walked around to the back of the trailer, where there was a patio table and a couple of benches made out of scrap wood. Odell sat on one and pulled out a cigarette.

Busto and I sat on the other bench. The other two men followed us and took up standing positions, blocking our path back to the van. The implications were obvious. The children reappeared at a different window, looking out at us.

"We like little...Nicki just fine," Odell said.

"It's Ricki," I said.

"Of course. Ricki. Don't worry, he's settlin' in good. Of course, keeping teenagers is darn expensive. You can understand why we need his pop to help with his upkeep."

"Mister Patton, you can't just take another man's child."

"Look here, boy, 'round these parts, Odell Patton is the law these days. The gov'ment don't come here anymore, and somebody's got to maintain order. Baxter's been stompin' on land that don't belong to him and poachin' the wildlife."

"Who put—"

Odell held up a hand. "Shut up!"

I stopped what I'd been about to ask. *Who put you in charge?*

Odell held up a finger. "I'm still talkin'. You don't watch your mouth, I'll knock your teeth out. As *I* was sayin', Baxter's been tresspassin' and pochin' on my land. Now, I *could* have shot him and would have been within my rights to do so. But me, I'm a restrained fella, and I says to myself, 'We should teach ol' Baxter a lesson so he don't do this no more. But a man has to feed his family. So, we'll let him go and take his boy instead.' And that's exactly what we done. Roger has to stay with us until his pop pays what's owed us."

"You mean Ricki."

"Boy, don't you have a mouth on you? Aint that what I done said, you smartass?"

I tried to relax my clenched fists. I'd dealt with men like Odell Patton before. He had an ego a mile high and thought he could do no wrong, and yet the world was falling to pieces around him.

"I've come to bring you payment," I said. "But I want to see Ricki first."

"He's just fine, but I don't know where he is. It might take a while to track him down."

I leaned back and folded my arms. "We'll wait."

Odell sighed and mumbled something unintelligible under his breath. He looked at one of the other men. "Winston, why don't you go see if you can find Nicki."

Winston, behind me, grumbled something and walked away.

"So, what did you bring us?" Odell said with a secretive smile.

I didn't say anything but instead shook my head and looked away from the man. We sat there freezing under the overcast sky. Odell finished his cigarette and took out and lit a second.

Ten minutes later, Winston returned with Ricki in tow. The teenager was still dressed in the winter clothing in which they'd taken him: wool pants, a heavy winter jacket, a knitted stocking cap, and worn leather boots.

"Hey, Ricki," I said. "Are you okay?"

The teenager had a tense look in his eyes, but he nodded.

"See, I told you he was fine," Odell said, blowing a plume of smoke almost in my face.

"Okay, I've brought you five gallons each of diesel and gasoline. You give us Ricki, then you get to keep the fuel. I'll even give you the cans."

Odell smirked and rolled his eyes. "I showed you the boy. Now, show me the fuel."

"I'll get it," Busto said. He excused himself and went back to the van. The third man followed him. I hoped he wouldn't see what Zeta was doing.

A minute later, Busto returned, lugging the two cans. He set them between Odell and me.

Odell opened the caps and sniffed the contents. Satisfied, he said, "This'll work as a downpayment. But you owe us more."

Destiny had warned us, so I wasn't surprised. I wanted to fight this man, but I had to remember this visit was about gathering intelligence, and enough time had already elapsed for Zeta to do what was needed. It was time to leave so we could plan the next phase of our rescue plan. "How much?"

"80 gallons of diesel and 20 of gas."

"We don't have that much."

"Then we'll just have to hold onto Ricki until you cough up what Baxter owes."

I sighed and rubbed my forehead. "Nobody has any fuel these days. The Kergans have disrupted the supply chain. You're asking for the impossible." It was, in fact, not too difficult, now that we had the complete base and nanoforge, but we didn't want the Pattons to know about that. We had to make this painful for them, or they'd try these same bullying shenanigans again.

"Not my problem. You tell your friend, Baxter, to stay

off our land."

"He was on national forest land. You have no right to keep Ricki."

Odell waved at Winston. "Get him out of here." He turned back to me, gripping his shotgun menacingly. "Boy, I don't typically deal with children like you. I don't care how you do it, but you're goin' to pay me what I'm owed."

I reached for the cans.

Odell flashed the shotgun in my direction. "Uh, uh, those stay. Unless you want us to get careless with your friend's son."

I estimated about thirty minutes had passed since we sat on these benches. I suspected it was enough time for Zeta to learn what she needed.

I wanted to scream in Odell's face and threaten him. But that would put him on edge. We needed him to feel strong right now. So, I swallowed my wounded pride and forced a pitiful look on my face. "Okay, Mister Patton, we'll do our best."

"That's more like it. Don't worry. We'll keep an eye on Richi for you."

I ignored his botching again of Ricki's name. Busto and I stood and walked back toward the van. "Destiny, let's go!" While we were still thirty feet away, I yelled to make sure she knew we were coming and got Zeta back into hiding.

Her head popped up from behind the van, then dropped again. The kids appeared at the front window, this time joined by a woman.

We got in the van. Destiny and Zeta were already inside. I started the engine. I turned us around and drove for the compound exit, the tires squelching through mud and bouncing over fallen tree limbs.

"Did you get anything, Zeta?" I said.

"Indeed, Consort. Ricki appears to be kept in the small trailer on the outer end of the clearing. After fearless Kory finished seeing him, Ricki was brought back there and locked into a closet."

"Damnation."

Destiny slapped her leg. "I bet even their little kids sleep with guns. But don't worry, we're *professionals*!" she said with a mock grin. "This will be a cinch."

29

We had a conversation with Ricki's parents after we returned to the secret starship base. Nobody wanted Ricki to be kept prisoner by the Pattons for any longer than absolutely necessary, so we needed a plan for going forward.

Zeta's intelligence revealed where Ricki was kept and how the Pattons configured their security. The Pattons liked to appear fierce, but Zeta learned that they didn't have good security. Though there were many firearms in the compound, the adults seemed casual about carrying them around and didn't appear to have any kind of organized watch in place. They acted like they didn't expect anybody ever to attack them.

"Zeta," I said, "what kinds of equipment can you manufacture that would help us if we decided to assault the Patton compound and rescue Ricki?"

"Hold on, Kory," Busto said. "Are you sure about that? Shouldn't we try and negotiate some more?"

"Gunny," Destiny said, shaking her head, "for an

experienced marine, you can be surprisingly naive sometimes. These are the sort of people who will give up Ricki only after they are sure that holding him will be of no further benefit."

"Destiny's right," I said. "I aim to convince them that that time is now. I want to hit them so hard they'll think twice before trying something like this again."

"But somebody could get hurt," Busto said.

"Somebody could also get hurt if we don't act," I said. "Every minute that those people are holding Ricki is a minute in which he could come to harm." I looked at Baxter and Lynda. "And, besides that, this would be a fantastic opportunity to put our team-building exercises to the test. What do you think, Gunny? Are we ready for something like this?"

Busto tapped his forehead. Despite his concerns, I counted on him to be professional and give me his genuine opinion on the matter. "Against these people? Yes, if we have the element of surprise. But like you said, we should hit them hard and make it painful. But let's not hurt them so bad that they'll want revenge."

"How would that work?"

"Somehow," Destiny responded, "we get them to realize we could destroy them, and then we don't. We recover Ricki and leave the Pattons alive in their compound to reflect on the wisdom of their choices."

"They've got children," Busto said as if it was an accusation.

"Even better," Destiny said, holding her arms wide. "It means they've something of their own to protect. We'll threaten them and then show them mercy."

Busto shook his head and frowned.

"Don't worry, Gunny, we won't hurt any children." I

pointed to Zeta. "Okay, back to my question. Zeta, what equipment can you manufacture to help us pull this operation off?"

"Zeta recommends tactical combat armor, first and foremost, because you possess none," the alien said. "You do have firearms, though they are primitive. Zeta could manufacture flechette guns and laser pistols and a few other arms that would be more effective."

"I just got you guys trained to use our existing weapons," Busto said. "I don't want to swap for sci-fi guns right before we do a mission. However, the combat armor sounds like a wise choice."

"Come on, Gunny, no laser pistols?" I said with a smile. I would like to get my hands on one of those, but I knew he was correct to be conservative.

He ignored my comment. "How long would it take to make the armor?" Busto said.

"Less than a day," Zeta said.

"What are they made of?"

"The armored suits are composed entirely of protomatter."

"Protomatter?"

"It is a material consisting of specialized carbon nanobots organized into a flexible lattice that forms a solid surface. It can be reshaped upon command, forming flexible or rigid surfaces of any shape. Protomatter is an ideal fabric for use in protective garments. Your ship suits will also be made of it."

Programmable clothing. It sounded pretty cool. I looked forward to trying it.

"How much protection do these suits provide?" Busto said.

"An individual suit of protomatter tactical armor

protects against kinetic projectiles up to 10 kJ of energy and pulsed energy beams of up to 20 kJ. It is impermeable, heat and tear-resistant, and the nanobots actively control the user's air supply, filtering out poisons and other hazards."

"Is that good?" I asked Busto.

"Yeah, much better than military body armor," he said. "A medium machine gun bullet carries about 3 to 4 kJ of energy. If these...protomatter suits work as advertised, they can stop most rifle and all pistol bullets."

"I'm sold. Zeta, please start making the suits. Fabricate four of them."

"For Phoebe, too?" Busto said.

"Yeah, I think we should take her on this operation. It's her brother, she'll want to go, and we need the numbers. You okay with that?"

"Yes, she's done well in the training."

"Very well, Consort, diligent Zeta will commence immediately," Zeta said. She pivoted in the air and flew away.

I cracked my knuckles one at a time. We were going on a mission. Though it wasn't the sort of deed Zeta had intended for us to do, it was necessary to put these Pattons in their place and make sure they knew that screwing with my people would only lead to trouble. I needed us to secure our people.

30

"What do I do with it?" I said, staring at the gray nanofiber case.

I stood in the base armory at a table upon which the case containing my new protomatter suit rested. It measured about the size and shape of a small suitcase. I had just carried it from the nanoforge, where it had been fabricated. Busto and Destiny sat on a nearby bench observing.

I had volunteered as our test subject. I would be the first one of us to test it.

"Open the case," Zeta said.

I opened the latches and lifted the case's lid on its hinges. Hot air gushed out. Inside lay a formless mass that looked like black playdough. It was large, filling the entire case. As I stood there looking at it, it seemed to ripple and vibrate of its own accord as if it were a living creature.

"Why is it so hot?" I asked.

"The nanobots comprising the protomatter consume power."

"Sounds wasteful."

"They can be put into an inert hibernation state, though that takes several hours to transfer in and out of. It normally consumes a trickle of power when out of storage and ready for use."

"What's next?"

"Pick up the protomatter and place it on the floor next to you."

I reached out, positioned my hands on the edges of the dough-like substance, and hesitated. "Do I just grab it with my hands?"

"Yes. It is quite rigid in this state." Zeta flew closer until she hung over the case. She lowered herself until she nudged against the protomatter. It gave slightly but left no indentation when she backed off.

I reached the rest of the way in and picked up the black mass. I expected it to feel like warm bread dough but was surprised to feel something like sticky rubber instead. However, as I lifted it out, I noted that it was considerably lighter than rubber and emitted no odor. I gently set it on the floor at my feet. "Okay. What next?"

"Remove all your clothing," Zeta said.

"You want me to strip?"

"Indeed, remove everything. The suit design assumes the human being protected is naked. All jewelry must also be removed."

Destiny laughed and clapped her hands and began singing a lewd song.

My face burned. I pointed at the walls of the armory. "We need some privacy curtains in here." I wasn't a prude—few street people could afford to be—but as captain of our crew, I wanted to do this in a more dignified manner.

"My dear sir, I can remove myself if you require

privacy," Destiny said mockingly with a bad British accent.

"No, that's okay. You've seen me naked before." I unbuttoned my winter shirt and pulled it off. "What do I do after I'm naked?" I said to Zeta.

"To activate the suit, stand on top of the protomatter with both feet and hold still."

I removed my pants, socks, watch, and underwear. Feeling extremely exposed and vulnerable, I stepped onto the blob.

It immediately transformed from its semi-rigid rubbery state into a flowing gel, and my feet sank into it, disappearing below its warm surface. The protomatter flowed up my legs, covering them with a thick coating about a quarter inch thick. It ran up my calves, thighs, and groin and reached my belly when I realized if it kept going up, it was going to suffocate me.

"Hold on!" I cried. "I'm not sure about this."

"You are perfectly fine, gentle Consort," Zeta said. "If it makes you feel more comfortable, you can move your legs and arms. It will not trap you."

It continued flowing up, reaching my armpits. "How do I get it off if I wanted to?"

"If at any time you wish to remove it, simply grasp an edge and tug firmly on it as if you were trying to peel it off. The protomatter will detect your action and interpret it as a command to withdraw. You may try it if you wish."

I feared I was being a coward. "No, let's do this." I wanted to give a good demonstration.

The protomatter encased my entire body, except my head, in a formfitting envelope. When it reached my neck, instead of continuing to flow up along my skin, the gel pushed outward, leaving an air gap, and began forming a hard shell around my head. Unlike the lower suit, which was flexible, the shell was rigid and held my head firmly with an air pocket around my ears, eyes, mouth, and nose. A transparent faceplate covered the front, wide enough to give me good peripheral vision in all directions.

"How do you feel?" Busto said. Though the helmet covered my ears, his voice came to me perfectly clearly, as if nothing obstructed my hearing.

I moved my limbs, rolled my shoulders, and rotated my head. I felt good. Great, actually. "Fine. It almost feels like I'm wearing nothing." I rubbed my gloved hands down my suited arms and could feel the suit's texture. It felt as if nothing covered my fingers. "Amazing. The suit lets me sense touch."

"The protomatter suit has a haptic interface that accurately translates contact onto your skin," Zeta said. "The lower suit maintains a flexible state for ease of mobility, while the rigid helmet replicates and augments the protection your skull provides. The faceplate is composed of a diamond composite."

"A what-composite?" I asked.

"Diamond composite. Each protomatter nanobot is composed of several million carbon atoms encasing a nucleus of robotic nanomachinery. Transparent surfaces can be constructed when the nanobots organize themselves into a diamond lattice."

I tapped the faceplate with a finger. "Pure diamond. Wow."

"No, not pure. It encases the billions of robotic nuclei of which it is comprised. But those are so small that they do not interfere with the passage of visible light."

"And the rest of the suit?" Busto asked. "How do these nanobots...organize themselves."

"It depends on the intended effect, but it is typically

comprised of long chains of carbon nanotubes. It has exceptionally high tensile strength and will respond to impulsive loads by going rigid such that impacts are absorbed by the suit instead of the encapsulated body."

"Impulsive loads. You mean, like bullets?"

"Precisely. It is also self-repairing, though if enough of the suit is damaged, it will no longer be able to protect the entire body until it is replenished with additional protomatter."

I held up my hands to my face and studied the length of my arms. My entire body was covered with a seamless matte-black fabric. I tested my flexibility by squatting, standing, and jumping in place. The suit gave me no resistance, and my head actually bumped the ceiling with a *thud* at the top of my leap.

"Careful," Zeta said. "The suit will amplify forceful movements. It is subtle, but you could easily damage something unintentionally."

"This is great," I said. "I love it. And I bet the color is perfect for night operations."

"Ah, indeed. The suit has other features, lad. Look at the inside of your left wrist."

I rotated my left hand and looked. The faint outline of some sort of panel lay embedded in the inner left arm of my suit.

"Tap it with your finger," Zeta said.

I did. The matte-black panel suddenly transformed into a glossy black surface, and bright green text appeared: *SYSTEM MENU.* Underneath the text were positioned several icons.

Zeta told me how to navigate through the menus. I soon found a setting called *EN CAMO* with an empty box next to it. I tapped the box, and an X-mark filled it.

"Holy smokes!" Busto yelled.

Destiny gasped.

"What happened?" I said.

"You just disappeared," Busto said. He'd jumped to his feet and was walking around me. "When I move around, I can just barely see your outline."

I moved my arm.

"Yeah, that I can see, but it's difficult. Your suit coloring changed to match the background."

I looked down at myself and saw that my torso displayed a figure of the cabinets I stood in front of, and my legs and feet matched the floor.

Zeta showed me a few other features. The suit incorporated integrated comms, a tactical display showing the position of allies and enemies, and automated fire control to assist with weapons aiming. The faceplate also provided light amplification for low-light situations or wavelength translation to make infrared and ultraviolet visible.

"The next suit is completed," Zeta said.

"Me, me!" Destiny yelled as she jumped up and ran down the corridor toward the nanoforge. Five minutes later, she returned clothed in the newest protomatter suit. "This is so cool!" she said.

Over the next couple of hours, Zeta finished constructing the other two suits. By the late afternoon, Busto, Destiny, Phoebe, and I were all wearing protomatter tactical armor. Busto took us through several of the drills he'd taught us, but this time wearing our armor and using our embedded comms.

We practiced for hours, until long after nightfall, since the suit faceplates made the night appear like day. The suit interface was intuitive, and the tactical display—which appeared on the faceplate as a HUD—was easy to use.

The suits provided excellent grip in the snow for our feet and hands. Phoebe was the first to discover she could scale vertical surfaces without needing ropes or handholds. "Eat that, Spider-Man!" she yelled out with a whoop.

Around about midnight, we halted the training.

"Kory," Busto said, "I want to postpone the operation for twenty-four hours. People are tired, and I'd like to do a little more training tomorrow."

"Okay, it's your call," I said. I'd promised him command of ground missions.

We stopped our drills and headed back to our beds or to our stations for those who had watch duty.

31

The next day, Gunny Busto put Destiny, Phoebe, and me through additional drills to help us further familiarize ourselves with our new armored suits. These included several exercises inside the base to practice close-quarters tactics and teamwork using the confined corridors and compartments of the underground facility.

In the evening, we ate a large dinner, then spent several hours in the command room walking through various mission scenarios, the decisions we would make, who would have what tasks, and how we might respond to different kinds of unexpected events.

I had placed Busto in tactical command of our ground missions. Though I was the group commander, I recognized that Busto's experience far exceeded mine when it came to boots-on-the-ground small-unit tactics. I trusted him to get us through this operation alive.

We rested for a few hours, and then, in the early morning hours, we left the base in the van, leaving Baxter and Lynda on watch. They'd wanted to come too. Of course, they had. We were going to rescue their son. But I explained that they hadn't trained with us for this kind of operation, and they were likely to put us and Ricki in danger. They grumbled but finally agreed it would be best to stay out of the way and secure the base.

I pulled us off to the side of the road about a half mile from the Patton compound. We hiked the rest of the way from there, wearing our new suits, armed with M4 carbines and pistols, and carrying a small amount of other equipment attached to suit harnesses. Zeta floated along with us.

Busto ordered us to stay together as one team. "For an operation like this," he said, "I'd normally like at least two teams, with one acting as overwatch. But we're too few in number."

Busto took point, followed by Destiny and Phoebe on his two flanks, and I trailed them and provided rear security. Zeta flew in front of me.

Our enhanced vision made the dark terrain easily visible despite an overcast sky. We left the road, cutting through the forest and up the mountainside over some very rough terrain. At one point, the clouds became so thick we had to switch to infrared optics because there was too little light even for the light amplification.

At about 2 am, we arrived on the forest's edge outside the Patton compound. Busto guided us to the top of an adjacent hillock that allowed us to observe the entire property.

No lights illuminated the area. I switched to infrared. The three trailers leaped out in bright white from the heat they gave off.

For the next ten minutes, we stayed quietly crouched on the ground and did nothing else but observe. Zeta rested on the ground and propagated her nanobots through the soil and the air.

In all that time, not a creature moved in the compound. There was no sign of activity inside the trailers or evidence of the two dogs.

"Zeta has located friend Ricki," our alien ally said. "He remains imprisoned in a closet of the small trailer on the far side of the clearing."

"How many people are in that trailer?" Busto said.

"Zeta counts eleven, including Ricki. Seven adults and teenagers, and four small children."

"Geesh, they really pack them in," I said.

"Weapons?" Busto asked.

"Aye. Four of the adults are sleeping in proximity to firearms."

"Can you show them on our tactical display?"

"Good idea," I said.

"Zeta expresses profound regret," Zeta said, "She has not completed the interface that allows her to transfer data to your suits."

"That's an oops," I said.

Busto sighed. "That's why we never rush into ops, Kory. Even just one more day, with more practice, we could have learned of a problem like this."

I shrugged. "We'll mark it down as a lesson learned."

Busto rested his M4 on his lap and rubbed his hands together. "If we storm into the trailer, they'll have their guns in their hands within seconds and be firing. Maybe they can't hurt us, but it'll put Ricki at risk, and I don't want anybody getting hurt if it's not necessary."

He rubbed his chin. "Zeta, what about the other trailers?"

"The other small trailer is similarly occupied and

armed," Zeta said. "Inside the larger trailer are twelve adults and teenagers, and five children. Observant Zeta counts six firearms in close proximity plus what appears to be a fairly large stash of weapons stored in one of the rooms."

"Good lord in a handbasket," Busto mumbled. I feared he was going to call off the operation. He could, if he wanted to, even if the rest of us wanted to go forward. I'd given him that prerogative as the ground tactical commander.

"What if we create a distraction?" I suggested before he called for an abort. "Something that would get the armed ones up and out of the house. Then we could sneak in and grab Ricki."

"No, not good enough," Busto said. "All it takes is one person staying behind and seeing us take Ricki. Remember, we've got to hike out of here with Ricki in tow. It's not gonna be easy, and I don't want a bunch of crazy-angry Pattons on my tail."

"What about a hostage?" Phoebe said from my side.

Busto leaned over to look at her. "What do you mean?"

Phoebe pointed at the large trailer. "I bet Grandma Patton is sleeping in that double-wide. Suppose instead of snatching Ricki, we grab Grandma and make sure everybody sees us doing it. Then we hold her and threaten to harm her unless they turn over Ricki."

"Ooh, that's harsh," Destiny said. "I love your idea, Phebes." She chuckled.

Phoebe's head jerked around. "I know what it sounds like, but they took Ricki! It's what they deserve. I want them to feel like how my parents feel right now."

"Zeta, can you locate an elderly lady?" Busto said.

"Aye, there is a female of advanced age sleeping in the large trailer. She sleeps in a bed with two small children and an adult middle-aged female. A small pistol rests on a table next to the bed."

Busto crouched there in silence for a minute. Then he looked up at us. "Okay, this is what we're going to do." He mapped out his plan. After absorbing it, we all agreed to it.

32

Destiny, Phoebe, and I crouched underneath the exterior of the window leading into the bedroom where Grandma Patton slept. Zeta remained behind on the hillock where we had been observing the compound. Somehow, we had not anticipated needing to communicate via radio with Zeta, so she was out of contact for now.

Busto was out of sight, taking care of our distraction.

"Okay, the charge is ready," Busto said over the suit comms. He was about a hundred feet away, planting an AN-M14 thermite incendiary grenade on a wrecked semi-tractor parked outside the ring of trailers. The grenade was one of the goodies he'd stolen from the bandits.

He promised us that if the truck still had any oil and fuel in its tank and engine, then it was going to burn spectacularly and give us our distraction. Once it got the Pattons' attention, we'd burst through the window and grab Granny and anybody else we could.

"Go ahead," I whispered into the comms. "We're in position."

"It's lit."

I watched my tactical display as a blue dot representing Busto began moving toward us. When it was almost on top of our three dots, he appeared out of the dark, just ever so barely visible through his camouflage.

"We should have brought some marshmallows," Destiny said.

For a minute, nothing happened. The trailer blocked our view of the truck. But soon, I noticed a faint orange glow reflecting off the snow and the clouds. Gradually, it grew in intensity, and soon, we also heard the sound of a vigorously burning fire. The scent of burning diesel and hot metal flooded our senses.

We stayed still, waiting for the Pattons to wake up and do something. What if they didn't notice until morning?

A door in the distance slammed open, and seconds later, a man came running around the corner of the trailer, almost stepping on me, though in his rush, he didn't even notice I was there. He ran to the trailer porch and started pounding on the door. "Odell! Wake up! Fire!" He pounded some more. "Dammit, fire! Fire!" He moved over and pounded on the windows.

I heard a commotion inside the trailer. A moment later, the front door opened, and two men came running out half-dressed with their boots unlaced.

"The old Kenworth is burning!" the first man said.

I recognized Odell's voice. "Okay, calm down. You'll wake up Grandma!" The three men went running, thankfully, this time in the other direction around the trailer from where we crouched. A few seconds later, another man and two women ran out of the trailer headed in the same direction.

"Ready?" Busto said.

The rest of us replied that we were.

"Okay, on three, I'm going through that window, and you're following me." He pivoted on the ground, slung his rifle over his shoulder, and faced the window. "One...two...three!"

Busto jumped up and smashed his armored fist into the window. Glass shattered. He grabbed the edges of the window frame and yanked himself with great force up and through the window. I heard a crash in the room and screams.

Next, Destiny went through. Phoebe and I stayed outside the window, with our M4s ready and guarding our retreat.

Women cursed inside the room, and children started crying.

"Please! Please! No!" a woman screamed.

A door opened.

"What the hell?!" a man said.

"Drop it, or she dies!" Busto screamed. "I mean it!"

I wished I could take a look, but I was supposed to keep my attention on our rear. I knew Gunny wouldn't actually hurt Grandma, but somebody else could do something stupid.

"Damn you!" the man said. "It's goin' to be okay, Mama. I swear to God if you hurt her..."

"Out of the room! Now!"

I heard an elderly woman cursing vile words at Busto.

Movement in the corner of my eye. I looked. Destiny stood at the shattered window holding a child dressed in pajamas and wrapped in a filthy blanket—a little boy or girl of about five who was crying and frozen in terror.

"Close the door!" Busto yelled. A moment later, a door slammed shut. "We got to move," he said over the comms.

"Phoebe, help Destiny," I said. "I've got this."

Phoebe slung her weapon and turned to the window. Destiny handed the child down to Phoebe, who set them down between me and her. Next through the window came an old woman with long silver hair and most of her teeth missing. She looked more resigned than terrified.

I grabbed her arm and pulled her against the wall of the trailer.

She struck me ineffectually with a skinny arm. "You sons of bitches! When I get back to my boys, they'll kick your asses so hard you'll find yourselves in China! I may be old, but I know a bastard when I see one!"

I prodded her with the muzzle of my rifle. "Shut up!"

Following Granny through the window came a middle-aged woman cradling a toddler, who was also crying.

Last, Destiny and Busto jumped back out. He moved off and told us to follow him. Destiny held the arm of granny and Phoebe, the mother, with the toddler. The older child clung to the mother. I came in the rear.

"Watch where you step, you idiot!" Granny yelled. "You're walking right through my daisies and dianthuses!"

I tried to ignore the elderly woman's cursing and complaining.

"Okay, next step," Busto said. We followed him around to the other side of the trailer. I felt bad for our prisoners, who were walking barefoot in ankle-deep snow.

"Kory, watch our rear," he said. I was grateful for the reminder because I'd become distracted by the rusting semi-truck that had become a raging bonfire. It was fully engulfed in flames, and thick black smoke rose into the sky in a tall column. The entire compound was lit by the light of the fire.

I kept my attention on our rear but caught glimpses of the setting. A dozen adults surrounded the fire with buckets and were trying to throw their contents onto the truck. But the heat was so intense they couldn't get close enough. That didn't stop them from running back and forth from a well, where two others furiously pumped, rocking up and down on the manual pump arm.

We approached the group of people with our prisoners between them and us, our weapons threatening them. Busto stopped about thirty feet away. Nobody had yet noticed us.

"Odell Patton!" Busto yelled. "Don't even try to put it out. It won't work!"

Odell whipped around, holding a bucket. Sweat ran down in beads on his face into his beard. At first, he looked confused. But then our prisoners registered in his consciousness.

"Who are you?" Odell said. "What is this?"

"You're going to have to let that fire burn itself out," Busto said. "I made sure that once it started burning, nobody would be able to extinguish it."

"Grandma? Are you okay?" Odell took a step toward the prisoners.

"Stop!" Busto yelled. "Not another step closer." He prodded Granny with his M4. The old woman stood proudly with her chin held up high. The mother cringed and held her crying babies close to her.

Odell froze in place.

I saw movement near the double-wide. A man came running carrying a shotgun.

I was forced to make a split-second decision. I aimed and fired a single bullet.

The man jumped, slipped, and fell as the bullet flew over his head, as I had intended.

There was another flash of movement to the side. Yells. My attention was still focused on the man I'd shot at. But in one smooth motion, Destiny dropped her hand to her sidearm, drew her pistol, aimed, and fired.

When I turned around, I saw a man flailing on the ground with a pistol lying next to him. He was bleeding from his right chest where Destiny had shot him,

"Clear!" Phoebe said.

"Clear!" Busto said. "Hold your fire!"

Two men and a woman dropped to their knees next to the wounded man. One of the men pressed his hands to the bleeding bullet hole while the others dragged him away.

I took several steps toward them and picked up the dropped pistol, a large revolver, a true hand cannon. I said a mental prayer of thanks for Destiny's quick reaction. I hadn't even noticed this guy. He could have possibly killed one of us if he'd gotten close enough.

"Don't shoot!" Odell yelled. "We're unarmed!"

Busto pointed his rifle threateningly at him. "Are you?! Are you?!"

"Everybody just calm down!" Odell said. "We got women and children out here!"

"I don't want to see any more guns, or somebody else will get shot. You hear me?"

"Yes, sir. We got no money if that's what you're looking for. Who the hell are you, and what do you want?"

"We want what you took," Busto said. "Give us Ricki Brooks. Him for the lives of Granny, the woman, and these children. Return the boy unharmed, and nobody else has to get hurt."

I wondered what kind of terrible sight we must have appeared in the darkness. I had expected more resistance from the Pattons, but between the fire, the shock of us taking the family matron, and the wounding of one of their men, everybody was quite subdued.

"Winston!" Odell yelled. "Bring the Brooks boy."

I knew I had to do something to make sure the Pattons got the message that my people were not to be threatened ever again.

"Destiny," I said over comms. "Cover our rear. Let me have the old woman."

We switched positions until my towering figure stood behind Granny. I reached down and disabled my camo. I slung my rifle, drew my pistol, and held it to Granny's head.

"Odell!" I yelled. He turned to look at me. "Do you remember me?"

The man's face looked puzzled.

"The friend of the Brooks. We spoke yesterday."

His face drooped, and he licked his lips. "Look, the boy is fine. We were never gonna hurt him." His face hardened, and he pointed at our prisoners. "Look at them! They're gonna catch pneumonia! They're standing in the snow in their bare feet! How could you animals do this?!"

"They'll be fine as long as you move quickly. We'll be on our way once Ricki is in our hands."

"And then what?"

"Then we're going to walk in that direction," I pointed toward the hillock where Zeta was hiding. "And once we get into the woods and we don't see anybody following us, we'll release them."

"Now —" Odell started to say.

"I'm not done. After that, you're going to leave us and the Brooks alone. If you ever mess with our business again, then next time, more people will get hurt. Maybe killed. Do you understand?"

Odell nodded. "Yes, I do."

"You can keep the fuel," I said.

Winston appeared from one of the small trailers,

hauling Ricki by the arm.

"Let him go," Odell said.

Winston did, giving the teenager a slight shove.

Ricki noticed us and came to a halt, looking with startled eyes. I realized he couldn't recognize us.

"Ricki, it's Phoebe," his sister said. "It's okay." She gestured to him, and Ricki ran until he was in her arms.

"Clear out people!" I yelled. "Back to your trailers! We're not leaving until you're all inside."

Odell clapped his hands. "You heard him. Come on, what are you waiting for?! Grandma and Stacy and the kids are freezing out here."

The adults moved quickly after that, returning to their trailers, leaving the truck blazing. The fire showed no signs of letting up. Already, the nearby snow had melted, turning the ground into a muddy quagmire that stank of rot.

As soon as we were alone with our prisoners, Busto said, "Let's move out."

"You animals!" Granny screamed. Like she and her family had any right to call us that. They lived in such squalor that they were little better than animals themselves. "You better crawl back to the hole where you live and hide. Because if my boys ever find you, you'll wish you'd never been born!"

I replied, "The quicker you move, the sooner you go home."

She slipped and slid on the muddy and snowy ground as we crossed the clearing while I gripped her upper arm firmly to keep her upright. We reached the edge of the woods and the foot of the hillock. After verifying that Ricki was okay and ensuring nobody was following us—easy to notice with the infrared mode of our visors—we released our prisoners.

We went up the hillock until we found Zeta. Then, we watched the prisoners to make sure they returned to safety, which they did. Each of them slipped and fell multiple times. I hoped Granny didn't break a hip.

From there, we hiked back down the mountain to the van. Ricki couldn't see a thing and we had to practically carry him out of there, especially through the roughest parts of the terrain. But he was skinny, and the suits noticeably enhanced our strength.

We made it home a little before 4 am to the overjoyed welcome of Baxter and Lynda.

By the time we made it to bed, it was past 6 am.

33

I opened my eyes and didn't recognize my surroundings. Square walls, no windows, it felt like a cell. The only illumination came from the dim red digits of a bedside clock.

Then I remembered. I was in my quarters in our base. I was still getting used to having my own room to sleep in. I also still found it strange to sleep separate from Destiny, though her sleeping quarters were beside mine.

It was 11:13 am, and I felt like a bus had run over me. I got out of bed, stripped off my pajamas and underwear, wrapped myself in a bathrobe, and grabbed a clean set of underwear and coveralls from a drawer. The synthetic cloth apparel came from the nanoforge. The coveralls were simple yet practical, and all of us had begun using them for daily wear around the base.

I opened my door and stepped into the empty hallway. No natural lighting from outside reached us underground, and the hallway lighting was still set to nighttime mode. "Hall, lights on." Full spectrum lamps embedded in the ceiling turned on. I blinked in the bright light and perambulated toward the shared bathroom and shower at the end of the corridor. The cold quartz surface of the corridor floor met my footsteps.

The living quarters, including the mess, were on level two of the base, below level one where the armory, hangar, nanoforge, workshop, and control room were located. At present, we had only three bedrooms. Zeta said that with time, as we gained tribute points, we could use those to expand the size of our crew and living quarters.

Tribute points were how the Collective Dominion's Ministry of War tracked the fighting record of insurgent warship crews who they supported. Whenever we completed a mission goal or destroyed Kergan capabilities, we were awarded tribute points that could later be exchanged for hull or base upgrades, better technology, or to increase the number of crew under my command.

We hadn't earned any tribute points yet because we hadn't engaged the Kergans. It was too bad our little mission last night to rescue Ricki didn't count for something. It had been an excellent experience for my team. Not only had we come out of it unhurt, but we'd gained experience and become more comfortable working with each other. At least that's how I felt. I hoped my friends thought the same.

I luxuriated under the shower's hot water. After months without access to a bath or shower, I was still becoming accustomed to having our own bathroom and shower, which I could use whenever I wanted. The advantage of having a fusion plant and deep wells was that we'd never lack fresh, hot water.

Was I really going to take my crew into battle against the Kergans? We were now as safe as we would ever be. With Zeta's help, Destiny and I had obtained what we'd always sought: reliable security, shelter, and food.

It seemed to me that going out to fight the Kergans

would threaten all of that. But I'd made a promise to Zeta. As the consort of a Heliacal Templar, I was obliged to use her help to fight for humanity's freedom. If I didn't, the consortship would be terminated, Destiny and I would be thrown out, and we'd be on our own again.

I turned off the water and toweled myself off. After brushing my teeth and dressing, I tossed the towel in the laundry hopper and went to the base mess.

The mess was big enough for all seven of us humans to eat at the same time. Even though the Brooks had their quarters above ground, we'd become accustomed to meeting for breakfast and dinner.

As fancy as the nanoforge was, as I previously said, we knew it could not produce most kinds of food, at least not any that was edible, except for the zetamilk. Simple ingredients, such as cooking oils, sugar, salt, and flavored beverages, could be fabricated. But flour? Ice cream? Pizza? Beef? The nanoforge failed horribly with these. Zeta said that I could assign somebody to learn how to program the nanoforge. But we had nobody to spare at the moment.

So, we continued to make trips into Wolf Jaw, carrying trade goods to exchange for food and other supplies that we couldn't easily fabricate.

The mess was empty. I must have missed breakfast, and nobody bothered to wake me up. But there was fresh coffee. I poured myself a cup. It was brewed from beans we'd purchased in town, so it tasted decent.

I prepared a plate of biscuits and bacon I found stored in the fridge and carried it with my coffee upstairs, where the rest of my people likely were.

I found Busto and Destiny sitting in the control room chatting.

"Sleepyhead is up," Destiny scolded me when I walked

in.

"Sorry," I said. "You should have woken me."

"And let you know what we were doing? Dude, you're such a slave driver that the only time we can chill is when you're sleeping."

I knew she was just giving me a hard time. "I'll remember that the next time you ask me to watch a movie." I sat in a spare chair and dug into my food.

She snorted. "As if we've seen any movies recently. Do you think Zeta can build us some kind of rec room with movies, video games, and stuff like that?"

"I don't know. You should ask her." The bacon was crisp and thick, just the way I liked it. Steaming white gravy dripped off my biscuits. "What's the plan for today?" I said.

"I don't know, boss," Busto said. "Our late-night operation threw our schedule out of whack."

"How's Ricki?"

"Seems fine. He said the Pattons mostly ignored him, though they did feed him a little."

"How did *we* do?" I asked him.

Busto propped a foot on the leg of Destiny's chair and leaned back. He yawned. "There's a lot of things that could have gone wrong that didn't. I'll just say that."

"Always the pessimist."

"We kicked ass, is what we did," Destiny said.

Busto guffawed. "Against unarmed men who were distracted by a raging fire, and old women and children." He pointed a finger at her. "I dare you to try what we did against that same compound when it's defended by trained Kergan soldiers who are expecting us."

Destiny glared at him. "I'll remind you that I took down the only armed man last night."

"There were actually two," I said. "I fired a shot over the

head of a guy with a shotgun."

"I know," Gunny said. "And you both did good. Excellent reaction times. But it was still nothing like the experience of facing actual Kergan soldiers."

"Gunny has a point," I said as I shoved a fork full of biscuits into my mouth and washed it down with a gulp of hot coffee. "We had surprise on our side and the advantage of equipment."

"Which reminds me," Busto said. "I'm meeting with Zeta in a few minutes to evaluate some potential upgrades to our small arms."

"Good." I looked at Destiny. "And you?"

"I'm making a supply run into town," she said. "Then I'm gonna stop by and see Aunt Judith."

I still hadn't had the opportunity to meet Destiny's aunt. "I'll come with you," I said.

"Sure."

"Let me just check in with Zeta really quick to see how she's doin' with the ship construction."

Destiny nodded. After breakfast, I took my dirty dishes to the mess and then went to find Zeta.

The cavernous hangar smelled of hot metal and ozone. The glossy cream quartz walls measured 70 ft square and 20 ft high. A trail of slimy nanobots streamed along the floor from the nanoforge to a hunk of metal that seemed to be growing out of the quartz floor.

I found Zeta floating nearby as she supervised the construction of our ship.

"Hey, Zeta," I said. "Do you ever rest?"

"Hello, Consort," she said. "Zeta does not require recuperative periods like humans do."

I wondered if other ignas were like Zeta. Sometimes, I

forgot that she was a living biological being, like me, not a machine.

I studied the objects on the hangar floor. Tendrils of nanobots almost wholly covered them, making it difficult to make out the shapes. I thought I recognized metal plates joined together in the shape of a lower ship hull.

"How's the ship going?"

"It is progressing well. The specialized construction nanobots Zeta required have been primed. Zeta predicts the cockpit will be completed by tomorrow. That is if Gunny Busto's request for new small arms doesn't impede progress."

"I understand your concern with the schedule. But give him all the help he asks for. It's important. We need to look after our security."

"Aye, but the sooner we have the cockpit, the sooner Zeta can begin training your crew for your intended missions."

I'd never flown in anything before and not even been a passenger on an airplane. And now I was going to learn how to pilot a starship. In picking me, the Dominion proved to have some strange selection criteria.

"Do you need anything?" I felt guilty about leaving so much work falling on Zeta.

"Nay, but thank you for asking, lad."

I knew the best thing I could do for Zeta was keep people out of her hair so she could work. But we needed those new small arms. Our current weapons couldn't penetrate our own tactical armor, which meant that they'd likely be unable to kill armored Kergans. Until we had that capability, our security was impaired. I kept thinking about the glimpses of black flying objects spying on us. I needed us to be prepared.

"Lad, Zeta has something else to show you," Zeta said.

"Sure."

"Come along." She floated out of the hangar toward the nanoforge, and I followed. We stopped in front of a closet in the corridor that was empty as far as I knew. "Open it."

I did and found a small walk-in closet with empty shelves. No, not entirely empty. I entered and found a shallow box filled with stacks of yellow bars and disks on a back shelf. I touched them. They were hard and cold. Metal. "What are these?" I picked up one of the bars, which was more like a chip than a bar, about the size of my thumbnail, but heavy. It had the image of a swan engraved on the front surrounded by the words, *The Perth Mint*. Below that was stamped *99.99% PURE GOLD 1 GRAM*. "Where did you get these?"

"Zeta has been extracting small quantities of gold from the spoil, knowing its monetary value to humans. She fabricated bars and coins to be used as currency in case it's ever needed."

"But this looks exactly like a gold bar from the Perth Mint." My eyebrows shot up. "You counterfeited their product?"

"It was easy enough, and this way, they'll be easier to sell if needed." She floated over my shoulder and nudged the box. "Look. Zeta has also made copies of 1-ounce American Gold Eagles."

I looked. The yellow disks were actually coins about the size of a quarter with the image of a goddess on the front. They were stamped with the date 2013. I'd never held a Gold Eagle before, but I knew it contained one troy ounce of pure gold. Each was worth many hundreds of thousands of dollars in that post-hyperinflation era. In truth, they were nearly priceless.

I picked them up and counted. There were twenty-six Gold Eagles and 203 Perth bars. "We need to lock this closet up."

"A wise decision, consort. I will secure this room if that is your wish."

"Do it. And don't tell anybody else about these. I'll tell the others once we decide what to do with them."

"As you wish."

Compared to an armed starship, the gold wasn't worth all that much. But it was hard currency with a solid value that we could use if someday we needed to carry something small around with high value. It might be wise if each of us carried a little gold around as an emergency source of funds. I'd need to think about it.

"What about other precious metals? What else have you mined?" I said.

Zeta spun on her axis. "I have also accumulated small reserves of silver, platinum, and palladium."

"See about converting those into bars and coins also."

"Yes, consort."

"Zeta, this was a good decision. Thank you for taking the initiative."

"You are most welcome, lad."

34

We found Destiny's Aunt Judith and Cousin Earline at home and doing fine. Judith was a black woman in her early fifties, thin and petite, like Earline and Destiny. Her eyes were fiery, and her back was straight. She shook my hand and wouldn't let go but instead gripped my forearm with her other hand. "Is this him?" she asked Destiny.

"Yes, Auntie, this is Kory," Destiny said.

Suddenly, she released my hands and grabbed me in a tight hug. I towered over her and must have weighed twice as much as her, but her arms felt like a vice. "Bless you, boy!" Then she kissed me on both cheeks. "God Bless you for what you've done for little Destiny!"

I blushed and patted her on the back. I didn't know what to say.

Destiny laughed. "Auntie, careful, you're going to make him pop!"

"Oh, shush you." She released me and took a step back. "All that time, you were homeless, and I couldn't imagine how you survived." She gestured to me with a hand. "But now I understand. You had this mountain of a young man looking out for you."

Destiny beamed a smile at me that melted my heart. She nodded. "That I did." She reached out and took Judith's hands, her eyes shining. "I owe him everything."

I held my hands up defensively. "Hey, we watched out for each other. Destiny's pulled me out of plenty of binds herself."

We visited with them for the next hour. Judith was a quiet woman, and most of the time together was spent with Destiny and Earline talking while Judith and I sat there. But I was at peace and didn't mind it. Just seeing Destiny happy and relaxed made the visit worthwhile. For the first time in years, it felt like we had turned a new page in our lives. Why that fact struck me at that moment and not earlier, I don't know. Maybe it was the smiles that Judith and Destiny had rewarded me with. This memory is one of my most treasured.

We returned to base in the afternoon to find that Zeta had finished fabricating new automatic rifles for us. Busto was outside testing one of them.

Getting out of the van carrying sacks full of purchases, I heard an unusual *crack, crack, crack* from the direction of our firing range. We carried the supplies down to the base mess. Then I ran back up to ground level and to the range.

When I arrived, I saw Busto aiming an unfamiliar black weapon and squeezing the trigger. Every time he did it, the weapon emitted an ear-splitting *crack* and bucked slightly. The weapon looked only somewhat like an M4 carbine. It was about the same length and had a barrel and stock, but from there, the appearance diverged.

"What is it?" I yelled so Busto could hear me through the earmuffs that protected his hearing.

He turned around, slipped one cup off his ear, and said, "What?"

"What is that?" I pointed at the weapon.

Busto smiled. "A new toy. Something Zeta made. It's an automatic flechette gun. Cover your ears and watch." He lifted the weapon to his shoulder and aimed it.

I cupped my ears with my hands.

Busto must have changed something because this time, when he pulled the trigger, instead of a single *crack*, I heard a *BRRRRRAAAP!* The trunk of a dead tree about fifty feet away disintegrated into dust, and the top fell to the ground with a crash. A sharp, sweet-smelling scent filled the air.

"Impressive," I said. "What does it do?"

Busto pushed a button on the gun, and a box dropped out of the middle. The top had an opening, and he pointed inside it at a linked chain of hundreds of darts. They were made of dark metal and had something that looked like a white plastic stub glued to the rear fins. "These are the flechettes. A battery pack shoots electricity into that white stub at the base which vaporizes it. The expanding gas pushes the flechette out the barrel at hypersonic speed."

"Hypersonic. Is that fast?"

"Yes, three times faster than the bullets from our M4s, according to Zeta. That weird smell, did you notice it?"

"Yeah, kind of sweet, like overripe fruit."

"Nitrogen oxide. The bullets move so fast through the air they make it burn."

"They burn the air?"

"Yeah."

"Wicked. But the bullets look kind of small."

"The flechettes? No, they're about the same mass as the 5.56mm ammunition we use in the M4s. It's just that they don't require a cartridge." He patted the flechette gun. "This baby uses caseless ammunition. Each magazine holds 96 rounds." He pushed the magazine back into the rifle.

"Did Zeta make any more?"

"Yeah, down in the armory. Go grab yourself one and come shoot with me."

After I found one of the newly fabricated guns and returned, we spent the next couple of hours practicing with them. Phoebe and Destiny soon joined us with the rest of the guns. We put on our tactical armor and went through our standard training drills, but this time using the flechette guns instead of the M4.

Zeta had also fabricated laser pistols, enough for all the humans to arm themselves. They were strictly short-range weapons because the atmosphere and distance quickly attenuated the laser beam. Still, at thirty yards or less, they were highly destructive weapons able to penetrate Kergan body armor and, at point-blank range, could even punch through light vehicle armor and obstructions, such as locked doors.

It was a good thing I had insisted on Zeta interrupting the fabrication of the ship to make the new small arms. My decision likely saved our lives, given what happened two days later.

35

"Waypoints are set," Destiny said from the cockpit seat to my right.

"Got it," I said. I gripped the flight controls in my clumsy fists and steered—or attempted to steer us—toward the icon on my helmet's HUD that overlapped my view of the cockpit windscreen.

We weren't actually flying. The cockpit was real enough, but the images on our display, HUDs, and through the windscreen were all simulated. We sat in the incomplete ship inside the base's cavernous hangar.

"Unknown airborne contact, range 103," Busto said. He sat in a seat behind Destiny. Zeta was strapped behind me into a special harness just for her.

We were on our second day of flight training, and it was our first exercise as an integrated crew. Previously, Zeta had given us one-on-one instruction for each of our roles. I was the pilot and ship captain. Destiny was the navigation and defensive systems officer. Busto, the sensor and offensive systems officer. Zeta, the ship engineer.

Other than Zeta, Destiny and I were complete novices, of course. Busto had some experience aboard US Navy ships employing certain parts of their weapon systems, but those skills didn't translate well over to his new role.

On my display, a gray square appeared, denoting the unknown contact. It was moving fast, perpendicular to our motion. We flew a couple thousand feet above the simulated ground. I was supposed to intercept the target and get close enough for Busto, or "Weaps," as I was supposed to call him, to get a visual ID with our optical sensors.

The vehicle started to drift to the right in a sideslip.

"Dammit!" I yelled. The ship could fly almost as well sideways as forward. It had inferior directional stability. Zeta said that was intentional because it led to outstanding maneuverability. But it also meant I still had difficulty making us fly in a straight line.

The vehicle wiggled around as I adjusted the flight controls, and I got us straightened out. Then we started dropping toward the ground. I groaned and corrected for my drift before we smacked into the simulated terrain. But by then, the contact had already passed in front of us and accelerated.

"Contact lost," Busto said a moment later.

"Continue to the patrol waypoint," Zeta said.

"Who made you boss?" I growled.

"Captain, when we are training—"

"Yeah, yeah, I know," I said. "You're the mission commander when we're training. I got it."

The simulation suddenly froze.

"Holding..." Zeta said.

"What is it?" I said.

"Zeta detects unusual activity near the base perimeter. This is not a drill."

I unstrapped from my ejection seat and hit the button to open the cockpit canopy. "I'm going to the control room to take a look," I said.

Destiny, Busto, and Zeta followed me as I ran down the corridor leading out of the hangar.

In the control room, I studied the displays that showed us a view of the base perimeter at ground level. On the display showing the road, something hulking, black, and wheeled moved slowly up it in our direction. "Kergan," I whispered. It was an armored Kergan patrol vehicle.

On another display that showed our southern forest perimeter, a matte-black ovoid aircraft flew through the air, following the edge of the road and undoubtedly shadowing the patrol vehicle. It was a blackhole. Perhaps *the* blackhole, the one I'd been spotting off and on for weeks.

"Put the base on alert," I said.

Destiny smashed her fist on a red button on the wall. A wailing tone sounded along with a strobing blue light overhead.

We ran to the armory. By the time I arrived, I'd already opened my coveralls and had them shoved down to my waist. I was stripped and naked, standing on my protomatter suit as it began covering my legs when Phoebe ran into the room and started removing her clothes.

It took us just a few minutes to get our armor on and prepare our weapons. I ran back to the control room, which, fortunately, was just a few steps down the hallway from the armory.

"Maybe they'll just keep driving down the road," Destiny said.

The Kergan ground vehicle was barely moving, creeping along at less than walking speed. The weapon turret on its roof pivoted back and forth, continuously examining the forest between us and them.

The blackhole had stopped hovering over the ground just at the southern edge of our glen. It was identical to the surveillance vehicle I'd shot down back in San Jose. I couldn't be sure, but somehow, I knew it had led the Kergan patrol vehicle to us.

"No, they're here for us," I said. "Phoebe, make sure your parents and Ricki are safe."

"They're locked up already in their panic room," she said from the doorway. She looked deadly, dressed in form-fitting black armor, cradling her flechette gun with a laser pistol strapped to her shapely hip. Like a black widow.

"Gunny, they're going to attack us," I said.

"How do you know?"

My heart thudded, and my mind raced. "I don't know, I just do. Call it a gut feeling. What do we do? We haven't ever talked about what to do if the base is attacked."

"Stay calm," Busto said. "What do you think I've been training you to do all these weeks?"

"Okay. But I don't want those Kergan to get inside this base. We meet them topside. No prisoners. No escapes. We need to kill all of them because if any of them make it back to their own base, they'll just return with reinforcements."

"Understood."

"We need to take out that aircraft first," Destiny said. "It's one of their spy bots."

"Agreed," I said. "Busto. How do you feel about that plasma cannon?" Yesterday, Zeta had introduced us to a new small arms weapon, though it was hardly small. It was a heavy weapon that fired bursts of high-velocity plasma. It was intended as an anti-material and a light anti-vehicle weapon.

"I think it's okay. You want me to use it against the spy

bot?"

"Yes. We'll cover you and keep the ground vehicle distracted."

We discussed a few more details of our plan to defend the base. Busto hauled the plasma cannon out of its storage shelf in the armory.

I checked the tactical map of my helmet HUD and was glad to see that the base control computer updated it with position information for the aircraft and ground vehicle. The Kergan armored truck was still a little down the road, moving slowly and hidden behind the trees. We could use that to our advantage.

"Let's do this!" I said.

I ran up the stairwell in the lead with Destiny and Phoebe right behind me. Busto brought up the rear, hauling the plasma cannon.

I opened the exterior door, exited, and ran for the trees on the north side of the glen, with Phoebe and Destiny following me. We kept our armor camo deactivated, waved our arms, and ensured we were visible to the scout blackhole.

Busto didn't join us. He activated his camouflage and dove into some nearby bushes.

I ran for the woods. The blackhole began to move again, coming toward us.

"Yes, just like that."

I reached the first tree and dove for cover behind it. Destiny and Phoebe dropped to the ground beside me and lay prone.

The blackhole skirted the edge of the glen, moving in a broad circle but coming in our direction. The armored truck picked up speed. A few seconds later, it appeared around the bend in the road briefly before disappearing behind the bulk

indicated it had moved to the far side of the outcrop after its colleagues were killed.

Busto's blue dot moved across the glen but further south of us, toward the road.

I gestured to Destiny and Phoebe to the north. We crept forward carefully to the northern shoulder of the outcrop. We would try to hit the truck from two directions.

Before we reached the flank, Busto said over comms, "I'm at the road and opening fire on the truck."

Moments later, bright flashes lit up the overcast sky. Dozens of small detonations sounded. Then a *braaaaap* roared from behind the outcrop.

We reached the flank. I peeked around it until the Kergan truck was in sight. It had come to a halt in the middle of the road, and its turret was aimed in Busto's direction and firing with a flechette cannon on full auto. Busto appeared to be pinned down.

"Gunny, you okay?" I said.

"Yeah. Damn cannon is ripping up my cover. I can't shoot him. My cannon didn't penetrate his armor."

"Roger. Let's try again. We'll draw his fire, then you shoot."

We opened up with long bursts of our flechette guns on the truck. Sparks flew off its armored sides, and the small viewports broke into starry patterns, but nothing seemed to penetrate.

The turret swung around and pointed at us.

"Take cover!"

I dove back around the outcrop just as rock and wood exploded, seemingly from everywhere. Something heavy hit me in the back and knocked my breath out of me.

The mini-detonations of the plasma cannon were sounding again.

After catching my breath, I got to my feet and returned to the flank. Destiny and Pheobe had left me and were already firing at the truck again, hitting it with crossfire.

A shadow moved deep in the woods to one side of Phoebe, where she was firing from the cover of a thick tree.

Without pausing to think about it, I aimed at the shadow and fired a burst of flechettes. Only after it was dead did I realize it was the third Kergan trooper. It had been trying to sneak up on our flank.

The truck's turret had stopped firing, and so had Busto, though Destiny and Phoebe continued to lay down fire. The truck began to creep backward down the road.

"I think their turret is damaged," Busto said, "but my cannon is out of ammo."

"We need to stop them," I said.

"Roger."

I swung my gun's strap over my head, hanging it on my back, and drew my laser pistol. "Cover me," I said. I didn't wait for a response and sprinted toward the moving truck.

As I approached the hulking metal vehicle, I looked for openings. Holes. Anything that would give me access to the interior.

I holstered my pistol, leaped onto the sloped frontal armor of the truck, and engaged the sticky grip on my hands and feet. I crawled up the surface, hoping nobody would shoot through the windshield at me.

I reached the roof and scrambled on my hands and knees. The turret had been turned into metal slag and charred composites. I pulled my pistol out again and aimed it at the roof.

I fired.

A blinding ray of yellow light illuminated the roof and cut straight through it. I kept my finger on the trigger and swept the pistol in a line that traced a square. At least, that's what I tried to do, but the pistol switched off when I only got past the first corner. An error message about overheating appeared on my HUD.

I didn't even know what I would do once I made the opening. Was I just going to drop through it and start shooting? What if they shot back?

A moment later, Busto appeared at the side of the truck, climbing it. "They're immobilized," he said. "One of the ladies shot out an axle."

He took out his own pistol and started where I'd left off. Between the two of us, we quickly opened a hole in the roof.

"So, who's going to—"

Before I could finish the sentence, Busto dropped through the hole with his pistol in hand. I expected explosions, screams, and angry words. Instead, silence met my ears. Ten seconds later, Busto's head popped through the hole. "They're dead."

"You killed them?"

"No, they were already dead. I think they suicided. The driver and the gunner. They're both dead."

"Why did they do that?"

"Who knows? Must be an alien thing. Maybe they're not allowed to surrender." Busto suddenly grabbed my shoulder and twisted my torso around, looking at something closely. "Holy smokes. Hold still. You're harness."

I flexed my muscles and moved my arms. I felt fine except for a mild ache in my back. "I'm okay."

"Your harness on the back is torn to shreds, and there are globs of metal sticking to it."

I remembered being hit in the back by something and being thrown to the ground. "Well, I'm fine." But I realized my suit had likely saved me from some terrible injury.

In the moment of reflection on my own health, as the adrenaline of the firefight began to taper off, I began to shake uncontrollably. "Doggone," I said. It was the only word I could get out. I'd just been in battle and had survived. And my friends and my sister were okay. We'd wiped out a Kergan patrol and would live to tell the tale.

"Take a breather, Kory," Busto said. "I'll be back in a minute."

I sat on the top of that armored Kergan truck and thought about the danger I had led my team into. I had given them orders that could have led to their deaths, and instead of calling me crazy and hiding, they had listened and obeyed, even though my commands could have killed them. Their trust in me could have been their end.

But we won the engagement. It had worked. Some god of war was smiling down upon us in that moment.

Just then, a black human pickup truck came around the bend coming from town. Here I was, sitting on a smoking Kergan patrol vehicle, with a fire burning in the woods from the downed blackhole and dead marac soldiers lying on the road.

I gathered myself into a crouch, placing the mass of the melted turret between me and the truck.

"We got company," I said over comms. "Find cover."

36

A black Ford F-250 pickup truck drove toward me at about 25 mph. The glare of diffuse sunlight on its windshield prevented me from identifying who was inside.

Could these be collaborators? The dead Kergans had come from the direction of town. Did that mean Wolf Jaw was now under the control of the Kergans?

I raised my gun and kept it aimed at the truck cab. Then I switched off my suit's camo, held my left hand up, and waved, signaling them to stop.

The truck came to a halt about 30 feet away from the Kergan vehicle. The driver's window lowered, and a head peeked out. I recognized the man. Archibald Andrews, from the Wolf Jaw police.

It was a police vehicle. I couldn't see the side of the truck, but it looked like the same one that had escorted us through town when we first drove through Wolf Jaw. I lowered my weapon. "I'm coming toward you."

I scooted to the edge of the truck roof and dropped the seven feet to the road surface.

Both doors of the pickup opened, and three people got out. Andrews from the driver's side, and from the passenger's side, a man I didn't recognize, followed by the mayor, Dora Best. All of them were armed. Andrews stood on the pavement looking at one of the dead marac troopers on the shoulder of the road.

I kept my flechette gun in the rest position, hanging from its sling. Busto, Destiny, and Phoebe hid in the trees not too far away, undoubtedly covering me. I approached Mayor Best with my hands held out and open disarmingly.

"Well, *you* look like a human," Dora said.

Dressed in my armored suit, she didn't recognize me. This was an unfortunate situation. We'd likely stopped the Kergan patrol before they could get word back to their base, but that wouldn't matter if the humans in Wolf Jaw learned of our base and reported us. "Dora, it's Kory Drake," I said and held out my hand.

She looked at it suspiciously, studying my figure and weapons, but then she took my hand. Unsmiling, with wide eyes and fingering the holstered pistol on her hip, she said, "What have you kids done here?"

"Defended ourselves," I said.

Dora and the second man walked past me so they could get a better look at the destroyed armored truck and dead maracs.

"These are the same Kergans who came through town an hour ago," the second man said.

"What did they want?" I asked.

"They wouldn't say, other than that they had business in the national forest." Dora rubbed her palms on her pants. "They ran through our checkpoints without stopping, destroyed one of the gates, and almost hurt some of our officers. They only stopped for a few seconds at One Stop."

"What for?"

"They wanted to know if there were any known insurgents in the area. I told them no. Which was the truth, as far as I knew it." Busto, Destiny, and Phoebe had walked out of the trees and stood about 40 feet away. Dora took note of them. "At least, I thought it was." Her face flushed. "What the hell have you done?"

"They were after us. We couldn't let them escape with word of our existence."

"And what is that? What are you?"

There was no way to hide what they'd already seen. And I wasn't about to make some of my fellow humans disappear. Especially not somebody like Dora, who'd always shown us kindness. "I think that should be obvious."

"Do you have any idea how much you've jeopardized my town?" Dora said, trying her best to pierce me with her icy glare. "The Kergans just lost one of their teams. They'll come looking for them. What are we supposed to do in Wolf Jaw? I've got over 5,000 people whose safety I'm responsible for, most of whom are refugees. The last thing I need is to be caught harboring guerrillas."

I shifted my gaze back and forth between Dora and Andrews. "Then walk away, forget about what you've seen here, and don't tell anybody about us. You weren't meant to see what happened."

"How could we not have?" Andrews said. "We heard cracks of gunshots, smoke, and explosions." He pointed to the burning spy bot. "You can see that column of smoke all the way from town. We came to investigate."

I kicked a pebble lying in the middle of the road. "I thought you didn't have jurisdiction out here? Why did you even come?"

"To see if there was a threat to the town."

"We eliminated that threat and no thanks to any of you. You've left us on our own out here to fend for ourselves. Just a few days ago, one of my people was kidnapped. Some help would have been nice from the police, but we knew there was no chance of that, so we took care of matters ourselves."

Andrews folded his arms. "Who was kidnapped?"

"Rikki Brooks. The Pattons took him hostage when he and his dad were out hunting."

"Is he okay?"

I moved closer to Andrews. "We recovered him. One of the Pattons was hurt, along with their ego."

Dora moved, so she stood in front of me. "I'm sorry about that, Kory, but we don't have the resources to protect the people living out here."

I held up an open palm. "That's fine by us, Mayor. But it means we also have to protect ourselves, which is what we just did. We're at war with the Kergan Empire. Humanity is. Whether you want to be or not. War was gonna come knocking on your door one of these days."

She sighed and shook her head. "So, you *are* guerrillas."

Andrews' gaze locked on the mayor. "I told you there was something fishy about them the very first day they came here. A working van, no desire to obtain food from the town, just wanting to move through it."

"I knew it, too." Dora looked at me. "But we *like* you kids. We really do. And the supplies you've generously traded to the town have been a huge help. I never suspected you were...soldiers!"

"We just want to be left alone," I said. "We wouldn't be any bother if everybody would just leave us alone." I stepped over to a dead marac and kicked it in its armored mantle. "This Kergan patrol came looking for trouble, and they found it."

"What is your group's intentions?" Dora asked.

"Like, what is our mission?"

She nodded.

"I can't talk about that, Dora. If it goes how it's supposed to, you'll never know we even exist."

"It's too late for that."

"No, it's not. If you three promise to keep our existence secret, we'll let you leave here and go about your business."

Andrews' hand dropped to his service pistol, and it looked like he was about to draw it. "Don't you dare threaten public officials!"

"We destroyed this Kergan patrol to keep word about us from getting out. I'm not gonna hurt any of you, but we can't just let you go back to town knowing you'll tell everybody about what you saw. I need guarantees!"

My three partners walked closer, with their guns at the ready, and positioned themselves to cut off the retreat of the town citizens. Busto came to my side and whispered, "What are you doing? I'm not going to stand for this."

"Just stay calm. I don't know what to do. I'm bluffing." I needed Dora, Andrews, and the second man to believe our threat.

I turned back to Dora. "But if you'll give us your word that you won't speak to anybody about us and what you saw, then we'll let you go."

None of the three of them responded immediately.

"You're not Kergan collaborators, are you?" Destiny said with her most haughty tone of voice.

Dora's face twisted in disgust. "The hell we are! We want to be left alone just as much as you do." She stomped her foot on the cold asphalt. "Damn you, kids!"

I held up a hand to signal calm. "We'll continue supplying you with fuel. Nothing has to change."

"Everything's changed! I've got a guerrilla band hiding in my backyard! But I suppose I don't have much choice, now, do I? This god damned invasion has set us back a century." She pressed her fingers into her forehead. "Yes, we'll keep this quiet. But I have conditions."

I rolled my eyes. "What?"

"You're not getting our silence for free. I've got 5,000 people to care for, and it's a mighty burden. What are you gonna do to help me with that? How much more fuel can you provide us? And what about other supplies?" She pointed at our suits and weapons. "You seem to be very well equipped."

"Let me speak with my colleagues for a moment." I gestured for my team to follow me and walked around the outcrop. "Zeta! I need you!" I called once we were out of sight of the townies.

"Aye, Consort?" Zeta said as she flew from the base entrance.

"Destiny, what do you think?" I said.

"They have no right to make demands," Destiny said. "Because they're so isolationist, we had to rescue Ricki ourselves. I'm mad at the police and the mayor. I don't want to give them anything."

Busto shifted his weight and raised a hand. "Hold on, there. These are civilian officials who are asking for our help. They're offering us increased security. I think it would be stupid of us to ignore them. It would only take one word in the ears of the Kergans to bring them down on us with a force ten times larger."

"I don't appreciate being blackmailed," Destiny said. "That's what this is. They know something about us that we want to keep secret. They're threatening to expose us unless we pay them. What's to stop them from returning in a month and demanding even more?"

The former Marine shook his head. "I don't think this is a shakedown. They truly need help in town. Haven't you seen all the refugees they have on their hands?"

"Last I checked, we hadn't signed up to become a charity service."

"Destiny," I said, "I don't think we have a choice. The honest truth is that I want to help the refugees in town. Surely, we have enough excess production capacity to make some kind of ongoing payment for their silence."

"It's a bad idea," Destiny said. "It sets a precedent we'll eventually regret."

"Listen, Mayor Best doesn't want to bring the Kergans here anymore than we do. I'm convinced the townies will protect our secret. If they become dependent on our supplies, they'll have every incentive to ensure the flow of those isn't interrupted."

"I agree," Busto said. "It'll be a symbiotic relationship. No, Destiny, I don't think this is blackmail."

"Fine, whatever. But they better not stop trading us meat at One Stop. And I want it ground and made into hamburger patties."

I sighed, but I knew I'd won her over. "Okay. I'll see what I can do." I looked at the igna. "Zeta, how much diesel can the base produce each day without interfering with our mission?"

"Give Zeta a few days to establish dedicated nanobots for the task, and we could comfortably produce 240 gallons daily."

"What about gasoline?"

"There is little difference between the two hydrocarbons. We could also easily produce methane and propane, though we must construct pressure vessels for storage."

"What about food? Could you produce large quantities of zetamilk and cooking oil? Sugar? Salt?"

"If we cut the production of fuel in half, to 120 gallons a day, then we could produce about 500 pounds of food per day, surplus to what we already produce."

"Okay. That's what the town really needs: milk, cooking oils, and sugar. They have easy access to fresh fruits and vegetables and some grains, but not that other stuff. I wish we could easily produce other high-protein foods besides the zetamilk."

"Lad, given time, we could develop that ability."

"Yes, but it doesn't help us now." I looked at my friends. "Okay, this is what we're going to offer them. 120 gallons of fuel per day and 500 pounds of food. They choose how they want everything split up between diesel, gasoline, propane, zetamilk, cooking oil, sugar, and salt. We let them come here to collect it once per week. Phoebe, can I put you in charge of organizing all of this?"

"Me?" I couldn't see her face, but her voice registered surprise.

"Yes. Gunny, Destiny, and I have our hands full training for our mission." I still hadn't told any of the Brooks family that we were building a starship. They probably still thought we were just a small band of insurgents. I didn't want to get Phoebe mixed up in it until it was necessary. And, besides, I'd noticed she was good at organizing things.

"I suppose I could if you need me, Kory."

"Yes, I need you. Remember, Wolf Jaw must still supply us with fresh produce and dried grains to feed us at the base."

"Okay, I'll try my best."

"Zeta, work with Phoebe. She'll be our liaison with the

townies."

"Yes, Consort."

We returned to Dora and the others.

"We agree," I said to the mayor. I told her what we could supply them with in exchange for their silence.

Dora's mouth hung open. "That is generous. I had no idea you were capable of so much."

"Dora, it's stretching our supplies. Let that be a sign of how much we need your silence. And understand this: if the town finds out about us, and we discover one of you three leaked it, our agreement ends."

"You have a deal. A weekly pickup of the supplies works for us."

I also obtained promises of silence from the two men. Dora and they got back into their truck and drove away.

I clapped my hands. "Okay, we need to clean up this mess before the Kergans see it." I wondered how we would make the massive armored truck disappear.

After finishing burying the marac bodies, I walked across the glen. Nanobots were digesting the armored truck and the debris from the blackhole, that being the easiest and quickest way to make them disappear.

Zeta intercepted me as I came abreast of the hangar entrance. "Consort, we must speak."

I was tired and didn't feel like talking, but I slowed and stopped, hoping this would be brief. "What is it?"

"On behalf of the Collective Dominion, Zeta congratulates you on your first victory against the Kergan Empire," Zeta said.

She was correct, of course. This was our first time as a team fighting the Kergans. And we won. "Thank you, Zeta. We couldn't have done it without you. They were tough.

Without the armor and weapons you've fabricated for us, we would have been killed or captured."

"Lad, that is the intent of the Heliacal Templars: to unite the technology of the Collective Dominion with the fighters of repressed peoples. Humans are superb fighters. Zeta carries good news."

I shifted on my feet and tilted my head up. "Oh, yeah?"

"You have earned tribute points from this victory."

I hadn't even thought of that yet. But we had defeated a Kergan unit in combat and were supposed to be rewarded for it. "Excellent. How did we do?"

"The Ministry of War has awarded you 5.5 tribute points. 2.5 points for the dead Kergans and 3 points for the destroyed vehicles."

I turned and paced slowly toward the base entrance with Zeta flying next to me. "What can we do with that?"

"It is a small quantity of points, but we could make a couple of base upgrades. For 1 point, Zeta can add a passive base perimeter defenses. For 5 points, she can make a tenfold increase in the capacity of the base power plant. You don't need it yet, but you will in the future. For 3 points, Zeta can add an automated medical bay to the base."

I thought about the difficulty we'd had taking out the armored truck. "What about improved weapons?"

"Zeta has no options that are immediately available. The least expensive upgrades are a laser point defense system for the starship and plasma grenades to supplement your small arms. Each requires 8 tribute points."

I opened the door of the stairwell and began walking down it. "How much to expand the base with three more sleeping quarters?"

"That would require an additional residential pod, which costs 6 tribute points."

I stepped into the armory, pushed my fingers into the seam between my helmet and suit, and the protomatter retreated and began flowing down my face and neck. "What's this base perimeter defense consist of?"

"An 8.3 ft fence topped by razor wire with an integrated psionic near-field emitter, motion detectors, and cameras."

"What is a psionic near-field emitter?"

"It causes psychological distress in organisms possessing nervous systems, deterring them from approaching the fence."

"So, it won't stop a full-blown Kergan attack."

"No, but that is not its purpose. The intent is to provide security against trespassers and spies."

I picked the blob of protomatter off the floor and put it away in its protective case. I slipped into my underwear and coveralls. "Okay, I've decided. Build us the perimeter defenses and the medical room."

"Very good, Consort, Zeta shall commence immediately." She turned and flew deeper into the base.

Now, we could more easily keep undesirables like the Pattons off our land. And we would have a way of dealing with medical problems. What would we have done if one of us had been injured in the firefight? Why didn't the basic version of the base not already have a medical facility? Well, at least we would have one now.

37

It looked like a giant shark.

I stood in the base hangar with Destiny. Our starship was completed. Zeta had just notified me, and Destiny and I had come immediately.

The ship's skin was a gleaming silvery gray. It was about 60 feet long and the body 20 feet wide, including the fins. The vessel had no wings, just the stubby fins.

Walking around it, I noticed differences from how a shark looked. Four fins in an X configuration were located midship, with two angled downward and the other two upward. An oblong pod was attached to the end of each fin.

At various points on the streamlined skin were clusters of small lobes. The cockpit was familiar because we'd been entering it and using it over the last week, but the rest of the ship had been hidden from view because it had been submerged in thick nodes of nanobot fabricators.

The ship rested on four delicate legs. The upper fins rose above our heads, stopping a few feet from the hangar ceiling.

There was also no tail. The body was streamlined like a shark's body, with the four fins located at the center of gravity, but the back of the ship tapered to a tailless point. There was no sign of any rocket nozzles or control surfaces.

"Where are the engines?" I asked Zeta.

"Zeta believes the lad is asking about what produces motive force?"

"Uh...yeah."

"The pods on the end of the fins are reactionless tractor engines. The chromatic battery powers them."

"What does it mean that they're reactionless?"

"In a reaction engine, such as a rocket or jet engine, some kind of matter is accelerated and ejected out the back of the engine in the opposite direction toward where the vehicle is to move. This produces an accelerating force on the vehicle.

"In these reactionless engines, they accelerate the space-time fabric surrounding them rather than matter. This produces an accelerating force without the need to expel fuel."

I rubbed my chin. "So, we don't need any fuel?"

"Indeed. Only energy."

"Sounds pretty smart."

"It is an advanced technology based on physical laws that humans were likely still several decades away from discovering."

"What's the ship made of?"

"It is constructed of crystals of doped silicon carbide, except for viewports, which are pure silicon carbide. The material provides high strength at high temperatures and is further reinforced with atomic force—"

"Yeah, yeah," Destiny said, "you guys can nerd out some other time. I want to know when we get to fly it."

"Your crew requires more training yet before you will

be ready to take the ship out."

"How much more?" I asked.

"No less than three more weeks."

I clapped my hands and rubbed the palms together. "Well, we better get at it. Where's Gunny?"

Over the next month, my crew and I underwent an intensive training regimen. We spent three hours with Gunny Busto each morning doing physical exercises and tactical drills. Next, we'd spend an hour studying spacecraft engineering under Zeta's direction. After a 30-minute lunch break, we'd spend the next nine hours with more classroom instruction and in the cockpit running through simulated scenarios.

Zeta instilled in us the importance of cross-training for each other's roles. This meant that in the event one of us became incapacitated during a flight, other crew members could seamlessly take over. As a result, both Destiny and Busto spent many hours in the pilot seat, while I took over for navigation or weapons. Our additional training hours for cross-training were a testament to our dedication and determination.

We also were required to learn Zeta's crew role as the chief engineer. This took many hours of classroom work, learning propulsion, power, and flight engineering. My lack of a high school education was telling and slowed me down.

I felt envious of how quickly Destiny and Busto learned the material while I seemed to be wallowing. As the crew commander, I thought I should set a good example of academic success. Instead, I was constantly playing catchup. I tried not to let it bother me, and Zeta was a patient teacher who never expressed worry at my slower pace. But it was embarrassing.

Why had Zeta selected me as her consort instead of Destiny or Busto? Or another one of the billions of humans living on the planet. I seemed like an odd choice. A homeless eighteen-year-old, uneducated boy wouldn't have been *my* first choice as captain of an alien warship. More like my last choice.

Nevertheless, after a month of training, I could see the improvements in myself. Not only was I in the best physical condition of my life, but I understood the ship's systems inside and out. Maybe I didn't know enough to construct one myself, and I certainly didn't understand much of the technical theory of operation, such as for the chromatic battery and the tractor pods and atomic bolsters, just to name a few. However, by the end of that month, I felt like I knew how all the important systems operated and how to tune them under different conditions to get the most out of them. It was a significant growth from where I started.

Finally, after rigorous training, we received Zeta's approval for our first flight. The anticipation was palpable as we prepared to take the ship into the blue skies. We were ready, we were prepared, and we were about to embark on an endeavor that would test our skills and our resolve.

38

"Watch your speed!" Zeta cried out over the intercom.

I pulled back on the stick axis, the one that translated into forward acceleration using the tractor pods. Pressure built up on my shoulder straps as the ship decelerated.

"Better," Zeta said. "If we are to remain silent, you must not exceed the speed of sound."

Flying the ship for real was so much more exciting than the simulations. Real forces were imposed on our bodies. The tractor pods gave us incredible maneuvering abilities, and Zeta's training over the last few months prepared me well for using them. "Yes, you've told me before. I got a little carried away, sorry."

We flew up a remote valley in the Sierra Nevada Mountain range, approaching a mountain pass. The ground around us was covered with thick snow. I brought our airspeed down to 500 knots while banking and turning to follow a curve in the valley that took us over a frozen lake.

I had to fly in a manner that kept us off Kergan and human sensors. The ship produced a tiny radar cross section and thermal signature and had active camouflage over a wide range of the EM spectrum, but exceeding the speed of sound created a multitude of pressure and density phenomena that could hypothetically be picked up by Kergan sensors if they were actively searching for us. And pushing our airspeed even higher, to hypersonic velocities, would almost guarantee we would be detected because of atmospheric ionization and thermal bloom. While we could easily accelerate to those speeds, going that fast was only to be used in emergencies or combat.

"I'm tired of calling it 'the ship,'" Destiny said. "It needs a name."

"You have a suggestion?" I said.

"*Shadowfax*."

"You want to name it after Gandalf's horse?" Busto said. By his tone of voice, I guessed he didn't favor the name.

"Busto? Do you have a suggestion?" I said.

"So, she wants a horse's name," Busto said. "Okay. How about *Mister Ed*."

Destiny turned around in her seat and gave Busto a dirty look. "You're so weird. We're not naming our warship *Mister Ed*."

I laughed. "Okay, since you guys can't agree, I'm picking. I've got one. *Thunder*."

"*Thunder*," Destiny said. "I like it."

"Then *Thunder* it is," Busto said. "Do we need to smash a bottle of champagne on the bow when we return?"

"Zeta, you okay with *Thunder*?" I said.

"Captain, Zeta's civilization does not follow the human custom of naming our ships. Humble Zeta has no preference."

"Starship *Thunder*!" I yelled. We became momentarily weightless as the newly christened *Thunder* zoomed through the mountain pass, and I steered our trajectory downward to keep us skimming close to the terrain.

Destiny yelped.

"New high-altitude contact bearing 192 by 20, range 334, FL 930," Busto said. "Designating Bravo-one-niner." The new contact's gray icon appeared on my tactical display, one of over a dozen other unidentified contacts, all lacking transponders. Almost certainly, Kergan vehicles of some type.

"When are we going to space?" I asked.

"Not yet, Captain, you require additional training," Zeta said. "And this vehicle is capable only of reaching Low Earth Orbit."

"Ah, but we're a starship. We can't call ourselves that if we can't go into space."

"Patience, Captain. Without additional upgrades, this ship lacks sufficient delta-v to do much more than a LEO orbital insertion."

"What do we need?"

"Zeta recommends an upgrade to your chromatic battery back. For 4 tribute points, she can double its capacity."

"Hey, you didn't tell me about that option when we had those points to spend."

"Zeta did not because it would have been pointless to increase the delta-v of the ship when you couldn't even fly it yet. The missions you will conduct in the near future do not require entry into space."

"Well, next time, tell me *all* of the options. I want to be fully informed before making decisions."

"Aye, Captain."

I found it still strange how Zeta called me "Consort" when we weren't on the ship and "Captain" when we were.

I wondered if it was a regulation. She also insisted on us calling each other by our ship role when we were on the ship. Destiny was Nav. Busto was Weaps. And Zeta was ChEng for Chief Engineer.

"When do we fly our first mission?" Destiny said.

"If this test flight produces no anomalies, then we can select and plan your first mission," Zeta said. "Captain, after that dry lakebed ahead of us, turn around and return to base."

"Roger, ChEng." Zeta still had command authority because this was a test and training flight.

We flew over the bone-dry salt bed of a desiccated lake somewhere in Nevada. At 500 knots and fifty feet over the ground, the flat, featureless terrain was nothing but a blur. No objects were in view, leaving me without a sense of our height above the ground, forcing me to depend entirely on my instruments for flying.

The eastern edge of the lakebed flashed below us. I banked *Thunder* steeply to the left, putting us into a tight turn that pressed us into our acceleration couches. The legs and hips of my protomatter suit squeezed against my skin and massaged my muscles, stopping blood from draining from my head under the extreme acceleration I was subjecting us to. "Woohoo!" I yelled gleefully.

Destiny groaned next to me.

After completing the turn, Busto announced yet another new unidentified contact, this time somewhere far to the east.

We weren't a starship crew yet. We'd have to earn that by actually taking our ship into space. And regardless, at that time *Thunder* could barely be called a ship. Its cramped interior provided no space for moving around. Once we were strapped into our acceleration couches, we could not move except for Zeta. She could reach a few places inside the hull from her seat, but that was because her body was much smaller than us humans.

Thunder was currently configured as a strike fighter called a Raider. Zeta had told me that the Corvette class was the next hull upgrade we could obtain. The latter was a proper starship, with the endurance for multi-day missions, possessing small cabins, a head, and an engineering space. However, we would need a whopping 250 tribute points to purchase the technology. That seemed like a long way and dozens of missions in the future.

In the meantime, we could use some of our tribute points to upgrade *Thunder*'s weapons and defensive systems. In its basic un-upgraded configuration, the Raider class possessed a magazine of four anti-ship missiles, twenty light intercept missiles, and a plasma cannon in a fixed mount in the nose. It also was equipped with passive defensive systems that used battery energy to reinforce the hull structure. One of the first upgrades I planned to purchase was the laser point defense system or LPD. I also wanted to upgrade to an expanded missile magazine and add a ventral-mounted railgun.

But first, we needed to fly our missions and succeed in them. We had to go and fight the enemy. I had never wanted to be a soldier, and I still didn't want to be one. But somehow, over these last few months, training with Zeta and my crew and watching the base and starship be built had led to me feeling a growing excitement and sense of achievement. Maybe going off into the wilderness to hide from the world wasn't the only option open to me.

The question for me was, *what am I fighting for?* Was I going to fight for me and my crew? For the Collective Dominion? Or for humanity? Was I just doing this to have a safe place to live and access cool technologies? Or was I doing this for a goal that was bigger than myself? Was I maybe doing this to honor the memory of my parents?

It was challenging to think about this when I'd spent all my life living in orphanages and on the streets. I'd always been on the guard for myself and, in the last five years, also for Destiny. Thinking about the needs of society was anathema. Society was doing just fine. We were the ones, Destiny and I, who were oppressed.

Except, now we weren't. The Kergans had caused human civilization to collapse. My crew and I were doing much better than most other humans. Was I going to selfishly hide away in the mountains and strive to protect my new family and ignore the rest of humanity? Or was I going to do something about the Kergans?

I didn't feel like I had to make this decision yet. Right now, my goal was to protect my team and ensure we had reliable shelter, food, and safety. If conducting these missions on behalf of the Collective Dominion was what I needed to do so that we continued receiving the help we had so far, then I would do it.

39

Destiny, Busto, Zeta, and I were in the armory, suiting up for our first mission. Our flight suits were the same protomatter suits we used as tactical armor, though reconfigured to better serve as spacesuits.

The armory also served as our mission briefing room. Not that we'd had any serious missions yet, but it was where we did our briefings before training.

"Your quest is to patrol the west coast airspace, intercept incoming Kergan freighters, and if the fates favor you, destroy them with your armaments," Zeta said.

It was a mission we had now simulated a dozen times. In theory, we knew what to do. But there was always a first time for any action, and this was one we hadn't yet done in real life. My heart fluttered, and my muscles felt tense.

"We're the ambushers," Destiny said.

"We're a wolf," I said.

"No, more like a jaguar," Busto said. "An ambush predator. We will go hunting, keeping silent, and when we find worthy prey, we will take it down."

"How do we know there won't be humans on these ships?" I said.

"The assumption is that Kergan merchant ships approaching Earth are crewed only by members of the Kergan Empire," Zeta said. "Dominion intelligence indicates that departing ships are heavily laden with cargo and captives, but arriving ships are empty."

"Yeah, it would be pretty bad if we murdered our own race that we're supposed to be protecting," Busto said.

"I still wish I knew for what purpose the Kergans were taking so many humans captive for," I said. "Destiny almost got taken."

"Oh, who knows," Destiny said. "Maybe if I'd stayed with them, I'd be enjoying myself right now at a resort, drinking a margarita on the beach."

I grinned. "Yeah, I hear the Kergan masseuses are the best in the galaxy. You know, because of all those arms."

"Or," Busto said, "they could be eating us."

"Way to go, Gunny," Destiny said. "You know how to keep the moment going."

Busto and I laughed.

Busto's eyebrows lifted. "But, what if I'm right? They could be eating us."

Someday, we would learn that the truth was so much worse than the Kergan maracs using us as a food source. But that's a story for another time.

With my helmet on, I walked to the base vestibule with my crew following me. We crossed it to the door on the opposite end, which led directly into the hangar.

Thunder loomed over us, filling almost the entirety of the hangar. My figure reflected in the nearly mirror-like curved surface of its hull. As I walked toward the cockpit in the bow, I brushed my hand on the surface.

We climbed into the cockpit using the protomatter nodes on the nose of the ship. These configured themselves into convenient ladders and then stowed themselves flush against the ship's skin when not in use.

I turned on my cockpit instruments as Zeta powered up the rest of the ship. *Thunder* had few moving components, so there were no noises to indicate the ship was ready to go except for some indicators on my displays. That would change as soon as we began moving.

This was a real mission. I was finally in full command. "Open hangar," I said.

"Roger," Destiny said, and her fingers flew on her invisible haptic interface, pressing what seemed to me to be imaginary buttons. But I knew that from her perspective, they were perfectly visible in her HUD, and her suit simulated the feeling of real controls under her hands as she pushed buttons and moved levers.

The *clunk* of disengaging locks sounded outside the ship, and a sliver of light appeared in the hangar ceiling above us. The gap widened as the heavy hangar door—4-foot thick quartz—lifted up above the ground and then slid to the side, exposing *Thunder* to the outside.

"The hangar and airspace are clear," Busto said after he checked our sensors.

"Launching," I replied. I pulled on the controls to accelerate us slowly in a vertical climb. *Thunder* slid out with only a few feet of space separating its furthest edges from the hangar threshold. But the ship was completely stable, and I felt no risk of losing control and hitting something.

My HUD gave me all-around visibility just by looking in the direction I wanted to see. Even straight through the floor and the rear.

Thunder rose above our hidden glen. Active camouflage was enabled, and I knew that anybody looking up at the sky in the ship's direction would see nothing but an odd warping of the air, if they even noticed that. It would look like a mirage on a hot day.

"Proceeding to patrol area," I said. I rotated *Thunder* on its vertical axis until we pointed to the northeast and accelerated forward.

The hangar door below us slid shut. From up here, the glen looked like an empty mountain valley. The hangar door and base stairwell were disguised as mounds of exposed stone. The Brooks' home was hidden mostly by the trees, and what was visible was also disguised as rocks.

Thunder flew over the Sierra Nevada Mountains, keeping low. Our patrol area was in the foothills of the western Nevada desert. It took us about 40 minutes to travel to the location. We had no potential targets on the sensors, so I brought *Thunder* in for a landing on the top of a low mountain. From there, our sensors still had a clear view of the sky, and it saved us energy and reduced the risk of detection.

We didn't wait more than ten minutes before Busto cried out, "Contact bearing 293 by 30, range 430, FL 1020. Designating Charlie-one."

A gray icon appeared on my tactical display. It was 430 nautical miles away but closing rapidly.

"They're moving fast, at Mach 19, and putting out a massive heat signature," Busto said.

"Nav, plot a silent intercept for Charlie-one," I said.

"Roger, plotting now," Destiny said.

"Weaps, tell me when you've got a visual confirmation on Charlie-one."

"Roger," Busto said.

"ChEng, how do our systems look?"

"The board is green," Zeta said.

Several waypoints appeared on my tactical display, and a virtual pipe in my HUD indicated Destiny's plotted intercept path. We needed to leave in twenty seconds if we were going to make the intercept without exceeding our stealth profile.

"I'm launching," I said. "Keep trying to get that visual, Weaps." *Thunder* leaped from the mountaintop, retracted her undercarriage, and accelerated toward her first waypoint. Charlie-one was now toward our tail and high in the sky, still hundreds of nautical miles behind us but closing fast as it re-entered the atmosphere coming down from orbit.

Destiny's intercept tract kept me at subsonic velocities right until just before the point of closest approach. At that point, we would have to decide whether to accelerate to a velocity that would permit us to follow the contact—and become visible on Kergan sensors—or abort and return to our patrol area.

My biggest concern was our intercept being countered by Kergan strike craft, possibly interceptors from orbit or the ground. Most Kergan merchant ships were unarmed.

"Captain, I've got a visual," Busto said.

An image appeared on one of my displays showing what looked like a fireball, but upon closer examination, it was a rectangular-looking ship shrouded by waves of plasma on the surfaces facing into the airstream. It looked just like the images of Kergan merchant ships Zeta had shared with us previously.

"Looks like a merchie to me," Destiny said.

"I agree," I said. "Weaps, compute a target solution. Nav, continue on this intercept course. Watch out for enemy sensor emission signatures."

"Aye aye, Captain." She laughed. "I always wanted to say that for real."

"You sound like a pirate," Busto said.

"Very funny," I said. "Now cut out the chatter. We're going into battle."

A minute later, Busto said, "I have a missile launch solution."

I looked at the image of our target again. The plasma bloom surrounding it had dissipated, though the massive ship's edges glowed orange, red, and even yellow in some spots as it radiated the heat of reentry back into the atmosphere. They were moving at Mach 4.5 now and only a few tens of nautical miles away.

"Okay, decision time," I said. "Are we doing this, or not?"

"Damn right we are," Destiny said.

"Hell yes," Busto said.

"Affirmative, Captain," Zeta said.

"I'm accelerating." I pushed the tractor pods to almost full power, and *Thunder* sprang forward, pressing me deep into the cushioning of my acceleration couch. The ship vibrated around me as it fought through Earth's atmosphere. Within moments, we had accelerated through the sound barrier, climbing nearly straight up to catch the target.

"Weaps, fire two ASMs."

"Aye, Captain."

I wondered what it would feel like when the missiles launched. We had yet to test the tubes. This would be *Thunder*'s first time firing in anger. Seconds later, the ship jumped slightly, and two black darts separated from the ship and accelerated ahead of us. The missiles also used reactionless drives, just like *Thunder*, so there was no missile rocket plume. Nevertheless, they quickly pushed up to hypersonic speeds, and soon, they glowed brightly as they plowed through the atmosphere.

"12 seconds until missile impact," Busto said.

"We're being illuminated by a search radar out of Adaven," Destiny said.

"Roger. Let me know if you see anything trying to intercept us."

"Splash!" Busto yelled.

The ship was still too far away to see with my naked eyes, but a pair of flashes in the distance indicated the missiles had hit their target.

The visual sensor showed the Kergan merchant ship billowing smoke out of its tail. It also looked like something had taken a bite out of it. But it kept on flying and began maneuvering, steering away from us and accelerating.

"They're running," Busto said. "Holy smokes, I can't believe they just ate two of our ASMs and survived."

"Hit them again, Weaps. Two more."

"Aye, sir."

Two more missiles launched from our tubes and accelerated toward the ship.

"8 seconds."

I checked the interface for *Thunder*'s plasma cannon and prepared it to fire. But, in the end, it wasn't needed. The second pair of missiles hit the ship in the tail as it tried to flee.

The merchie belched a massive fireball out its tail and debris flew off it. It started to tumble. Soon, contrails of condensed water vapor curled around it as the aerodynamic forces built up on its surfaces. The colossal vehicle began an uncontrolled plunge through the deeper portions of the atmosphere.

"I hope that doesn't hit anybody," Destiny said.

"Charlie-one is down," Busto said.

"I've got a target acquisition radar tracking us," Destiny said.

"Okay, time to get low and slow." I put *Thunder* into a steep descent and canceled all acceleration, letting natural atmospheric drag slow us down.

As we descended, we watched the cargo ship fall from the sky and hit the empty desert, producing a massive ball of flame and dust. "Whoo, yeah!" Busto yelled.

"*Thunder* has a confirmed kill!" Destiny said.

"I've got two contacts moving fast in our direction," Busto said. "It looks like we pissed them off. Range 500."

"We'll be long gone and silent by the time they catch up," I said. I pulled us out of our dive and flew us over the rolling desert hills at 550 knots, heading west.

"Captain, Zeta recommends returning to base," Zeta said.

"I know we're out of ASMs, but we still have twenty intercept missiles," I said.

"IMs will likely be ineffective against large merchant ships, and the plasma cannon is intended as a weapon of last resort."

"I suppose you're right. Plus, they know we're out here now and are alerted."

"Indeed."

"Okay, Nav, plot me a course back to home."

"Aye aye, Captain," Destiny said. I could hear the smile in her voice.

40

Back at the base, we had a celebration. It felt so good to hit back at the Kergans, even though it had only been a helpless freighter. Still, it was one less enemy ship to carry away humanity's wealth and people.

The Brooks met us inside the base mess for a feast. We prepared some venison steaks we'd had in the freezer for a week, waiting for a special occasion. Busto fried up potatoes, and I made a salad.

"The only thing we need is beer," Busto said.

"Naw, no need for that. You know how I feel about alcohol," I said.

"Captain, you're gonna cause a mutiny," he said, but with a laugh.

"You named the ship!" Phoebe said as she walked up behind me and nuzzled my neck. I felt myself blush. That girl would just not give up. Sure, she was pretty, but just not my type. I liked being friends with her, but she seemed to want more.

"It needed one," I said.

"But *Thunder*? It's kind of boring."

"No, it ain't. That's the perfect name for a warship. And it's too late, anyway. It's a done deal."

"When are you gonna let me join the crew, *Captain* Drake," she said with a hand on her hip, fluttering her long eyelashes.

"You know we don't have enough space on the ship, Phoebe. You'll have to wait until we upgrade to a bigger hull."

"But you could still train me. Couldn't you?"

"I suppose we could. What do you think, Zeta? Can we train Phoebe to operate the ship?"

"Zeta thinks that would be wise, Consort," Zeta said.

"That reminds me. Zeta, how many tribute points did we just earn?"

"You destroyed a *Loyich*-class freighter, massing 20,000 tons empty. You have earned 25 tribute points."

I threw my fist in the air triumphantly. "Hey, that isn't half bad. Not at all. Let's add the LPD system to *Thunder* and I want the grenades for our small arms stores." The additional missile tubes would have to wait until we had more tribute points.

"Aye, Consort."

Busto stepped over and faced me. "I want a man-packable anti-vehicle missile of some sort in case we run into another armored vehicle."

"How much is that?" I asked Zeta.

"Zeta believes the technology you want to unlock is the Zacir anti-armor flechette gun. 10 tribute points. Zeta warns you it is a heavy weapon that would prevent the user from carrying any other weapons except their sidearm."

"Well, if my math is correct, the LPD, grenades, and

anti-armor gun put us at 26 tribute points. More than we just earned. Sorry, Busto."

"Captain, you had a previous balance of 1.5 points, bringing your total to 26.5 tribute points. Would you like to allocate them in the way you just described?"

I looked at my teammates. "Any arguments?"

"I think we should save up until we have enough for the bigger ship," Destiny said, glancing at Phoebe.

"I understand," I said, "But we need to be able to protect ourselves. All these upgrades will make us more deadly in a fight on the ground and help us defend ourselves against intercepting fighters. That's why we didn't stay and fight more today; the missiles are the only defense we currently have against interceptors."

Destiny distributed plates. "If we had a bigger ship, it would make us harder to kill."

I finished adding the last of the ingredients to the salad. "True, but to get the bigger ship, we need to survive enough missions to earn it. And I don't think that's likely if we continue as we are."

Destiny shook her head. "It was easy enough today. We only need another ten missions like that to have enough for the Corvette."

Busto took the pan of potatoes off the stove. "They won't always be that easy. We caught that merchie by surprise. Now the Kergans know that somebody is out here."

Destiny looked at Zeta. "Aren't there supposed to be other guerrilla cells doing the same thing we are?"

Zeta spun. "Friend Destiny, this is true, but Zeta does not know the details because those are kept secret. From how unprepared the Kergan defenses were today, Zeta's humble guess is that your cell is one of the first to become operational."

"So, that means our missions are only going to become more difficult going forward," I said, thinking about how hard it would be to intercept a freighter if enemy fighters were shooting back. "I also think we got lucky today. Honestly, I'm terrified of being intercepted by a Kergan fighter."

"You are right to feel this way," Zeta said. "Kergan strike craft, especially their interceptors, are formidable."

I looked at Destiny, pointed at Zeta, and nodded. "We need better defenses. And we were lucky to take out that armored truck the way we did. If it hadn't been for Gunny on the plasma cannon, we would have been screwed."

Busto carried the bowl of potatoes over. "I got the sense that those soldiers weren't very good. I wasn't impressed by their fighting abilities."

I took the bowl from him. "Are they all like that, you think?"

Gunny wiped his hands on a towel. "We can only hope. But it doesn't seem possible. Otherwise, how did they manage to beat all the world's militaries in just a month?"

"With their technology."

This reminded me of the days right after the start of the invasion. I had always ignored the news because it was irrelevant to my life. But it was difficult to do this when American society was in a panic as our armies and navies and air forces were defeated and surrendered, one after another, all around the world.

"Some of America's military survived the invasion," Busto said. "But all those people and equipment are now owned and controlled by the Kergan military government."

"So, we could run into American weapons," I said.

"Correct. It may be an American fighter you must face in *Thunder*, like an F-22 Raptor or an F-35 Lightening."

"Zeta, can our sensors pick those up? They're stealth aircraft."

"Some of our sensors, yes," Zeta said. "It will not be a problem."

41

Zeta unlocked our new technologies and manufactured the upgrades. We spent time in the forest training with Busto on using the new grenades and anti-armor flechette gun. We made a racket, which drew more attention from the citizens of Wolf Jaw, but our new perimeter fence did its job and kept the curious away.

The town fully exploited their agreement with us for food and fuel. Every Saturday, they arrived with two trucks to load up supplies we had manufactured and stored during the week. The townies soon became accustomed to our "facility" up in the mountains. We were on friendly terms with them and could go into town whenever we wanted to and be sure of peaceful encounters.

Zeta upgraded our ship with the new LPD system. It consisted of four small laser blisters on the ship that were tied into Destiny's defensive systems console. They could engage missiles and projectiles at close range and attempt to vaporize them before they impacted us. It gave us a third level of protection above and beyond the atomically reinforced hull and the intercept missiles.

My crew spent several days training with Zeta on performing space missions. Flying in space was not like flying in the atmosphere. For one, velocities were generally a couple orders of magnitude higher. Also, vehicle control was wholly dependent on the tractor pods because there existed no atmosphere that could be manipulated by control surfaces.

Operating in space was also energy-expensive. As it was currently configured, *Thunder* had enough energy in its chromatic battery to provide up to 20 km/s of total delta-v. That was enough to get into orbit, perform some simple maneuvers, and then return from orbit without using the atmosphere for braking, i.e., avoiding atmospheric heating that Kergan sensors could detect. Because of all these expenses, going into space didn't leave much energy margin remaining for combat.

Of course, once we got into orbit, we stayed there until we returned. Theoretically, we could park the ship in orbit and remain there indefinitely, so long as we didn't expend all our energy. But *Thunder* was not equipped for long endurance flights. Not only did it have no crew sleeping quarters, but there was also no head or mess. We were all confined to our acceleration couches from the start of the flight until we returned to base.

Without question, I was proud of *Thunder*, but in its current form, it was barely worthy of being called a starship.

Zeta spent several days training us in simulation to perform operations in LEO. We also performed one test flight to qualify for the job.

"Hurray, we're astronauts!" Destiny yelled as we decelerated back into the atmosphere.

I was being careful because, as I have said, we were never supposed to allow the atmosphere to decelerate *Thunder*. After all, it produced a vast thermal signature easily detectable by the enemy. Instead, we decelerated while still in space until *Thunder* could safely enter the upper atmosphere without producing an ionized trail of gases.

"Sorry, but I doubt NASA is handing out astronaut wings anymore," Busto said.

It was a fantastic experience. We'd done two orbits of the Earth and were flying eastbound in the upper atmosphere over the central Pacific. *Thunder* faced opposite our direction of motion so I could decelerate without throwing us forward into our harnesses.

"And Weaps threw up twice. Doesn't that disqualify you?" Destiny chided.

"Shut up, Nav," Busto said. "Even astronauts sometimes vomited in space."

The three hours we'd spent in weightlessness had been enjoyable. Busto had suffered a short bout of space sickness, but Destiny and I had gotten through it with nothing worse than momentary nausea.

"Two contacts bearing 169 by -25, range 897, FL 2430. Designating Echo-one and Echo-two," Busto said. "They're descending on our same reentry track."

Though this was a training mission, *Thunder* was fully armed, and we were authorized to engage targets of opportunity. Busto had spotted potential prey below us and in front.

I reduced our deceleration to allow us to maintain a higher velocity and get a closer look at the contacts.

"Huge thermal blooms. Definitely Kergan freighters, though smaller than the one we shot down. Putting them on visual now."

On my display appeared the box-shaped Kergan freighters. These were more cube-shaped instead of the long rectangle of the one we'd destroyed. They were descending toward the west coast of California. Destiny's navigation plots predicted they would land somewhere in Southern Utah.

"Can you visually confirm they are Kergan flagged?" I said.

"No need, Captain," Destiny said. "Their transponders are squawking, and they indicate a Kergan port as their registered base."

"Well, that's convenient. I didn't know we could pick up their transponders."

"Zeta taught me how to do it a few days ago."

"Can you plot an intercept course?"

"Aye, one moment."

"Weaps, I want to fire a pair of missiles, one at each, once we're in range."

"Aye aye, sir."

"Captain, the only intercept I can find requires us to pursue them at hypersonic velocities," Destiny said.

"Okay, hold for a moment. ChEng, how are we on energy levels?"

"Chromatic battery charge is at 47%," Zeta said.

"Okay, that will be enough. Nav, lock in that intercept." I clapped my hands. "All hands, prepare for action. We're chasing a pair of Kergan merchant ships. They're about to have a bad day."

It was quiet in the cockpit for the next several minutes as everybody busied themselves, configuring their consoles and preparing their assigned systems for battle.

"Going hypersonic," I said. I whipped *Thunder*'s nose around so it pointed in our direction of travel, then pressed the stick forward to accelerate us. I dipped the nose down to plunge us deeper into the atmosphere.

Soon, blankets of orange and yellow plasma erupted along the edges of *Thunder* that were plunging through the atmosphere. By now, we would easily be visible on Kergan sensors even from a long distance.

"I have a missile firing solution for Echo-one and Echo-two," Busto said. "We'll be within range in two minutes thirty seconds."

The thickening atmosphere began to roar against *Thunder*'s hull. Drag pushed back against the ship, obliging me to increase the power of the tractor pods to counteract it. We reached Mach 9 and were gaining rapidly on the targets.

"An early warning radar is tracking us in Hawaii, and a second smaller one from somewhere up in orbit," Destiny said.

The threat icons indicating the radars appeared on my tactical display a moment later.

"30 seconds until missile launch. Four new contacts have launched from Travis Air Force Base in California. They are on an intercept course with us. They're not a threat yet."

"Roger," I said. "Keep a close eye on them."

Our targets adjusted their course, aborting their reentry, and began to climb and accelerate. "They've seen us," I said. "They're trying to run."

"Vampire, vampire!" Destiny cried out. *Vampire* was our codeword for an enemy missile launch. "One of those freighters is armed. It just launched two ASMs, which are inbound to our position. 25 seconds until impact."

"Roger, Nav, engage them with IMs and LPDs."

Thunder jumped two times.

"ASMs away," Busto said.

A few seconds later, two smaller thuds sounded as Destiny launched a pair of intercept missiles at the approaching enemy ASMs.

"Okay, I'm going evasive," I said. I turned *Thunder* into a right-hand bank and pulled us in a curve that would present our side to the incoming missiles.

One of our IMs intercepted an enemy ASM, and they both disappeared from my tactical display. Our second IM missed and began circling, searching for its target. Its icon blanked out several seconds later after Destiny issued a self-destruct command so it wouldn't accidentally lock onto *Thunder*.

"Enemy ASM five seconds away," Destiny said. Rapid *crack-crack-crack* sounded through the hull. "LPD is firing... trash one!" A *boom* sounded, and the ship bucked. "Both enemy missiles were intercepted!" Destiny clapped her hands.

Busto called into the intercom, "Missile impact in three...two...one...BAM!"

Both ASMs we launched impacted at the same time. Echo-one broke in half from the explosion and began to disintegrate midair, becoming a long rope of debris burning up in the upper atmosphere.

Echo-two endured its hit better, staying intact, but it immediately began decelerating and went into a ballistic trajectory. Clearly, they'd lost engine power. Smoke billowed from their stern, and they began to tumble.

I steered *Thunder* toward the crippled Echo-two, wondering if I would need to strafe them with the plasma cannon. Oh, what I'd do if I had a railgun. With one of those, I could pop a hypervelocity dart into them without getting any closer.

But it proved unnecessary. Echo-two's uncontrolled

hypersonic descent into the atmosphere caused it to sustain severe damage. Pieces of the outer hull soon began peeling off, first in a trickle, then in a stream, as the ship's own forward motion squeezed it against an impenetrable wall of compressed ionized gasses.

"Echo-one and Echo-two are down," Busto said.

"Multiple airborne search radars are tracking us," Destiny said. "It's those contacts that launched from Travis."

"I see them," Busto said. "They are range 200 and closing at Mach 2. Definite hostiles. I'm designating them X-ray-one through -four."

"Should I run from them?" I said.

"I don't think we have much choice. They're between us and home," Destiny said.

"But it's four-against-one."

"Let's see what they are," Busto said. "I'll have a visual soon."

I kept our speed at Mach 4, heading east-southeast at an altitude of 65,000 feet. Chromatic battery levels were now down to 39%.

"I have visual. Four F-22 Raptors are on an intercept course with us."

"Humans!" I said.

"We don't know that," Destiny said. "There could be Kergan pilots flying them."

"Maybe," Busto said, "but my money is on them being human collaborators. Ex-Air Force pilots who are working for the Kergans now."

"We could easily outrun them," I said.

"But we'd leave our signature painted across the entire west coast leading right back to base," Destiny said. "I think we should deal with them."

"ChEng, will our ASMs perform well against human fighters?"

"That is a good question, Captain. Our ASMs are optimized for inflicting damage to large targets with low maneuverability. You should use the IMs against these fighters."

"Vampire!" Destiny called out. Then a moment later, "Vampire...vampire!"

I saw three new tiny icons on my display showing the position of the three enemy missiles.

"Nav, Enable the LPD, and shift energy to the atomic bolsters."

"Aye aye, Captain."

"Weaps, target one IM per enemy, but don't launch yet."

"Aye aye," Busto said.

"We're engaging." I decelerated *Thunder* and put us into a corkscrew dive that would end with us passing through the formation of Raptors.

The enemy Raptors responded by scattering to the four winds, cutting their speed, and turning in an attempt to get on our tail.

"Weaps, fire!"

Four brief shudders later, our intercept missiles were away, screaming into the distance after the air dominance fighters. I tried not to think about the human pilots who were likely flying those machines.

"Trash one!" Destiny said as the LPD shot down one of the enemy missiles.

Then, a few seconds later, she called, "Trash two! Brace for—"

She never finished her sentence. A fist punched me in the back, and *Thunder* entered an uncommanded left bank. My helmet smacked into the back of my seat. Somebody yelled something unintelligible. Red lights lit up one of my displays, and alarms sounded.

I sucked in a breath and forced myself to calm down and focus on one event at a time. Evidently, we'd been hit. My displays indicated damage to the lower-right fin and tractor pod, though the latter still seemed functional. In the meantime, while I was stunned, two of our missiles hit their targets, and a pair of Raptors became nothing but balls of smoke and fire.

One of the surviving Raptors was on my tale, lining up for another shot.

"ChEng, are we safe for hard maneuvering?" I asked.

"Aye, Captain. There is slight mechanical damage to one of the fins, but self-repair procedures are already underway. You are under no g-load limits."

"Roger." I pulled us into a loop, carrying us vertically, accelerating through the turn.

"Vampire!" Destiny called.

The LPD cracked in its staccato rhythm.

"Trashed!" Destiny said.

We were inside the minimum launch range for our IMs. The only weapon we had was the nose-mounted plasma cannon. Versus two F-22 Raptors. What could possibly go wrong?

I finished the half-loop, coming out of it and going in the opposite direction. The Raptor that had been on our tail passed beneath us, then entered its own loop.

I dove, pulling into another loop, but at the last second, twisted it sideways and converted Thunder's energy into a reverse turn so that we came out of it with the Raptor coming at us head-on.

In my HUD, I aligned by targeting reticule on the forward body of the Raptor—an aircraft so beautiful it almost made me cry—and squeezed off a short burst of high-velocity plasma pulses. *BRRAAAP!* The sound of the plasma cannon firing was louder than I'd expected, shaking *Thunder*'s bones.

The pulses ripped into the Raptor and tore it in half. We flashed by the debris a heartbeat later at 1200 knots closing speed.

"Vampire, vampire!" Destiny cried.

While we'd been busy dogfighting, one of the Raptors, the other—X-ray-three—had gotten himself lined up for another shot and let loose two more missiles.

"X-ray-three is running!" Busto said.

"I can't chase him. I've got to deal with these missiles," I said.

I maneuvered *Thunder* through the missile avoidance drills Zeta had taught me. These put *Thunder* through motions that maximized uncertainty in the enemy missiles' tracking logic and ensured I gave our LPDs good visibility of our pursuers.

A flash of white light erupted, followed by a small fireball far behind us. "Trash one!" Destiny said.

We still had one more missile chasing us. "Screw this." I accelerated away from it at 6 gs. "It's a human missile,"—I grunted under the strain of the forces pressing on my chest —"it's got to be on its final legs. How far can it go?"

Keeping just under Mach 3, I placed the missile on our tail. It had been launched at a long distance and below us, so it had already expended much of its energy, and its rocket motor was out of fuel. At first, it slowly gained on us, but then it fell behind, and a few seconds later, it wobbled and plunged into the sea.

Breathing a sigh of relief, I said, "Weaps, where's that last fighter?"

"He's doing Mach 2.5 and making for home. Already 50 nautical miles distant. We can hit him with an IM if you want."

"No, he's running away, and we're damaged and I want to stay silent. X-ray-three gets to live and fight another day." I turned to Destiny. "Nav, plot us a course for home."

"Aye aye, Captain."

A new set of waypoints appeared on my display a minute later, and I turned *Thunder* to follow it. It would be a leisurely 600-knot flight at 100 feet altitude for a couple of hours.

I thought about those Raptors we'd destroyed. Three of them. In their day when they were new, each had cost $100 million in old dollars—before hyperinflation hit. We'd just trashed over a third of a billion dollars in US military equipment. And I didn't care. They were defending the Kergans, who were stealing our world. They got what they deserved.

42

Our LEO training mission turned into an ambush on two Kergan freighters and a dogfight with four human fighters. Though an unplanned mission, it bagged us 30 tribute points for the two medium-sized freighters and 36 for the three fighters. We almost weren't awarded the points for the fighters because they were human craft, but Zeta convinced the Dominion War Ministry that the Raptors had been under Kergan military control attempting to counter our ambush.

I used the increased credit balance for three upgrades to *Thunder*. For 24 tribute points, a larger ASM missile magazine holding eight missiles; for 28 tribute points, a ventral-mounted railgun in place of the plasma cannon; for 12 points, I unlocked the ground attack missile—or GAM—that could be launched from our standard 1,000-pound missile tubes in place of the ASMs. The GAM could also be used against ships but was less maneuverable, had reduced range, and its warhead was larger and optimized for penetrating soil and rock on a delayed fuse.

These purchases left us with just 2.5 tribute points remaining, and I decided to save those toward our Corvette hull upgrade. The good news was that when we eventually upgraded *Thunder*'s hull, all our technology upgrades would convert to it.

Post-flight analysis of Thunder's telemetry indicated an American Sidewinder missile hit it on the lower starboard side of the hull. The missile detonated about three feet from the hull and propelled a cloud of metal rods into us. The atomic bolster did its job reinforcing the crystal matrix of the silicon-carbide hull plates, and no permanent damage was done. The experience gave me new confidence in the robustness of *Thunder*. A 20-pound bomb detonating right next to it bounced off without so much as tarnishing the ship's mirror-like hull. The jolt had caused minor internal damage, but Zeta had easily managed it and repaired it back at the base.

The Dominion-technology IMs we used were about the same size as the Sidewinder but possessed a much more potent warhead. I asked Zeta about it, and she gave me a lengthy technical description, little of which I understood, other than that the IM warhead was somehow derived from the same chromatic battery as we used for the ship's power. The warhead initiated a catastrophic discharge of its battery, which vaporized its structure and converted it into a rapidly expanding ball of superheated plasma, many more times destructive than a chemical explosive of equivalent size. Our plasma grenades worked on a similar principle, as did the explosives in the ASMs and GAMs.

If the Dominion possessed weapons with that much explosive power, then the Kergans must also. Just because we'd easily withstood a 200-pound American missile didn't mean that *Thunder* could survive the detonation of a 1,000-pound Kergan ASM.

The night after we returned from this training flight, Busto, Destiny, and I had an invitation to dine again with the Bests. The invitation had come a couple of days earlier, and we'd already accepted.

"I'm exhausted," I told Destiny as we walked down the corridor outside the base command center. "I just want to go to my quarters and crash."

"Not so fast, you stinker," she said. "We've got dinner tonight with the Bests."

I groaned. "I forgot. Why don't you and Busto go without me?"

"Uh, uh. They're your friends too. And you're our fearless leader. You're not pushing this on me, bud." She poked me in the ribs.

"I don't know. It just feels like such a letdown. A few hours ago, we were in an alien spaceship fighting the forces of evil. But now we have to go have dinner with Dora and Neal."

She stopped and rested a hand on her hip. "Kory Drake, are your britches so big now you can't bother with your neighbors?"

I felt my face flush. Destiny was right. I was letting my ego tell me my own comfort was more important than my friends. That's who the Bests were. Friends. Without them and our other acquaintances in Wolf Jaw, we would likely never have succeeded in founding this base. Even though Dora and Neal weren't essential to our team, they were still part of our lives. I had to remember that I remained the same homeless kid who I'd been just two months ago. It was pure good luck that had gotten me and Destiny this far.

"Okay, you're right," I said. "Let me go shower and change into some clean clothes."

"Okay, but I call dibs on the first shower," she said and

sprinted for the stairs leading to the lower levels.

"Oh, you..." I said and chased her, but I was smiling.

We spent the next three days resting, training, and recharging *Thunder*'s chromatic batteries. The ship carried only one battery, but we possessed two spares, which we kept fully charged—each battery took ten hours to fully charge from the base reactor—so we could rapidly swap in case we needed an emergency resupply. The same went for our missile stocks. Zeta kept the nanoforge occupied, producing additional munitions so that we always had sufficient inventory to rearm the ship multiple times in a row.

Two days after the fight with the American fighters, we received notification from the Ministry of War of our next mission.

"Consort, we shall partake of a joint operation," Zeta said. She, Busto, Destiny, and I were meeting in the base command room.

"What does that mean? Joint operation?" I asked.

"Multiple insurgent cells shall undertake a coordinated air attack on a Kergan installation. Our cell has the honor of being selected because, at this hour, we possess ground attack capabilities."

Fighting as part of a larger group of friendly ships sounded complicated. "I don't think we're ready. We've never encountered another insurgent ship before."

Zeta spun 180 degrees. "Zeta understands your reservations. But we have today and tomorrow to train for the engagement."

I glared at her. "That's all?"

"It is something."

"So, the mission is tomorrow?"

"Tomorrow night. The raid shall be conducted under the cover of night so as to impair participation by human collaborators."

I looked at Busto and Destiny. They had said nothing, but I recognized confusion in Destiny's eyes and worry in Busto's. "How many cells will be participating?" I asked.

"Four cells."

"From where?"

"That information was not provided for security reasons."

"How many ships?"

"Zeta does not know, but she presumes it is one ship per cell."

"When do we meet them?"

"We don't."

I threw up my hand. "What?! How are we supposed to coordinate?"

"Prior coordination would be wise, but for purposes of operational and cell security, there can be no contact between you and the other cells until right before the mission begins. On the battlefield, you shall be able to communicate with each other via radio, but that is all."

"This is gonna be a mess," Busto said. "One *never* conducts a mission with marines with whom one has not trained with before."

"Zeta recognizes the situation is not ideal, but these are the orders we have received," Zeta said. "Of course, Consort, as the cell leader, you could refuse the order. As insurgents, you are not within the Dominion military chain of command. However, Zeta's advice to you would be to follow these orders. Refusing them would set a bad precedent for your relationship with the Ministry of War. Up until now, they have been pleased with our results. We were one of the first cells operational within North America, and we have already conducted two successful armed raids. A decision on us participating in this operation was not arrived at lightly. It is a sign of trust in us and confidence in our abilities. And you, Consort, likewise must learn to trust Zeta's superiors."

I breathed in deeply. She was giving me a guilt trip. So typical. "I just wish we had more time to get our feet wet," I said.

"There will be more opportunities for solo missions," Zeta said. "This particular mission is against a critical facility that is—using an English metaphor—too tough of a nut to crack with one cell."

"What is it?" Busto said. "What's the facility?"

"It is an underground Kergan command and control nexus. The nexus is responsible for coordinating air and space defenses across northwestern and central North America. It is located at Malmstrom Air Force Base in the state of Montana."

I shook my head. "You want us to *attack* an Air Force Base? That's crazy! They'll launch fighters on us before we can run away!"

"This attack is part of a larger operation. Several other cells shall launch diversionary attacks on Kergan merchant traffic in the region. This will pull defenders away from the base. That is when your four cells will attack. You shall fly in at low level and silent, firing your missiles only at the last second, and then you shall flee. It shall be done using hit-and-run tactics that do not permit the enemy enough time to recall defenders."

Busto stood and folded his arms. "Something like that might work. I know we weren't an air unit, but my Marine Raider unit was well-trained at executing those types of strawman diversions to nullify defending forces. What happens to us if the diversions don't succeed?"

"Then your attack will be aborted," Zeta said.

I nodded. "So, we're gonna hit Malmstrom. I've never heard that name before. What do they do up there?"

Busto smirked. "That's a Minuteman base. Nukes. Ballistic missiles."

"Oh, my lord," Destiny said. "We're gonna bomb a base full of nukes. Surely, nothing could possibly go wrong."

I shrugged. "Bring plenty of sunscreen."

43

I piloted *Thunder* north-northeastward under the black moonless sky. My view of the outside was provided by infrared optics and low-probability-of-detection spread-spectrum synthetic aperture radar. We had just crossed from Idaho to Montana and were maintaining an airspeed of 500 knots.

In our mission briefing, I learned from Zeta that our initial rally point was east of the Highwood Mountains, about 30 miles from Malmstrom. That was where we would meet with our fellow raiders for this mission.

My tactical display indicated a high level of traffic in the North American airspace, much more than we were accustomed to seeing. That could be good if the hoped-for diversions was causing it, or bad if it was because the defenders were on alert.

Zeta had confirmed with the War Ministry that there would be four Raider-class Dominion strike craft, like ours, in the raid, each from a single insurgent cell. Supposedly, all crews in our flight were veterans of at least one successful mission. That still didn't make me feel comfortable going into a fight-to-the-death with strangers at my sides, but at least they were legit comrades in arms.

As we approached the rally point, I called out on our designated rendezvous radio frequency using an LPD spread-spectrum waveform—the only safe means of communicating when we were so close to the enemy. "This is Warlock-two calling Warlock flight, over." Warlock was the callsign our flight had been designated. Warlock-one was the flight leader. It disappointed me not to be chosen for that role. I hoped whoever was in charge didn't screw us over.

I repeated my call over the radio, but again receiving no response. We must have been the first ones to arrive. I put *Thunder* into a slow orbit around the rally point, keeping a close eye on the airspace.

A flight of two F-35 Lightnings appeared on my tactical display, taking off from Malmstrom and heading west at high speed. Then, a minute later, another contact took off from Malmstrom, also headed in the same direction but at an even higher speed.

"Look at that son of a bitch go!" Busto said over the intercom. "Check out the infrared signature on that bastard."

I looked. It showed a cylindrical craft of large size with a hollow in its base packed with weapons apertures and missile tubes. "What is it?" I asked.

"That is a Kergan armored frigate," Zeta said.

"Good grief," Destiny said. "I wouldn't want *Thunder* to meet that thing."

"That would be advisable," Zeta said in that dry tone she always used. "That warship is specifically designed to counter strike craft like *Thunder*. It carries just enough armor to resist your weapons while deploying a multitude of IM tubes."

"Well, I'm glad it's not hanging around here," I said as I watched the frigate quickly recede to the west in hot pursuit of something. "It looks like the diversions are working. But where is the rest of our flight?"

At that moment, my radio sounded with a woman's voice, "Warlock-two, this is Warlock-one. Do you copy?"

I pressed the transmit button. "Warlock-one, this is Warlock-two, I copy you. Good to hear you."

"Warlock-two, Warlock-one, I have the rest of Warlock flight in formation. Engage your combat transponder."

Over the intercom, I said, "Zeta, how do I do that? What's the combat transponder?"

"I'm on it, Captain, one moment," Zeta said. "Okay, it's engaged."

I transmitted on the radio, "Warlock-one, Warlock-two, roger, transponder is engaged."

Three blue icons appeared on my tactical display, labeled with my flight's callsigns: Warlock-one, Warlock-three, and Warlock-four. They were also orbiting the rally point. They had been here the entire time, and our sensors hadn't seen them. These Raiders really were silent ships!

"Warlock-two, Warlock-one, I've got you now. Join up on my port flank."

The combat data links had been enabled as soon as we turned on our transponders. The links enabled the sharing of telemetry and sensor data between the members of the Warlock flight. With the link came new information on my flight displays and my HUD, including visual outlines of the nearby ships.

I banked *Thunder* and climbed toward my flight, easing into a position flanking Warlock-one, placing it off our starboard bow.

The other three vehicles looked nearly identical to *Thunder*, except that none showed evidence of having the ventral-mounted railgun we'd recently installed. I wondered how they had configured their ships using their earned tribute points.

I wished we could have landed somewhere secret and met face-to-face with the other crews. The information we could share with each other might save lives and make us into more effective fighting units. I hated these cell rules that kept us out of contact with each other.

"It's good to meet all of you finally," I said over the radio.

"Warlock-two, this is Warlock-four. It's nice to meet you also," a deep male voice said.

"Warlock flight, cut the chatter," said the cold female voice of our flight leader.

Okay, be a cold witch if you must, but that doesn't mean I can't make nice with the others.

The flight continued to orbit the rally point for a couple more minutes. I wondered what was holding us up. As the flight leader, Warlock-one must have been in direct contact with our superiors, whoever those souls were.

It had been a few minutes since I'd seen the last departing units from Malmstrom. The Air Force Base was lit up like a Christmas tree on our threat sensors. Search and acquisition radars, lidar, radio traffic, the thermal signatures of hot engines, and building exhausts. The SAR was picking up reflections from ground vehicles and pedestrian traffic.

Our target, the underground nexus, was located about two miles east of the center of the base. It was a newly constructed network of bunkers installed by the Kergan to house the staff who monitored the airspace over this part of Earth.

I suspected that one of the reasons—or perhaps the only reason—we'd been selected for this mission was because we now possessed GAMs. *Thunder*'s missile magazine was loaded with eight of them, all intended for use against this target. We had only the twenty IMs for self-defense, plus our railgun and LPDs. We'd lost the plasma cannon when we installed the large railgun.

"Warlock flight, Warlock-one, the mission is go. I am proceeding to the target waypoint. Maintain formation until final approach and engage the enemy per your briefings."

Warlock-one banked hard to the left and entered a tight turn. I followed her, watching Warlock-three, who was off my starboard fins. Warlock-four trailed behind Warlock-three.

We flew around the northern edge of the Highwood Mountains, flying at 600 knots and barely 50 ft above the local terrain. We passed over a mountain lake, then raised our altitude slightly to fly over a spur of foothills projecting to the north. After leaving the foothills behind, we settled down again to fly just over broad empty fields.

As we approached the town of Shepherd Crossing, I heard over the radio, "Warlock flight, Warlock-one, move to attack formation."

This meant moving into a line-astern formation with about a quarter-mile spacing between each of us. Warlock-three and -four slowed down slightly to put distance between them and us, and I eased *Thunder* over to starboard, so I was directly astern of Warlock-one and about 30 ft higher.

"Warlock flight, Warlock-one, 20 klicks to target. Weapons free, I say again, weapons free."

We were now free to fire as soon as we had a target lock. After that, it would be a free-for-all; each ship would be responsible for defending themselves and fleeing the area.

"Weaps, how's it looking?" I said over the intercom.

"I'm acquiring the target now," Busto said. As the offensive weapon systems officer, it was his job to acquire our targets and program our GAMs.

"Nav, how's the threat display look?" I asked.

"Nothing notable," Destiny responded. "But that worries me. I know there's got to be something down there we don't know about that can hurt us."

"Understood. We'll find out soon enough. Approaching engagement range."

"Target identified," Busto said. "One moment…"

"Warlock-one is firing!" Destiny cried out.

The ship in front of us flared brightly as missiles departed her magazine at hypersonic velocities. Moments later, they impacted their assigned portion of the target, producing huge geysers of molten rock and dust.

Warning lights flashed on my threat display. Several new icons appeared.

"Vampire!" Destiny called out.

A ground-to-air missile launched from somewhere in the base and began tracking Warlock-one.

"I've got weapons lock. Permission to fire?" Busto's announcement pulled my attention away from the unfolding scene.

"Fire!" I yelled.

Thunder rocked as it released all eight of its GAMs. They roared away at Mach 6 in a beeline that connected with our assigned portion of the bunker complex. New geysers of broken soil and stone flew into the air.

"Get us out of here, Captain!" Busto said.

"Hell, I've got Kergan fighters inbound!" Destiny roared.

A pair of bright red icons appeared nearby, at a high altitude but descending fast. "Where did *those* come from?!" I said.

"They must have been hiding, just like us," she said.

I pulled *Thunder* into a tight left-hand turn and dropped closer to the ground. Then I pushed us forward with the tractor pods, accelerating up past Mach 2.

"Warlock-one has two fighters on her tail," Destiny said.

"What happened to the first missile?"

"Warlock-three's LPD took it out."

"Vampire, vampire, vampire!"

The leading Kergan fighter fired three IMs at Warlock-one. She would have only seconds to take care of them.

I altered our flight direction, so we approached Warlock-one's flight track they were attempting to escape down.

"Warlock-two, Warlock-one, maintain spacing!" the cold woman said over the radio.

I ignored her and moved us closer. I suspected Warlock-one didn't have LPDs.

"Destiny, get those missiles!" In my desperation, I forgot protocol and called her by her name. I couldn't accept one of our other crews being lost.

Flashes of white light illuminated the night like the world's brightest strobe light. "Trash one...trash two."

Our LPD burst blew up the first two enemy IMs, but we missed the third, which continued tracking and detonated near the stern of Warlock-one with a blinding flash.

More calls of "vampire" sounded on the radio from the other members of the flight. A half dozen missile icons were now in the local airspace, plus the two Kergan fighters. Destiny fired two IMs, hoping to intercept some of the enemy missiles.

I blinked the ghost of the flash out of my vision and looked again at Warlock-one. It was still flying! But its speed had dropped and entered a slow turn. They were probably dealing with damage.

"Warlock-three is down!" Destiny announced.

I hadn't even noticed the ship was in danger. "Dammit!"

"The crew ejected!"

I prayed that the crew of Warlock-three would make it to the ground safely and escape. The tactical display showed Warlock-four moving westward at Mach 5 with nothing and nobody in pursuit. *Lucky son of a gun.*

Running is what we should have been doing. It's what we were *supposed* to do. I was disobeying orders, but I refused to leave a comrade behind to die when my ship was still capable of fighting. At a rational level, I knew the Kergan fighters were dangerous, but emotionally I couldn't contemplate abandoning Warlock-one. Instead of fear, I felt swelling excitement and rage and determination unlike anything I'd felt before. At the time I didn't know it, but it was my first time being gripped by battle fever.

"We've got to get those fighters off of her tail!" I roared.

"But, Captain, our orders—" Zeta said.

"I don't care about what they say. We're not letting that ship die!" Warlock-one was doomed without our help.

I dove *Thunder* into a steep descent to gain airspeed and pushed the tractor pods to maximum acceleration, slamming and compressing us into our couches. *Thunder* rocketed forward. Then, as the ground approached, I pulled up sharply and was pleased to see the range to the two Kergan fighters closing rapidly.

"Weaps, get me IM solutions for those fighters."

"Roger, targeting Zulu-one and Zulu-two."

Over the radio, I said, "Warlock-one, Warlock-two, get out of there! Head eastward! We're engaging your tail!"

"Warlock-two, Warlock-one, negative! I say negative! You are to leave this area immediately and return to base!"

I executed a high yo-yo to bleed off airspeed, pulled to the left, and whooped when I discovered the move had placed us right on the tail of Zulu-two.

"Weaps, fire when ready," I said.

"Vampire!" Destiny called. "That one's coming at us!"

"Get it!"

Flashes of white light.

"Trashed!" She struck her instrument panel with the palm of her hand.

"Firing two!" Busto said.

Thunder vibrated as two IMs left our magazine.

"Weaps, charge the railgun!" I said. "Three-slug burst!"

White light lit up the night sky. One of our missiles disappeared, but the other tracked true and detonated off the side of Zulu-two. For the moment, the Kergan fighter continued on its course.

I brought us out of our descending turn and threw *Thunder*'s nose up to bear on Zulu-one. I thumbed a switch, and the targeting reticle for the railgun appeared on my HUD. The charging countdown decremented to three... two...one... with the reticle leading Zulu-one slightly, I squeezed the trigger.

Thunder was punched three times in the nose in rapid succession, jerking me forward against my seat straps. Bright lines of ionized air appeared between us and Zulu-one. Two railgun slugs connected with the Kergan fighter and punched clean through and out the opposite side of its hull in two huge bursts of sparks like exploding fireworks.

A moment later, Zulu-one detonated in a massive

explosion. I shoved *Thunder* into an evasive barrel roll to avoid the expanding ball of fire. *Wooomp!* The blast wave hit us and shook our ship seemingly halfway across the sky.

"Holy hell!" Destiny cried. "What were they carrying?!"

"Their chromatic battery likely suffered a short circuit," Zeta said.

"A short did that?!"

There was no time to observe the havoc we'd just unleashed. "Nav, what happened to Zulu-two?" I asked.

"It's circling. I think our missile damaged them. Warlock-one is headed eastward again at 500 knots. I've got multiple threats inbound!"

"Weaps, fire two more IMs at Zulu-two. I'll get us out of here!"

"Roger!" Busto said.

I pointed us southward and reduced our altitude, but we kept our speed up for the moment. There was no reason to go stealthy if we were about to fire more missiles.

"Firing," Busto said an agonizing ten seconds later.

Thunder vibrated. I dropped our airspeed down to 600 knots and brought us closer to the ground.

Moments later, Busto slapped his instrument panel. "We got them! Zulu-two is toast!"

I lifted my hands from the flight controls for a moment and clapped them. "Woohoo!" I reached over and clasped Destiny's left hand and held it momentarily.

The radio crackled. "Warlock-two, this is Warlock-one. Thanks for the assist. We owe you one."

"Warlock-one, Warlock-two, the drinks are on you." I chuckled. "Safe travels. I hope nobody was hurt."

"Thank you. All souls onboard are accounted for and in one piece. This is Warlock-one, signing off."

Warlock-one disengaged the combat data link, and the

icons for our comrades disappeared. We were on our own again.

Then I remembered Warlock-three. We had possibly lost comrades that night. I again hoped they'd reached the ground alive. Clearly, the diversion hadn't worked as well as it should have. It was almost like the Kergan knew something would happen at Malmstrom.

And Warlock-one *would* have been lost, too, if not for my decision to go back and help them. We'd been lucky that those two Kergan fighters had been distracted by Warlock-one. And that Zulu-one had failed to take any evasive action when I placed us on their tail. They must not have been expecting us to deploy a railgun.

On the long flight home, the adrenaline came down, and these thoughts stopped racing through my mind. We had survived a third mission and our most dangerous one yet. I put the ship on autopilot, tilted my head back, and closed my eyes for a moment.

"Zeta, any word on whether we destroyed that command nexus?" I asked.

"Nay, Captain. It will take some hours for the Dominion to perform a post-strike assessment. Zeta shall let you know once she receives the report."

Even insurgent guerrilla starship crews have to deal with bureaucracies.

44

I hated that we didn't have a dishwasher at the base. We were surrounded by all that advanced alien technology, but Zeta couldn't get the nanoforge to whip up a Maytag.

My hands were deep in sudsy water in the sink of the mess's kitchen as I worked a brush on a large pot we'd cooked pasta in. We had a rotating chore schedule, so everybody had to take turns, and tonight was my night. Seven hungry people produce a lot of dirty dishes.

While my hands were busy, my thoughts went to our last mission at Malmstrom. Zeta had received word from the Dominion Ministry of War that the target had been successfully destroyed. The field under which lay the Kergan nexus was nothing but a moonscape now, littered with dozens of giant craters and blasted rock.

Rather than being reprimanded for disobeying orders, my crew received a commendation in our record for coming to the rescue of Warlock-one. We also received 60 tribute points for the mission and 48 points for the two Kergan fighters we shot down. That put our balance of tribute points at 110.5. A lot, but, sadly, still less than half what we needed for the Corvette.

"What's the commendation worth?" I asked Zeta.

"It will increase the likelihood of your crew being selected for choice missions."

I grunted. "You mean, more likely, we'll be given the most dangerous missions."

"Consort, where does this cynicism derive from?"

"I suppose I have a problem with authority figures. I've yet to meet one who I could fully trust. They're always on the lookout for themselves, first and foremost. They don't care about my crew and me. Not as people. They only care about what we can do for them. They'll use us and abuse us until we're broken, then discard us and move on to the next crew. So, why should I care if we got a commendation? It just means we caught the attention of some big wig at the Ministry of War. I think that's a bad thing."

"You are mistaken, lad. You should feel honored by this commendation. You should feel pride in the great deeds you have wrought. The Collective Dominion nurtures its most valuable armsmen."

Zeta sounded so sincere I almost wanted to believe her. What she said made sense for a perfect world. She described a world that I would like to live in. But my life had proved that the real world didn't work that way. The strong took power and used it to benefit themselves and their friends without considering how it impacted the weak, or plain just not caring how they destroyed lives.

"Honestly, Zeta, I would rather have been awarded additional tribute points. A bonus. *That* would make me grateful."

The base intercom crackled. "Kory, Dora Best is at the gate requesting to meet with you," said Phoebe, who was on duty in the command station.

"Okay, give me a couple minutes. I'll be right there." I rinsed my hands in clean water, flicked and dried them, and walked to my quarters to grab my winter jacket.

I climbed the two levels of stairs to the surface and trudged through the snow covering the glen path. It hadn't yet been cleared of the most recent snowfall, though the hike to the gate was short.

Dora Best and a man I didn't recognize stood about 6 feet from the closed gate. Just far enough so the psionics didn't engage and drive them away.

I reached into the gate control box and commanded it to open. With the whine of electric motors, it slid to the right on rollers. Dora and the man walked through.

"Hello, Kory," Dora said with a cheerful smile. She handed me a small sack, and I took it. "I made you some oatmeal-raisin cookies."

"Oh, that was kind of you," I said, looking in the bag. There must have been two dozen. My mouth watered.

"It's my grandmother's recipe. They'll melt in your mouth, I guarantee it."

"Well, thanks. But I'm guessing you didn't drive all the way out here just to bring us cookies."

"No. I haven't been here since that...incident we won't mention. You've made some changes! This fence is new."

"Yeah, you know, after those two security events we experienced, we thought it wise to secure our perimeter. Sorry if it seems unneighborly."

She waved a hand. "No, it's fine, I understand. And where are my manners!" She gestured to the man who stood by her. An older man, short and round, with a scruffy brown beard. "This is Leonard Urbonas."

I nodded in acknowledgment. "Hi, Leonard. Kory

Drake."

"Hello, young man," Leonard said. "I've heard a lot about you and your group up here. You seem to be doing well despite everything else that's going on."

"We try our best." I looked at Dora. "What's this about?"

Dora lifted an eyebrow. "Leonard is an amateur radio operator and quite talented at it. The telephone network in Wolf Jaw has become almost unusable in recent weeks. I don't know what the Kergans are up to, but it's nearly impossible to call anybody. Leonard has devised a plan to issue table-top radio sets to a few of the town's citizens to give us some degree of long-distance communication when the phones are down."

"Sounds like an interesting idea. What's that got to do with us?" I said.

Dora nodded. "We have a transceiver set for you folks. We came to give it to you and show you how to use it."

"Mmm, okay. Sounds interesting. Let's see it."

Leonard removed his backpack, opened the top, and showed me the set he had brought. It looked like a couple of electronic boxes, cables, and dials. "The necessary antenna is in the back of Dora's SUV. We can help you install it and show you how to use it."

I wouldn't let them into the underground portion of the base. I didn't want anybody to know what we had there. Even the Brooks' home was off-limits, in my opinion. Its sophisticated construction would create uncomfortable questions, especially from somebody like Leonard, who was technical-minded.

"How about you show us here in the glen? Then we'll install it ourselves."

"Where are your shelters? Where do you sleep?" Leonard asked. Dora stood next to him, looking at me intensely.

"Oh, we keep them hidden. We've found that to be the best way to stay safe."

I wondered if Dora felt offended that we hadn't yet reciprocated with a dinner invitation for her and her husband. Surely, they were curious about what we were up to out here.

"I suppose I could show you here outdoors," the fat man said. "Do you have a table?"

"Sure, give me a minute."

I found a folding table, a couple chairs, and some power cords. Busto, Phoebe, and Ricki joined us while Destiny took over the security watch in the command center.

Leonard gave us a one-hour tutorial on ham radios, enough for us to operate this particular set. None of us were licensed, but the FCC no longer existed, so who would be checking?

By the time we finished, each of us could make and receive two-way calls with other citizens inside Wolf Jaw. Our set was assigned the callsign "Drake Glen," a name I didn't pick.

We thanked Dora and Leonard and saw them off. Then, we installed the radio set down in the command center. We assembled the 12 ft antenna on the ground above the base, and Zeta bored a hole through the roof to run power and signal cables to it.

"Dest, you're on duty. Give it a try," I said after we'd completed the job.

She turned on the transceiver, adjusted the tuning dial to the Wolf Jaw frequency, pulled the microphone toward her, tapped the transmit button, and said, "Wolf Jaw Central, this is Drake Glen. Do you copy? Over." She released the button.

We heard static coming out of the receiver. Then, a few seconds later, it popped, and a clear voice said, *"Drake Glen, this is Wolf Jaw Central. We copy, over."*

"Wolf Jaw Central, Drake Glen, copy. Please relay to the mayor that our station is on the air."

"QSL on your status and 73 from Wolf Jaw Central."

Destiny released the transmitter and laughed. "We need a cheat sheet on the wall. It's gonna take me a while to learn their radio jargon."

"I think I like this idea," I said. "Now we have an easy way to talk to the folks in Wolf Jaw without having to drive into town. Do you think your aunt has one of these?"

"I don't know. I'll have to ask."

The Kergans had thoroughly trashed humanity's telecommunications infrastructure—no wonder the supply chains were so disrupted. Nobody could talk to each other. Even the mail system was down. The only way to send letters was through private couriers, which cost a lot of money.

Americans were dying off like flies because of the disruption. The elderly, sick, infirm, and crippled had already died because the medical system was no longer able to sustain them. Pharmaceuticals were scarce. It was like living in the 19th century again. And maybe that's precisely how the Kergans wanted us to live from now on.

Dora and Neal had told us about the mass graves the town had had to dig to accommodate the hundreds of refugees that were dying each month. The supplies we'd been sending had helped, but the town could not keep up with the constant influx of new refugees who were permitted to pass the gates. There was starvation, disease, and violent crime among the refugees and their camps—malnourished children with marasmus. Cholera, typhus, and influenza killed young and old. Murder and rape were a constant threat. All the symptoms of a collapsed social order that had devolved into tribes of wild animals where the strongest fed on the weak.

The rest of humanity was becoming like us homeless people. Lacking a stable community, laws, or an effective economy. Failed private institutions. The young people were the most affected because that's who the Kergans seemed to focus on abducting. And still, nobody knew what the alien empire was doing with their captives.

Oh, there were dozens of rumors. They're used for medical experiments. No, they're taken to other worlds to be slave workers. No, to be eaten. They're hostages to keep the few remaining Earth governments faithful to their new overlords. They're being used to terraform alien worlds for the Kergans. They're *sex* workers (that was one of the weirdest rumors).

But none of these rumors seemed to be the truth. The Kergans were completely closed-lipped about it, and the Collective Dominion either didn't know or weren't talking.

45

Thunder climbed vertically at 550 knots, crossing the boundary between the troposphere and stratosphere, and continued climbing. Destiny, Busto, and I rested comfortably on our acceleration couches as our ship climbed like an elevator up and out of the atmosphere.

Our fourth combat mission was a raid on a Kergan orbital port the Empire had recently completed. The port was making it unnecessary for them to land their lumbering freighters. Instead, recently, they'd begun using smaller shuttles to move people and materials from Earth to space. Probably as a way to counter the guerrilla starship cells. There weren't many of us, and we could shoot down only so many shuttles. The number of shuttles was overwhelming us, and the small vessels were challenging to pick up with sensors, so Dominion Command had ordered us to hit freighters at the orbital port while leaving the port itself intact.

If it were up to me, I would have instead destroyed the port, but Zeta said it probably had a large human population on it.

Thunder passed the Karman line, indicating we were safely out of the atmosphere. I tilted the ship's nose down so we were level with the horizon, but kept the tractor pods pulling us up so we didn't begin falling. Then I accelerated us forward at a brisk 5 Gs. It would take us 3 minutes to reach orbital velocity at that acceleration.

"Anything on our scopes?" I groaned through the weight pressing on my chest.

"Threat displays are empty," Destiny said.

"Sensors are picking up some known orbital traffic and debris. No unknown contacts at this time," Busto said.

I didn't know why I asked them. The data they monitored was duplicated onto my tactical display. Maybe because I was worried about missing something in all the clutter of icons and curves, or perhaps because I didn't like the complete silence of being here in space where there was no atmosphere singing against *Thunder*'s hull.

"How's our thermal signature, ChEng?" I said.

"Our heatsink is active and good for the next couple of hours," Zeta said. "Vehicle surface radiation pattern matches the galactic background."

That meant we were quiet and invisible. That's why the Kergans were forced to defend important assets directly; they possessed no reliable way of seeing us coming from a distance. We could hit and run with impunity so long as we stayed quiet and always succeeded at the running part.

Thunder completed its orbital insertion maneuver, and I disengaged the tractor pods, putting us into free fall. The shell of a pistachio nut floated past my head, and I swatted it away. "Gunny Busto, clean up your trash."

"Aye aye, Captain."

The former Marine was addicted to pistachios. The food

shortages prevented him from finding new sources in town, but he somehow still had enough stashed away to leave empty shells all over.

Today, *Thunder*'s missile magazine was fully loaded with eight ASMs and twenty IMs. It would take more of them to destroy a merchant ship in orbit than on the ground or flying in the atmosphere. When in atmospheric flight, a severely damaged starship tended to tear itself apart and enter uncontrolled flight, resulting in impact with the ground and destruction of the ship.

But up here in space, you could punch a dozen large holes in a freighter, yet if critical systems weren't hit, it would keep flying. Maybe it wouldn't be able to enter the atmosphere anymore, but its crew and much of its cargo might survive.

What this meant is that we'd be lucky if we destroyed even one freighter. But space was where the sheep were gathering, so that is where we wolves had to hunt them.

Our target orbital dock was in a different orbital plane than ours. That was intentional. We wanted to make it as difficult for defenders to intercept us as possible. In planning our orbit, Destiny timed it so we would cross the dock's orbit just as they passed, giving us a *very* brief intercept window to fire our missiles. The combined closing speed would be in excess of 10 km/sec—just a blink of an eye. We would get only one shot at this.

"I have the port on sensors," Busto said. "Scanning for targets now."

"90 seconds until nearest approach," Destiny said.

"Weaps, I'm just along for the ride," I said. "This is your show."

I checked our batteries: 63%. Getting to orbit took a lot of energy, and we'd need more than half of what remained to return to Earth.

"Three freighters are docked. I have firing solutions for all three," Busto said.

"Fire all ASMs when ready. Allocation to targets is per your discretion," I said.

"Aye aye, Captain."

"Entering final run," Destiny said. "We're in the pipe. Here we go, boys!"

Our orbit had taken us over Earth's dark side. We observed the outside using infrared sensors, which rendered the surface of Earth in shades of green.

Like a movie running on fast forward, the giant spaceport appeared in the distance, racing toward us at 10 km/sec. *Thunder* shuddered as Busto ripple fired eight missiles. Then, the port whipped past us too fast to perceive any details except for some vague lumpy blurs that might have been space vessels.

"Multiple impacts!" Busto yelled.

On the display screen from the optical and thermal sensors, I saw a series of bright flashes surrounding the port, followed by quickly growing spheres of sparks exploding outward. A few seconds later, as the port grew almost too small to distinguish against Earth's background heat, an even brighter secondary flash erupted, momentarily outshining the sun.

"Something blew up!" Destiny said.

I studied my display, looking for our next scheduled orbital maneuver. In the back of my mind, I wondered if that secondary explosion had damaged the dock and what the consequence would be if that were the case.

"I've got a hostile contact on our tail!" Busto said. "Designating Whiskey-one."

"You sure it's following us?" I asked, watching my

tactical display and seeing the bright red triangle icon that had just appeared.

"Hell yes, they're accelerating at 20 gs!"

My heart skipped a beat. "How — how is that even possible?"

"Inertial dampers," Zeta said.

"Well, I want some. How do we get them for *Thunder*?"

"Only on larger ships, typically frigate-sized or larger."

The implications of her statement hit me. "Darnation! We got a big guy on our tail!" I fiddled with the configuration of my displays to get them ready for saving our asses.

"A targeting laser is painting us," Destiny said. "Can you break contact?"

"I'll try." I turned *Thunder* to face perpendicular to our orbital track and punched in maximum acceleration. We reached 10 gs, which was painful, even for short periods. How were we going to counter a ship that could pull 20 gs?!

After twenty seconds, I relaxed some of the acceleration before one of us burst a blood vessel.

"They're still painting us and closing," Destiny said.

"I've got a visual," Busto said.

A familiar shape appeared on the sensor display. The blunt flying cylinder with a hollow underneath one flat end that was stuffed with weapons and other gadgetry. "That's that Kergan frigate we saw at Malmstrom! Or one just like it!"

"Vampire, vampire!" Destiny yelled. "Two ASMs inbound. My god, they're accelerating at 100 gs! They'll be here in seconds! Firing IMs! Activating LPDs!"

Our hull shuddered, and the LPDs crackled.

This frigate had the advantage up here in space. *Thunder* was optimized for atmospheric flight. We were going to become interstellar dust if we stayed up here.

"Hold on, everybody!" I tilted *Thunder's* nose to nadir and accelerated toward Earth's surface at 10 gs. Within a few seconds, the bright glow of reentry plasma surrounded the vessel.

Thunder began to shake violently. The downward acceleration began to weaken and converted into a sideways force as we plunged into the thicker parts of the atmosphere.

"Captain, we are rapidly draining battery power to maintain the atomic bolsters!" Zeta yelled. "You must reduce velocity! I can't hold the ship together for much longer!"

I ignored her cries and watched the two ASMs that were tracking us. They turned to follow us into the atmosphere, still accelerating. One of them detonated about 10 km astern of us, the second a few seconds later at about the same distance. Maybe our IMs had hit them, but I suspected they had entered the atmosphere at too high a velocity.

"Both...missiles...trashed!" Destiny yelled, her voice barely recognizable because of the massive forces we were subjected to. By now, we must have looked like a shooting star to anybody observing our flight from the ground.

I let up on the tractor pods and applied force in our flight direction to get our speed down before we blew the bolsters and melted the hull.

But the enemy frigate was still chasing us.

We don't have a chance against that thing! I realized.

"Weaps, fire IMs at Whiskey-one!" I said. The small intercept missiles would likely not penetrate the Kergan frigate's armor, but we had to try something, and we had no ASMs left.

"Vampire, vampire!" Destiny yelled almost at the same

time as I felt a couple of our IMs leave their tubes.

Fortunately, inside the atmosphere, the enemy missiles were forced to travel much more leisurely, though they were still several times faster than human air-to-air missiles. We wouldn't have long before they impacted.

The LPDs fired continuously as I jigged and jagged *Thunder* across the sky in an attempt to confuse the missile targeting logic. Destiny also fired an IM at the enemy ASMs.

"Trash one!" Destiny said. Then a moment later, "Vampire...vampire...vampire! Blast them. How many missiles do they have?!"

I watched our missiles fly our flight path in reverse, moving toward the frigate. One of the icons blinked out when the frigate's own defenses intercepted it. Then, the other two blinked out in quick succession, long before they got anywhere close to the frigate.

"Trash two!"

That was great, but we still had another three missiles on us, and that frigate was still closing with us! It wouldn't be long before they could bring other weapons to bear upon us.

"Nav, where are we?"

"Somewhere off Southwestern Australia, over the Indian Ocean."

I had an idea. Probably a crazy one. "ChEng, can *Thunder* survive being submerged?"

"Aye, Captain, all Dominion-designed starships are rated for underwater flight."

"Why didn't you say something before!" I put *Thunder* into another steep descent, almost straight down.

"Trash three!" Destiny said.

Then, a giant kicked the ship. My helmet slammed into the canopy. Alarms whooped.

"We took a hit!" Destiny said.

"Damage to the stern orientation pods. Power converter three is destroyed," Zeta said. "Missile magazines are offline. The stern bolster is disabled. LPD-2 is down, and LPD-3 is rebooting."

"ChEng, maximum charge to the forward bolsters!" The mirror-like surface of the ocean raced up to meet us. I put on the brakes at the last second and hoped it would be enough. "Brace yourselves!" The sudden deceleration pulled me forward so forcefully that it felt like my eyeballs would pop out.

I watched the last missile chasing us, closing, knowing we couldn't survive another hit like the last one.

Thunder hit the ocean like a freight train hitting a brick wall.

I blacked out.

46

When I came to, it was pitch black in the cockpit and eerily silent.

Am I dead?

A terrible pain pierced my head, and my arms and legs felt like they'd been ripped out of their sockets. No way was I dead. It hurt too much.

"Anybody there?" I asked in a hoarse voice.

"Captain, *Thunder* is rebooting," Zeta said. "Ship power will be restored momentarily."

It was too dark to see anything. I reached my hand to the right and felt it brush up against the motionless body of Destiny. I shook her but got no response.

"Weaps?!"

A muffled groan behind me. "I'm here. Geez, boss, what did you do to us?"

"Saved us. I hope."

My instrument displays turned on. I reached up to a button above my head and turned on an interior light so I could check on Destiny.

She was unconscious, her body twisted inwardly in a way that didn't look healthy.

"Zeta has established neutral buoyancy, and we are currently stationary at 230 ft below the surface," Zeta said. "There was flooding in the stern, but Zeta has stopped it and purged the flooded spaces."

I studied my instruments and confirmed what Zeta had said. A ship schematic showed what must have been at least half the ship systems disabled or otherwise offline. "Can we still fly?"

"In a moment, Captain. Zeta is still recovering critical flight systems. She shall let you know when you can. But for the moment, though disabled, we are in no immediate danger."

I unstrapped from my acceleration couch and moved closer to Destiny. It wasn't by much because her instrument panel was in the way, but I was able to get my helmeted head down close to her chest. I could see she was breathing. I checked the suit interface on the inside of her left arm and looked at her vitals. She had high blood pressure and a fast heartbeat, oxygen saturation was a little low and dropping, and her respiration was erratic.

I shook her. "Destiny! Can you hear me?"

Her eyes fluttered open, then squeezed shut. She grimaced and tried to straighten out, so I grabbed her left arm and helped pull her straight.

"Aaagh!" she screamed.

"Did that hurt?" I asked, feeling helpless and realizing how stupid my question was.

She started to take a deep breath, then heaved like she was going to vomit. She screamed again. "Aaagh! I can't... breathe!"

I rubbed her back. "Take it easy. You just had a jolt

when we hit the water."

"No! Something's wrong! I feel a sharp pain in my chest every time I breathe, and I can't get air!" Her hands flung out, searching for something.

I grabbed one of them and squeezed. "Just give it a minute. You probably had the breath knocked out of you."

She nodded and was quiet for a minute, taking shallow breaths. But I could tell she continued to struggle.

"ChEng, are we flight ready yet?"

"No, Captain, Zeta is still working on it."

"Dest, talk to me. What hurts?"

"I feel like something is stabbing me in the right chest every time I breathe in or out," Destiny said through clenched teeth. "And I can't seem to get a decent breath of air. I feel like I'm suffocating."

"Let me see your suit controls."

She rotated her left arm so I could easily access them without leaving my seat. I rechecked her vitals. Her breathing was still erratic, O2 saturation was still falling, and she had rapid a heartbeat, and high blood pressure. I wasn't a doctor, but I knew it didn't look good.

I switched her suit interface to the air mixture controls and adjusted it to deliver pure oxygen. "Let's see if this helps."

"ChEng, we need to get out of here," I said. "We've got a wounded crewmate."

"Almost ready, Captain. Zeta is just waiting for the number 2 tractor pod to finish rebooting."

"Captain, how is she?" Busto said. I could hear the worry in the tone of his voice.

"Weaps, I suspect she has a chest injury of some kind that's affecting her breathing. We need to get her back to the base medical bay ASAP."

I'd let us hit the ocean with too much force. All of us were hurting, but in Destiny's case, something had broken. At least *Thunder* was still operational. I worried about the enemy frigate. Had they left us, or were they hanging around the area to see if we resurfaced?

With Destiny injured, she couldn't operate the navigation and defensive systems. Busto and I would have to split the tasks between us.

"Weaps, can you take over navigation?"

"Aye, sir." We all had cross-trained on each other's systems for this eventuality, and anybody could operate them from any of the couches, including the pilot controls, if needed.

"Plot us a course for home. I want it to be supersonic near sea level. Calculate the maximum speed we can travel at without expending the battery, leaving us a 5% reserve."

"Are you sure?"

"Yes. I know it increases the chances of us being detected, but only slightly. I'll risk it if it means getting Destiny back to base quickly. Just have us slow to subsonic once we make landfall over California."

"Aye, Captain. Give me a minute."

It was quiet for a while as Busto worked his instruments, doing something that probably would have required only a few seconds of Destiny's time.

"Captain, the ship is ready for flight," Zeta said.

"Okay." I turned again to Destiny. "Dest, how are you feeling?"

"A little better. It's not so hard to breathe, but my right chest is killing me. Do we have any pain meds?"

I asked Zeta. No. We didn't even have a simple first-aid kit inside the cockpit. What a stupid oversight. We needed to remedy that and also install survival kits in *Thunder* in case we ever had to eject or abandon the ship.

"Sorry, honey, we don't have any," I said. "We're gonna make a supersonic dash for home. We'll have you in the medical bay before you know it. Busto, Zeta, and I have everything under control. You just lay back, close your eyes, and try and forget about the flight."

"I'll try," she said weakly.

My heart thudded in my chest so hard it felt like it would break. My palms were clammy, my movements jerky. Looking at Destiny's pale, expressionless face filled me with more worry than I'd felt since that time one of Muffin's gangbangers had abducted her a year ago.

"Captain," Busto said, "I've worked those numbers. You can maintain a speed of Mach 4.1, and we'll have enough juice to make it back, plus a reserve."

"Okay, good job, Weaps. We'll make the passage at Mach 4," I said. "Here we go. Let's hope that frigate didn't decide to stick around, or this will be a *really* short flight."

I engaged the tractor pods, lifting us toward the water's surface. Sunshine illuminated the depths, yellow rays making a school of fish in the distance flash like a sparkler. The surface approached the windscreen, shimmering until we made contact, and *Thunder* burst through the waves, shedding water.

I placed us in a hover just over the water and let our sensors scan our surroundings. No contacts in the air or on the surface. At least that we could see. That frigate could be hiding, staying silent, just like us. But I had hoped that in hitting the ocean surface as hard as we did, that the Kergans would assume we were dead.

Sea birds glided in the air. There were scattered cumulus clouds and a stiff breeze—no sign of land.

I steered us to the northeast and accelerated. I didn't go

instantly to Mach 4 but brought our speed up gradually, keeping an eye on the threat displays, the ones that Destiny would typically be monitoring. One of our LPDs was destroyed, but Zeta had managed to get the other damaged one back up and running.

Within a few minutes, I had raised our velocity to Mach 4. We flew at a low level, as low as I felt comfortable flying. We soon left the ocean and crossed the Australian coast, flying over its barren interior. Moving this fast through the troposphere, we were leaving behind a powerful density, sonic, and thermal signature, but apparently not strong enough to warrant attention. Nobody seemed to notice us.

Destiny was asleep or unconscious, one or the other. I couldn't tell. I worried for her, but I could do nothing until we got home.

Flight distance: 15,200 km, nearly halfway around the world. Crossing the width of Australia from southwest to northeast and over the eastern edge of Papua New Guinea, then the width of the vast Pacific Ocean. Moving at Mach 4 near sea level gave us a speed of 5,000 km/hr. We made the trip in a little over three hours, and with the chromatic battery charge depleted to 6.8%. It truly boggled my mind how huge the Earth was.

When we arrived and landed in the hangar, my injured sister did not stir, even when I touched her shoulder. Nor when I squeezed her hand. She was truly unconscious.

Destiny, my dear sister, became my team's first medical emergency.

47

"Our order is for 60 gallons of diesel, 50 of gas, and 15 of propane," the man on the radio said.

"Roger, Wolf Jaw Central, I have you down for…" Phoebe repeated back the order she'd received for supplies from the mayor's office. She was on watch in the base command center, and I was hanging around and chatting with her.

She and the man on the radio were still conversing when I received a notification on the electronic tablet Zeta had provided me a few days ago.

Destiny Austin has received medical clearance and will awake momentarily.

I jumped out of my chair, tapping Phoebe on the back as I ran out of the room. "Got to go!" I hissed.

She looked back at me with raised eyebrows but quickly turned back to the receiver when a new burst of words came through.

I trotted to the medical bay on the second level but tiptoed into it when I arrived. Destiny lay sleeping in the last medical pod of the three we possessed. Her coffin-like pod was sealed with a transparent top.

She lay with eyes closed, her long, curly black hair fanning out like a halo. A thin sheet covered her nakedness, stopping at her chin, with her arms exposed. One of them was connected to an IV and other instruments.

She'd been unconscious for two days, firstly because of her injury, secondly because of the subsequent chest surgery, and thirdly to keep her sedated so her body would heal.

A minute after I arrived at her side, a chime sounded in a calm but repeating sequence.

Destiny opened her eyes.

She blinked at the bright light and raised her left hand to rub at her face.

A mechanism inside the pod clicked, the top raised with a sigh and pivoted up. One sidewall of the pod opened and hinged down, exposing her side and legs.

I grasped the hand of the arm with all the cables in it. "How do you feel?"

"Where am I?" she said with a hoarse voice.

I rubbed her knuckles under my thumb, outlining the ridges and valleys. "In the base medical bay. Are you feeling better?"

"I'm thirsty." She rubbed her eyes.

I got her a water bottle and helped her lean her head up to drink from it.

"How long have I been here?" she asked.

"What do you remember?" I replied.

She fingered the IV where it entered her arm. "I remember you driving *Thunder* into the ocean. Then I hurt my chest"—she rubbed at her right chest—"and couldn't breathe. That's the last thing I remember. We were still in the ocean."

I spread my arms out. "Well, as you can see, we made it back. You've been sleeping for two days."

"Geesh... How's *Thunder*?"

"It's fine, but don't worry about that." *Thunder* had suffered significant damage to its stern and several of its internal systems. Zeta was still busy with repairs and said the small ship would be out of commission for three more days. "The important thing is you're gonna be okay."

I heard footsteps behind me. "Look at this!" Busto cried out as he rushed in. "Our sleeping beauty is finally awake!" He stopped at my side, reached out a hand, and rubbed one of Destiny's legs.

"Why did I sleep so long?" she said.

"You had surgery," I said. "You suffered an injury called flail chest."

"Flail chest?"

"When we impacted the ocean, your harness crushed your rib cage and fractured about a half dozen of your ribs. Broke clean through them. A part of your right rib cage became detached and was interfering with your ability to breathe." I slapped my hand on the medical pod. "The pod here had to perform surgery on you to reattach the ribs and repair damage to your lungs."

Her face paled. "Sounds serious."

The truth was, she'd almost died. She'd been in a coma when we'd finally landed in the hangar. We made it home just in time to save her life. "It's behind you now. The pod says you're okay to get up and move around. But no heavy lifting or exercise for three more days."

"That's it? After it opened up my chest and put me back together, I only get to rest for three days. You guys suck!"

There was my girl. I smiled. "Your blood is flooded with

medical nanobots helping your body heal. It's another one of the Dominion magics we earned when we added the medical bay."

"Gross! I've got that goo in my veins?"

"Your kidneys will flush them out gradually over the next few weeks."

"Speaking of kidneys, I need to pee." She looked down at her barely covered body. "And where are my clothes?!" She shooed us away. "Get out of here, you guys, and give a girl some privacy."

Busto pushed closer. "Not so fast." He leaned down and kissed her on her smooth forehead. "I'm so glad you're okay, Dest."

Destiny scowled and shoved him. "Calm down, Romeo!" But when she turned her head, I noticed her lips were upturned in a pleased expression.

We used the time while Destiny was healing and *Thunder* was being repaired to work on our tactical small-unit skills.

I also spent time in the cockpit with Phoebe, training her as a crew member. She wasn't officially registered with the Dominion as a combatant, so I couldn't take her on any missions. Still, we had an understanding between us that as soon as *Thunder* was commissioned as a corvette, she would become part of the crew. I was training her to replace Destiny, who I wanted to promote to executive officer and train as an additional pilot.

Between the last two successful missions, we had built up a healthy balance of tribute points. Our balance now stood at 155.5 tribute points. But I wasn't spending them. I was saving up for the corvette upgrade. We'd reached and surpassed the halfway point.

That frigate, Whiskey-one, had scared me. I knew how

vulnerable *Thunder* was to a ship that powerful. We needed something bigger that could counter it.

I also wanted a larger crew and the ability to operate in the field for multiple days. The corvette would give us these things. It would have a hugely increased range and be easily able to reach the Moon and back, though it wouldn't have an FTL drive. We wouldn't get that until we upgraded from corvette to frigate. That was too far in the future to even plan for.

I finally altered my decision and purchased the expanded fusion power plant for just 5 points, leaving us with a balance of 150.5 tribute points. We would need it to keep the corvette fully charged because it would use a vastly greater amount of energy than the Raider-class did. Zeta was busy for several days expanding the power plant chamber and upgrading the fusion plant. In truth, we kept the old plant as is and built a second, much larger one next to it that had ten times the generation capacity.

A few days after the repairs of *Thunder* were completed, we took it into combat again. Over the course of the next two weeks, we conducted three attacks on merchant ships, two of which were successful and bagged us three more kills of large freighters and one defending Kergan fighter.

Our balance of tribute points ticked up to 244.5 points. We were just one easy mission shy of having the 250 tribute points needed to take the plunge and upgrade *Thunder*'s hull. The entire crew was buzzing with anticipation, their excitement palpable.

48

I parked *Thunder* on top of some unnamed mountain peak in northwestern Nevada. The position gave the sensors a clear horizon-to-horizon view for over fifty miles in each direction while conserving the charge in the chromatic batteries. *Thunder* sucked in data from dozens of optical, infrared, microwave, radio, magnetic, and particle sensors. We scanned the western approaches from Earth orbit into the Western and Midwestern US, looking for the movement of unescorted Kergan cargo ships.

I sat in the pilot's chair, relaxing while occasionally monitoring the status of the primary flight systems. We'd been sitting here for two hours without sighting any potential targets.

"Weaps, who was that cute thing you were sitting with last night?" I said over the intercom.

"Don't know what you're talking about, boss," Busto said.

I shook my head. "Don't give me that. The brunette with the blue eyes who was sitting right next to you after dinner with the Bests. What was her name?"

"You see?" Destiny said. "Even *he* can't keep their names straight."

"Oh, you mean Nadia," Busto said.

I laughed. "You've been making—"

Busto cut in. "Stand by. I've got two contacts in atmospheric reentry, bearing 13 by 21, range 1300, closing at 5700. Designating Alpha-one and Alpha-two."

I tapped the control of my interface, feeling the contact with the imaginary buttons through my haptic gloves. The display switched to a copy of Busto's tactical situation map. In it, he highlighted two triangles from hundreds of other known civilian contacts that *Thunder* was currently tracking.

"What are they?" I asked.

"Still too far away to get a silhouette, but their thermal bloom is massive. They're big, and they're coming in steep."

"My projections predict them landing somewhere in Nebraska or Kansas," Destiny said.

"Could be warships."

"If they are," I said, "they're big, like cruiser-sized, and I've never seen a pair of them descend into the drink like that together before. It looks to me like a small convoy of freighters."

"Empty freighters," Destiny said, "coming to rape us some more."

I thought about how close we were to earning the ship upgrade—just 5.5 more tribute points to qualify for the corvette. Destroying two Kergan freighters would easily push us over the threshold. Even one would be enough. Though I loved *Thunder* as it was, its cramped confines and small battery limited our operational endurance and firepower. I wanted more. And Destiny was likely correct;

these were Kergan merchant ships coming to Earth for another load of our minerals, crops, or, worst of all, humans. We needed to stop them.

"Weaps, compute an ASM firing solution," I said.

"Roger that," Busto said.

"Nav, plot a silent intercept."

"Roger," Destiny said.

"ChEng, we'll be departing on a pursuit in just a minute."

"Roger," Zeta said, "all systems are go. May the fates favor our blade!"

And maybe that blade would draw some blood today, I thought with a smile.

New traces plotting an intercept trajectory appeared on the tactical map. "Your intercept solution is up," Destiny said.

"Okay, folks, here we go." I grabbed the control sticks, and *Thunder* immediately responded by rising vertically from the mountain peak. I retracted the undercarriage and used the tractors to accelerate us forward at a brisk 2 gs. "Weaps, you have that firing solution yet?"

"Still working on it, Captain," Busto said with mild irritation. "They're moving at Mach 13 and are still over a thousand klicks away. It's going to be a little while yet."

"Roger." I steered us eastward, keeping us subsonic but climbing steeply. If the contacts continued on this trajectory, they would pass overhead in just a few minutes. "Weaps, do you have that silhouette yet?"

"Should be coming up in a moment...got it. Our contacts are two Kergan freighters, bulk carriers. Massive ships."

"And no escort," I said. "Any threat emitters?"

"No, Captain," Destiny said.

I paused to think. These were the biggest cargo ships we'd ever seen—bulk carriers. We insurgents had become a scourge on the Kergan merchant fleet. I had difficulty believing they'd send two ships like that in a convoy completely unescorted. "Zeta, I would think the Kergans would be sending more escorts to Earth, considering how many of their merchant ships we've destroyed in the past months."

"The Kergan Empire is currently executing several military campaigns within the galaxy," Zeta said. "Earth is a relatively low priority compared to others. The Empire's forces are spread thin. This is to your advantage, Captain."

"Sure. I just don't understand why they keep sending unarmed freighters to Earth when we just shoot them down. It doesn't seem rational. And that bothers me. They're not acting like I would."

"They aren't human, Captain."

I snorted. As if being human gave us any particular advantages over other races. "Sure, ChEng, that explains everything."

I set the flight controls on auto, released the control sticks, and stretched my arms. My right hand brushed Destiny's flight suit, and I reached out and squeezed her shoulder.

She reached up, patted my hand, and then went back to tapping at her interface.

"Weaps, anything on sensors to be worried about?" I asked.

"I've got hundreds of signatures. Almost all of it is likely human. If there is a threat, they haven't shown themselves yet."

It was quiet for a minute, and then Busto said, "Captain, I have an ASM firing solution on both contacts. Ready to fire on your command."

I took my controls back in hand again. "Prepare to release three ASMs at each contact. Fire on three... two... one... now."

Thunder thumped as the missiles were released from its dorsal tubes and accelerated away.

The ionized gasses left in the hypersonic missiles' wakes would immediately appear on Kergan threat-warning systems. We were no longer silent, so I pushed the translation stick forward and felt my body pushed back into the seat cushion as we accelerated up to hypersonic velocities.

My tactical display showed the missile tracks closing rapidly on our two contacts. Several of the missiles went wide and then circled around so that the six missiles approached their targets from different angles.

Then abruptly, a third contact appeared right on top of the trailing freighter, Alpha-one.

"New contact!" Busto yelled over the intercom. "Kergan frigate!"

A squat cylinder, looking like a stack of pancakes, with a hollow in its base from which projected weapons and instruments and other unidentified gadgets. It out-massed *Thunder* twenty times over. It was Whiskey-one! Or something just like it. An armored frigate.

"Where the hell did *they* come from!" I responded.

"We're being scanned," Destiny said. "I recognize that spectrum. That's Whiskey-one!"

"I'm designating the new contact as Whiskey-one," Busto said calmly.

"Whiskey-one is firing LPDs," Destiny said. "We are being targeted."

We couldn't stand up against this frigate. Whiskey-one

had nearly killed us the last time we encountered them. We hadn't even tried to fight them, but had run as soon as they attacked us, and still we barely escaped. Armored frigates were designed explicitly to kill ships like *Thunder*.

"Damn! Where did they come from?!" I yelled, momentarily uncertain what to do. I wanted those additional tribute points! I didn't want to run!

I watched the threat display as our missiles closed on our targets. Maybe an ASM would squeeze through and destroy one of the bulk carriers. Then, one of them blanked out as Whiskey-one's LPDs intercepted it. Then, a second disappeared.

I put *Thunder* into a tight turn away from the three-ship convoy, trying to buy us some time while I decided what to do. We needed to kill those freighters! They were our ticket to a bigger and better *Thunder!*

"Captain, Zeta looked at a recording of our millimetric radar when Whiskey-one appeared," Zeta said. "The signature of the trailing freighter increased substantially for several seconds. Evidence indicates the frigate was stored within the freighter's hold, and they launched when we fired upon them."

I groaned. "Maybe the Kergans are more clever than I thought." They'd used one of the freighters like a massive starship carrier.

The tracks of our four surviving missiles crept along on the tactical display, closing on the giant bulk carriers as those continued to decelerate through Earth's atmosphere. Then, another of the missile symbols blanked out.

"I've lost three missiles," Busto said. A moment later, he said, "There goes another."

"We can't fight a frigate," I said.

"Cautious Zeta concurs," Zeta said. "Live to fight

another day, Captain."

"All our missiles have been intercepted," Busto said. "The merchant ships are unharmed."

"We're out of here." I banked *Thunder* and depressed the nose toward the ground, then applied reverse acceleration through the tractors, quickly cutting our forward velocity to nearly zero. The crew were thrown around awkwardly as the G-forces twisted in unusual directions. Destiny groaned next to me.

"Vampire, vampire!" Destiny yelled. "Whiskey-one has released two missiles... No! Make that four! They're on an intercept trajectory with us. Those aren't normal IMs. They're huge ASMs!"

"Nav, defensive systems are released. Save us."

"Roger that," Destiny said with steel in her voice.

Now, we would really see how much our IMs and LPDs were worth. Maybe I should have invested in the larger IM magazine, but *Thunder* didn't have the volume for them and the LPDs. They would have used up a third of our upgraded ASM magazines. Yet another reason we needed the corvette.

I dove *Thunder* at the terrain below. The exterior view glowed orange as the dense atmosphere compressed. It rebelled against the Raider's aggressive velocity as it tried to punch through the air and gain time for the LPDs to eliminate the enemy missiles.

Thunder shuddered as Destiny launched four IMs at the enemy ASMs.

"Nav, let me know as soon as you take care of those missiles," I said. I would put our small ship into silent mode as soon as we stopped firing. Of course, I was assuming we would destroy those missiles. There was no alternative except for death. Undoubtedly, those were military-grade ASMs pursuing us, intended to destroy warships. Just one of them would turn us into dust.

"Roger," Destiny said.

"Captain, I've got an ASM firing solution on that frigate," Busto said. "Should I fire?"

I thought about it. Our missiles were unlikely to get through unless we released our entire magazine, which I didn't want to do. We still had two ASMs left and sixteen IMs. We might need them. But maybe we could distract them and buy us a few seconds. "Fire the remaining ASMs. At your discretion."

One of the enemy ASMs disappeared when an IM hit it. Then, a second was destroyed a moment later. Destiny called out the successful intercepts over the intercom.

"Firing," Busto said. With a rumble, our last two ASMs left their tubes and accelerated back along our trajectory.

A staccato clicking sounded through the bulkhead. "LPDs are firing," Destiny said. The sharp clicking continued. The battery indicator dropped slowly as the LPDs sucked our energy and poured it into the rapidly approaching enemy missiles. "One down!"

I banked hard to the left and pulled us into a tight turn, hoping to give the LPDs a better angle on the remaining missile.

"Enemy Missile will impact us in nine seconds!" Destiny yelled.

The crackling of the LPDs continued.

"Whiskey-one has eliminated both of our missiles!" Busto said.

"Three enemy missiles down!" Destiny said. "Five seconds!"

"Max power to bolsters!" I yelled.

"Roger that!" Zeta said.

"Three... two..." Destiny said.

I braced myself for impact. I don't know why. Our death would be so fast it wouldn't even register in my brain before it was vaporized.

A *crack,* then a *Bang! Thunder* rocked forward.

"Yes! Four down!" Destiny yelped.

I released the breath I had been holding. "Going silent! ChEng, rig for silent flight!"

"Roger," Zeta said. "Captain, we've suffered damage to the battery. Power reserves have dropped to just 10%."

"Understood, we'll deal with it in a moment," I said.

I pulled back on the stick, and my body was flung forward into my harness as *Thunder* rapidly decelerated.

"Active scans are off," Destiny said. "LPDs are stowed."

"Weapon apertures are sealed," Busto said.

I dropped our altitude until we practically touched the grassy plains somewhere in central Colorado. Our velocity reduced until we were moving no faster than a ground vehicle. *Thank the fates for our agility.*

"Any signs of pursuit?" I said.

"Possibly," Destiny said. "They're headed west now at Mach 2, but they're high. They must have lost us in ground clutter and are extrapolating our location."

Our power reserves were low. That near miss from the last enemy ASM had damaged something in our chromatic battery. We couldn't stay in the air much longer. We needed to get back to the base and swap batteries.

"Nav, can we make it back to base?" I asked.

"Just a moment," Destiny said. "I project that if you maintain a subsonic velocity, we would have enough power to make it back home. Flight time will be 55 minutes. Shall I plot a course?"

"Yeah. We don't have the power to hang out here and hide. Let's get home and get recharged. But keep an eye on that frigate."

"Roger."

A moment later, a new course popped up on my tactical screen. I accelerated toward it, taking care to move *Thunder* in a way that made it look like a civilian aircraft. Soon, Zeta had us emitting a valid civilian transponder to mask our true identity.

"Did any of our missiles make it through?" I said. "I lost track."

"No," Busto said. "The frigate shot them all down."

"Damn," Destiny said.

That was precisely what I was also thinking. The freighters had escaped. We'd lost out on the chance to upgrade the hull. And all of us would need to clean our soiled suits after the scare that the frigate gave us. Well, except for maybe Zeta. Did she even get scared? Ever?

"They might be following us," Destiny said. "Whiskey-one is continuing on a course that roughly parallels our own."

"Are they keeping their distance?" I said.

"Aye."

"It must be a coincidence. Surely, they don't know where we are now. We're running quiet. I'm maintaining our course. We don't have any other choice; we need to get back to base and resupply. Otherwise, we'll just be that frigate's whipping boy."

49

We slowly flew westward across Colorado, Utah, and Nevada, back to our base in Wolf Jaw, flying barely faster than a human passenger jet.

My chest clenched, and my hands shook as the adrenaline began to wear off. I put the controls on auto, leaned back my head until my helmet rested against the headrest, and closed my eyes for a moment. I was *not* ready to die for my country or humanity. Destiny and I were supposed to be living in comfort by now, but somehow, we'd allowed ourselves to get intertwined with Zeta's goals. There was that constant drive to earn more tribute points to improve our safety and standard of living. It had almost gotten us killed today.

Whiskey-one continued to parallel our course, though keeping their distance and slowly creeping ahead of us because of their higher velocity. They were also flying at 90,000 feet while we were down at 31,000 following a commercial aircraft corridor.

When we neared Wolf Jaw, Zeta disengaged our

transponder, and I put *Thunder* into a rapid descent to get us down into the Sierra Nevada Mountains surrounding the valley. I began to recognize landmarks and guided us over Huntington Lake and then around Sunset Point to descend its south slope.

"Beginning final approach," I said.

"Hangar main hatch is opening," Destiny said.

Through the canopy, I watched the rock and soil at a distant point lift out of the ground and then pivot away, revealing the maw of our base's subterranean hangar. It was broad daylight outside, but *Thunder*'s active camouflage was engaged, which should hide us from the curious eyes of anybody in Wolf Jaw who happened to be looking in this direction.

I flew *Thunder* slowly over to hover above the hangar, brought us to a stop, and then eased us down vertically through the hatch, deploying the undercarriage at the last second. We touched the hangar floor with a slight bump and bounce as the undercarriage absorbed the last of our kinetic energy.

"Shut it all down, people. Weaps, get on the base sensors, and monitor Whiskey-one."

"Roger," Busto said. "Just as soon as I use the bathroom, Captain."

I nodded and returned to the control panel I had been busy with as I checked our status. "ChEng, swap our damaged battery ASAP."

"I'm already on it, Captain," Zeta said. "I'm also reloading the missile magazines."

The canopy popped and hummed as it began to pivot up. A *clunk* reverberated through the hangar as the main hatch seated and sealed itself above us.

My shutdown tasks were completed. I lifted the

faceplate of my helmet and breathed in. I smelled ozone, hot metal, and a slight ammonia scent that must have been residual off-gassing from the hull plate seals after our hypersonic dash through the dense lower atmosphere.

I unstrapped myself and stepped out of the cockpit onto the airframe. I tapped on the hull thrice, and protomatter extruded from an orifice to form a rigid ladder leading to the floor. I climbed down the last few rungs, jumping and walking quickly to the base control room.

Grabbing a protein bar from the small fridge, I sat in front of the large situational display of the surrounding area. Busto hadn't returned yet from the bathroom, but Whiskey-one was already highlighted. It seemed to be moving toward us.

"Uh... Guys!" I yelled. Where was everybody?

I ran back to the hangar. "Zeta!"

"Here," her voice said from somewhere behind *Thunder*'s tail.

"It looks like we may have company soon. How's it going with the swap?"

"Almost done. Zeta shall be right with you. Rearming will take longer."

I jogged back to the control room and found Busto and Destiny there. "Am I correct?" I said. "Is Whiskey-one approaching?"

Busto focused on the display and didn't turn to me as he said, "You're right. They are descending and decreasing in speed. They're 100 klicks away. ETA is about five minutes."

I cursed at myself for not having purchased any of those base defenses, like the retractable railgun turrets and MPDs. If the enemy knew where our base was, we would be sitting ducks.

But what were the chances of that? They would have

had to have had direct visual observation of the hatch opening and us descending into it, but our active camouflage would have made us look like a smudge in the landscape.

Where was Zeta? I needed her advice. "Should we ignore them and hope they're just being suspicious and don't actually know where we landed?"

"I don't know," Busto said.

Zeta floated into the control room. "Consort, Zeta advises hiding for now. Chances are very slim they detected this base. They may try to flush us out, hoping we'll panic and run. Stand firm. We are in the right, and right is might."

I rolled my eyes at her declaration. "Okay, we'll stay here. But keep *Thunder*'s systems energized in case we need to leave quickly."

We remained in the control room for the next several minutes as we watched the slow approach of the frigate. They flew cautiously. We had an excellent visual feed of the warship.

Whiskey-one looked a bit like a steel plug, like an especially thick flying saucer. The ship's base was hollowed out and filled with various devices and projections, which I thought might be its primary weapon systems. That meant they were expecting trouble to approach from the ground. The armored frigate flew a little to the north of and above our base, moving on toward Wolf Jaw.

"What are they doing?" Destiny said.

"They don't know where we are," I said and relaxed.

"But they have a pretty damned good idea," Busto said. "Look, they've stopped."

He was correct. Whiskey-one came to a stop hovering over Wolf Jaw's tiny downtown, floating 900 feet above the ground. Our base sensors gave us an excellent visual recording of the frigate.

I had no idea how the citizens were responding to this unusual attention, but it couldn't be good.

A sudden flash overloaded the video feed for a second. Filled with horror, I realized what had just happened as Destiny said, "They're firing!"

A few seconds later, a second flash erupted.

"What's our damage?" I asked.

"They're not shooting at us. They're shooting at something else. I think they're firing on the town!"

White smoke began to rise from somewhere in Wolf Jaw as something burned. Not long after that, a second column of smoke began to climb the sky.

"Well, that sucks," Busto said.

I thought of all the friends we had made in town. Neal and Dora at One Stop. Destiny's aunt and cousin. All the people who had willingly traded supplies with us, so we didn't have to always eat zetamilk. "I bet they'll be okay. They've *got* to be," I said lamely.

Destiny turned to me and folded her arms. Her lips clenched together, and her pupils dilated. Her eyes begged me without her needing to say a word. I knew she was thinking of her aunt and cousin.

As if understanding what Destiny and I were communicating with our eyes, Zeta said, "Consort, your priority is to protect *Thunder*. We should consider evacuating."

I stomped a foot. "To *where*? This is our home!"

"Your ship and crew are critical to Earth's resistance movement, more important even than Wolf Jaw. Every Kergan ship you destroy equals dozens of Wolf Jaws being saved."

I knew the Templar was correct in her assessment. It

made logical sense. But why did it feel so wrong? In the past, I'd never had a problem with abandoning people and going it on my own. Everybody important in my life had abandoned me—except for Destiny. I didn't owe anybody else anything. Sure, we'd had some good times with the people of Wolf Jaw. They'd helped us out when we'd been in a difficult situation before Zeta got our base up and running. But we'd paid them back many times over. I hadn't sworn my life to protect them.

Destiny stepped closer to me and took my left hand in hers, then she turned to look at the display.

Whiskey-one continued to fire randomly into the town. A hatch in the frigate's side opened, a Kergan assault shuttle exited, and began to descend.

"No! They're landing troops!" Destiny said.

Phoebe strolled into the room. "Kory, the magazines are rearmed." She jerked to a halt. "Damn! What's going on!"

"Whiskey-one followed us home," I said.

"Consort, we *must* prepare to evacuate," Zeta said. "Those Kergan troops are going to interrogate the town folks. They'll soon be led to the base. We cannot delay."

"Where will we go?" I said.

"It doesn't really matter so long as there are sufficient resources. Almost anywhere would work. We can create a new base. This one is lost. You can't fight that frigate."

I held my hands to the side of my head. "And here I thought you were all about facing overwhelming odds to show the righteousness of your cause."

Zeta hung quietly in the air for a second without responding. Her body inclined to the left and then to the right. "We must preserve our strength so we can fight another day. You and your crew are too valuable to lose in a one-sided battle."

Static suddenly sounded from the ham radio receiver, and a voice called out. It was filled with worry. *"To anyone listening, this is Wolf Jaw Central! We are under attack by Kergan forces!"*

It sounded like Neal Best. I wondered what help he could be hoping for that could face a Kergan frigate. The situation was hopeless.

The voice continued on the radio. *"Please, anyone, please respond! The Kergans are attacking our town! They're killing people in the streets and shooting at buildings!"*

"Kory!" Destiny moaned. "Are we going to at least say something to them?"

"Zeta advises against it," Zeta said. "Any transmission from that primitive radio would be detected and instantly triangulated to this location. Consort. *Captain!*" I yanked my head up to look at her. "It is time to evacuate. The ship is ready. There is still time for us to slip away unnoticed."

"Unnoticed?" I said. "And what about the Brooks?" I pointed at the Brooks' daughter. "What about Phoebe? And Ricki? They won't fit in the ship!"

"We can only rescue the crew. The frigate is far enough away that if we fly the ship slowly along the ground, they will unlikely be able to detect us."

"If we could somehow ambush them," Busto said, "maybe we could hurt them enough they couldn't shoot back."

Zeta and Gunny's last comments planted the seeds of an idea in my brain. In a stand-up fight, *Thunder* wasn't even close to being in the same weight class as that frigate. They'd eat us, spit out our bones, and ask for more. But it didn't have to be a stand-up fight. We were guerrilla warriors resisting the invasion of our world. Honor didn't require us to fight fairly.

At that moment, I realized that Destiny, Busto, Zeta, and I were a shield for humanity. I felt *pride* in myself for the first time in my life, satisfaction with the work and trouble we'd caused the Kergans and for the humans we'd protected. We had saved lives. There were people alive and healthy that day because of our actions. Maybe the adults in my life had failed to protect me as they should have, but that didn't mean I should follow their example. Dora Best and Judith Fulton showed me the good that humans can do when they care about their community and the people who live in it. And even more importantly, they had shown Destiny and me that we could be a part of such a community and be welcomed. And last of all, and most importantly, I wanted my parents to be proud of me, just in case they were watching me. If I died protecting other humans, would that be such a bad thing?

I was *not* going to turn my back on my town. I was *not* going to abandon the Brooks. I was *not* going to betray Destiny's aunt and cousin. If I did, perhaps I would live to old age, but I would die with words of regret on my last breath. *That* would be worse than an early death.

"We're going to help them," I said.

Destiny jumped up and down, clapping her hands, and then she hugged me. "I knew you would do it!"

Busto shrugged and said, "We're probably going to die, you know. But I'm in. You guys are my family now."

Zeta made a moaning sound. "This is a poor use of Dominion military resources. But you are Captain. And Zeta cannot fault you for your valor."

"Everybody, get to the ship," I said. "I'll explain my plan while we launch."

50

Thunder whispered around us, ready to stalk its prey like a wolf hunting in the forest. Only our current target was the equivalent of a grizzly bear instead of a deer.

"ChEng, can our railgun penetrate that frigate's armor?" I asked.

"Only at close range, and even then, it will have a low probability. Warships of that size have very powerful atomic bolsters," Zeta said.

"Is it possible to overcharge the railgun?"

"Yes, but I do not recommend it. Overcharging could damage or destroy it."

"But would it be more likely to penetrate?"

"At close range, yes, it would likely penetrate if you overcharge by 100%. But doing so would almost certainly damage the weapon."

We were facing a more powerful foe. We should be running from them, not looking for a fight. But I would not abandon our friends in Wolf Jaw to the Kergan wrath we had brought down upon them. We had to confront this frigate, but on our own terms.

"Okay, this is my plan. We will approach Whiskey-one from a very low altitude and speed so that if they see us on sensors, they'll think we're a ground vehicle. Once we get below the enemy ship, we'll overcharge the railgun, then I'll raise *Thunder*'s altitude until we're immediately adjacent to Whiskey-one, inside their minimum missile firing range, and I'll fire the railgun into its side."

"You're gonna shoot it at point-blank range?" Busto asked.

"Yes. Overcharged, that should punch through its armor and bring down its bolsters."

"Then what?" Destiny asked. "It'll be too close for firing missiles."

"I don't know. We'll play it by ear. Any suggestions?"

"I'll deploy the LPDs," Destiny said. "We may need them to hold off any Kergan troops who landed if we encounter them on the road."

"Fine. Open the hangar hatch."

Daylight appeared above us moments later. I engaged *Thunder*'s camouflage and lifted it out of the hangar, bringing us to a hover just barely off the ground. We were so low that the lower hull almost brushed the tops of grass stalks.

On my tactical display, Whiskey-one appeared as a bright red triangle about two miles away, hovering over Wolf Jaw. The optical sensors showed it was still firing at ground targets. There was so much smoke that it seemed like half the town must be burning.

I tried to think of *Thunder* as if it were a large truck. I glided over the ground toward the gap between the forest and outcrop leading to the forest service road. It wasn't quite wide enough for the ship, and we slammed into several trees, which toppled. Then we forced our way through the too-narrow gate in our perimeter security fence, bringing down two sections of it.

I entered the road, turned right, and flew *Thunder* down it toward Wolf Jaw at about 45 mph and a couple of feet above the pavement, following the faint yellow line in the middle. It was slow going, and I had to reduce speed when going around a couple sharp bends. We were so wide we took up both lanes. Anybody driving a vehicle coming toward us was in for a huge surprise.

Whiskey-one continued terrorizing the townies, which angered me, but the distraction kept their attention off us, allowing us to creep closer.

We arrived at the northern checkpoint and entered town. The checkpoint had been abandoned, the guards undoubtedly having moved into town to deal with the Kergan troops.

The plywood gate was still in position, blocking the road. Just like our gate, I rammed it with *Thunder*'s prow, punching through it like it was tissue paper.

The streets in town became narrower. *Thunder* was so wide its sides overlapped onto the shoulders of both sides.

We passed a burning business that was fully engulfed by flames. A Wolf Jaw fire engine with flashing red lights was parked next to it. Firemen were spraying water into the flames. They gaped at us as we silently floated by them, taking a turn in the road at 20 mph.

We encountered two cars parked on the shoulders in opposite directions, leaving too small of a gap to pass through. I pushed through anyway, cringing at the screech of metal rubbing against metal as I used *Thunder* to shove the cars to the side.

There were bodies in the streets. Civilians were shot down either by the frigate hanging over our heads or by the

Kergan shore party that had just landed. The bodies were charred and mutilated by high-energy blasts. There were children and women among the dead.

The elementary school property was empty except for several motionless bodies lying on the pitted and charred front lawn. Many windows had shattered, and one wing was smoking from some as yet hidden fire.

We were about half a mile from my goal when we encountered the first team of four Kergan troops. They floated out of a side street in their flying armored suits, armed with cannons. One of them fired at something across the street. They didn't seem to notice us.

"Contact!" Destiny yelled.

In these confined streets, the LPDs cracked like the sound of thunder as she opened fire. Thin threads of laser beams connected with the soldiers one by one, punching holes in them and dropping them before they could respond.

I focused on driving *Thunder*, letting Destiny and Busto worry about the enemy.

Another Kergan team came into view. They saw us, dropped behind cover, and began firing. Flechette projectiles bounced off of *Thunder*'s hull. One of the troopers opened up with a rapid-fire plasma cannon. It hit us in the windscreen but did nothing except slightly increase the energy the bolsters drew.

The LPDs fired again, punching through concrete and passenger vehicles to reach the Kergan soldiers hiding behind them. I was surprised at how effective the LPDs were as anti-personnel weapons. They effortlessly mowed down the Kergan troopers.

We glided past One Stop. One of the fuel pumps was burning, producing a thick column of black smoke. Nobody was fighting the fire. About half the windows of the store were shattered. The roaring flames licked at the side of *Thunder* as we passed. I wanted to stop and help them put the fire out, but nobody could safely do that until we took care of Whiskey-one.

I knew we probably couldn't kill the Kergan warship, but that wasn't my immediate goal. I just wanted to damage them and get them away from Wolf Jaw. They were here for us, not the citizens of the town.

"Weaps, how's Whiskey-one looking?"

"They still haven't noticed us. They seem to be working over the power distribution center next to the hydro turbine hall."

"Charge the railgun to 100% overcharge."

"Aye aye, Captain!"

I brought up my aiming reticle on my HUD for the railgun and watched the countdown tick away.

We arrived at the point in the town that was my goal, almost directly below Whiskey-one. We were so close that I could pick out sensor apertures and windows at the bottom of the warship.

It was hard to believe they couldn't see us, but so far, we'd observed no response.

Our camouflage and the haze of smoke in town masked us from view. Even if they *had* seen us, I expected we would have been mistaken for a truck.

The charging timer hit zero.

"Here we go!" I said.

I pushed *Thunder* up at 2 gs, and we rocketed into the sky. Whiskey-one seemed to race toward us, though I knew it was us that was moving, not them.

I reversed the tractor pods and brought us to a heart-stopping halt right next to the frigate's hull. Or bow was perhaps only fifty feet away. I didn't even need to aim. All I saw through the targeting reticle was a wall of matte black hull plating.

"Firing!" I squeezed the firing stud.

A fist seemed to smack *Thunder* in the bow, slamming us backward.

A flash of white light exploded in the direction of Whiskey-one, saturating sensors and temporarily blinding us.

I applied forward thrust to counteract the recoil from the railgun, which had thrown us backward several hundred feet. The flash had left ghostly images in my vision, which I was trying to blink away.

"Status!" I said.

"The railgun has suffered damage to its main power supply and is disabled," Zeta said. "Zeta is trying to reroute power."

"Do we have an ASM solution?"

"We're too close, Captain!" Busto said.

My vision cleared, and I got a view of Whiskey-one. It still hovered over Wolf Jaw, but it now sported a gaping hole in its side, from which black oily smoke poured. The ship was also slowly sinking to the ground.

The frigate was likely disabled only for a short while. I felt the temptation to run while we could, but if I did, it would open up the range enough for the frigate to fire a salvo of missiles at us. Being at point-blank range like this was the safest place for us.

"Threats?" I said.

"Whiskey-one's active sensors are acting erratically. Either we're too close, or we damaged them."

"Do we have *anything* we can shoot them with?"

Whiskey-one's sink halted, then it started to glide up again. The ship rotated on its vertical axis slowly. They were acting like they didn't even know we were there. They must have been still reeling from the blow we'd delivered.

"How's that railgun coming?" I asked.

"Zeta shall require a couple of minutes," Zeta said.

"I'm going to fire the LPDs, Captain," Destiny said.

"Good, aim for the hole in their side."

"Roger."

Flashes of lasers arced between us and Whiskey-one as Destiny began to fire the LPDs at the frigate. Maybe we would get lucky, and a laser beam would hit something vital.

Suddenly, the frigate accelerated eastward, leaving *Thunder* hovering alone above Wolf Jaw.

51

The frigate was running. They'd even left their own troops behind.

"Wow!" They had done exactly what I'd wanted. I could just let them go, or we could secure our future safety by chasing them down and trying to kill them. I pondered the decision only for a heartbeat before I slammed the flight controls forward to pursue Whiskey-one.

They were accelerating at only about 3 gs, well under what I knew they were capable of. We had damaged something.

I managed to follow them so closely that neither they nor we could open fire with missiles. The LPDs continued to fire into the side of the frigate.

Then, a lone LPD on the frigate opened fire on us. Only one of them, but it was accurate. Laser beams began to dig at our bolsters, though our battery was having no trouble keeping them charged for now.

Whiskey-one fled across the snowy tops of the Sierra Nevada range, smoke pouring out of its side, with *Thunder* in close pursuit. The two ships continued firing their LPDs at each other.

The frigate raised its altitude but only got to about 12,000 ft before leveling out. A large piece of its hull fell away.

Then, the cylindrical ship pivoted until the hollow end —the one filled with weapons and instruments—pointed at us.

"Uh oh!" Destiny yelled.

I jinked *Thunder* to the side, but not quickly enough. The end of a tube in Whiskey-one flashed, and our little ship jolted. The status display indicating hull integrity flashed yellow around *Thunder*'s bow.

"The bow atomic bolsters are at 50%," Zeta announced on the intercom.

The tube on Whiskey-one flashed again but missed this time.

I reduced airspeed slightly to put a little more distance between us, though not so much that they could fire missiles at us. Of course, neither could we. I was counting on Zeta getting the railgun operational again.

In our wild chase eastward, we crossed over the California-Nevada border. Then Whiskey-one altered course southward, traveling in a southeastern direction.

"Railgun is online!" Zeta said. "Now, these beasts will feel our teeth!"

"Railgun is charging," Busto said.

I continued to jink the ship around, dodging the occasional return fire from Whiskey-one. It seemed to be some kind of railgun. They were firing no other weapons, even though I knew they had them. We'd evidently damaged something important. Whiskey-one now sported a wide hole blown completely through one end and out the other.

My HUD indicated the railgun was ready. Aiming at Whiskey-one's center, I squeezed the firing stud, and *Thunder* jumped. A bright flash of light burst on the frigate's hull. A second later, I fired another. Then another.

Whiskey-one jinked around, but they were such a large target at this close range it was almost impossible to miss. However, the enemy ship's thick armor seemed to deflect many of my shots. Nevertheless, I continued to pour railgun fire into the other ship.

As we flew south of Las Vegas, I flinched from the impact of a Kergan railgun slug. *Thunder* suddenly slewed to the left. I moved the flight controls to compensate, but the response was sluggish.

"Captain, the fiends have disabled our upper port tractor pod!" Zeta said.

I managed to get our ship back under control, but losing one of our four tractor pods had noticeably reduced our agility and speed.

Wisps of smoke ran from a dozen holes that had pierced Whiskey-one, streaming behind the wounded frigate like blood.

Desolate desert lands passed below us. To the east, a strip of blue and green wandered through the brown sand —the Colorado River. We were approaching the Arizona border. Where was Whiskey-one headed?

Thunder bucked up and down, and we slewed again, but this time to the right. Our speed also dropped off.

"Upper starboard tractor pod is disabled!" Zeta reported.

I wrestled with the flight controls, trying to keep us in controlled flight. *Thunder* zigged and zagged across its flight path, making it difficult to aim the railgun. We also began to fall behind.

Despite the difficulties, I continued firing the railgun at our prey each time I managed to get the nose of the ship pointed in the correct direction. Pieces of Whiskey-one were now falling off the ship. Whether from our slugs' impacts or aerodynamic forces, the frigate was falling to pieces.

"Captain, bolsters are at 10%!" Zeta said.

I thought about turning around and returning to base. This frigate absorbed all the damage we inflicted on it and yet continued to fly. But I sensed it was close to dying. I didn't want them to get to their base and report on Wolf Jaw. I feared that if we didn't kill them, they would return within days to finish us off.

But we were falling further and further behind, even though I had the flight controls almost pressed to the stops. The problem was I couldn't keep us flying in a straight line. The constant jinking was bleeding off our airspeed.

We took another hit. A loud bang sounded inside the cockpit. I felt the roar of the atmosphere. Alarms sounded, and red lights flashed on one of my displays.

"The hull is open!" Busto yelled. "Zeta is hit!"

"ChEng! What is your status!" I yelled.

There was no reply, though I still felt my link to my consort.

"Aaaargh!" I screamed in frustration. "Weaps, compute an ASM solution, and prepare to fire all our ASMs at Whiskey-one!"

"Aye, Captain," Busto said.

I squeezed off two more railgun slugs and watched one of them strike the frigate. I backed off on the controls and allowed the distance between us and the frigate to open up. "Fire when ready!"

When Whiskey-one was about half a mile ahead of us, *Thunder* shuddered as it ripple-fired all eight ASMs. They shot forward and closed the distance in just a second.

A series of explosions burst from the enemy frigate, and debris flew outward.

Something hit *Thunder* with a sharp *bang*. Our ship started to vibrate and shake so hard I feared we'd be thrown from our seats.

A cloud of smoke momentarily hid whiskey-one, but then it flew clear.

One side of the frigate had a massive hole that looked like a monster had taken a bite out of it. The hollowed-out section was a smoking ruin.

Whiskey-one began to lose altitude. It went into a slow tumble.

"We got it!" Destiny said.

I ignored her because it took all my concentration to keep *Thunder* in the air. My status display was filled with red lights, reporting multiple system failures. We'd lost two of our main tractor pods plus several clusters of mini-tractors used for attitude control. Auxiliary flight controls were also damaged. Multiple openings in the hull indicated where the bolster had weakened and allowed the internals to be damaged and destroyed. And worst of all, my ChEng, my consort, was unresponsive! I needed Zeta!

Whiskey-one made an uncontrolled plunge toward the desert a few miles east of the Colorado River.

I looked for somewhere to set *Thunder* down. It was becoming uncontrollable; systems were failing one after the other, and I needed us on the ground before I lost complete control and painted the landscape with our ship.

Below us, the enemy frigate hit the ground, moving at around 400 knots. A huge fireball vomited flames and dust into the sky.

Destiny and Busto cheered.

I wrestled with the flight controls as we flew eastward over a small chain of mountains, gradually losing altitude. Suddenly, we were flying straight at the side of a mountain.

I put us into a tentative turn. *Thunder* didn't want to respond. We were flying right at a wall of solid rock!

At the last second, our ship stopped fighting me, and I got us to enter the turn. The nearly vertical granite side of the mountain flashed by our hull with only 80 ft to spare.

We circled around the shoulder of the mountain, and a wide valley opened up in front of us. I allowed our speed to drop off more and entered a slow descent. "I've got to set us down! Brace for a crash landing!"

I no longer had the ability to hover. We would have to land at high speed.

An open stretch of thankfully flat, arid desert appeared ahead. I aimed the ship at it and put us into a steep glide. *Thunder*'s fins acted like stubby wings, allowing us to glide, though more like a rock than an airplane.

I extended the undercarriage, but an error popped up on my screen. *The undercarriage is damaged!*

Our approach to the improvised landing field seemed leisurely, at first. But as the ground approached, its apparent motion increased until it was whipping by too fast to make out individual details. We were coming in at 150 knots, far too fast. Too late, I wondered if we should have ejected.

"Brace for impact!" I yelled.

We hit the ground. The motion threw me forward into my seat straps.

My helmet smacked into one of my displays, shattering the latter.

The violent shaking threatened to tear *Thunder* into pieces. It went on and on. I couldn't see anything. Debris pounded into my poor ship's hull with *bangs* and *booms*.

52

I must have been stunned. The next thing I remembered, silence surrounded me, and Destiny shook me.

"Kory! Are you okay?" she said.

The canopy was gone. Either one of the crew had ejected it, or it had been ripped loose. Hot, dry wind blew against my body.

I couldn't sense my link to my consort. "Zeta!"

I fumbled with my straps, exited my chair, stepped onto the upper hull, and crawled back to Zeta's seat.

The hull next to Zeta had a crater in it that passed entirely through and into the cockpit.

Zeta's capsule was damaged. There was a hole in it, blackened, with melted edges, like somebody had pressed a white-hot poker into it until it burned through.

Zeta did not respond. I could no longer sense her presence through our consort link.

Busto said, "What can we do?"

I had not the slightest clue about how to treat a wounded igna. "She told us that the capsule contained her body. I can't sense her. I think…she's gone."

I felt like I was walking along the edge of a chasm and tipping over. My heart felt dead.

Destiny crawled to my side and put an arm around me. "We'll find her," she said, resting her head on my shoulder.

"I think she's lost. Is she dead?" I wondered, because we had no body, just this empty capsule.

I hit the release for her seat, and Zeta's capsule came free. I cradled her in my arms. She no longer glowed and she felt so light compared to the last time I held it, like the empty husk the capsule was, far lighter than the one other time I picked it up when we found her by the dumpster. It seemed so long ago.

We didn't know if Zeta was dead, only that she was gone. And I couldn't sense her through our link. That link had become such a steady companion over the preceding months that I had forgotten about it until it was gone. My heart felt as empty as Zeta's capsule was.

The igna was missing in action and likely dead. We didn't know how to deal with a dead warrior of the Dominion, so we treated Zeta's capsule as if it were her lifeless body. We buried her next to the crash site, piling rocks on top of the spot in the barren desertscape. Busto said a few words as a memorial to our friend but I can't remember any of it.

Thunder was as dead as Zeta. I circled the wreck on foot. The lower hull was shattered, cracked into hundreds of pieces. Both lower fins had been ripped off. The ship had left a deep furrow almost 500 yards long in the desert, filled with pieces of her structure that had broken off.

"Dest, what was our last position fix?" I asked.

"We're in Western Arizona, about 20 miles northwest of Kingman, Arizona."

I surveyed the terrain. Arid desert surrounded us, covered by sparse bushes. Flat, dry, and a little hot even though it was the middle of the winter. Distant mountain ranges spanned the western and eastern horizons.

"Let's get the survival gear out of *Thunder*," I said. Each of us had a small survival pack integrated into our ejection seats. They contained water and food for a few days, maps, a compass, a reflective blanket, a knife, and other odds and ends. We also each had hidden a couple of Gold Eagle coins and a dozen Perth gold chips on our bodies. "I suspect water's gonna be our main problem." *Unless they take gold.*

We were hundreds of miles from the base without transportation or any prospect of rescue. Was our work as insurgents over and done with? I no longer had a Dominion consort. Would the Dominion abandon us out here in the middle of nowhere? Did the Ministry of War even know what happened?

At least we still had our protomatter suits. Each of us also had a laser sidearm and a flechette rifle stored in the hull. If we got into a fight, we could handle ourselves. But water and food were the most significant problems.

We were once again homeless with nowhere to go. But I was not going to give up. We would get back to the base and then figure out what to do next.

I didn't know how we would do it without Zeta. She understood how to operate our base's nanoforge and the fusion plant. I regretted not taking the time to learn any of the necessary skills. If I had the chance, I would remedy my ignorance.

Destiny studied her map and estimated our position as about 9 miles west of a tiny town called Elkins, which rested on a small county road.

I gave Busto the lead, and he ordered us to begin the

march to Elkins soon after. Moving at a cautious pace, he estimated we would arrive there before sunset.

As we trudged through the barren landscape, I reflected on my actions that day. At least we had killed that Kergan frigate. We had protected the citizens of Wolf Jaw and our base. We hadn't been cowards. *How many tribute points did we earn from killing that frigate?* I wondered. It must have been a lot. We had undoubtedly earned our corvette hull if only we could return to base and reestablish contact with the Dominion.

If we could contact the War Ministry, maybe they could send us another Templar consort to replace Zeta. Not that Zeta could be replaced. I mourned for her. But I was trying to be practical, which meant we needed a new military adviser. Then we could rebuild *Thunder* into a corvette.

I wasn't going to just cut our losses and disappear. I was done with being homeless and scared all the time. I was done being selfish and thinking only of Destiny and myself. Fighting the Kergans these past months had given me a hunger to see them kicked off of Earth and for humanity to be free.

If Destiny and Busto were still willing, we would find a way to rebuild *Thunder* and continue the fight.

THE END

Kory Drake and the crew of *Thunder* continue their adventures in the next *Starship Thunder* book: **Lindblad Liberation**.

Please rate or review this book online. As an indie author, I *depend* on your reviews to legitimize my books in the eyes of those who have not read them.

About Joseph McRae Palmer

Joseph McRae Palmer writes speculative fiction. He is also an engineer in the telecommunications industry and holds a Ph.D. in Electrical Engineering from Brigham Young University. Joseph was born in Provo, Utah, but raised in Sitka, Alaska, and graduated from high school in 1993. Later, he served as a missionary for two years in central Mexico. He and his wife of more than two decades, Beatriz Palmer, are parents of one son and three daughters, and as of 2023 they reside in northern Utah, USA.

Joseph's fiction site: www.josephmcraepalmer.com

Printed in Dunstable, United Kingdom

67869163R00238